THE DAY OF THE DEAD

Maurizio de Giovanni

THE DAY OF THE DEAD
THE AUTUMN
OF COMMISSARIO RICCIARDI

Translated from the Italian
by Antony Shugaar

Europa
editions

Europa Editions
214 West 29th Street
New York, N.Y. 10001
www.europaeditions.com
info@europaeditions.com

Copyright © 2010 by Fandango Libri s.r.l.
First Publication 2013 by Europa Editions
Second printing, 2016

Translation by Antony Shugaar
Original title: *Il giorno dei morti. L'autunno del commissario Ricciardi*
Translation copyright © 2014 by Europa Editions

Library of Congress Cataloging in Publication Data is available
ISBN 978-1-60945-187-5

de Giovanni, Maurizio
The Day of the Dead

Book design by Emanuele Ragnisco
www.mekkanografici.com

Prepress by Grafica Punto Print – Rome

Printed in the USA

To Giovanni and Roberto,
for giving me the most marvelous gifts of fear.

THE DAY OF THE DEAD

I

As the dawn was beginning to extract the outlines of things from the night and the rain, if someone had happened to pass by the foot of the monumental staircase leading up to Capodimonte, they'd have seen a dog and a child. But they would have had to look very closely; the figures were hard to make out in the uncertain light of early morning.

The dog and the child just sat there, motionless, indifferent to the fat, cold raindrops falling from the sky. They were sitting on the stone bench in the ornamental recess just above the bottom of the staircase. The staircase itself was a rushing torrent, transporting leaves and branches from the wooded palace grounds.

If someone had walked by and stopped to look, they might have wondered why the stream of water and detritus rushing downhill seemed to respect the dog and the child, flowing around them without touching them, save for the occasional splash. The alcove offered some slight shelter and protected them from the rain: only the hair on the dog's back quivered every now and then, like a shiver of wind.

Someone might have wondered what the dog and the child were doing there, sitting motionless in the cold dawn of a rainy fall day.

The little boy was gray, his hair plastered to his head by the rain, hands in his lap and feet dangling an inch or so from the ground, head tilted slightly to one side, eyes lost as if in a dream or in some thought. The dog seemed to be sleeping, its head resting on its paws, fur spotted with sopping wet patches of dark brown, one ear raised, its tail at rest along its side.

Someone might have wondered if the dog and child were waiting for somebody. Or if they were thinking about something that had happened, something that had left its mark in their memories. Or perhaps if they were listening to a sound, some faint music.

Now the rain starts drumming louder, thundering like a revolt against the rising sun; the dog and the child remain motionless, indifferent to the water's fury. From the child's nose and the dog's lifted ear stream icy rivulets.

The dog is waiting.

The child no longer dreams.

II

T he call came in at 6:30 A.M., an hour before the end of the night shift.

Ricciardi didn't mind staying overnight at the police station, when he was assigned that shift; for the most part they were quiet hours, time he could devote to reading or a pleasant kind of repose somewhere between waking and sleep on the sofa in the room next to his office. And it was rather rare for his rest or his thoughts to be disturbed by a policeman knocking on the door, requesting his presence.

Murders happen at night, but they're discovered in the morning; so the danger hour was exactly then, just as the light of day was lifting the veil on the depravities of the darkness.

Ricciardi had just finished washing up in the sink at the far end of the hallway when he saw Brigadier Maione dragging himself up the last flight of stairs.

"Commissa', you didn't think they'd let us finish our shift in peace, did you? A phone call's just come in, a gentleman from the Tondo di Capodimonte. He says that there's a milkmaid with a nanny goat who's crying."

Ricciardi reflected on the matter as he dried his hands.

"So now they're calling us about crying milkmaids? And I'm not sure I understand: who's crying, the milkmaid or the nanny goat?"

Maione threw his arms open wide, still panting after racing up the stairs.

"Commissa', you can joke if you like; meanwhile it's raining buckets out there, and since we've got another hour left in our shift we're going to have to make it all the way to Capodimonte in this downpour. It's serious business: apparently there's a dead boy on the monumental staircase. It was the woman who found him, as she was walking down from a farm on the hill with her little nanny goat to sell milk, she says that this is her route, and she saw him there, motionless, and she gave him a shake but he didn't move. So she went to the nearest building to get help, and this gentleman who rang us up was the only one who had a telephone. Now I ask you, couldn't this have happened a couple of hours from now? Then the one hiking through the rain would be Cozzolino, who's young and eager, whereas the minute I get even a little bit wet, I get a backache so bad I have to walk bent over at the middle."

Ricciardi had already thrown on his raincoat.

"In other words, you really are getting old. Come on, let's go see what this is all about. It might just be a prank—you know how people love to see cops running around in the rain. Then you can go home and dry off."

The way from the police station to Capodimonte was the same route that Ricciardi took to go home. A long walk that, at a certain point, took on such a steep incline that it left you gasping. You had to walk the length of the Via Toledo, with its imposing aristocratic residences, cross the Largo della Carità and walk past the Spirito Santo building, walk alongside the National Museum: a border line with, on either side of it, uphill and down, the impenetrable narrow alleyways, or *vicoli,* of the Spanish Quarter, the port, and the Sanità neighborhood, bubbling over with life and grief, cheerful energy and poverty.

Ricciardi had the same thought every time he passed this way, every morning and every night, feeling on his skin the suspicious eyes of those who had to conceal the way they earned their living: that street said a lot about the city. It said everything there was to say.

And it always changed, season after season, offering variously a torrid summer picture in which filth baked in the sun, or a fragrant image of spring, with fruit and flower vendors displaying their wares for wealthy passersby, or the artificial wasteland of winter, when all the dodgy dealings retreated into the ground-floor apartments, or *bassi*, lining the street, sheltered from the icy wind that never seemed to die down.

Now, on this damp autumn morning, the long street had as many rivulets running through it as there were *vicoli* intersecting it, carrying garbage and filth from the distant hillside down toward an unreachable sea.

Maione leapt nimbly to avoid the deeper puddles, in a futile attempt to keep his boots dry.

"She'll kill me. Guaranteed. My wife will kill me. Commissa', you can't imagine what a savage beast she turns into when she has to clean mud and filth off my boots. I tell her, don't worry about it, I'll clean them myself, and she says, now don't talk nonsense, she says, I'm a brigadier's wife and it's my job to clean his boots. In that case, I ask, why all the complaining? And she says, it's my job to clean them, but would it kill you to be a little more careful?"

As they walked, he did his best to ward off the rain with a big black umbrella he held over his and Ricciardi's heads. The commissario, as usual, wore no hat, nor did he seem to be paying any attention to the bad weather. Maione easily changed the subject:

"I don't understand you, Commissa'. I don't mean the umbrella—you might think of carrying one, seeing as it's been raining for three days now, but I can see how a person might get tired of carrying it and decide to leave it at home—but a hat at least, couldn't you try wearing a hat? You may be young but believe me, when you're my age, every single drop of rain turns into a stabbing headache."

Ricciardi walked briskly, his hands plunged into his raincoat pockets, his gaze fixed straight ahead of him.

"You know I can't stand wearing a hat: it gives me a migraine. Plus I grew up in the mountains, I don't mind the cold and the damp. Don't worry about it; worry about your own health, and about keeping your boots clean."

They'd reached the part of the walk that Ricciardi especially disliked. This was the bridge that the Bourbon monarchs had built, so they could reach the royal palace, the Palazzo Reale, without having to pass through the Sanità quarter, which had always been one of the city's most dangerous neighborhoods. For some strange and inexplicable reason, from the day it was built that towering viaduct, that riverless bridge that sank its pillars into the narrow *vicoli* beneath it, had become a favored spot for suicides.

What Ricciardi inwardly referred to as "the Deed," his grievous curse to perceive the last thoughts of those who had died violent deaths, became an intolerable burden near the bridge. There was always at least one lingering ghostly image, ready to lift its gaze as he passed and speak to him the words with which it had been forced to abandon its existence of flesh, bones, and blood. A farewell message with one recipient alone: him.

On that rainy morning, perfectly visible to the eyes of his soul, there were two adolescents perched precariously, hand in hand, on the parapet. The young man's neck was broken, and his face was looking backward, as if his head had been put on the wrong way around; he was murmuring: *not without you, never without you.*

The girl's chest was crushed and the front of her head had been virtually obliterated by the impact. A thought came to him out of the bloody pulp that had once been her face: *I don't want to die, I'm too young, I don't want to die.*

Ricciardi mused to himself that perhaps love had claimed more victims than war. Actually, he could leave out the "perhaps," he decided.

Farther on, on the same parapet, a fat old man with a stove-in skull was saying: *I can't pay you back, I can't.* Debt, the commissario thought as he hastened his step, leaving a panting Maione behind him. Another incurable disease. God, he was tired. Nothing ever changed, it was always the same things.

They finally arrived at the Tondo di Capodimonte, where the monumental staircase began. It hadn't been easy to make it all the way up here; the last stretch of road had been a raging river of branches and leaves through which they'd had to fight their way upstream. Maione had finally given up trying to spare his boots, and his face had taken on an expression of grim silence. Ricciardi carried with him the image of the suicides and was grimmer still.

A knot of people had gathered at the foot of the staircase, above the first flight of steps. The mushroom patch of umbrellas hid from view whatever it was that they were looking at. The arrival of Maione and Ricciardi, accompanied by a pair of policemen, immediately scattered the assembled crowd. Maione snickered:

"As usual. The only thing stronger than curiosity is the fear of getting mixed up in some trouble with the law, the second the police show up."

Ricciardi immediately spotted the little boy, sitting on the stone bench at the foot of the left-hand buttress. He was small, his feet didn't reach the ground, and he was dripping wet. Rain ran down from his hair, drenching his tattered clothes, the clothes of a *scugnizzo*, a street urchin. On his feet were a pair of wooden clogs, the marks of chilblains clearly visible. His lips were purplish, his eyes half-open and staring into empty air.

He was especially struck by the boy's hands, lying fallen in his lap like a pair of dead baby birds. White, much lighter than the complexion of his legs, livid from the cold, they appeared to the commissario as a mark of surrender and misgiving. He instinctively looked around, and saw no trace of ghostly images: the child's death couldn't have been a violent one; perhaps he'd frozen to death, or starved, or succumbed to some disease. Abandoned, he thought: to his own devices, to the elements, to random violence, to loneliness. The child had had no choice in the matter.

If there was one thing he hated, it was seeing dead children. The sense of sheer waste, denial, lost opportunities. A people, a civilization is defined by the way it cares for its children, he'd once read in a book, back in his university days. That city certainly didn't come out looking very good, by those standards.

Maione roused him from those thoughts:

"Before leaving headquarters, I gave orders to call the hospital and summon both the medical examiner and the wagon to remove the body; they'll be here any minute. The milkmaid's over there, the one with the nanny goat on a rope. Do you want to talk to her? Standing near her is the man with the telephone, that gentleman with the umbrella. I told him we don't need him and that he's free to go, but he won't leave. You want me to bring them both over to talk to you?"

The milkmaid kept her eyes on the ground. Her lips were quivering, and she had a scarf tied tight around her head. She was quite young, little more than a girl; with one hand she held a piece of rope tied around the nanny goat's neck, in the other she held a metal milk can. Stuttering with cold, fear, and shyness, she told her story in dribs and drabs, how she had been coming down the staircase to make her rounds selling milk, taking care not to slip and fall, when the nanny goat had leapt to one side. There was a dog, lying on its side at the top of the bottom flight of steps, snarling.

"There it is, you see it? It moved when I came back from

the gentleman's house, after calling you, and it hasn't moved since."

Ricciardi saw, some sixty feet away, a dog sitting on its haunches, still as a statue, watching them intently. It was a little mutt, the kind you see dozens of every day, its dirty white coat spotted with brown, its muzzle pointed and one ear cocked.

The young woman went on with her story, telling how, after trying to determine whether the little boy was asleep or was sick, she'd gone running over to the nearest apartment building and summoned her customer the accountant Signore Caputo. The accountant, a dapper middle-aged man, short, with a pair of gold-rimmed glasses, took a step forward and tipped his hat.

"Commissa', with your permission, I'm the accountant Ferdinando Caputo, at your service. This girl, here, whose name is Caterina, comes by every other day. I can only digest goat milk, cow milk gives me a stomachache and then I'm sick for the rest of the day. In any case, this morning the girl, here, Caterina, runs into the courtyard of my building and starts screaming, hurry, hurry, help, there's a little boy on the stairs and he's not responding. I'd only just woken up, I was still in my nightshirt, I rushed from the bed to the window . . . "

Maione snorted in annoyance:

"Okay, okay, Accountant Caputo, let's get to the point if you don't mind, no disrespect intended but we really don't care what you wear to bed. What happened next, did you go downstairs?"

"No, Brigadie', what was I going to do, go downstairs in my nightshirt with my nightcap on my head? No, I told the girl, here, whose name is . . . "

" . . . Caterina, we know. The police officer, here, whose name is Antonelli, even wrote it down in his report . . . "

The accountant glared at Maione.

"What is this, Brigadie', are you making fun of me? I was

just trying to be precise, for your benefit. To make a long story short, the girl came up and I called police headquarters. And that's that."

Ricciardi waved his hand.

"All right, all right, thanks to you both. The officer has taken down your names and addresses, if we need anything we'll send for you. Probably not, though. You're free to go."

Once they were alone, they drew near the corpse. Ricciardi wondered why, by that time of day, there was still no sign of a family member or an acquaintance out looking for such a young boy if he hadn't come home the night before. Maione, squatting, was eyeing the dead body with interest.

"Commissa', we'll have to find out whether this child even has a family. The clothes look like he dug them out of the trash; look here, the trousers are so loose on him that the twine around his waist had to be wrapped around twice just to hold them up. And his shirt is made out of burlap. Look at the clogs, he's practically barefoot in this weather. This is a *scugnizzo*, trust me. A kid with no friends and no family."

Ricciardi turned to look at the dog, sitting motionless ten feet from them, watching every move the two of them made.

"Family, maybe not. But he had at least one friend; too bad he can't tell us anything. Ah, here we are, the health authorities are finally here. Now maybe we'll learn something about the death of our lonely little boy, here."

III

The public health authorities, on this occasion, were represented by Dr. Bruno Modo, who was leaping from one foot to the other in the water, doing his best—and it was no easy feat—to keep from getting too wet while holding an umbrella, his leather doctor's bag, and a sheet of paper. As soon as he spotted Ricciardi and Maione he headed straight for them with a bellicose glare.

"You two, eh? How could I ever have doubted it? A phone call first thing in the morning, as soon as I've gotten my trousers dry after getting soaked on my way to the hospital, a mile and a half upstream fighting this goddamned river they call Via Nuova Capodimonte, and who do I see? Laughing-boy Ricciardi and his skinny squire, the noble Brigadier Maione. Can we put an end to these special personal requests, Brigadie'? Look, read this: the immediate presence of Dr. Bruno Modo is requested and required. Let me ask you, wouldn't any other doctor do? Did you really have to call me specifically?"

A sardonic smile appeared on Maione's face.

"No, Dotto', it's just that the commissario is never happy unless he has you here. He only trusts you. When that other doctor comes, the little young one, I don't know, somehow the commissario just doesn't seem satisfied. The way you handle corpses, no one else comes close. And so we ask for you special; why, aren't you happy to see us?"

Modo turned to look at Ricciardi, waving the sheet of paper

with the phoned-in formal request in a mock-threatening gesture.

"I can't wait for the morning that your request sheet shows up on my desk. The one that's going to say: two police detectives found torn to pieces by a Fascist enforcement squad. Ah, if only! The day that happens, even I'll enroll in the party, I will!"

Ricciardi's expression hadn't altered, but he was clearly amused.

"Have you ever thought about getting into vaudeville, the two of you? A nice little act at the Salone Margherita, the doctor and the brigadier, oom-pah-pah . . . Listen, shall we get this examination underway, so we can all get out of the rain? Based on an initial assessment, in any case, I don't see any signs of violence on this corpse."

Modo shot him an offended look.

"Oh, right, now you're the one who decides when there are signs of violence and when there aren't. Look, you've brought me all the way out here, my long underwear is wet right up to the knees; we might as well do this examination right. Where is the corpse? Ah, here it is. A little boy. Very young, couldn't be more than seven, eight years old. Ah, what a shame."

The doctor started moving around the child, carefully lifting the clothing, tenderly touching the hands and legs. Ricciardi noticed from a distance that the dog had gotten to its feet and now had both ears cocked, as if waiting to be called; all the same, it seemed to sense how delicately Modo was working and, remaining vigilant, didn't move from where it stood.

The doctor examined the position of the corpse, crouched down to palpate the feet, inspected the face. He took notes on the back of the memo requesting his attendance. As he worked, Maione held the umbrella over him, doing his best to anticipate the doctor's rapid movements.

When he was done, Modo went over to Ricciardi, drying his hands on his handkerchief.

"Now then: the corpse is stiff and cold. If you ask me he died yesterday evening or in the middle of the night. You're quite right, there are no marks of violence on the body, at least nothing that could have proved fatal: old bruises, a few abrasions here and there, but nothing that was concurrent with death. He's sitting up because he's leaning against the wall, otherwise he would have fallen over. In my opinion, he's seven years old, but he could be a little older; these street kids get very little to eat and develop rickets, so they can be a couple of sizes smaller than what's normal for their actual age. He may even be ten or twelve years old. That's something you're going to have to find out."

Ricciardi asked:

"About the time of death, are you certain?"

Modo shrugged.

"You can never be certain, when it's cold and raining. The corneas are already opaque, glazed over, and I'm pretty sure I'm seeing black at the edges of the pupils. You can see hypostasis, that is, red blotches from the settling of blood due to gravity, along the right side of the neck, on the pavilion of the right ear, under the thighs, and on the legs, like socks. You see? If I press on the flesh with my fingers, it doesn't turn white. The corpse stayed in this position for a long time."

"And the cause of death? Agreed, no violence. So what killed him?"

Modo fell silent for a moment as he looked at the boy.

"I couldn't say. It looks to me like a simple case of cardiac arrest. I told you, they're weak, undernourished; every cold turns into pneumonia. They have no medicine, no one takes care of them. This is the third one I've seen this month. They found one of them at the train station whose ribs stuck out so much that you could examine his skeleton without even opening him up. Another one, a girl, was so hungry that she fell into the street at Sant'Eframo and a car ran over her like she was a bag of rags. It's heartbreaking, I know. But it's just one of the effects of poverty in this city that's still waiting for the rising sun of the future."

Maione listened, shaking his head.

"I feel tremendously sad for these poor creatures, Dotto'. Used to be every family would take in one of them. They called them the children of the Madonna. And they were even treated better than the other kids; people said they brought luck. But now, with the poverty you see these days, who can afford to have an extra mouth to feed?"

Modo never missed an opportunity to slip into his favorite topic of conversation.

"But doesn't everyone say that we now live in a perfect country? Read the newspapers, Brigadie', and all you'll read about are parties, receptions, inaugurations, ship-launchings, and military parades. Foreign princes and kings visiting our country, happy, cheering crowds. But you and I, and our friend Ricciardi, here, all know perfectly well that matters are quite different. That children like this nameless boy are allowed to starve to death on the side of the road."

Ricciardi raised his hand to stop him.

"Have mercy, Bruno. I beg you, no politics this morning. I can't take it. I spent most of my night shift filling out reports and I'm even more disgusted with our political system and bureaucracy than you are; but I think that, with this fixation you have on Mussolini and the Fascists, you're going to get yourself in trouble sooner or later, and very serious trouble, too."

Modo ran his hand through his thick white hair and put his hat back on his head.

"So? You think that at my age I could really be afraid to speak my mind? After what I did in the Great War, for my country? For my reply to you I'll borrow a reply of theirs: *me ne frego*! I don't give a damn!"·

Ricciardi shook his head.

"You don't understand. Or perhaps I should say you pretend you don't understand. Men like you do a great deal of good for their people. You're the best doctor I know, and not only because you know what you're doing and you're good at it, but also and especially because you feel pity. I was watching you, before, as you were examining this poor corpse; you showed respect for it, as if it were still alive. Do you think it would be the best thing for them, for us, if people like you, who are few and far between, were yanked out of circulation because of a phrase or even a single word uttered in the wrong place at the wrong time? Don't you think it's better to try to change things day by day?"

Maione added, from under the umbrella:

"The commissario has a point, Dotto'. In any case, I have to do my duty as a spy, and in five minutes I'm going to turn you over to the proper authorities, so that they can send you off to internal exile in a hot, dry place, and I'm doing you a favor, at that."

Modo burst out laughing, and waved to the two morgue attendants who had accompanied him.

"It's no use, and more the fool I for even trying in the first place: you can't have a serious conversation with a couple of cops. It's as if I were trying to talk to a pair of oxen, except that they'd at least pretend to listen to me, without making idiotic jokes. Okay, okay, I'm heading back to the hospital; at least the dead don't have a bunch of smart retorts. And I'm going to send this poor child to the graveyard, so that he might rest in peace, even if I can't."

The rain had turned to a faint drizzle, indistinguishable from fog. The two attendants lifted the corpse, laboriously straightening the stiffened limbs. Ricciardi saw them start toward the wagon, which was drawn by an old black horse glistening with raindrops. The child's head lolled to one side and a rivulet ran down his neck. An involuntary mechanism of memory recalled to Ricciardi's mind the image of a lamb that he used to play with as a child, after it had been sacrificed by the farmer for Easter dinner: the same head lolling to one side, the same tender neck. Two defenseless little animals. Two victims.

In the spectral atmosphere of death and fog, the dog howled once, briefly. Ricciardi felt a shiver run down his back.

Impulsively, he called out to Modo, who was walking away with the undertakers.

"Bruno, listen to me, I need you to do me a favor: Don't send him to the cemetery. Have them take him to the hospital, perform an autopsy on him. I want to know exactly what he died of."

Modo looked at him in surprise.

"What do you mean, what he died of? I told you, cardiac arrest. These children have practically no immune system to speak of; he could have died of anything. Why do you want to subject him to further torture? Besides, you can't imagine how much work I have to do at the hospital! With this weather, two out of five doctors are sick, and people come streaming in with bronchitis, pneumonia, and bruises from falls and accidents."

Ricciardi laid his hand on the doctor's arm.

"Please, Bruno. I never ask you for anything. Do this for me: as a personal favor."

Modo grumbled:

"That's not true, that you never ask me for anything. To be exact, you're an unbelievable pain in the ass. But fine, fine. I'll do you this favor. But remember, you owe me one."

Ricciardi grimaced in a way that was vaguely reminiscent of a smile.

"Fine, I owe you a favor. When the warrant for your arrest

finally lands on my desk I'll take the long way around the city when I come for you, that way you'll have time for one last visit to the bordello where you take your pleasures."

The doctor burst out laughing.

"You know that the whores in this city couldn't live without me, eh? *Guagliu'*, hold up there, there's a change in destination. Take the child to the hospital for me. He's a client of mine, now."

Once the cart had set off, Maione stepped closer to Ricciardi.

"Commissa', I don't get what you're doing here. Hasn't that poor child suffered enough already? Is it really worth it to inflict more cruelty on him now that he's dead, if there weren't any marks on the body?"

Ricciardi said nothing; he stood watching the dog, which had never once taken its eyes off them and had stayed where it was, even after the cart with the corpse had departed. He shrugged his shoulders.

"What can I tell you, Maione. It just seemed wrong to put him in the ground without even knowing what killed him. Come on, let's head back to headquarters, so that we can finally draw this night shift to a close."

IV

In a break with his routine, the deputy chief of police Angelo Garzo was already in his office at 8:15. This had thrown special patrolman Ponte, who had been promoted to serve as the official's personal assistant, into a panic.

Was it really a promotion after all? Ponte had serious doubts about the benefits of the new post. Sure, they'd tacked on a few lire to his salary, which didn't hurt when it came to making ends meet; and he no longer had to go out on patrol, which eliminated the discomfort and inconvenience of braving the elements, with all the aches and pains that inevitably resulted, especially on damp days like the ones they'd been having lately. And finally his new position had won him a certain grudging respect from his colleagues, who, well aware that the main reason for Ponte's promotion was his willingness to rat out his fellow officers, steered clear of him.

In exchange, Ponte had to put up with his superior officer's moods, the most unpredictable elements in all creation. Moments of groundless euphoria came on the heels of bouts of depression, during which poor Ponte had to guess what Garzo wanted from the expression on his face. Arrogant benevolence, which might prevail for example after some words of praise from the police chief, would quickly give way to furious dissatisfaction, and at those times it was best for Ponte to make himself scarce, because Garzo invariably took it out on him with memorable tongue-lashings.

But this was by far the worst period he could remember.

This is how matters stood: a month earlier, word had come down by telegraphic dispatch from the Ministry of the Interior announcing the Duce's decision to deliver the address to the nation from Naples. Prime Minister Mussolini, accompanied of course by the highest-ranking government officials, would be visiting the city on the third and fourth of November. Local government officials would be expected to provide the maximum cooperation, and the spotlight would be focused first and foremost on the local police and judiciary, of course.

Ponte had been the first to read that dispatch, handed to him by the telegraph operator at police headquarters so that he could take it directly to the chief of police; but since he knew very well that Garzo would skin him alive if he failed to tell him about a matter of such importance before he informed anyone else, Ponte had run headlong to his office.

He wouldn't soon forget his commanding officer's reaction. First Garzo had turned pale, then violet, and then white again, with a few lingering blotches of red on his neck and his forehead. He'd leapt to his feet and the sheet of paper had fallen from his trembling fingers. He'd stared down at it, muttering something incomprehensible, and then he'd dropped back into his chair, waving weakly for Ponte to take the document to the chief.

From that moment on, Garzo had becoming increasingly difficult with each passing day. He locked himself in his office for hours on end, checking and rechecking police reports and depositions from months earlier, terrorized by the possibility of an inspection; or else he'd burst into the sentry post, shrieking in falsetto that the sheer slovenlinesss of the room was unbelievable. And now he was actually showing up at police headquarters shortly after sunrise, when all poor Ponte wanted was to sip a cup of ersatz coffee and smoke his morning cigar in peace. Ponte glanced at the calendar: eight more days of this would really be more than he could bear.

Garzo glanced at the calendar for the fourth time in half an hour, and decided that he simply couldn't take eight more days of this tension. Il Duce. Il Duce in person, the Great Condottiere, the Chief of the Italian Nation, the Man of Destiny to whom the Italian people looked with boundless faith would be here, perhaps in his office, standing right in front of him. He might even smile at him, reach out to shake his hand. For the thousandth time since he first read the telegram from the ministry, he felt faint. The Duce's safety was the responsibility of the army and the secret police; that, at least, wasn't his concern. But the chief of police had stated it in no uncertain terms: the cleanliness and appearance of police headquarters and of the city in general were Garzo's personal responsibility.

In short, it was up to him, and him alone, to ensure that the Duce, the interior minister, and all the functionaries who would be coming down from Rome found Naples to be the perfect Fascist city, free of crime and anything unsightly. And he was determined to make sure that that was exactly the kind of city they would find.

Once again, for what must have been the thousandth time, he opened his pocket mirror and checked his mustache—grown recently at his wife's suggestion—to make sure that not a single hair was out of place. His wife, a woman who was as energetic as she was despotic, had been uncompromising in her view that when it came to a man's career, his physical appearance was an important calling card. And she knew whereof she spoke: her uncle was retired on a prefect's pension, after scaling all the summits of a ministry career.

Garzo knew that he wasn't a particularly astute investigator; he'd always felt a certain disgust for the criminal mentality, and he hated having to dirty his hands by interacting with thugs and hooligans. But he compensated for this with his considerable talent for personal relations, adhering to the tried and tested principle of being firm with the weak and weak with the strong: kissing up and kicking down. This approach had allowed him to free himself of actual duties and take on a series of executive positions, in which he had employed his God-given skills as an organizer. He knew how to see problems coming and prevent them, isolating the causes and carefully removing them.

And what, he mused, could the problems be now? What could possibly come between him and the Duce's praise, the minister's compliments, the chief of police's grateful embrace? His thoughts turned immediately to Ricciardi, and to his usual sardonic expression.

It was a fine time for the Duce's visit. There were no investigations under way, no unsolved cases, no unrest. For once, everything was running smoothly. So why did he feel so uneasy?

Ricciardi was a good detective, no doubt about that. He'd solved complex cases, some of which had been real stumpers; Garzo had once remarked to his wife that if you asked him, Ricciardi owed his successes to the simple fact that deep down he was a criminal himself, so he thought like the people he arrested. This assessment aside—and even Garzo wasn't entirely sure of it—the fact remained that Ricciardi was untamable, elusive, enigmatic. He lived with his aged *tata*, his childhood nanny. He had no bad habits, no friends, no woman in his life. A man without vices, he thought, cannot possess great virtues. And then, those eyes of his: those unsettling green eyes, clear as glass, that never blinked; those eyes that challenged you without challenging you directly, that put you face-to-face with the worst part of yourself, the part you'd rather not know about, the part you didn't know was there. Garzo shuddered.

Recently, moreover, there had been the widow Vezzi. That was another complication. The deputy chief of police couldn't understand why a woman who was so beautiful, wealthy, and well liked, and with friends in such high places (he'd even heard that she was close to the Duce's daughter), should make no secret of the crush she had on a character like Ricciardi.

She would pay him visits at headquarters, unblushingly, brazenly; and the less interest he seemed to show, the more shamelessly she courted him. Her presence, and the ascendant social position she had occupied in Naples's high society since moving there, gave the commissario an added layer of protection. Protection? Garzo asked himself. Yes, protection, he replied inwardly. Because he knew that if it weren't for her, he'd gladly take Ricciardi out of the picture; he'd rid himself of him, sending him off to do his investigating somewhere else, in a small town in the province, far from police headquarters and his own ambitions.

He stood up and started arranging the untouched law tomes that decoratively lined his office bookshelves so that the colors of their covers harmonized properly with the color of his carpet. He just couldn't put his mind at ease: Ricciardi was bound to cause trouble, he could feel it.

Still, come to think of it, the widow Vezzi's courtship of the commissario might prove useful to him. Word had it that the woman planned to hold a soiree in her new Neapolitan home, an exclusive reception in honor of the Duce's visit. Perhaps, he mused, he might be able to use his position to wangle an invitation, and maybe even attract notice. He'd heard that the Duce's daughter, Edda, was his favorite child and that she had considerable influence over her father; perhaps she'd find him charming and put in a good word for him.

He could see himself now: chief of police, in the royal box at the Teatro San Carlo, affably waving to the city's most prominent aristocrats. He smiled at the thought of turning the presence of a pain in the ass like Ricciardi to his own advantage.

Seized by a new wave of euphoria, he shouted: "Ponte!"

V

Livia Lucani, the widow Vezzi, took pleasure in the way
that her new apartment in Naples was coming
together; and it corresponded perfectly to the way
she'd envisioned it, when she'd first decided to move to the
city.

It was the first place she'd lived that she could call entirely
her own. She'd moved out of the home of her parents, heirs to
a noble and wealthy family in the town of Jesi, to go live with
an aunt in Rome and study singing. At the beginning of a
promising career as an opera singer, just as her lovely contralto
voice was starting to attract notice and critical praise, she'd
met Arnaldo, one of the century's greatest tenors, and married
him; and so, she realized, this was the first time that she'd chosen and furnished a home just for herself.

But perhaps she wouldn't be alone for long, she thought
with a smile as she sipped her coffee. Perhaps someone would
come along sooner or later to fill her bed, her home, and her
life. Perhaps someone with green eyes.

With effort she turned her thoughts back to the things
she'd need to do that day, and to her apartment. She'd chosen
a place in the center of town, with a little help from Ricciardi,
whose advice she'd sought. As usual, he hadn't wanted to
accept any responsibility toward her, and was very careful to
avoid entanglements; but she was patient, willing to wait, and
certain that sooner or later, as naturally as night follows day, he
would realize that she was the right woman for him, the one

who could pull him out of that strange quagmire of solitude in which he stubbornly insisted on living.

Instead of the lovely hillside of Posillipo, from which you could see the Gulf of Naples, or the new construction up in Vomero, with its cool air and greenery, she'd decided to move to the neighborhood near Via Toledo, choosing an elegant apartment on Via Sant'Anna dei Lombardi. She liked living downtown, amid the theaters and cafés, so that she could stroll past the chic shops and the ancient churches.

She fell in love with that city even before she fell in love with Ricciardi; she loved its cheerfulness, the way it changed its appearance and its colors according to the season, the swarms of street urchins who clung to the sides of the rattling trollies; she savored its constant music, the fact that at any time of day or night, whatever the occasion, there was always someone singing, either at the top of their lungs or under their breath; she enjoyed its food and its mild climate though she knew the weather could be capricious, as it had been recently, with days of rain. In that city, she was incapable of feeling unhappy.

Her girlfriends in Rome called her on an almost daily basis, asking her just what could be so wonderful in Naples that she had actually decided to go down there to live. Truth was, she thought with a smile, they were just eager to uncover the real reason for her move.

Livia had been a central figure in the high society of the capital. It was truly a rare thing for such a lovely and charming woman to win over even the ladies with her amiable personality, the women in those circles being inclined to jealousy and afraid of losing their husbands' affections. But Livia, open-hearted and sincere, sailed nonchalantly through the reefs of gossip and backbiting, and in the end succeeded in charming everyone, men and women alike.

There were a few people with whom she shared genuine friendship. One of these was Edda, the Duce's favorite daughter. The girl was barely twenty, a decade younger than she, and a fickle, capricious young woman; but she had taken a liking to the fascinating signora, who was a paragon of elegance and class. The two women liked each other, and when her schedule of official commitments allowed, Edda would call Livia for long, amusing phone conversations. This was one of the reasons Edda had asked her father if she could accompany him on his visit to Naples, even though she had her hands full getting ready to move to China with her new husband, a diplomat she'd married the year before.

Livia had decided to host a small, intimate party; it was a way of officially opening her home to Neapolitan society, and of showing her friend that the city was not the chaotic and dangerous slum that some people liked to portray it as.

Not that it would be a simple matter, to host the Duce's daughter. It would require extraordinary security measures and would attract the notice of both the city's aristocracy and its politicians. Still, it would be fun to open her drawing room to the elegant set and observe the behavior of certain self-important notables she'd had occasion to meet at the theater over the past few days.

She attended the theater by herself; she wasn't interested in being squired around by just anybody. Not that she wouldn't have had her pick of the town: almost every day her servants brought her enormous bouquets, some of them sent anonymously, others accompanied by ardent billets-doux with unfamiliar signatures. She stood up and, tightening the sash of her silk peignoir, she approached the mirror, admiring her shapely figure and her dark complexion, her raven hair and lustrous ebony eyes. My beauty, she thought. How much damage has my beauty done, to me and to others?

It had been her beauty that had captivated Arnaldo, a self-centered man accustomed to getting whatever he wanted. It had been her beauty that had caused two of her admirers to take leave of their senses; she'd spurned both their advances, and they'd gone so far as to challenge each other to a duel a few years earlier. It was her beauty that kept her from enjoying friendship with men, who, sooner or later, all decided that she must be theirs.

And now that, for the first time, it was she who wanted to cast her spell on a man, take him for her own and keep him at her side, he turned out to be the one man who was capable of resisting her beauty. Livia could tell that Ricciardi was hardly indifferent to her. Just the opposite: she could sense the tension, the way his body quivered silently whenever she approached, but there was something holding him back, making him keep his distance.

Once Ricciardi had told her that his heart belonged to another. That there was another woman in his thoughts. And so she had asked him whether he was married or engaged, and he had sadly shaken his head no.

That changed everything, she had thought to herself, emerging from the abyss of despair into which she had felt herself sink for a moment. No other woman could lay claim to him, he was a free man, and therefore he could still be hers. If he'd been otherwise committed she would have let him go: too many times she'd been the victim of her husband's philandering and two-timing, she'd suffered too many humiliations to want to inflict the same thing on some other woman. But if the strange, attractive commissario was unclaimed, then there was nothing wrong with implementing a strategy to conquer him.

Strategy? Conquer? Livia smiled into the mirror; those were words used in war, not in love. But deep down, she thought, isn't love a form of war? More like hunting than war, perhaps: but that did little to change the basic facts.

For the thousandth time she asked herself what it was about that man that moved her so deeply. His eyes, no question: two pieces of emerald so bright they glowed in the dark. And the tousled hair hanging over his forehead, the way he had of brushing it out of his eyes with a quick sweep of the hand. His hand, thin and nervous: that hand she'd so gladly feel on her body on one of those rainy nights.

She started brushing her hair. She wanted that man. She wanted him with every fiber in her body, in a way she'd never wanted anyone before. Throughout her life, she'd been guided, manipulated, and managed by others: her parents, her teachers, her husband. Now, for the first time, she had a home of her own, a place she'd chosen for herself, and a life all her own, full of the things she'd always desired; it was only natural that she should try to bring the man she wanted into that life and keep him close to her.

Gazing at herself in the mirror, she wondered what her unknown rival looked like, the woman whom Ricciardi said he loved. Not that it made a difference to her, against her blunt determination; she just wondered whether she was blonde or brunette, tall or petite.

Apprehensively, she feared that she might be prettier than her.

VI

Somewhat disheartened, Enrica looked down at the sleeping boy with a pen in his hand, his head resting on a sheet of paper and a streamer of drool at the corner of his mouth. He was snoring. It was the third time he'd dozed off that morning.

Of all the students she tutored, Mario was the most challenging: the boy's habit of suddenly falling asleep had caused him to be expelled from every state school in the kingdom of Italy, and his father, a wealthy cured-meats merchant, had confided in Enrica's mother, a regular client, that he'd reached his wit's end. The woman had immediately recommended her daughter, a certified schoolteacher, whose patience and stubbornness seemed perfectly suited to the challenge.

And so Enrica found herself spending most of each morning trying to wake up Mario, who was otherwise an upstanding young man, when he fell asleep on his schoolwork. She was hoping to present him at the equivalency tests for a junior high school diploma with some chance of passing them, as long as he didn't start snoring during the written portion of the exams.

But today, at least for a few minutes, Enrica was going to let her scholar sleep. She had something else to do.

Taking care to be quiet, she pulled a sheet of paper out of her skirt pocket and adjusted her myopic glasses on the bridge of her nose. Enrica wasn't beautiful, but she had a natural gracefulness and a femininity that expressed itself in her gestures and her smiles, which were attractive in spite of the fact that she was maybe a little too tall, with long legs hidden by the folds of her skirts, old-fashioned in their cut, the way she preferred. Her introverted personality, gentle but stubborn, allowed her to avoid arguments—especially with her mother, who tried to impose her own beliefs on her—and to do as she liked, thanks in part to the support of her father, a highly respected hat seller with a shop on Via Toledo.

The man dearly loved Enrica, his eldest, so similar to him in her reserved manner and tactiturn personality, and who at the age of twenty-four had never had a boyfriend. And yet she'd had her opportunities, most recently the son of the wealthy proprietor of a shop near her father's, but Enrica had refused to see him, sending her mother, who was terrified that her daughter would find herself an irremediable old maid, into a rage. I'm in love with someone else, Enrica had said: just like that, straightforward and unadorned, she had uttered this terrible piece of news one Sunday at lunch, before beginning her bowl of pasta with ragù.

Giulio Colombo, Enrica's father, had had his hands full trying to calm his wife over the next few days. They had been unable to find out anything about their daughter's phantom inamorato, except for the minor detail that he was not a married man: well, at least that's something, her mother had said, fanning herself nervously. No other information. What do you intend to do? she'd asked the girl, knowing that she'd stick to her plan, whatever that might be. I'll wait, she had replied, with her customary quiet determination.

When she made up her mind like that, she was best left to her own devices.

Life at home had returned to its usual routines. Enrica had resumed tutoring, cooking her father's favorite dishes, and embroidering after dinner, sitting by the kitchen window and listening to the faint sound of the radio playing in the living room. And shooting furtive glances at the window of the building across the street, where one could make out a slim dark silhouette, watching her as she did her needlepoint.

Enrica had learned who that silhouette belonged to a few months earlier. She'd received a summons to appear at police headquarters in regard to a murder she had nothing to do with, and when she walked into the office she found herself face-to-face with the man of her dreams, the unknown man who watched from the window: Commissario Luigi Alfredo Ricciardi. Their first encounter hadn't gone too well, truth be told. The fact that she'd been unprepared for the meeting, less carefully dressed and groomed than was customary for her, without a trace of makeup, had irritated her, and she'd reacted by displaying an aggressivity that was quite unlike her. For days she'd wallowed in the painful conviction that she'd never see him again.

Things had more or less worked themselves out in the weeks that followed. They'd gone back to gazing at each other from afar, even exchanging a hesitant wave of the hand, a nod of the head, a half smile. Enrica was patient. She knew how to wait. And her waiting had been rewarded just a few days earlier, with the arrival of the letter she now held in her hand, as little Mario snored away.

She smiled as she remembered how her father, returning from work, stood checking the mail the doorman had given him. He'd paused when he came to that one, furrowing his brow, and then he'd called her into another room, away from his wife's prying eyes. At last, he'd given her the letter, without a word, except to say:

"It's not postmarked."

What he meant by this was that someone had hand-delivered the envelope, or else they'd slipped it into the building's postbox. Then he'd left her alone, without asking her anything about it, neither then nor later. That's the way it was between them: discretion above all else.

She'd felt her heart bursting in her chest. In her bedroom, she'd waited almost half an hour, staring at the envelope and imagining all the possibilities. She didn't doubt for a second that it was from him, that he'd finally decided to step forward; at the same time, she was afraid of being disappointed, that it might contain a chilly formal greeting and nothing more.

Rereading it now for the hundredth time, she thought that to a certain extent, that's all it had been. But, in the end, it was still a way of reaching out to her.

Gentile Signorina, he began; *I am taking the liberty of writing to you, lest you think me rude for having the impudence and forwardness to make your acquaintance through a window. All the same, our meeting was so unexpected that I hardly had the presence of mind to introduce myself as I ought to have done. My name is Luigi Alfredo Ricciardi, I am a commissario at police headquarters, and, as you know, I live across the street from you, directly across from your window. This short letter is written with the sole intent of learning whether you would object to my greeting you, when I happen to see you from across the way. But I must add, in all sincerity, that I would be very glad if you did not object.*

I would be very pleased to hear from you. In the meantime, my fondest wishes,

Luigi Alfredo Ricciardi

Objectively, it wasn't much, but what Enrica valued greatly was what *wasn't* written in that letter; namely, the fact that there was nothing about any prior commitments, for instance with that beautiful and sophisticated *signora* she'd seen him with once at Caffè Gambrinus—otherwise he'd never have written to her. And the fact that he was not indifferent to her. And finally, that he was courteous, reserved, and shy, just as she'd imagined.

And now? she asked herself anxiously. Now it was up to her. It was her turn to reply, without being too forward, but also without being too standoffish, otherwise he might think that there was no interest on her part, as she feared he might have assumed based on her behavior the one time they'd met. She had to think, and she had to think quickly: if she let too much time go by before answering, he might take it as a sign of annoyance.

And how should she arrange to get her answer to him? She certainly couldn't be seen with an envelope in hand lurking around the postbox in his building, seeing as everyone in the neighborhood knew her; and mailing it would mean an enormous delay. She realized that she knew the elderly woman who lived with him by sight, a fat and good-natured woman who did her grocery shopping at the same place Enrica did; she'd have to screw up her courage and stop the woman, introduce herself, and talk to her. She'd have to be brave.

She put the sheet of paper back in her pocket and sighed, looking down at Mario, lost in his dreams. She coughed once; the boy woke up and looked at her with a bovine expression, barely recognizing her. She smiled at him and said:

"Now, where were we?"

And she shot a tender glance at the window across the way.

VII

Standing by his office window, Ricciardi was doing his best to dry himself off with his handkerchief. He watched the wind and the rain hammer down on the piazza, sweeping the streets clean of everything that wasn't anchored to the ground. The holm oaks were shaking their naked branches at the sky above, and people sought shelter in doorways and tried to save their umbrellas, useless against the fury of the elements.

As usual, the window reminded him of Enrica doing her needlepoint; a picture of peace and quiet, one in which he took refuge when he felt anxious and upset. Enrica. And the letter he'd written her.

Even though he knew that he hadn't been overly demonstrative, he was still deeply unsettled. For someone like him, so disinclined to engage in human relationships and displays of affection, it had truly been revolutionary to pick up pen and paper and contact her so directly, especially given the fact that they'd never been properly introduced. He shot a look at the chair in front of his desk, where the young woman had been sitting on that regrettable occasion when they'd first met. What a miserable fool he'd seemed. She must have thought he was an imbecile, an unfortunate idiot.

And what if the letter that I wrote her, he thought, strikes her as an intolerable intrusion into her life? Then I won't even be able to look at her from the window, to observe her simple, slow, serene gestures. Normal. Normality, that strange condition that was unknown to him. He remembered how he'd watched her secretly for months: there was something about the way she embroidered, the unhurried way she moved through her small world, that made the scene such a pleasure to watch that it had become his main reason for coming home at night, after work. Now he was sorry he'd written to her. But there was no taking it back: there was nothing he could do but wait.

In the rain-lashed piazza, he saw cars going by. In the distance he could see a woman holding a little girl by the hand, the two of them standing motionless in the middle of the street, incongruously dressed in light summer clothes. He remembered the accident, which had taken place a month and a half before, during the last whiplash of summer heat: the little girl had dropped something, a toy, perhaps, and she'd made her mother stop just as a Fiat 525 turned the corner and shot onto the piazza; the driver was looking the other way and ran them both over, stopping only after the rear tires had thumped over their bodies. From that distance Ricciardi could see that the woman's legs had been taken off neatly at mid-thigh, while the little girl's head was crushed from the neck up. The woman was still saying: *hurry, they're waiting for us.* Who knows who was waiting for them; whoever it was, they'd wait forever. The little girl was saying: *the top, I lost it, my top.* A wooden toy top. The cause of death was nothing more than a cursed little wooden top.

Even though they'd been bloodied and ravaged by the car's tires, the woman and girl were the only ones who had stayed dry under the driving rain. Death's little privileges, Ricciardi mused ironically. But the privilege of hearing their words even from a distance and watching their corpses dissolve slowly, day by day: now, that was something he had all to himself. That's who I am, Enrica. A man destined to walk surrounded by grief and pain, to be deafened, sickened, and suffocated by it. What can a man like that offer you? What kind of life? What kind of love? What a selfish wretch I was to write you a letter, even a pointless letter like that one.

The little girl and her top made him think back to the corpse that had started his week. The fact that he hadn't seen the boy's specter, and what Modo had said about it being certain he had died of natural causes. But, Ricciardi wondered, how natural could the death of such a young boy really be? Didn't that child have a right to enjoy the thrills, the triumphs, and the sorrows of a full life?

He could still see the back of the boy's neck, rain-streaked, the head dangling in empty air as the morgue attendants carted him off like the carcass of some stray animal. What was the boy's name? What games did he like to play, who were his friends? Was there a mother, were there brothers and sisters weeping in despair at his loss, or was he as alone and abandoned in life as he was now, in death?

Now Ricciardi saw another little boy in his mind's eye, another little boy playing with a wooden spade in a vineyard, twenty-five years earlier; he could hear the steady murmur as the boy described to himself the fantastic world around him, the world of his imagination. And he reflected on the thought that loneliness is a disease that spares not even the wealthy, and that spreads from childhood to adulthood and even old age.

These musings were interrupted by a discreet rap at the door, followed by the entrance of 265 pounds of wet brigadier.

"Nothing yet, Commissa'. We have no reports of a missing boy; it seems no one's noticed that the child's gone. Or at least, no one's thought to call the police about it."

Maione was cleaning himself off with a small hand towel, examining his mud-caked boots with resignation.

"Nothing, and this filth won't come off; now who's going to calm Lucia down? It's just my luck, right at the end of my shift. Otherwise I'd at least have time to let them dry off a little;

instead now I have to go home in this state. I'm sorry, Commissa', were you thinking? Am I interrupting?"

"Why, are there times when you're not thinking? No, I was just wondering about that little boy. Whether he had someone who cared about him, or if he was alone in the world."

"To judge by his clothing, if you ask me, he was alone. There's not a mother alive that would send her little boy out in this rain in wooden clogs, take it from me: even the poorest mother would at least have wrapped his feet in footcloths. When I was a boy my mother spent half an hour every morning wrapping me and my brothers' feet in the winter. Those footcloths were better than a pair of boots, let me tell you. And she'd wrap them so tight that our feet fell asleep and we'd have pins and needles all day long, I can still remember it. But they never came undone, you can be sure of that."

"Our little friend, on the other hand, had no footcloths. And his feet were covered with chilblains, did you notice? I'm very curious to know what killed him; what did Modo say, when will he let us know?"

Maione wasn't convinced that the autopsy had been the right choice, and he made no secret of the fact.

"He said that he'd call us, maybe tomorrow even. But Commissa', I have to tell you: this business about having the little boy autopsied, I can't say I was pleased with it. I don't like the idea of putting him in the ground cut up into pieces, after the doctor is done rummaging around in his guts looking for something that's not there. I know that you had only the best intentions, but you know that in this city little children die in the street all the time. It's nothing new, unfortunately."

Ricciardi turned his back to the window.

"I know. But you, you're a father, and I'd hardly expect to hear you say such a thing. The little boy is dead, that's true. And believe me, I don't like seeing corpses carved up any more than you do. It's just that I can't stand the idea of never even knowing how he died, that's all. A child that young shouldn't be tossed out like some old clothes. We need to give him a first and last name, and the doctor needs to give him a cause of death; at least that way we'll be burying a person, not a thing."

Maione smiled.

"I understand what you're trying to say. As someone who's lost a son, I know what it means never to see your child come home again. And even if we never talk about it, when Lucia and I look at the children that are left, we always think of Luca, and we'll think about him forever: I know it, and she knows it. And now that the Day of the Dead is almost here, we think about him even more. This rain, this neverending rain, it gets into your bones and makes you feel even sadder . . . And now the office is starting up, too; it's become a living hell!"

"Why? What's happened?"

Maione spread his arms wide.

"Oh right, I always forget that you never talk with a soul in here but me. And you're smart not to, believe me. Well, as you know, Mussolini's coming to town on November 3, and Garzo's going out of his mind. He's been saying that if anything goes wrong, he'll send us all to work as prison guards at Poggioreale; he's been arranging and rearranging the furniture in his office, over and over again; he's been having the stairs mopped several times a day; he sent both the automobiles to the garage for an overhaul, on the off chance that Mussolini wants to go for a drive; he looks at his mustache in the mirror constantly—and he thinks no one notices, but everyone's laughing behind his back. In short, a disaster!"

Ricciardi shook his head.

"How can people be such idiots? So Mussolini's coming; so what? Leaving aside the fact that he won't even end up visiting headquarters, what difference does it make anyway? Won't people go on dying, won't the same horrible things keep happening, out in the streets?"

Maione pounded a fist into the flat of his hand.

"That's exactly the point, Commissa': no, they won't. That is to say, that idiot Garzo is telling everyone that things have to function smoothly in this city, that there can't be any unrest or crime; that this is the ideal Fascist city, where all citizens live in peace and tranquility. In other words, we can't have any unsolved crimes or investigations under way, at least until Thunder Jaw, the *Mascellone*, heads back to Rome, and we'll thank God when he leaves."

Ricciardi gave him a dirty look.

"If he thinks that we're going to start covering things up or wasting time that we could be using to solve cases just so he can pretend that all's well, then he's really lost his mind. You can even send your friend Ponte to tell him: we're not going to stop doing our work, Mussolini or no Mussolini."

Maione burst out laughing.

"Fucking hell—my friend Ponte: I'd drop him down a man-hole and let him drown in the sewer, that two-faced rat! True, lately he's been Garzo's main victim, and it serves him right; if you could see him running back and forth, he's even more ridiculous than usual . . . Anyway, I knew you'd say that. I was thinking, though: working as a guard at Poggioreale can't be much worse than staying here, right?"

VIII

From the autopsy room in the hospital, Dr. Modo could hear the rain beating down on the roof and the windows. The overhead lamps illuminated the marble tables; it was finally evening after a long, difficult day. The wards were filled with every disease imaginable; he asked himself how people survived in the hygienic conditions that prevailed in most of the city.

The rain made matters worse: lungs, throats, and bones all absorbed the dampness like sponges and suffered serious damage. The common folk, accustomed to scraping by and concealing their misery with dignity, only showed up at the hospital when the situation had advanced beyond any remedy and there was nothing left for the physicians to do but try to alleviate their pain.

Modo thought about the torrents of filthy water gushing out of the backed-up city sewers and pouring into the ground-floor *bassi*, carrying waste and dead animals onto the floors where children played. He shook his head and shuddered; it was a miracle that so many people were still alive, to be sure. Often, after his regular shift was over, when he was so exhausted that his eyes refused to close, he'd wander the city's alleyways and *vicoli*, administering medical care to those in need of it. Old women tried to kiss his hands, but he recoiled: he wished there were more he could do. He wished he could give them medicine, but he only managed to pilfer a few doses here and there, when those people needed cartloads of it.

Tonight, for instance, I'd be much more useful out there

than in here autopsying a corpse, he thought as he looked down at the little boy spread out naked on the table, bruise-blue in the spectral light, his head resting on a wooden block. But he couldn't bring himself to tell Ricciardi no, and so instead of comforting the living, he found himself digging around inside a dead body.

He mused about the strange nature of his friendship with the commissario. They certainly weren't kindred spirits: Modo was outgoing and overly emphatic, while Ricciardi was reserved and rarely laughed; but in some strange way he felt closer to him than anyone else he knew. Perhaps it was because they were both loners: perhaps it was because they both observed the times they lived in with the same disenchantment and melancholy. Or perhaps it was because they felt the same pity for that teeming city and its desperate populace. Each of them chose different battles, though: the doctor opted for the path of explicit dissidence, the commissario for silent action.

He pulled the pocket watch out of his vest fob: ten o'clock. It had probably been about twenty-four hours since the little boy's death. He checked his surgical tools, clean and arrayed neatly in a metal tray next to the autopsy table. As always they looked ordinary and inoffensive: needle and thread, scissors, knives of various gauges and lengths, a handsaw and a pair of hacksaws, a bone chisel and a hammer. He thought of his father, a skilled carpenter who had worked until he was seventy so that Modo could attend medical school. You see, Papà, we're not all that different in the end. In the end, I saw, hammer, and chisel, too.

Ricciardi, Ricciardi: damn you, and damn your stubbornness. He remembered something from the Great War, on the Carso front, where he'd been the battalion medical officer. He'd met a lieutenant, a Calabrian named Caruso. He was a slight man of few words, swarthy and dark haired, constantly on the move. The two men had hit it off and they spent long evenings together in the trenches, listening to the distant rumble of artillery, swapping stories about women and the faraway cities they called home.

Caruso had a gift: he knew before anyone else what would happen in battle. He'd say: now watch, they're going to move over here, they're going to maneuver in thus-and-such a direction, they're going to try to outflank our machine gun emplacements. And right on schedule, as if Caruso himself were directing the whole operation, the chiefs of staff and the Krauts would do exactly what he'd predicted. But it didn't stop him from taking a bullet right between the eyes, one September night: that was one thing he hadn't seen coming.

Ricciardi reminded him of Caruso: the same sad half-smile, the same tense, active hands, the same gaze lost in contemplation of who knows what distant grief. The same strange ability to interpret reality according to his own subterranean streams, currents invisible to everyone else. There are people who go through life taking the burden of everything onto their own shoulders, even though they lack the necessary strength.

He focused on the little boy. He'd completed the external examination. He'd gone over the clothing: a shirt made of coarse linen, several sizes too big, threadbare and filthy, and a pair of oversized short britches, fastened at the waist with a length of twine on the verge of breaking. No underwear, no cuts, no recent rips or tears. No violence, at least not enacted on the clothing.

Then he'd examined the epidermis, every square inch of skin. As he'd announced after his initial survey, there were no signs of recent wounds. Marks aplenty, no doubt about that: on the neck, belly, and legs. Contusions, bruises, hematomas. Life wasn't easy for *scugnizzi* like this one. But there was nothing that could have caused his death, nothing very recent.

War, thought Modo. War and death. There was something absurdly exciting about war, he had to admit: the uniforms, the rifles, the bullets, and the bombs. Sure, there were hunger, filth, and infections: but there was also the knowledge that you were fighting for your country, for your homeland. Ridiculous concepts, he saw that now: a distant border, people who had never stopped speaking other languages no matter what flag was flying over city hall; but when you fight, you think of your own home far away, your traditions, the things that belong to you.

But the war that you fought, he mused, looking down at the body on the table, was one of neither glory nor grandeur. It was a war for survival, a war to live long enough to see the sun come up the next day, or to wake up to the feeling of rain on your skin. A war for bread, a war against the cold, a war for a dry place to sleep. A war that has no borders to defend, no bridges to destroy: the war of life.

He took his scalpel and made a Y-shaped incision, starting from the collarbone and running down to below the sternum, and continuing to the pubic bone with a detour around the navel. Beneath the skin, the layer of fatty tissue was virtually nonexistent, and Modo was not a bit surprised.

He decided first of all to perform a thorough examination of the abdomen, convinced as he was that the child's death had been caused by a straightforward cardiac arrest, possibly triggered by a congenital malformation combined with the generally poor state of health: the little boy was light as a baby bird. If he discovered the cause of death, he hoped to spare the victim the next step: the opening of the cranium for an examination of the encephalon.

Now, once again, the talk was of war: in the speeches of the head of state, in the newspapers, in idle conversations in the bars and cafés. Nothing explicit, of course; no one ever spoke about war openly. But if you observe carefully, thought the doctor as he applied the retractor, you realize that war is in the air, and how. All this talk about greatness, empire, history, ineluctable destiny. About mastery, dominion, and colonies. If that's not war, then I've never seen one before.

But I have seen war, you know that, child? I've seen war. And trust me, that's not easy either.

Now the Man of Destiny himself is actually coming here, to Naples. He's coming, and all the people like you will crowd the piazzas and clap and cheer on command. They might even put on their best clothes, as if it were a holiday, as if it were a special occasion. There might be a few petty thieves who'll take advantage of the excitement to slip their hands into a few pockets, I don't deny it, but there won't be many. For the most part, everyone will feel better for it, stronger, less hungry. The destiny of greatness. The empire: sky, sea, and land. And this time, just like before, no one will have the courage to say that the fault lies with this man and the others like him, arms akimbo, hands on hips, eyes flashing and jaws jutting, that it is they who spread hunger and death in the name of nonexistent ideals.

I've seen plenty of dead people, child. And I still see them, every day. Today it's you on this table, with the skin of your chest held up over your face by a couple of forceps, and these few little white bones splayed out. Tomorrow it could be anyone else. It could be your mother, who doesn't even know you're dead, or one of the brothers or sisters you've never even met.

Tell me, child: are you happy about Mussolini's visit? Are you as eager as everyone else to kiss his shiny boots, to get a nod of approval from that massive bovine head? Do you think too that we'll conquer the world together, and that Mussolini will restore the legacy of power and wealth that others took from you?

He picked up a large pair of surgical shears and started cutting through the ribs, on either side of the sternum. The ribs were soft and yielding, like those of a lamb. It broke his heart.

No, he murmured. You don't care about the Duce's visit anymore. Nothing matters to you; not now, my little one.

And he went on cutting, not realizing that his eyes were red with tears.

IX

It was around nine in the morning when they finally learned who the child was, or at least who he could be. Ricciardi had been in the office for almost two hours. He'd expected to find a note from the hospital waiting for him upon his arrival, or a woman sobbing and screaming at the foot of the stairs leading up to the sentry post, but there was no one. He started working on the report he'd have to file concerning the discovery of the body, but there was a sense of disquiet growing inside him: it wasn't possible that no one had noticed the child's disappearance.

The feeling of anguish was heightened by the fact that the dog he'd seen where the boy's body had been found was following him: he'd noticed it outside his apartment, on the other side of the street, sitting in the rain, one ear cocked. He'd set out for headquarters with the dog trailing behind him, some thirty feet back, on the opposite sidewalk. He'd stop and the dog would stop, too. He'd start walking again, and the dog would start again, too. In the end, he'd decided to simply ignore it, and he hadn't looked back again. When he got to headquarters the dog was gone, but it had left him swathed in a sense of some unfinished business.

That feeling vanished, in fact, a couple of hours later, when Maione appeared in the door and politely cleared his throat.

"Commissa', there's a priest here to see you who says that

he might be able to identify the little boy from Capodimonte. *Prego*, go right in, Don . . . ?"

A priest walked into the room. He was a nervous, pudgy man, of average height, his ragged tunic buttoned up the front and a round hat in his hand. He was wiping a mixture of sweat and rain from his brow.

"Don Antonio Mansi, parish priest of Santa Maria del Soccorso at Santa Teresa."

He spoke in a dolorous tone, as if he felt sorry for someone, probably himself. Ricciardi took an immediate dislike to the man.

"*Prego*, Padre, come in. My name is Ricciardi. Have a seat. Maione, you stay too. Tell me, what can we do for you today?"

"As I was telling your warrant officer here . . . "

Maione corrected him. He was punctilious about his rank.

"It's brigadier, Don Antonio. Brigadier Raffaele Maione, at your service."

"Forgive me, of course, Brigadier Maione; in any case, I have reason to believe that this child, so regrettably deceased, the one who was found at Capodimonte, is one of mine."

"One of yours?" Ricciardi asked. "What do you mean by that?"

The priest had taken a seat with his hat on his knees, and he'd slid the handkerchief back up one of his sleeves. He spoke in a subdued voice, his hands resting on his belly.

"In my parish, among the other good works we carry on, we take in a number of the orphans from the quarter. I house them in a building behind the rectory; right now we have six. One of them, the youngest, is named Matteo, and we haven't seen him since the day before yesterday. Seeing as he's never been away this long, I thought I should come report the matter to you."

Ricciardi was thrown by the priest's untroubled tone of voice. He sensed neither tension nor worry in the man's words,

words that were uttered, moreover, in the sniveling whine that he'd immediately noticed.

"But Padre, didn't you notice the child was missing before? Why did you wait until this morning to come to us?"

"Well, you see, Commissario, I'm not running a boarding school. What I have is just a shelter for these children who have neither a home nor a family. They're free to come and go as they like, they learn a trade, or they beg in the street; I certainly can't keep track of what all six of them are doing, twenty-four hours a day. Sometimes it happens that they stay out all night. These are children accustomed to life on the streets, unfortunately: but they're perfectly capable of looking after themselves. Some- times they just leave and don't come back, they find someplace else to stay, and they don't even come to say thank you for what we've done for them. But I don't do it to receive gratitude, I do it only for the glory of God."

Ricciardi and Maione exchanged a glance: it struck both of them as a speech the man had used on more than one occasion, a speech he kept handy in case he needed it.

"Well then, how did you come to the conclusion that the boy we found is . . . what did you say his name was, the child who lives in your shelter?"

"Matteo is his name. Matteo Diotallevi, but we assign them a surname ourselves when we don't have any other, just so we can register them with the office of vital statistics. He's the youngest one, I think he must be seven or eight; I can't say for sure, because they come to us not knowing when or where they were born. I thought it might be him because until now, as I told you, he'd never been away for so long. This morning, when I didn't see him, I asked the others and then inquired a little around the neighborhood, and no one had seen him in the past few hours. That's when I decided it would be best to report him as missing, to be safe. Then, when I got to police headquarters, the brigadier told me about the body you found at the Tondo di Capodimonte. Perhaps, if I saw him, I'd be able to confirm."

Ricciardi studied the priest's expressionless face.

"Forgive me, Padre, if I may take the liberty of saying so, you don't seem especially concerned. Resigned, perhaps, if anything. Why is that?"

A moment of silence followed. Both the priest and Maione were surprised by what the commissario had said, in such flat and direct terms. At last, the man heaved a sign and replied:

"That's not the way it is, believe me. I care deeply for the children I help, and the fact that I keep the house going, at great personal cost and sacrifice, and receive nothing in return is the proof. But these times we live in aren't easy, and who would know that better than you? The conditions the poor live in are terrible, and the ones who suffer most are the weakest, the elderly, and the young. They're vulnerable to accidents, diseases. They die on the streets, in the *vicoli* and in the *bassi*. The brigadier here was telling me that the boy you found probably died of natural causes; if it's Matteo, and I still have some hope that it isn't, he'd probably still be alive if he'd stayed home, with me. But these things happen."

Ricciardi was unwilling to dismiss the death of a child so glibly.

"They shouldn't happen, though, should they, Padre? It's up to us, to keep them from happening."

The priest smiled a melancholy smile. Never once during their conversation had he moved his hands, which rested on his belly, fingers knit.

"No, indeed. There are a great many things that ought not to happen but still do. What does the state do for these children? I'll tell you, Commissario: nothing. Nothing at all. It's all left to us, to the Church, or to the charity of the few wealthy people who still have a conscience. In twenty years, I must have lost at least ten or twelve of these boys. They've fallen off trolleys, drowned in the sea in the summertime, or been run over by a cart or a carriage. Or else killed by a fever or an infection, caught by eating who knows what, or cutting themselves in any of a number of ways. And the minute a place is vacated, there are a hundred more to bring in off the streets. We can only do what we're able, and that never changes. Perhaps that's why I seem resigned to you, my dear commissario."

Another silence ensued. Even though Ricciardi instinctively disliked that man, he had to admit that his reasoning was impeccable; he even felt irrationally at fault, as a representative of a government that was doing little or nothing for these children. For some reason, his thoughts turned to the dog that had followed him that morning, the young dead boy's last friend.

"Padre, if the child does in fact turn out to be Matteo Diotallevi, I'll have to ask you some more questions. But what we need to do first is proceed to the identification, so you'll need to come with us to take a look at the body, at the Ospedale dei Pellegrini."

This time, it was the priest's turn to be thrown.

"The hospital? But didn't you say the boy was dead when you found him? Perhaps you meant to say the cemetery."

"No, the corpse is at the hospital. I asked the medical examiner to examine the body, to determine exactly what caused the boy's death. I see that it's still raining out; Maione, call down and have them bring up a car."

The brigadier shook his head regretfully.

"No, Commissa'. Both cars have been sent to the garage to get spruced up for the Duce; I told you yesterday. Seems we're going to have to go on foot this time, too."

And he looked down sadly at his boots: polished and gleaming, but not for long.

X

The walk to the hospital wasn't long, but the rain made it unpleasant. As Don Antonio walked, he kept the hem of his tunic lifted with one hand and held his hat to his head with the other, taking care not to stumble into any of the numerous puddles of unknowable depth that had formed on the sidewalks. Maione had the same problem, and he muttered curses under his breath, so that they would not reach the priest's ear, while trying to hold up the umbrella to shelter Ricciardi, who, as usual, seemed indifferent to the water drenching his uncovered hair.

They finally reached their destination and stood dripping in a waiting room, where they were met by Dr. Modo. The physician was dropping on his feet, his face creased with wrinkles and stubbled with in a day's growth of whiskers. Ricciardi felt a stab of remorse for having forced him to take on that extra, no doubt draining task, which would probably turn out to have been pointless.

"Ah, there you are," said the doctor. "I would have called you later, I'm waiting for the results on some tests that I've ordered from the lab. And after that, with your permission, I'd like to head home and get at least twenty-four hours of sleep. Who is this gentleman with you?"

Maione hid a smile: Modo never missed a chance to display his nonconformist views, especially his anticlerical ones. Don Antonio looked back at him offendedly and then turned to Ricciardi, waiting for the commissario to introduce him.

"This is Don Antonio, the parish priest of Santa Maria del Soccorso. Did I get that right, Padre? He runs a small shelter for orphans and he thinks that the child you have here with you might be one of his, a little boy who disappeared a couple of days ago. He'd like to take a look at the corpse to see if he can identify it. May we?"

Modo ran a hand through his hair, a habitual gesture.

"Yes, I would think so. I'm done with him; I'll tell you the findings later."

Don Antonio squinted, in an expression of mistrust. He spoke not to Modo, but to Ricciardi.

"Excuse me, Commissario. What does the doctor mean when he says that he's done with him? Just what has been done to the child?"

The doctor answered brusquely:

"We've done what we thought necessary. We performed an examination to determine how this child died, while those who ought to have been keeping an eye on him were doing other things. That's what was done."

The priest took a step back, blinking.

"We look after these children for as long as they allow us to. If they go out and wander the city by themselves, that's hardly our fault. Can I see him, now?"

Modo, still glaring angrily at the priest, turned and led the way back to the hospital morgue.

The boy's corpse had been reassembled and dressed in the tattered clothing he'd been found in. Even though Ricciardi was hardened to terrible sights, he still felt his heart break when he saw the body, which looked so tiny on the marble table. The signs of the restitching done after the autopsy were clearly visible, on the head and on the shoulders; from there, the incision disappeared underneath the boy's shirt.

Don Antonio rocked back on his heels; his eyes filled with tears. He took a step forward and approached the corpse. He made the sign of the cross over the child's forehead, then murmured a prayer and a benediction. Then he ran his thumb over the incision on the top of the head and gave Modo a cold, hard look. Finally, he said to Ricciardi:

"It's him. This is Matteo, little Matteo. But someone is going to have to answer for this, this thing that's been done to him. This massacre."

Maione, hat in hand, shot a glance at Ricciardi as if to say: I told you so. The commissario returned the priest's look with a level gaze.

"Well, report me, if you're going to report anyone, Padre. I'm the one who arranged for the body to be examined further, and I take full responsibility. Neither the doctor nor Maione, here, thought it was necessary. But I felt a need to know how the child died, and so I ordered the autopsy."

The priest hissed:

"And now, do you know how he died, at least? And, more importantly, does it make a difference?"

Modo was about to break in, but Ricciardi gestured to him to be quiet.

"Forgive me, but that's still under investigation. It's not something we can share with the public. But would you please be so good as to return to headquarters now? Brigadier Maione will accompany you. I'll have to stay behind for a few minutes to talk with the doctor, but I'll meet you there shortly."

Don Antonio seemed to have calmed down, but his expression remained fierce. He nodded a brusque farewell, directed midway between Modo and Ricciardi, and left the room, escorted by Maione.

The doctor lit a cigarette.

"The very idea of bringing a priest here. You know, they bring bad luck, from my experience. I never want to see one in my hospital if I can help it."

"But the place is full of nuns, I see," said Ricciardi.

"What does that have to do with anything? They're nurses, and they're first-rate nurses, too. The best, believe me: even in wartime, at the front, they were tireless. That might be a form of fanaticism, too, but at least it's useful fanaticism."

"All right then, what can you tell me? Do you know what killed the little boy?"

Modo gestured for Ricciardi to leave the room. A muscle in his jaw was twitching. His exhaustion aged him.

"Come on, let's get out of here. I need some fresh air, even if it's raining."

They found a place to talk under an awning at the entrance to the wing where the morgue was located. From behind a couple of scrawny saplings being whipped by the rain came the calls of the strolling vendors in the market. Ricciardi guessed they were calling their wares in vain: there couldn't be a lot of people out in this weather.

"Well, Bruno? What can you tell me?"

The doctor said nothing for a moment, then replied:

"No, first you tell me. Why did you insist on this autopsy? What made you suspicious?"

Ricciardi, his hands shoved in his pockets, his hair plastered to his forehead by the rain, replied:

"You know, Doctor, the work you and I do is based on intuitions. That's what you always say, isn't it? The clinical picture steers you toward one diagnosis, but then you glimpse another: and you pursue that other diagnosis, and in the end you're either right or you're wrong. That's the way it is for me. It was just an instant, when the morgue attendants were carrying him off. The way his head was dangling, all that rain. The pity of it. I don't know: it was just an impulse."

Modo went on smoking in silence. He looked out at the rain falling on the trees. Then he said:

"Sure, intuitions. Things you can't put your finger on. But

you know what an autopsy is like. It's sheer butchery. I was hoping I wouldn't have to open up the child's head. But I did. I even had to carve into his back, to gain access to his spinal cord."

"If you're worried about the priest, don't be, Bruno: I take full responsibility, whatever the outcome . . . "

"I don't give a damn about the priest," the doctor snapped, "I don't give a damn about him, the bishop, or the pope himself. It's the child, the fact that he couldn't complain. If I hadn't found anything, then I would have seen him at the foot of my bed every night, demanding an explanation, asking why I'd sent him to his grave chopped into little bits."

"So you're telling me you found something?"

The doctor laughed.

"And out comes the policeman. Straight to the point, eh? Okay, yes, I found something."

"I knew it! That means we'll have to do a full investigation; we can start with the priest and . . . "

Modo interrupted him:

"Don't get all worked up. I said that I found something, not that there's something to investigate."

"But what does that mean? Tell me, then, what killed this child?"

"Let me tell you the whole story. First thing, I took a look at the heart, and it was in the systolic phase, as I expected: big as a watermelon. And then there was the rigor mortis, extreme and much longer lasting than normal. The cyanosis and the spotted bruises . . . In other words, there were just too many signs pointing to convulsions. So then I had to resign myself to assessing the nervous system."

Ricciardi was listening very attentively.

"Why, is there some connection?"

"Of course, if there are convulsions then it's quite likely that the nervous system is responsible in some way, don't you agree? And in fact both the meninges and the spinal cord were full of blood. I even found a few areas that were outright hemorrhagic. Our young friend didn't die peacefully. Not at all."

"And yet he seemed so serene, in the position he was in when we found him."

Modo shrugged.

"That doesn't mean anything; you know that. An instant before dying, he might have relaxed, and perhaps the only reason he was sitting up and not flat on the ground is that the wall was supporting him. In any case, at that point I took samples from the brain and from the spinal cord and I sent them to the laboratory, where luckily a friend of mine was on duty. He was on his regular hospital shift, fully paid, and I was on a special shift ordered by Commissario Ricciardi, working completely free of charge."

Ricciardi made a face.

"You're getting really obsessed with money in your old age, you know that? Fine, I'll buy you a pizza at the Trattoria Da Nannina, around the corner."

Modo snickered.

"Well, I'll be! Then it's true what they say: you're filthy rich but still a skinflint. Anyway, as I was saying, I sent those samples in for analysis, along with the food remains that I found in the stomach and duodenum. I'm still waiting for the written results, but an hour ago my friend came to see me in the autopsy room and told me what he'd found."

Ricciardi waited.

"Well? Are you going to tell me what the hell killed this child or not?"

The doctor crushed his cigarette butt under his heel and exhaled the smoke in a theatrical plume.

"You were right. He didn't die of natural causes, he didn't die of an infection, malnutrition, or some disease. He was in bad shape, there's no denying that, but he was strong and he would have gone on living for many years to come. But I was right, too, when I brought up the possibility of accidental death with you earlier."

"Which means what?"

"The child died from poison. Strychnine, to be exact. He must have simply ingested a handful of poison bait, those little clumps of sugar and flour that they put out to kill rats."

Ricciardi stood there openmouthed.

"Rat poison? The boy ate rat poison?"

"Surprised, are you? Well, that's because you don't see the things I see, day in and day out. They eat everything they find. You eat or you die. They dig through the garbage, they fight dogs for scraps. They'd eat the rats themselves, if the rats were easier to catch. I've seen this kind of thing before, though I have to say that they usually stop before they ingest a fatal dose, because strychnine has a bitter taste; but such a frail child would only have to eat a tiny amount for it to kill him. And then those bastard shopkeepers, to protect their disgusting merchandise, they hide the poison in bait balls made out of bread and cheese or sugar: a tasty little morsel, in other words."

The commissario was perplexed.

"But couldn't someone have given him the poison? Intentionally, I mean."

Modo gave him a long hard look, then said:

"Listen, Ricciardi: I don't know why you're devoting so much time to this child and his death. You know I admire your dedication, and I feel as much pity, if not more, for the poor people who die of privation in this city that the Fascist regime has made so utterly perfect. Unfortunately, for a child to die from accidentally eating some rat poison is a normal turn of events. The dead should be left in peace; and the world this little boy spent his short life in is far too murky and filthy for us to delve into. I told you that this is a case of accidental death, and I have no intention of writing anything else in the report. Please, just accept it."

Ricciardi had nothing more to say. He squeezed the doctor's arm.

"You're probably right, Bruno. I just have a couple more questions for our friend the priest and then I'll be done. Thanks again, and let me know when I can buy you that pizza."

With the doctor's gaze following him, he headed back to headquarters. In the rain, by the hospital's main entrance, he saw a dog looking in the direction of the morgue.

XI

Rosa Vaglio fastened her hat in place with a couple of hatpins, picked up her umbrella, and went out, double- and triple-locking the door behind her. She was only going to do a little shopping in the neighborhood, but she wasn't taking any chances: even if people said that everything was safe these days, it was still a rough quarter.

Actually, the whole city scared her. They'd moved there ten years ago, and she still wasn't used to all those people, all the hustle and bustle, and the fact that you could go out every day and walk around for hours and never run into anyone you knew.

Back home, in the village of Fortino, in the southern part of the province of Salerno, almost in Lucania, things were quite different. Everyone knew everything about everyone: they never had strangers visit from other towns, or when one happened to pass through, they looked at him as if he had two heads, until he felt so uncomfortable that he left, and then everyone heaved a sigh of relief. There was no need for strangers, back home.

What's more, there was respect. When she walked down the main street of town (the only street, for that matter) everyone doffed their hats at the sight of the Barone di Malomonte's *tata*. She knew it, and she strode proudly, head held high, eyes straight ahead. No one dared to address her, unless she spoke to them first. She had been chosen to raise the next baron, and that was all anyone needed to know. She made her rounds of the farms and workshops, checking to make sure that no one was stealing, that everyone set aside the finest products—the fattest hogs, the best cheeses—for the family that lived in the castle. That's how it was meant to be, and that's how it was.

Circumspectly walking down the staircase of the apartment building, Rosa sighed as she thought about what it must be like back there, now that everyone had been left to their own devices. In the past, her mere presence had been enough to make big, strapping farmers tremble; they knew all too well how capable her sharp eyes were of detecting even the slightest deception. But then, someone had to look after things. The baron had been dead for years, and the poor baroness, the Good Lord love her and keep her in glory, had never been up to such duties.

As always, the thought of that gentle, petite woman brought a smile of tenderness to Rosa's lips: her childlike face and lovely green eyes. Immediately after meeting Rosa, at the time a twenty-year-old housekeeper with strong arms and red cheeks, the baroness had decided that when she became a mother, this would be her child's *tata*. Many years went by before that came to pass; in the meantime Rosa had helped the baroness to keep things running smoothly during those long periods when her migraine headaches and lethargy forced her to stay in bed. But then the baby boy was born.

Her baby boy.

Rosa had immediately set about caring for him, with simplicity, and without any ado. From the very beginning she dedicated her life to him, as if she'd been born for this purpose, as if the years she'd lived before setting eyes on him had been nothing more than a long period of preparation.

She'd loved him unreservedly, unconditionally, unquestioningly. As the baroness had told her—before her extended stay in the hospital, culminating in her death—Rosa would have to be the child's mother in her place; and so she had been.

Not that she understood him, she thought as she looked out at the water pouring down. She'd never understood him. His habitual silences, the way he stared into empty air, his sudden bouts of melancholy. In every respect, and for all intents and purposes, he was just like his mother, with the same clear green eyes, looking out at a world that they alone could see. But it wasn't Rosa's job to understand Luigi Alfredo Ricciardi, Barone di Malomonte; her job was to take care of him, to make sure that he lacked for nothing.

And that was what worried her. Time was passing: she was past seventy and he was thirty-one years old, an age by which most men had already established a family and were raising their children. And he hadn't even found a fiancée.

Simple soul though she was, Rosa understood that there were emotions stirring in that tightly closed heart. She saw him night after night, looking across the way at a certain window, when he thought she was asleep in her bedroom; instead she got up and, on tiptoe, she'd peer through the crack in the door, which he purposely left ajar so he could listen to her snore.

So why did he persist in this absurd loneliness? Even though she knew she was looking at him through the eyes of a loving nanny, she found him very handsome, sensitive, and good-hearted. And wealthy, too, though he was absolutely (and, to her eyes, culpably) disinterested in his estates. He had everything necessary to charm the best woman in the world.

But the *signorino*, the young master, as she called him, behaved as if he'd taken a vow: no woman, no family.

She believed it was her duty to perpetuate the Malomonte name. She considered it a crime to knowingly bring such an old and venerable family to an end. But what could she do?

A few months earlier, she had noticed that under a certain loose tile in his bedroom, the *signorino* had hidden a book. Laboriously, because she knew only her numbers and capital letters, she'd copied the title. Then she'd gone to ask the hairdresser who'd attended parochial school for a couple of years and had learned to read from the nuns to confirm it for her. And in fact, the title was: *Il moderno segretario galante*. She'd asked around and had discovered that it was a collection of love letters, to be used as models.

She didn't know how to read, but she could put two and two together. In the window across the way, she knew that it was Enrica Colombo who sat embroidering, the eldest daughter of the owner of the hat shop on Via Toledo. And her *signorino* watched her embroider.

She didn't know whether he had actually made use of the book after buying it, but she certainly hoped he had: the girl seemed good-hearted and honest, and she came from a good family, as far as she knew. The hairdresser, who was a sort of living neighborhood newsletter, had maliciously told her all about how Enrica had spurned a potential fiancé whom her mother was encouraging, a rich and handsome young man: Rosa had heaved a sigh of relief, inwardly commenting that there was no one as handsome as her own *signorino*. What she couldn't tell though was whether the hairdresser was a two-way street: that is to say, whether or not Enrica also had occasion to hang on the hairdresser's words, whether she had learned of the interest expressed by Donna Rosa, Commissario Ricciardi's old *tata*, in this affair of the heart.

After pulling her shawl tight around her neck and opening her umbrella, Rosa ventured out into the rainy street, thinking that the damp weather was inflicting a decidedly harsh punishment on her aching bones. She needed to take action, she thought to herself. Fate does as it pleases, but sometimes it needs a little push. The girl was sitting across the street, reservedly, clearly waiting for him to make the first move, while he waited for his own shyness to melt away. It was slow to melt! In fact, it would probably never melt, and in the end the girl was bound to get sick of waiting and accept some other suitor.

And they'd both live unhappily ever after, some fifteen feet apart, lacking the courage to ever speak to each other.

But what could she do? she wondered as she zigzagged through the rain to the spice and grain shop to buy some chickpeas. How could she strike up a conversation with the young woman and explain to her that that blockhead of a *signorino* of hers loved her in silence, from a distance, but lacked the courage to live his life?

As she was crossing the street a pair of eyes, from behind a pair of glasses and a window, caught sight of her. The owner of those eyes then hurried to her closet where she grabbed the first hat that came to hand and an umbrella, and then galloped down the stairs.

Rosa was just thinking that Ricciardi didn't even wear a hat, so she couldn't arrange for him to visit Enrica's father's shop, when, right in front of the grocer's, she found herself face-to-face with Enrica, who was courteously stepping aside for her.

Smiling brightly, she looked her in the face. It's now or never, she told herself.

XII

Water.

Water that doesn't clean.

Water that flows down in a thousand rivers without a sea, washing mud up to the front doors of the *bassi* and then inside, spreading filthy fingers over the rammed-earth floors, into the blackened straw of the pallets. Water that beats against the windows and stirs the sleepers, or carries specters of ancient sorrows into dreams. Water that leaves black marks on the high tufa-stone walls, finding its way into old buildings to undermine their foundations. Water that muddies polished shoes and tears umbrellas out of hands, because it wants to eliminate all obstacles that prevent it from entering people's souls, bringing with it the damp of depression.

Water that separates.

Water that becomes a cold wall between lovers, removing the smile from their eyes and hearts. That keeps people away from school, the workshop, and the office, creating a sea between them, a sea that's impossible to navigate. Water that turns streets into slippery rivers, that sucks any chance of encounter down into its whirlpools. Water that takes toys away from children, forcing them into imprisonment on a chair or in a room.

Water that steals.

There will be no one to buy from the vendors' carts, to give alms to the poor, to be defrauded. There will be no one to buy balloons or toys in the Villa Nazionale. There will be no one to listen to the *pazzariello*, the street crier, announcing in song the opening of some new shop. There will be no one, and there will be nothing to eat.

Water that frightens.

Frightens with the thunder that rattles the night, with the lightning that illuminates the silence. Fear that makes your heart lurch in your chest, that makes you draw your head between your shoulders, waiting for the worst. Water that makes the walls creak, and makes you think that nothing is a sure thing, that nothing will ever end.

Water that never ends.

Ricciardi was walking back to police headquarters, through the rain that never seemed to stop falling. The question that filled his mind, leaving no room for any other thought, was this: Why wasn't he there? Why didn't I see him?

The cause of the child's death had been poison. Strychnine. There were no other causes, Modo had ruled them out decisively: the boy would have lived many more years, he'd said. But in that case, if he'd died from poison, why hadn't Ricciardi seen his ghostly image?

The terrible company of the Deed had marked his whole life, from the time he'd seen the first dead man to speak to him in his family's vineyard, when he was five years old. God only knows how many times he'd wished he could be spared from this curse.

In contrast with what he usually did—try his best to forget what he'd seen—Ricciardi summoned up memories of the poison victims he'd seen in the past. He thought of the first one, a classmate at boarding school who for who knows what reason had eaten an entire box of matches; perhaps it was on a dare, some stupid game with a friend. He remembered the boy, smiling and translucent in the recreation yard, immersed in an incessant retching gush of blood and a perennial diarrhea, saying over and over again: *I won, did you see? I won the bet.* And the convulsions of his two university friends who had gorged on mushrooms purchased from a street vender, one of which was poisonous—just one. The specter of one friend, trembling like a vibrating guitar string, his eyes rolled back in his head, was saying to the other: *good, aren't they? And they were so cheap.* And then there was the brokenhearted suicide he'd seen just a few months earlier from the San Martino belvedere, clutching his belly and vomiting a yellow froth as he said: *I can't live without you.*

He saw them, the poisoned dead. There was no doubt about it. So why hadn't he seen the little boy?

He knew the Deed, and its few but exceedingly strict rules. He saw the image of the dead person the way they'd died, repeating their last thought in the very place their broken life had flowed out of them. Therefore, only one answer could be possible: the child hadn't died where they'd found him.

The thought exploded in his head just as there was a crack of thunder, an accompaniment to the pelting rain. If he hadn't died there, it meant someone had moved the body.

This didn't necessarily mean that the boy had been murdered, Ricciardi realized. But it did mean that someone, for some reason, had decided it would be worth the trouble to move the body and leave it in a place where the child's presence might seem to be the result of chance. Who could have wanted to do such a thing?

On the opposite side of the street, through the curtain of rain, he could make out the dog's spotted coat. He decided that he'd hunt down whoever it had been to move the body and find out why they had done it. He'd do it because it was the right thing to do, and because a child isn't just a disposable thing.

And because there was something about that dog that made him determined to keep going.

Rosa entered the shop, followed by Enrica. The heavy rain had forced the proprietors—the husband manning the counter, the wife at the cash register—to light their oil lamp. There were no other customers. The shopkeeper, a strapping, jovial man with thinning hair and missing teeth, greeted Rosa affectionately:

"Here she is, the beautiful Donna Rosa! How are you this morning, my lady? Have you seen how hard it's raining?"

"*Buon giorno*, Don Gera'. I've seen it and I've felt it, in all the aches and pains in my body, in every last bone. Now, better be quick, I've got a whole kitchen to put together, this morning I haven't done a thing and it's already ten. Give me a slice of lard, six fresh eggs, two kilos of chickpeas, and make sure they're good this time; last time I had to throw out half of them. And two cups of olive oil: good olive oil. Give me two kilos of mixed pasta, wrap it up nicely so it doesn't get wet, with all this rain. And beans, I almost forgot, two kilos of beans. A little sugar, too, and a quarter kilo of tomato paste. Ah, and one more thing: a quarter kilo of roasted coffee."

Gerardo followed her orders, moving nimbly from one recipient to the next behind the counter.

"What should I do, send these things up once the boy gets back from his deliveries?"

Rosa snorted.

"No, absolutely not, that way I won't get my groceries until two this afternoon! I have cooking to do; when my *signorino* gets home he expects to find food on the table! No, just give it here, I'll carry it up myself."

It was then that Enrica coughed once and then said, practically under her breath:

"If I'm not intruding, Signora, I'd be glad to give you a hand carrying your groceries. I'm Enrica Colombo, I live right across the street . . . "

Rosa turned to look at her:

"Yes, yes, I know who you are. Your windows are right across from ours, aren't they?"

The young woman blushed visibly but held her gaze.

"That's right. If you'd like, I can help you up the steps: with all these things, your umbrella and your bag . . . I mean, if you like, I'd be happy to do it."

The shopkeeper and his wife exchanged a conspiratorial glance. The woman smiled and pretended to count the money in the cash register. Rosa nodded her head.

"It would be a pleasure, if you'd like to give me a hand. I'm not as young as I once was, you know, and the more the years go by the worse my back gets. But I just can't wait for Don Gerardo's delivery boy to come back. Thank you, Signori'. I'll carry the pasta myself."

XIII

From the armchair in her living room, Livia watched the rain streak her window. The tracks of the raindrops across the glass enchanted and distracted her from the continuous chatter of Anna, an old friend of hers from Rome who'd been talking her ear off on the phone for almost half an hour.

"Now *you* tell me, Livia: you left us, one night you were here and the next morning you were gone, you just abandoned us all! You know, just yesterday I ran into the Marchese della Verdiana, you know, that tall handsome man with the handlebar mustache: the same one who used to court you so relentlessly, the one who sent you the enormous bouquets of roses every morning, remember? Well. He stopped me, if you can believe it, while I was walking down the Via del Corso, just rears up in front of me, just think! He makes a nice little bow, he clears his throat, and he says to me, he says: Signora, how enchanting to run into you like this, and on and on, why, what a pleasure, you've brightened my day, and so on and so forth . . . Livia? Livia, are you even listening to me?"

"Yes, of course, Anna, I'm here, I'm listening."

"Good! Because this story is interesting, you know? So, to get to the point, the marchese says to me: that friend of yours, the Signora Vezzi, hasn't she come back from her trip yet? *Capisci*, Livia? Everyone in Rome is talking about your move, and he pretends to think you're just off on a jaunt to another city!"

Livia wished she had a good excuse to put an end to that conversation: she knew that Anna was just telling her the story in the hopes of extorting more information from her about the reason for her disappearance from Rome. Smiling as she lazily twisted the cord of the elegant white telephone around her fingers, Livia decided to keep her on tenterhooks for a while longer.

"And you? What did you say to him?"

"Ah, I just told him the truth: that I had no idea, that you left without telling me when you'd return, and that any day now I expected you'd let me know. You know, poor thing, he seemed so distraught and eager to know when you'd be coming back that I couldn't bring myself to tell him that you'd sent a crew of roustabouts to get your things and shut down your apartment in Rome."

Livia burst out laughing.

"And who told you that? Did you hire a private investigator to watch the entrance to my building? You're fantastic, you know that, Anna? You take gossip to the level of fine art!"

"Livia, you know you're not being fair, and you're hurting my feelings! You're one of my dearest friends, I'm allowed to miss you, no? And it's only natural for someone who wants to know how you're doing to ask me, don't you think? We always used to go out together, you and I. So, come on, I'm begging you: tell me why you left. I would think I'd have a right to know! Did something happen, here in Rome? A quarrel, a lover . . . A married man, perhaps? Come on, just tell me, please!"

"Why, did someone tell you I was having an affair with a married man? And when could I have had this affair, with you checking on me constantly? Come on, Anna, just accept it: there's not always a reason for everything. And if a woman leaves a city, it might be because she's running away from something, but it also might be because she's searching for something, no?"

On the other end of the line, Anna loudly blew out her cheeks.

"There, you see? You're trying to make a fool of me again! But what sane person decides to leave Rome for Naples? And you of all people, perhaps the only woman with full access to every drawing room and salon in the city, and a personal friend, no less, of Edda Mussolini—or I suppose I should say, Edda Ciano, now that she's married. By the way, have you spoken to her? I heard that she might travel down to Naples with her father and her husband in a few days for the address."

"Yes, I talked to her and we might see each other. But she for one has never scolded me for moving away like you've been doing, you know. In fact, she told me that it was a wonderful idea, that this is a stupendous city, and that she even envied me, just think of that."

Her girlfriend sighed resignedly.

"There, now even the Duce's daughter is on your side, poor me. I have no choice but to believe the lies you tell me, that you're actually interested in someone in Naples. Though that's odd too, because a girlfriend of mine who lives in Naples—and I won't tell you who she is or else I'll lose even this source of information—she wrote me and told me that she hadn't heard anything about a man striking your fancy."

A pair of green eyes flashed through Livia's mind and were gone, like a lightning bolt.

"Or maybe there is a man, and he's just not interested in me."

A loud, screaming laugh came through the receiver.

"A man who doesn't want you? You? Livia Lucani, the widow Vezzi? Now that's something I'd like to see! I wish I had ten lire for every man I've seen mooning after you, you lucky thing. No, that's impossible, if I needed proof that you're talking nonsense, now I have it. Fine, I get it: you've decided to stop confiding in me. But I love you just the same, so just know that if you want to talk to me, I'm right here."

"I love you too, *cara*. Kissses, *arrivederci*."

At last, thought Livia; and she went back to watching the raindrops on the glass, thinking about those green eyes.

Ricciardi stared at Don Antonio, trying to discern his emotions. The priest had a pained expression on his face, but he seemed to have no intention of dropping the matter of the autopsy.

"I'd like to know from you, Commissario, who authorized you to massacre that child's dead body. If there had been reasonable doubts about the cause of death, then I would have been the first to urge you to get to the bottom of it. But the doctor himself says that there's no reason not to believe in the accidental nature of the misfortune, it seems to me that that's what I heard. And in that case, why on earth did you decide to carve up that poor corpse?"

"Padre, I can tell you now: the child died, not of disease or infection, but of poison. He ingested strychnine, rat poison, along with the bait it came in. This is worth a little further investigation, don't you think? If only to ensure that such a terrible thing doesn't happen to any other children."

Don Antonio seemed struck by this information; he shook his head sadly, and ran a hand over his face. Even Maione started in surprise.

"This too is something I've had to see before. It happened five years ago: two of my children found some food that had gone bad. We never found out what it was they'd eaten. They fell ill, they got worse; then one died, the weaker of the two, while the other one survived, but he was never the same. He stopped talking and he was committed to an institution. These are terrible accidents, but they happen."

Ricciardi nodded.

"Yes, Padre. It happens. All the same, if you don't mind, I'd like to know a little more about this child, his life, the things he did."

The priest became defensive:

"Really? And why would you want to know that, Commissario? If you yourself say that it was all a terrible accident, then all I need to do is ask the other boys where Matteo might have found the poisoned bait, don't you agree? That way, you can go look into it and make sure nothing like this ever happens again."

"It's routine procedure, Padre. The child died of other than natural causes, and we have to justify our intervention."

Don Antonio sighed, momentarily resigned.

"Fine. Go ahead and ask."

"Why don't you go ahead and tell me, Padre. Tell me about the child, his personality, his friends, the kinds of things he did. Anything that comes to mind."

"All right: his name was Matteo, but everyone called him Tettè. Because—poor boy—he had a terrible stutter. First he'd get excited, then anxious, and then he wouldn't be able to speak. Sometimes he'd get stuck on a single letter and have to give up entirely, just stop talking. He was small for his age, he must have been at least eight, maybe older, clever but a loner, perhaps because of the stutter. He had a little dog. I can't have the boys keeping animals, you understand, for hygienic reasons. So he'd leave the dog outside, and whatever the weather, the dog would wait for him. They were always together."

Ricciardi asked:

"A dog with a white coat and brown spots?"

Don Antonio nodded.

"That's right, you must have seen it yourself. Was the dog in the area where . . . where you found Matteo?"

"Yes, Padre."

"I'm not surprised, it never left his side. Who knows what'll become of that dog now. Anyway, we all loved Tettè so much: everyone doted on him. Since he was the smallest, the other boys protected him, and anyone who dared to lay a hand on him had the boys to answer to. And, I'll admit, I always had a special fondness for the boy myself. No one would ever have harmed a hair on our Tettè's head."

A huge thunderclap shook the windowpanes. The rain started coming down even harder.

XIV

Seven days earlier: Tuesday, October 20

Tettè wakes up early. Daylight hasn't begun filtering through the closed shutters yet.

It's cold out. The others are all sleeping fully dressed, wearing every article of clothing they own. Tettè lets his eyes adjust to the darkness. He can make out the shapes of the bodies on the pallets around him.

He's having trouble breathing; his nose is clogged with mucus. He tries to swallow, but his throat is sore. He pushes aside the burlap sacks that serve as his blanket, careful not to make a sound. His feet touch down lightly on the icy floor, but Tettè doesn't feel the cold: he's accustomed to walking barefoot, and the soles of his feet have developed thick calluses as a result, like the soles of a shoe.

In silence, moving as stealthily as a cat, he reaches a corner of the large room and leans close to the wall. He checks again to make sure that everyone is still asleep, taking a quick look around him.

He crouches down on the floor and counts the bricks in the wall. Two, five, six. Silently mouthing the numbers with his lips. Brick number eight sticks out ever so slightly from the wall. With both hands, very slowly, Tettè eases it out and removes it. He sticks his hand into the hole and pulls out a small packet of newspaper. Along with the packet comes a large cockroach. Tettè jerks in surprise and disgust, then crushes it with his bare foot.

Holding the cockroach in his left hand, he uses his right hand *to unwrap the newspaper packet. Inside is a pastry, a bit stale and slightly nibbled around the edges. Tettè looks at the morsel and smiles tenderly. After a moment's hesitation, he breaks off a tiny piece and starts to lift it to his mouth.*

He feels a large hand from behind around his neck, squeezing hard. He struggles to breathe, mouth gaping as he gasps for air. Now two hands spin him around, pinning his back to the wall. Standing before him is Amedeo, the eldest boy, teeth clenched in anger, eyes red with sleep. Behind Amedeo stand the other four. Amedeo loosens his grip a little, and Tettè inhales and exhales loudly.

"What's wrong, you rotten cacaglio*?" he says, using the derogatory dialect word for a stutterer. "Having trouble breathing? Maybe that's how it ought to be, maybe you don't need to go on breathing. Maybe I should drown you, with my own two hands."*

Amedeo hisses like a serpent. No one can hear him outside the door of the room, but to Tettè's ears, it's like a lion's roar. He shakes his head, terrified.

"No, eh? You don't want to die? Why not? What's the point of you going on living, can you tell me? Why should people like you be alive? I'd be doing the kid a favor if I killed him, don't you guys think so?"

The twins laugh. One of them, the one missing his front teeth, says, yeah, come on, Amede', kill him, please. Squeeze his throat until his eyes bug out, the way you did that time with the orange cat.

Without taking his eyes off Tettè's face, Amedeo delivers a well-aimed kick to the twin's belly; the boy rolls on the floor without emitting so much as a groan and throws himself on the pallet, bent at the waist.

"Shut your mouth, you idiot. I told you never to talk about these things. Not even when no one's here. All right, then, cacaglio*, where were we? What were you hiding in the wall? Show me, or else I'll tear that bastard hand of yours right off your arm."*

He still has his hand wrapped around Tettè's throat; again the boy can't breathe. His vision is starting to blur. He sees lots of tiny lights blinking before his eyes. He feels as if he's falling asleep and having a dream.

Cristiano, the last one to arrive at Santa Maria del Soccorso, lays his hand on Amedeo's arm.

"Amede', that's enough. Keep it up and you'll kill him, can't you see he's not breathing? Let him go."

"Yeah? And who are you to give me orders? You want a little taste for yourself? A good hard kick in the balls like I gave that moron over there? Or should I just choke you, too?"

Cristiano keeps his distance, but he knows how to handle Amedeo.

"Think it over. If you kill him, we'll lose lots of things, and you know it. And anyway you've put the fear of God in him now, you'll see that he won't make the same mistake twice."

Amedeo looks at Tettè with disgust; he lets go of his neck and lightning-quick grabs the packet out of his hand. The twin who's still standing moves cautiously forward to get a look at it, but Amedeo shoves him away. He sniffs at it, samples a piece.

"Phew, that's disgusting. It's moldy and cockroaches have been eating it. The cockroaches are just like you, rotten cacaglio: they hide in the dark, they scuttle away along the wall. And when I see one, I crush it. Remember that, cacaglio: I'm going to crush you."

He spits out the piece of pastry he had in his mouth, dumps the rest on top of it, and crushes it underfoot. Then he turns and walks away. The twin lunges at the mess on the floor, scrabbling at it with his fingers and eating it, looking at Tettè derisively.

Tettè's eyes fill with tears, but he doesn't cry. He gets to his feet, runs his hand over his neck. He would like to say something, but he knows that the words wouldn't come out. From across the room, Cristiano watches him, expressionless. Tettè smiles at him, but the other boy turns away and walks off.

A shaft of gray light starts to filter in through the shutters.

XV

Ricciardi, having taken note of the priest's laundry list of happy memories and the idyllic picture he had just painted of the dead boy's life, asked:

"And you, Padre, when was the last time you saw him?"

Don Antonio tried to think back, with some difficulty.

"Now then, let me recall. Yes, I'd say on Sunday night, after the seven o'clock service. I remember that he was there, even if he wasn't the one who served mass. Yes, yes. I remember clearly, he was sitting in the second pew, on the left, looking from the altar."

Ricciardi looked at the priest, then he said:

"And could you tell me who he was with, Padre? Who was he sitting with at Mass?"

"With the other boys, I believe. With all the other boys. They all attend the evening Mass every Sunday. They know that's what I want."

"What about after Mass? Where could the child have gone? Don't they eat dinner, after the service?"

"Yes, certainly, after the service they go to dinner. I have no way of knowing, Commissario, where they . . . "

Ricciardi bore in:

"But, Padre, don't you dine with the boys? If you were with them, you'd surely have noticed whether or not Matteo was there. There are only six of them in all: that's what you told me, right?"

Ricciardi's question fell into silence. A pained expression had appeared on Don Antonio's face. He stood up.

"Forgive me, Commissario, but now I really must go. I've been away from my parish too long as it is, and the faithful need me. Moreover, as you can well imagine, I've got to arrange for poor Matteo's funeral. I must also inform his companions of his death; as I told you, he was very well loved."

Maione had stood up with the priest, in a show of respect, while Ricciardi had remained seated.

"I actually haven't finished yet, Padre. There are quite a few things I'd still like to ask you."

The priest remained standing.

"Then we'll just have to finish this conversation of ours another time, Commissario. And as long as we're talking about it, it would be best to establish some ground rules regarding this matter."

"Meaning?"

"Meaning that, however heartbreaking and terrible, what happened to Matteo was an accident, the result of a tragic twist of fate. That neither I nor anyone who lived with him and helped him, all without asking for anything in return, is to blame. That I do not personally fall under your jurisdiction, and therefore unless I choose to do so of my own free will, I need not answer any questions you might have: that I owe you neither my time nor anything I might or might not know. On this point, Commissario, bear with me if I repeat myself: it's up to me to decide whether I wish to answer your questions or no. It's up to me, and me alone. And one more thing: it's my duty to inform the curia of what's happened, both Matteo's tragic death and the fact that you ordered the dissection of the child's body without requesting any kind of authorization."

Ricciardi objected vehemently:

"No, Padre, what we did wasn't a dissection! It was an autopsy, and it was ordered to learn the cause of death. It was a necessary examination."

"That remains to be seen. And I assure you, Commissario,

that the curia is not about to stand by and watch as servants of God are treated like criminals off the street, held against their will by the police and interrogated like common murderers. I believe that you would be well advised to proceed very carefully: the bishop is in regular contact with your superiors."

The priest's diatribe, delivered in a voice as calm as if he'd been giving a Sunday sermon, had stunned Maione, who was standing openmouthed, cap in hand, by the door. But not Ricciardi, who hadn't moved an inch.

"As you think best, Padre. Take all the steps that you consider appropriate. But I can tell you one thing from my own experience: the only people who try to avoid questions are those with something to hide. Remember that. And keep one other thing in mind: as far as the fate of poor Matteo is concerned, you ought to be more concerned than I am. Good-bye; you're free to go."

Don Antonio nodded his head in farewell and left the room.

After shutting the door behind the departing priest, Maione turned to look at Ricciardi.

"Commissa', forgive me, but this priest strikes me as very dangerous. Did you hear what he said?"

Ricciardi snorted.

"The things that priest says to scare me are like water off a duck's back, Maione. If he didn't know there was something strange going on, do you think he would have put on such an act? And plus this whole fairy-tale world he has these children living in doesn't square to my mind with the fact that Matteo goes missing but it takes him two days to come tell us about it."

Maione scraped the floor with one foot, the way he did whenever he wasn't entirely in agreement with Ricciardi.

"Still, the priest does have one point: if it was an accident, then why all the questions? To tell the truth, if I'm being honest with you, Commissa', I wondered the same thing myself.

The autopsy, the investigation, the site inspections—we don't do all these things even if we find a dead body with a bullethole between the eyes. It seems to me we're attracting a lot of unnecessary attention."

Ricciardi shook his head.

"What, are you turning diplomatic on me now, too? Since when have we let a few threats scare us, instead of following through on an investigation?"

"Commissa', it's not a matter of getting scared or being diplomatic: this is something else completely. Mussolini's coming to Naples. They're already putting up posters all over town, haven't you noticed? And that puts the fear of God in everybody, you've got people running this way and that. The one running hardest is Garzo, and you know how much that imbecile cares about his relationships with important people; when that fortune-teller was killed, you remember, and the duke and duchess of whatever-it-was were implicated, he came this close to throwing us in jail ourselves, he was so scared of getting complaints. So just imagine if he gets a phone call from the bishop, the day before Thunder Jaw pulls into town!"

Ricciardi wasn't about to give up.

"Well, so what? If the child was poisoned, it's our duty to . . . "

"No, Commissa', careful: the boy poisoned himself, the doctor even said so. We don't have the grounds for an investigation. Even the autopsy, as I told you more than once, was going too far. Do me a personal favor, just this once: let's call a halt to this right here. Then maybe later, once Thunder Jaw has left town, we can walk over to the parish together, and we'll see what kind of conditions these kids live in. You know me, I'm the first to get angry about these kinds of things. But we can't keep this up, not right now."

Ricciardi stood up and went to the window. In the falling rain, not far from where the little dead girl was asking her mother to fetch her top, he glimpsed a dog sitting as if it were waiting for something. Without turning around, he said:

"I want to talk to Garzo. Do me a favor, call Ponte and ask for an appointment."

XVI

Rosa observed Enrica, who was sitting stiffly on the sofa, as if she'd swallowed a broomstick, holding a demitasse of espresso. She hadn't drunk a drop.

She'd been sitting like that for five minutes now, not saying a word, eyes downcast, knees together, perched precariously on the seat, far from the backrest. Rosa wondered how to break the silence, which was starting to become awkward.

When they'd reached the landing, the young woman had stopped at the threshold holding the groceries, dripping rain onto the floor. The *tata* had immediately invited her in, but Enrica hesitated, as if she were afraid of something; in the end, she had made up her mind and walked through the door, eyes on the floor until she got to the kitchen. She set the groceries on the table, being careful not to look around lest she seem to be prying. At that point Rosa had invited her into the living room, while she made a pot of coffee. When Enrica protested, stammering that she didn't want to impose, the *tata* brusquely pointed her to the sofa: if she wanted to offer the girl a cup of coffee, she wasn't about to tolerate objections of any kind.

In the meantime Enrica was inwardly experiencing a bout of panic. The minute she'd found herself on that landing, outside that apartment, all the courage and determination she'd built up over the past two days, endlessly repeating to herself that the only way to get beyond that impasse was to make contact with Ricciardi's *tata*, had melted away like a gelato in mid-August. She'd thought about it so much, dreamed about it so often that now she was terrified: the phantom of a possible dis-appointment, the thought of hearing bad news, of learning that he was engaged or something even worse, gripped her by the throat, literally suffocating her. So she sat there, at the center of her heart's temple, silently gasping for air with a demitasse in her hand, praying to be struck dead then and there.

Rosa, unaware of these thoughts but realizing that the young woman was struggling, finally said to her:

"Signori', if you wait any longer, we're going to have to toss it out, that espresso. It's very good, you know; I make a good cup of coffee."

Enrica started when the old woman said this, coming close to spilling most of the good coffee on the carpet. She drank half of it in a single gulp, burning her tongue in the process.

"Really very good, very good, *grazie*. *Grazie* again. I only wanted to help you carry the groceries upstairs."

Rosa blinked: the situation was worse than she'd thought at first. Enrica was truly distraught; it would be no simple matter to make her feel comfortable.

"And what do you do, most days? Do you stay at home, do you study, do you work?"

"No, I . . . that is, I have my high school diploma, I'm a teacher, but I don't teach. No, I mean, I teach, but the fact is that I teach at home, I tutor children at our apartment, not at a school. I help them prepare, and then they take their exams at school."

She realized she was acting like a complete idiot. She needed to get a grip on herself, or this was going to end badly.

"But I do housework, too, of course. That is, I help my mother, I give her a hand around the apartment. I especially like to cook, and my father says that I'm very good at it, too. And I embroider."

Rosa liked that surge of pride, and smiled approvingly. A woman who knows how to keep house instinctively recognizes another like herself. A kind of informal sisterhood.

"Really? That's nice. My *signorino* lives here, did you know that? I look after him, but he's the master of the house."

That direct reference to the object of her thoughts and dreams shattered Enrica's mounting equilibrium with the force of a hurricane uprooting a delicate young sapling. She started stammering again.

"Ah, is that so? I had no idea . . . that is, I knew, but . . . of course, I live across the street, and I'd seen a man, but I didn't think . . . not that I was looking through your windows intentionally, but you know, living right across the way . . . "

Rosa was afraid the girl would burst into tears right in front of her. She decided to go all in, relying on the no-nonsense approach of her birthplace:

"Signori', I know that you already knew it. And I also know that the *signorino* Luigi Alfredo, my young master, is perfectly aware of who you are and where you live. I doubt that you failed to notice that every night after dinner, for I don't know how many months, if not years, he stands at the window in his bedroom, which is right through that door over there, and watches you do your needlepoint. And if you're here today it's certainly because you know it, and you don't mind at all if he watches you. Am I right?"

Enrica felt like a little girl caught with her hands in the marmalade jar. She wished she could jump to her feet and run, and keep going until she reached the water's edge, or even beyond. But a second later she realized that he had been just as incapable of concealing his interest in her from his *tata*, and she found this fact to be quite encouraging.

She smiled uncertainly and sighed. Then she looked up, squared her shoulders, pushed her glasses up the bridge of her nose, and said:

"Yes, Signora. That's right. And I don't even really know why I'm here. Maybe it's because I need help. I need *your* help."

Rosa settled into her armchair, satisfied. The girl wasn't a striking beauty: in fact at first glance, she seemed rather mousy and insignificant. But now that she was getting a closer look at her, she could detect an attractive figure, with long legs and a nice bust, and regular features; her eyes, too, shone with the light of intelligence and wit, behind her myopic glasses.

"He wrote you a letter. I don't know if he ever gave it to you, but I do know he wrote you a letter. I'm positive of it."

"Yes, he wrote me. I received the letter the day before yesterday. It's not exactly . . . Well, I'd have to say he's not a man who makes bold declarations. He simply asks whether I would object to his greeting me if he sees me, that's all. I was happy, but now I'm not sure what I should do."

Rosa ran a finger under her chin pensively.

"Signori', I've never been married. There was someone, when I was young, not a worn-out old lady like I am now, and he made it clear that he might be interested in me, but I sent him away, and I wasn't very nice about it, either. Because all I wanted was to care for my *signorino*, his *mamma* had entrusted him to me; she died young. And I've dedicated my whole life to him. I ought to tell you that he is, by nature, just a little closed off, as they say . . . a little reserved, a little shy. In other words, he's not the type to put himself forward. If you ask me, he's afraid of rejection. But I'll tell you one thing: in all these years, I've never seen him the way he is about you. This business with the window, and the letter: it's very significant."

Enrica felt as if she were in a dream; here she was, in the place where he lived, pouring out her heart to a complete stranger, an old woman who spoke with an accent from a distant province, talking about something she wouldn't have revealed to her own parents even if she were being tortured. And yet she said:

"I know, I understand him. Because I'm the same way, not the kind of brazen woman who lets a man know that she likes him. Instead, I wait, hoping that he might, I don't know, ask my father for permission to take me out. So for the past year I've been sitting there doing my needlepoint, and he watches me, and nothing happens. And in the spring, I was summoned to police headquarters because of some investigation or other, and I found myself face-to-face with him. I don't know, it seemed wrong to me. So I lost my temper, I was harsh with him, and then I didn't want to see him at all, not even through a window."

Rosa nodded seriously.

"Eh, I remember that period. He was in terrible shape, he thought I didn't notice but I could see it, of course I could see it. So then what happened?"

Enrica smiled at the memory.

"A lovely blonde lady came to see me, Lucia, the wife of the brigadier who works with him. She told me that life goes by, and what passes you by never comes back. That she, for the grief of losing her son, had almost lost her other children and her husband. She told me not to be foolish, and not to turn my back on love. In short, she persuaded me, and I went back to sitting in the window. And I waited. Then my parents got it into their heads . . . They introduced me to someone, and I told them that I didn't want anything to do with him, and that I cared for another man. My mother didn't like it. She said that she expected me to become an old maid, and she may be right. But if I can't have the one I want, I don't want anyone in my life at all."

Rosa listened to Enrica talk; she liked the quiet, soulful sound of her voice. The better she knew her, the more convinced she became that Ricciardi's intuition about her was correct.

"If you ask me, you did the right thing, Signori'. It's just that with someone as hardheaded as my *signorino*, you have to be patient. You have to let him come out a little at a time, as if it was his idea. When he was small and I wanted him to wash up, for example, because he was always out playing in the yard and he got filthy, oh so filthy, if I'd say to him, go get washed up, he absolutely refused. But if, instead, I said to him, *mamma mia,* how horrible it is to see a dirty man, only little boys and babies are ever dirty, not grown-ups; then you should have seen him run for the tub. I think all men are that way: they need to think that they're making their own decisions, and it's our job to make them decide what we want them to do."

Enrica laughed, then she asked:

"And in your opinion, what should I do, now?"

Rosa replied:

"You need to write back to him, a nice letter. You need to tell him that you're happy to have him send his regards, and that you send your regards to him as well. And you have to find some way of conveying the idea—I couldn't tell you how because I only know my numbers—that you aren't engaged to be married, that you're not interested in anyone else, but that you'd like a family in your future. That way he'll understand that he can't dawdle forever, he has to get moving. Because, as you can see, I'm an old woman, and I can't stand the idea that after I'm gone he'll be left all alone, with no one to take care of him. You can't imagine, Signori': he's like a baby, he doesn't know how to do anything for himself."

Enrica impulsively reached out and caressed the older woman's hand.

"Signora, you'll live to be a hundred. I know it, I can feel it. And we'll become good friends, I'll come to see you every afternoon, when we're sure he won't be home, and I'll keep you company. That way, you can teach me to cook better."

Rosa slapped a hand to her forehead:

"Ohhh, *madonna santa,* you're right! I'm sitting here chatting and I haven't even made lunch! Come with me to the kitchen, and I'll show you how the *signorino* likes his chickpeas. Are you familiar with the cooking of the Cilento region?"

XVII

Ponte stuck his head in the office door and, with his eyes trained on the portrait of the king, said:

"If you please, Commissario, Deputy Chief of Police Dottor Garzo is ready to see you."

Ricciardi sighed in annoyance. He didn't know exactly why that little man was so uncomfortable around him, but the fact that Ponte could never bring himself to look him in the eye irritated Ricciardi in a way that few things could.

"Fine, Ponte. Would you do me a favor and let Maione know? I'd like him to come, too. We'll meet in Garzo's office."

Taking those instructions as a dismissal, Ponte withdrew his head like a tortoise retreating into its shell, shutting the door behind him with unmistakable relief.

Ricciardi was hardly overjoyed to be meeting with "Deputy Chief of Police Dottor Garzo," as Ponte pompously described him without fail. The commissario considered Garzo to be a fool, and a conceited one. The man cared about nothing but himself and his career, and was incompetent when it came to the challenging job of overseeing multiple investigations. Still, Ricciardi thought, perhaps that position really should be filled by someone like Garzo, who could act as an intermediary between the politicians and agents in the field, like himself. Even the police chief, whom he'd glimpsed only a few times, was nothing more than a government official. The war against criminals—criminals not entirely to blame for being such, or for being so numerous—was a war that had to be fought by beat cops and detectives.

Nevertheless, this time he really needed to talk to Garzo. He had to make it clear to him how important it was to get to the bottom of this case and find out what had really happened to that child. Of course, he couldn't tell him the real reason for his convictions: as he walked down the corridor, he almost smiled at the thought of the face Garzo would make if Ricciardi told him that he wanted to continue with an investigation because he *hadn't* seen the dead person's ghost. But all the same, that's the way things were, and he had to find a way to ascertain why the body had been moved, and from where, and above all, to conceal what.

As he reached the door of the deputy police chief's office, an out-of-breath Maione caught up with him, and shot him an imploring look.

"Commissa', it's not too late. Let's forget about this. I mean, if you insist, I can put out the word and see what comes of it, but on the q.t. Let's not give this idiot a chance to pin us down. You know how I feel about him."

Ricciardi squeezed Maione's arm reassuringly and knocked on the door.

Garzo was at his desk, with a pen in his hand and a blank sheet of paper in front of him. Maione immediately suspected that the scene was staged, because his reading glasses were lying on the desktop. The official looked up. He was a little worried about this reversal of the usual course of events: he was generally the one who had to request the presence of the commissario so that he could be brought up-to-date on the progress of some investigation. Now it was Ricciardi who had requested a meeting. What the devil could he want? Garzo had wondered.

He didn't like finding himself face-to-face with that man. His eyes seemed to burrow into him. And he always had that

air of superiority, or at least of a disregard for Garzo's author-
ity: and that was something Garzo found intolerable.

"Oh, here you are. Well, Ricciardi, what is this about?
Ponte tells me that you need to speak with me."

While Ricciardi was perfectly at his ease with the man, he
still didn't count a conversation with Garzo among his favorite
pastimes. He decided to come straight to the point.

"Dottore, I know you're very busy and I don't want to take
up too much of your time . . . "

Garzo was delighted to have this opportunity to lay out the
extent and the nature of his present responsibilities.

"That's certainly true, *caro* Ricciardi, it's certainly true.
This upcoming visit of the Duce, with all the officials and
functionaries from the Ministry of the Interior who'll be
accompanying him, rests entirely on our shoulders. At least in
terms of the city's appearance and presentation, of course.
You can't even begin to imagine how many things need to be
checked out, once, twice, as many times as necessary, to make
sure that His Excellency doesn't leave with a distorted
impression of the state of law and order that we've managed
to establish in this city. Luckily, the visit will be taking place
at a time when there are no major investigations under way,
no?"

Ricciardi noticed that on Garzo's desk a pretentious solid
silver desk set was on display: a letter tray with a mirrored base
and an elegant little surround, an engraved inkpot, a penholder,
and a boat-shaped blotter paper holder. Everything was gleaming and spotless, as if shining with a light all its own. He
thought back to the paperweight made from a fragment of an
artillery shell from the Great War, the only concession to aes-
thetics in his own office, and how glad he was to be so different from the deputy chief of police.

"That's exactly what I wanted to talk to you about, Dottore.
That's not precisely the current situation, at least not as you're

describing it. There is one case that, in our opinion, would repay further investigation."

A long vertical crease appeared immediately in Garzo's forehead.

"What are you talking about? I can't think of anything. Let me take a look . . . " and he pulled out a pile of reports that he kept in a desk drawer, far from prying eyes, and began leafing through them: "You see, there's nothing. Of course, run-of-the-mill administrative issues, a brawl in a tavern with a couple of patrons complaining of contusions, two tourists held up at Mergellina, but the stickup artist, a fisherman, was immediately arrested and everything he stole was recovered. Three horse-drawn carriages operating a taxi service outside the central train station without a license. But after all, this is a big city, it would seem strange if little things like these weren't happening, wouldn't it?"

Ricciardi was beside himself. Could it be that Matteo wasn't even filed among the police reports that constituted run-of-the-mill administrative issues?

"There's the case of the little boy who was found dead at Capodimonte, Dottore. I forwarded the report to you yesterday myself."

At this point, Garzo put on his glasses, opened another drawer, and pulled out a file.

"Ah, yes. Here we are: Diotallevi, Matteo, officially identified by Don Antonio Mansi, parish priest at Santa Maria del Soccorso. But that's another matter entirely; there's nothing for us to do at all. This is a case of accidental death, and here I see the medical examiner's report, from your friend, Dr. Modo: by the way, isn't he a little bit of a—how shall we say—a dissident? In any case, this is something that doesn't concern us. That's why the report isn't in the other drawer."

Maione shook his head: as if the fact that a sheet of paper was in one drawer rather than another changed the material facts of the case. This deputy chief of police really is a cretin, he decided.

Ricciardi took a deep breath, reminding himself to be patient, and then went on calmly:

"Dottore, this little boy died of strychnine poisoning. I believe it's important that we dig a little deeper into just how and where this poison was administered, also to ensure that such a misfortune doesn't repeat itself. I feel sure that . . . "

Out of nowhere, Garzo slammed the palm of his hand down on his desktop. The blast of noise was like an explosion, followed by the prolonged tinkling of all the newly purchased silver.

"What's this I hear? 'I believe,' 'I feel sure'? This is police headquarters, and we are policemen. We go by the facts, damn it! And all the facts are written right here: accidental death, due to the ingestion of poisonous bait for small animals. Rat poison! Ordinary rat poison! And you come into my office, to bother me while I'm trying to make sure the city is the very picture of order for the visit of no less than His Excellency the Duce, with these dreamed-up, nonexistent investigations?"

The commissario wasn't even slightly intimidated by Garzo's tantrum. He'd fully expected it.

"I don't dream up investigations, Dottore. I simply think that when the root cause of something is unclear, it's necessary to dig deeper, that's all. On the other hand, if the fact that we're talking about an orphan, with no one to care about whether he lives or . . . "

Garzo turned red as a beet:

"How dare you suggest such a thing? I have two children of my own, you know!" and he pointed to his family portrait in a silver frame, temporarily moved from his desk to a shelf on the bookcase, to give a greater impression of efficiency. "I put children above all else! But I'm also a man who looks at the facts; and the facts tell me that this is a purely accidental death. I also read that from the first examination no signs of violence were found, and so I wonder, and I ask you: why was an autopsy ordered?"

Maione scraped his foot on the floor. Ricciardi replied:

"I decided that it was the best course of action. Precisely the fact that there were no visible marks of violence left considerable doubts about the cause of the child's death."

"Doubts? What about you, Maione, did you have these same doubts?"

Maione opened his mouth, shut it, and then opened it again.

"I'm with the commissario, Dotto'; and when the commissario makes a decision, it's not my job to question it."

Garzo snickered.

"That says it all, it seems to me. Not even the brigadier is willing to state unequivocally that he agrees with you: and that's a new one on me. And not even Dr. Modo, in his report on the autopsy results, makes even the vaguest reference to anything intentional about the ingestion of the poison. Nothing at all. This time, Ricciardi, there's a simple answer, and it's backed up by the documents. The answer is no. You may no longer investigate this regrettable accident, because that's what this was: an accident. I forbid you to waste any more time on it, especially at such a crucial time for our city and for the police department. You'd just be digging in vain."

Maione looked at the floor. Ricciardi slowly shook his head; he'd taken into account the possibility of the official's refusing his request outright.

"You're right, Dottore. I probably just need a little rest, if you want to know the truth. To that end, I wonder if I could have your permission to take some time off, say a week or so. That way I won't bother you at this crucial moment with my bad mood."

Garzo was stunned by the request: as far back as he could

remember, Ricciardi had never missed a day of work, either due to sickness or for a vacation, not even in the summer. It was just another one of the mysteries that made him dislike that man so heartily. In his uncertainty, he decided to do what he did best: he tiptoed gingerly around the question.

"Why on earth this request? It wouldn't be because you're planning something, would it? Ricciardi, let me remind you: even when you're on vacation you remain a commissario of the royal Italian police of Naples, and anything you might do while not in the office will be subject to disciplinary sanctions, which could be serious; no, let me correct that: which could be dire. I'm inclined not to grant you this time off. It might be better to have you where I can keep an eye on you."

But Ricciardi had foreseen this as well, and he knew what strings to pluck in Garzo's soul.

"As you think best, Dottore. It's too bad, because that means I'll have to tell Signora Vezzi that I won't be available to help her out. She'd asked if I would do some shopping with her and help draw up the guest list for some reception or other that she's planning a few days from now. It seems to be something important."

The deputy chief of police instantly sat up straight in his chair. His tone of voice altered, but remained cautious.

"Ah, I've heard about this reception. And just how is dear Signora Vezzi? Have you seen her recently?"

Maione disguised a chuckle with a loud cough.

Ricciardi replied:

"Yes, quite recently. Well then, Dottore? What do you say, about this time off I'm asking for?"

Garzo tapped his pen on the blank sheet of paper.

"All right, Ricciardi. But just one week; and I expect you to keep me . . . informed, concerning Signora Vezzi's reception. You know how it is: we need to always be aware of everything that goes on in this city. Especially when it comes to certain events that might involve prominent individuals. We have to guarantee the utmost security."

Maione took a step forward.

"Dottore, since we're on the subject, could I have a few days off, too? That would give me time to take care of a few minor matters of my own."

Garzo snorted in annoyance:

"No, Maione, not you. I need all the manpower available to me in the next few days. Moreover, you've already taken your holidays. And it seems to me that Ricciardi, here, won't really need your help with whatever he'll be doing on his days off. Am I right, Ricciardi?"

The commissario didn't bother to respond to the broad hint.

"All right then, Dottore. I'll see you in a week, here in the office—or perhaps sometime before that, on some other occasion. Have a pleasant day."

Garzo smiled broadly.

"That's right, perhaps on some other occasion. *Arrivederci*, Ricciardi. And listen closely: I don't want to hear any news about you while you're away; especially in connection with this poor dead little boy."

XVIII

Maione followed Ricciardi into his office, walking in directly behind him. He stood there, cap in hand, motionless as the commissario shuffled the papers on his desk together into a single pile to create the appearance of order.

After a few moments, seeing that the brigadier was still hesitating, Ricciardi said:

"Well? Do you have something to tell me?"

Maione, who had been examining the tips of his boots, looked up.

"Commissa', you saw for yourself, I tried to wangle a little vacation time for myself, too; I wanted to give you a hand. But what I don't understand is, doing what? What is it you want to look for, what is it you're trying to understand? I'm still on your side, no matter what, and you know that. It's just that I can't help you if you won't tell me what you're looking for."

Ricciardi looked at the man, so big and strapping and confused, and felt a surge of tenderness. He sat down and did his best to explain, at least in part:

"Well, you see, Raffaele, Modo asked me the same questions. I don't have a satisfactory answer, and I didn't have one for Garzo just now, either. All I can tell you is that I sensed something when I saw them carrying away that corpse yesterday morning. There was something about that poor little dangling head being discarded like that, like a lamb on Easter. I realized that the boy'd been so alone that there wasn't a soul who cared whether he was dead or alive. I just thought that that was wrong. That the same way we ought to look after children when they're alive, we shouldn't let them pass out of this life without leaving a trace behind. And so, on instinct, I requested the autopsy. Then, once we'd established the presence of strychnine, it seemed to me that we ought to find out where he got it so that it wouldn't happen again. That's all there is to it."

Maione looked him in the eye as he spoke, not missing a word. He had no illusions about himself: he knew that he was ignorant. But he'd developed his instincts over the years, and how; and his instinct told him that there was something else making Ricciardi dig into Matteo's death and refuse to give up.

He also knew that he'd be unable to drag any more information out of the commissario, so he nodded seriously and said:

"I understand. All right, Commissa', let's see if we can take advantage of the fact that that stinker Garzo wants to keep me here. As you do your investigating, let me know what you've found out and what you need. From here, making use of our facilities, I can still give you a hand, right?"

Ricciardi almost smiled.

"All right, Raffaele. I assure you that if I need anything, and I almost certainly will, I'll call on you. There is one thing you can do for me starting right now, though: try to intercept any complaints that may come in from the curia. I have the impression that our friend, Don Antonio, as soon he sees my silhouette appear on the horizon, will run straight to the cathedral to talk to the bishop."

"Don't worry, Commissa'. But I want you to promise me something in return: if you see a dangerous situation, don't go charging into it. Wait for Brigadier Maione to show up: he's lucky and as long as he's there, nothing bad can happen to you."

Before Ricciardi had a chance to reply, there was a knock at the door and, after the sentry announced her, Livia Lucani, the widow Vezzi, entered the room, accompanied by her usual cloud of dizzying cinnamon-spice perfume.

On her gray cloche hat, decorated with a large cloth flower on one side, one could see the pearly drops of rain that had penetrated the coy cloth umbrella now dangling from her wrist. She wore a long black overcoat with a wide silver fox fur collar, a gray that matched her hat. She looked happy.

"Hello, hello, one and all! *Caro* Brigadier, how are you? Just as charming as ever!"

Maione felt as if he were hoeing dirt right there and then, a feeling that always seemed to come over him in Livia's presence.

"*Cara* Signora, *buona sera*. What a nice surprise, we're not accustomed to such beauty around here."

Livia laughed a silvery laugh.

"What gallantry. What a pity that you're already taken, otherwise I'd court you shamelessly. *Ciao*, Ricciardi. I understand that you're happy to see me too, but keep your excitement under wraps, or else what will the brigadier think?"

Ricciardi had remained seated, caught off guard by this unexpected visit. Now he got to his feet.

"*Ciao*, Livia. A surprise, to be sure: we weren't expecting you. Has something happened?"

Livia was taking off her long black gloves.

"Why do you ask? Does something need to have happened for me to come pay a call on you? No, nothing's happened. I've been out doing some shopping, and the poor chauffeur is parked downstairs in a car overflowing with packages and bags. But I'm helpless to resist, you see, because your city is so full of such *charmant* shops. And on my way back it just occurred to me, yes, what I've been missing is a bit of the doleful and the grim: I'll just go see Ricciardi, who must certainly be sitting in his office at police headquarters, mulling over the details of some horrid crime. And here I am!"

She'd taken a seat in one of the two chairs in front of the desk, unbuttoning her overcoat to reveal an elegant knee-length skirt and jacket beneath. She crossed her legs and pulled a cigarette out of her purse. Maione hastened to offer a light.

"*Grazie*, Brigadier. You could give someone I know lessons in gallantry, he could learn quite a bit from you. Well, what are the two of you up to?"

Ricciardi, in turn, sat down.

"In effect, it's a good thing you dropped by. I have to tell you that I used your name without asking permission, a little while ago. I should tell you that we found a little boy dead, and I . . ."

He was interrupted by the entrance of Garzo, his eyeglasses perched on his nose and a sheet of paper in his hand. Maione and even Ricciardi immediately realized that their superior officer had been informed of Livia's arrival and had come running; it didn't take an exceptional intuition to figure that out, since it had been years since the deputy chief of police had last ventured down into the offices of the floor below. The brigadier shot a blazing glance at Ponte, who was rubbernecking from out in the hall: Ponte immediately took to his heels.

"All right, Ricciardi, here's your authorization for that time off. Oh, what a fortunate coincidence! None other than the Signora Vezzi in person! Did you know, Signora, that we were just talking about you earlier?"

Livia extended her hand for Garzo to kiss it, launching a curious look at Ricciardi.

"Yes, Dottore, Ricciardi was just telling me about it. And concerning what, if it's not rude to ask?"

"Why, concerning the time off that the commissario has requested, so that he can help you with some party or other that you must be having. Or did he lie for some dark motive only he knows? Tell me, Signora, because if he was lying, I'll have him thrown into a cell!"

This attempt at wit was met with a grim silence from Maione and Ricciardi, while Livia shot him a smile and replied:

"In effect, I have to admit that Ricciardi is very useful to me, a latter-day Virgil guiding me through this chaotic and beautiful city of yours. Did you know that I chose my new apartment with his help? Not far from here, on Via Sant'Anna dei Lombardi: that way I can keep an eye on all of you without much trouble."

Garzo smiled, running a finger over his new mustache and hoping that the Signora might notice it.

"Of all the many beauties that we have in our city, I can now include you. We have Ricciardi to thank, then. Also for helping you to plan this famous reception I've been hearing so much about."

Livia looked first at Garzo and then at an embarrassed Ricciardi, and decided that this was just too tempting an opportunity.

"Yes, Dottore: it will be quite the event. It would be my pleasure if you could attend, with your wife, of course. For that matter, your lovely chief of police will be there, too, so you'll be among friends. The guest of honor will be my close friend Edda, the Duce's daughter. And perhaps, who can say, His Excellency himself might put in a surprise appearance. Please, help me out: issue a direct order for Ricciardi to assist me and to attend: you know how uncooperative he is, when it comes to social occasions."

Garzo glowed as if illuminated by a shaft of bright sunlight. In a voice quavering with delight, he said:

"Signora, I can't tell you how grateful my wife and I are to you, for this marvelous invitation! Ricciardi, *caro*, *carissimo* Ricciardi, I order you to put yourself on permanent regulation duty at the service of Signora Vezzi. With no other distractions, let me make that clear!"

Livia stood up, smiling.

"Now I really must go. Will you see me down to my car, Dottore? I'm afraid to go downstairs in these heels, but on the arm of a man like you . . . *Buona sera*, Brigadier. Ciao, Ricciardi, now remember: obey the orders that you've been issued."

And with that she was gone, leaving the office filled with cinnamon perfume and a feeling of apprehension.

XIX

Wednesday, October 28

E very day of the week, whatever the weather, Rosa woke up at five in the morning: a habit that she'd developed back home, when she'd been responsible for looking after the animals on the farm where she lived before going into service with the Malomonte family.

She didn't mind it: it gave her a chance to say her prayers, to calmly plan everything she planned to do that day, the meals she would cook; and then she liked to watch her *signorino* leave for work, be sure that everything was in order, that he was nicely dressed. He was so distracted. How many times she'd had to chase after him, to button his jacket, tie one of his shoes: when he was little, and even now that he was an adult.

She was surprised to see him still in his nightshirt at seven in the morning that day. She immediately asked him if he felt well. He had a grim expression on his face that worried her right away. He reassured her with a smile.

"Don't worry, I'm fine. I just took a few days off from work to take care of a few matters. So I'll be spending a little more time at home."

Rosa, who was all too aware of Ricciardi's complete lack of interest in his own business affairs, was at a loss. As far back as she could remember, with the possible exception of a funeral or a wedding involving the distant relatives he still had back home in Fortino, Ricciardi had never missed a day of work.

There must be something else to this; she was willing to bet on it. She'd have to be on her guard. Moreover, her recent meeting with Enrica, to whom she'd taken an instant liking, had set in motion the beginnings of a strategy; and the closer the tabs she kept on Riccardi, the more likely it was to be successful.

Ricciardi, on the other hand, was determined to find out what had happened to the little boy, and he'd decided to start with the place he'd lived: the parish church of Santa Maria del Soccorso.

The church was just a few hundred yards from his apartment building, going in the direction of Capodimonte. That morning, too, the weather was ugly, as it had been for days. It wasn't raining yet, but dark black clouds hung low as a cellar ceiling, and thunder could be heard in the distance, drawing closer.

When he reached his destination, he realized that no service was being held. The church wasn't big, with a single aisle and a few small side altars; a few elderly women were saying their rosaries in the first few pews, the ones closest to the main altar. The scent of incense and candles, and a great deal of dampness.

He spotted a door in the back that presumably led to the sacristy, and he opened it. One of the old women shot him a hostile glare. He stepped over the threshold, and saw a narrow corridor leading to a brightly lit room, where he found Don Antonio putting a stole away in a cabinet.

The priest's reaction was interesting: he narrowed his eyes, as if he couldn't be sure of what he was seeing; then a surge of disheartened resignation seemed to wash over him; and finally he assumed a decidedly irritated expression, though he adopted a tone of icy courtesy.

"Commissario, what a pleasure to see you here. For one thing because, if I'm not mistaken, you're one of my parishioners, aren't you? You don't live far from here, I seem to recall. And yet I don't think I've seen you here in church all that often."

Ricciardi wanted there to be no misunderstanding about why he was there.

"That's right, Padre. I live nearby, but I don't come to church often. I'm one of those people who believe that the Good Lord is everywhere. Do you disagree?"

Don Antonio closed the cabinet with a bang.

"Certainly, I agree. But what's not everywhere is community. It's one thing to pray, quite another to pray together. But if you're not here to pray this morning, then may I ask you the reason for this visit?"

Straight to the point.

"Let me begin by saying that I'm not here on official business, Padre. There is no police investigation under way, in other words. But, as we said earlier, both you and I are very interested in making sure that an accident like the one that befell Matteo doesn't happen again. And so I'd like to see if I can find out—perhaps by talking with a few of the other boys or by taking a look around the place where he slept or kept his things—where he might have found the poisoned morsels of bait that killed him. I promise not to disturb your parish activities."

Don Antonio eyed him intently, doing his best to figure out the commissario's real intentions, all talking aside.

"I see. Of course, as you said, I'm just as interested as you are in making sure that another misfortune like the one that befell poor Matteo doesn't happen. Let me therefore allow you to conduct this—what would you call it?—this 'non-investigation.' But I'd like for this to be a one-time visit; I can't accept any further meddling in the life of my parish, among other reasons because it would interfere with all the other things that I have to do. Otherwise, I'll have to inform the curia, as I've already told you."

Ricciardi put on a show of confidence that deep down he didn't feel:

"Certainly, certainly, I understand perfectly. But you'll see that it won't be necessary, Padre. All I want is to take a look around and have a quick chat with some of his friends. That's all."

"All right then. Wait for me here, Commissario. I'll go see if any of the boys are still around. You know, they all have apprenticeships so they can learn a trade, and they leave pretty early in the morning. With your permission . . . "

The priest left the room, and Ricciardi looked around. It was a cramped space, with a wall covered with cabinets, a chair, a prie-dieu, and a little table on which lay a missal and a Bible. Everything you'd expect to find in a sacristy, crucifix included. A short while later, the priest returned, accompanied by a boy who looked to be about thirteen, very swarthy with dancing dark eyes, his hair cut extremely short, almost to the scalp.

"This is Cristiano; as I told you, we all loved Matteo, but Cristiano might have been the one who was closest to him. Cristiano, say hello to Commissario Ricciardi."

The boy looked Ricciardi steadily in the eye, with an air of defiance more than of curiosity. Perhaps introducing him as a police detective had been deliberate, Ricciardi thought. The priest continued:

"*Prego*, Commissario: ask your questions."

Ricciardi didn't have the slightest intention of talking in the priest's presence, knowing that the boy's answers would be strongly influenced.

"I don't want to take up too much of your time, Padre. Perhaps Cristiano could show me where Matteo slept, and on the way I can ask him a few questions. That way you'll be free to get back to your work."

The priest seemed undecided; he looked at Cristiano with a vague expression of concern, then he pulled a watch out of his tunic pocket and said, with a hint of annoyance:

"Yes, all right, in any case I have a service in a few minutes. Now, Commissario, listen carefully: don't go beyond the limits that we agreed upon. And don't keep our young Cristiano too long. He's assigned to cleaning the dormitory room; it's his turn today."

Ricciardi said his farewells with a nod of the head and left the sacristy with the boy. Next to the church was a small courtyard, beside which was a low building that looked like a warehouse. The boy walked ahead of Ricciardi to the door, and the commissario noticed that his clothes were similar to the ones Matteo had been wearing when he was found: an old unbleached linen shirt; short britches tied at the waist with a length of twine; a pair of wooden clogs under calves blue with cold, riddled with scars, insect bites, and chilblains.

Once he was inside, Ricciardi took a look around. A single room, roughly twenty feet long and a dozen feet wide, at the far end of which stood a wooden screen that hid a latrine in one corner and a washbasin in the opposite corner. Set against the walls were two rickety cots and four straw pallets, the cloth linings torn in more than one place. The general impression was one of neglect and desuetude.

Cristiano stopped in the middle of the room and pointed to one of the pallets. In the middle of the bed, he could see the impression left by Matteo's small body.

XX

Seven days earlier, Wednesday, October 21

T*he boys are getting ready to go out and start their work-days as apprentices with various artisans, for which they receive a few cents a week; all but Cristiano, who's been fired by the cobbler for his disrespectful manners. Cristiano always has a smart answer. Cristiano won't obey.*

The door flies open and in comes Don Antonio, beside himself with rage. The door slams against the wall with a bang as loud as a gunshot; Tettè, who is washing up, jumps in surprise.

The priest strides into the middle of the room, then shouts: "Everyone here, in front of me!"

The boys rush to get into position. Amedeo and Saverio, the two oldest, who have a right to the two cots, are the first to jump into line. Tettè sees the two boys exchange a glance, and starts to get scared.

When they're all standing in a line, the priest says: "Do you know what's happened now? Three apples are missing. Three apples from the pantry: and I'm sure of it, because I put them there myself, only yesterday, and I counted them one by one!"

The six boys keep their eyes on the floor. They know from experience that the best thing to do now is keep quiet, because whatever they say, the rest will pay for it. Tettè clutches his shirt, which he had no time to put on, tight to his naked chest. The downcast heads are all shaved bald, to ward off lice.

Don Antonio resumes:

"Who did it? I'm only going to ask you once. If whoever did it confesses, then he will be punished, and no one else; if on the other hand the culprit doesn't step forward and admit that he stole from the house of the Lord, which is a mortal sin, then you'll all be punished for it. Also because if you know that someone has committed a sin and you don't say it, then you go to hell just the same. I'm going to let you go without food for two whole days. You know me: I'll really do it. And the culprit will be punished, you can be sure of that. He will be punished."

Terror fills the room, like a gust of wind. Everyone knows what will happen to the culprit. The broom closet. He'll be put in the broom closet.

In the dark, in the cold. Surrounded by a thousand nameless creatures that crawl on your skin, with quick little feet. If you go into the broom closet you come out with boils and rashes on your skin, and you scratch and scratch for days on end, but the itch still stays with you. And it's dark as the blackest night in there, only you can't move around because there's no room, not even enough room to breathe. It's a terrible place, the broom closet.

The other boys are breathing hard and loud. Tettè hears his own heart beating in his ears. He looks at his feet, on the rammed-earth floor. They're purple from the cold. A minute goes by. Then two minutes. Then Amedeo takes a step forward.

Don Antonio looks at him.

"Speak up, if you have something to say."

Amedeo's metamorphosis as he stands before the priest is an incredible sight. He sinks his head down between his shoulders; he seems to shrink; his legs bend at the knees. Even his voice changes, becoming as faint and small as a child's.

"Padre, forgive me. I don't like playing the spy, but this is something I have to tell you. I don't want to go to hell."

Silence. Everyone's eyes remain on the floor, except for Cristiano's, which flash angrily for an instant as he glares at Amedeo, then look down again. Don Antonio demands:

"Well?"

Without looking up, Amedeo points a trembling finger at Tettè.

"The cacaglio. It was him, that rotten cacaglio. He thought no one was watching, but I saw him. Last night, he ate them, the apples. Last night, in his bed."

The serpent of horror rises up from Tettè's stomach and coils around his throat from within. He never even saw the apples. He looks up, tries to say something, but can't speak. The serpent coils tighter.

"Really? And do you know what happens when you accuse someone without being able to prove it? Do you?"

Don Antonio's voice is menacing. Nanni, the sexton, has come in through the door, and he's rubbing his hands together. He likes it when punishments are handed out. Everyone knows how much he likes it.

At last, Amedeo looks up and nods. Then he turns around and walks over to Tettè's pallet. He lifts it with a confident gesture and grabs something; then he walks back to the priest and opens his hand. The priest takes the object and shows it to everyone: an apple core, cleaned all the way down to the last bite. Two ants fall to the floor.

Tettè feels like shouting out in desperation: it wasn't me, Padre! Can't you see that it wasn't me? I never even went into the kitchen! Why don't you ask yourself who helped make dinner last night, and you'll have your answer! Please, Padre, not the broom closet. I'm afraid of the darkness and the bugs and critters there!

But the serpent is coiled tight around his throat, and all that comes out of his mouth is a guttural gurgling sound. One of the twins can't stop himself from laughing, out of relief for having dodged a punishment and because Tettè can't speak, and the sexton slaps the back of the twin's head. No one laughs this time, as the twin rubs his hand over the shaven stubble on his head, the way he does when the lice make his scalp itch.

Don Antonio goes over to Tettè. He gazes down at him sternly. "Again. And yet you of all people shouldn't be stealing. People give you things for free. You're a lucky boy."

Tettè would like to tell the priest that he's not a lucky boy at all. That every time he comes back, the other boys take everything away from him. Everything, down to the last crumb. But the serpent keeps squeezing, and he feels like he's suffocating.

With a sudden gesture, the priest grabs his left ear between his fingers and twists hard. Tettè emits a groan that sends a shudder through everyone in the room. Cristiano looks at Amedeo, whose eyes are still fixed on the floor. The other twin covers his ears with both hands. Now Don Antonio practically lifts Tettè off the floor. The child waves his hand in the air, trying to loosen the priest's grip, but he maintains his hold on the ear, which is now bloodred.

Tettè is dragged out of the room, out into the cold rain. Everyone follows him and the priest, like a procession on its way to witness an execution. At the far corner of the courtyard, there's a door that leads into the broom closet, a dark little space no more than three by three feet. Still holding the boy by the ear, Don Antonio reaches into his tunic pocket and pulls out a key. He opens the door, throws Tettè inside, and shuts the door behind him, locking it.

First he feels relief that his ear has been released, then waves of terrible, lacerating pain. Tettè massages the ear hard. He can't hear a thing on that side, just a deafening ringing hum. He drags himself into a corner, grabs a rag, and brings it to his head. He can hear the feet of little animals scurrying in the dark, but he can't see them. He kicks at them to keep them away. He wants to sob and shout, but his throat is locked tight.

He sees his angel, standing right before him. He hears the angel's voice: when something bad happens, think of me, think of my smile. Think of it, Tettè. Think of it as hard as you can, and you'll see, everything will be all right.

He thinks as hard as he can, his eyes squeezed shut under the filthy rag, it wasn't me, it wasn't me, he shouts in the silence inside him. Please, I beg you, tell me that you love me. Just tell me once that you love me, my angel.

The thunder shakes the door of the broom closet. The rain beats on the door and drips inside. Tettè kicks out when he feels the icy little snouts touching him. He knows that if he falls asleep, the snouts and the quick little feet will become bolder, and he'll wake up to bites and stings.

He hears something scratch at the door, once, twice. He drags himself over, and finds a gap between boards; he breathes through it. He sees something close to the crack, and after a moment he realizes that it's a dog's nose.

He manages to poke out a finger and strokes the dog's muzzle. All he can do now is wait.

In the big room, Amedeo and Saverio sit on the cots and pull out an apple apiece from under their mattresses. Exchanging a sly glance, they bite into them and laugh.

Cristiano clenches his hands into fists but then tells himself: mind your own business.

XXI

Ricciardi approached Tettè's straw pallet, his hands in his pockets, eyes focused on the faint imprint that showed where the little boy had slept. Here you are, he thought. Here's where you dreamed your dreams; here you thought your thoughts, just small matters, no big ideas, no great hopes. Perhaps you thought about food. Or else you tried to imagine your father's face, your mother's caress. But probably not even that, since you'd never experienced the touch of a loving hand.

He extended his foot and touched the pallet with the tip of his shoe; a cockroach bolted out at a run, zigzagging. The commissario and Cristiano watched it run along the wall, until it slipped away into a crack.

Ricciardi addressed the boy:

"Was Matteo a friend of yours?"

No answer. Cristiano shrugged indifferently and continued staring straight ahead.

Ricciardi walked over to a little nightstand made out of wood from fruit crates, next to the bed. He opened it, crouching down to see what was inside.

Not much. A few articles of clothing. Carefully folded. Nicer stuff than what he'd had on when they found him, perhaps to be worn on a special occasion: a sailor's jacket, a little cap, a pair of shorts. Worn but very clean. Even a pair of sandals with pressed cardboard soles.

An old book, held together by a few cotton threads, with pictures of automobiles. The countless marks where the pages had been touched by grubby fingers. Who knows how many times you leafed through it in search of your dreams, thought Ricciardi. A little wooden car, broken in multiple places and inexpertly reassembled, with metal washers in place of the four wheels. Colored with a pencil: behind the wheel, a woman with blonde hair.

A woman's handkerchief, white, folded into a triangle, finely embroidered with a monogram that he had a hard time identifying, perhaps two letters intertwined.

Ricciardi sighed, putting everything back in its place and getting to his feet. He looked Cristiano in the face, a long searching look, and then said:

"Where are the other boys? What are they doing now?"

Once again, the boy shrugged and looked over at the corner where the cockroach had disappeared. They stood there in silence for a while, until Ricciardi decided that it was time to change his tone.

"Now listen to me and listen good. I'm a police detective. I can take you in on any charge I like, I just have to pick one. And I can have you sent to jail and make sure you never get out. And that's exactly what I'll do if I think you're trying to hide something from me. So, to my mind, it's in your interest to talk."

Threatening a kid: no question, he'd sunk pretty low. But he intuited that this was probably the only language Cristiano understood, unfortunately; and in fact, after a few seconds, the boy spoke.

"So what do you want to know?"

"Why don't you start by anwering the question you were asked: where are the other boys, and what are they doing?"

"Everyone serves as someone's apprentice. There are six of us . . . five, now. They're all out working, except me, because that bastard of a cobbler fired me."

He'd spoken in an undertone, with something that sounded

like an edge of anger. He kept his thumbs tucked into his belt, standing with his legs wide, his feet braced solidly. On the whole, he looked like he was ready to flee, or attack.

"Were you a friend of Matteo's?"

He shrugged again. Then he thought it over and replied:

"Tettè didn't have friends, and neither do I. But I felt sorry for him. He was little and he was a *cacaglio*, it took him an hour to say anything, so he mostly shut up and didn't talk. The less you talk, the better, in here."

Ricciardi wanted to know more.

"And what kinds of things do you do together, when you see each other?"

"At night, after we're done working, if no one goes out and about on their own business. But since we get dinner in the evening, and it's cold out, we all come back here. When the weather's better, some of the kids like to sleep out on the streets, instead of in here. It gets really hot in here."

"And you don't do anything else?"

Cristiano thought it over, then said:

"There's school, twice a week. On Tuesday and Thursday. The two ladies come, the old one and the young one, and they tell us stories, try and get us to read and write. I get sick of it pretty fast, I stick around for a minute or two, then I leave, unless they bring something to eat as a prize, even though I never win."

"And how was Tettè doing?"

"I told you before, he was a *cacaglio*, he couldn't talk, especially when he got worked up. But he was good at writing, and even better at drawing. Sometimes he'd get the prize, but even when he did, the bigger boys would take it away from him, and the rest of us would eat it. That's the way it works in here."

Interesting, thought Ricciardi. All this loving harmony the priest had described, in the end, was a fairy tale. Not that he'd ever believed it.

What remained to be determined, aside from what Don Antonio and others had told him, was just where Tettè had died.

"Do you know how Matteo died?"

Cristiano shook his head, in a very grown-up gesture.

"He was just a fool, the *cacaglio*. A little runt and a fool."

"Why do you say that? And how do you mean, he was a fool?"

The boy smiled sadly.

"Why, what else would you call someone who eats rat poison?"

Ricciardi took a look around: no sign of Matteo's phantom. Wherever he might have died, it hadn't been in here. Nor in the church or the sacristy, for that matter.

"Do you have any idea where he might have found the poisoned bait?"

Cristiano shrugged. Then he suddenly said: "Maybe. And I can take you there. But what'll you give me, if I do?"

"What I'll give you is I won't haul you off to jail, that's what I'll give you. And that strikes me as generous."

Cristiano sighed, gestured with a nod of the head, and set off. Ricciardi followed behind, passing through the courtyard with the locked door of the dark, cramped broom closet.

Since he was unaware of its existence, it didn't occur to Ricciardi to look inside.

From the writing desk she'd installed in her bedroom, Livia looked out at the city through the rain. The trolleys passed each other with cheerful toots of their horns, the handcarts pushed or pulled by strolling vendors continued in spite of the downpour, as their proprietors called out to potential buyers to look at their wares, even though those wares were kept hidden under tarpaulins.

Through the half-open door came the sound of the maid singing in the kitchen, on the far side of the apartment:

Saccio ca t'aggia perdere
Sento ca t'alluntane,
Ca tu te ne può gghi' primma 'e dimane
Pe' nun turna' cchiù a mme. . .

Livia loved that Neapolitan propensity for sound and song. In other cities, silence reigned: if you heard anything, it was the sounds of motors, the neighing and whinnying of horses, but not real sounds. Not music.

She tried to turn her thoughts back to the guest list she was drawing up. It was no easy undertaking: she had to keep the invitees down to a limited number, but she didn't want to make too many people unhappy. At the same time, she wanted to ensure that at least the people she liked would be there.

She sighed when she caught sight of the stack of letters that her girlfriends still hadn't gotten tired of sending her, letters that criticized her decision while trying to wheedle information about her new love. Love. What an absurd word that was.

Had she fallen in love? She really wouldn't know how to answer that question. No doubt, this was an unprecedented situation she found herself in: she was courting Ricciardi, without a thought for who might notice. She wondered whether she would have acted this way back in Rome. Would she have shown up at police headquarters to say hello to him, the way she had done the evening of the day before? Would she have dared—in the potential presence of everyone she knew, and at the risk of running into a dozen of her dear tongue-wagging girlfriends—to stride brazenly into the place he worked, without a blush?

She decided she was in love. She wasn't the kind of hypocritical woman who was afraid to look her own emotions in the face.

Not that he gave her much cause for hope: this time once again he'd been more embarrassed and surprised than elated. But this made the man that much more alluring, not less. Plus, she'd noticed when she sat down that he'd glanced at her legs, blinking rapidly before hastily averting his gaze. He liked her, she was sure of it; but in that case, why did he keep concealing the fact?

With an effort she refocused her mind on the guest list, writing Garzo's name, with a note that his invitation would include his wife. She didn't like him much, but that had been a small price to pay to rope in Ricciardi.

The guest list would have to be ready by seven o'clock that evening. She remembered what Edda Mussolini's secretary had told her over the phone that morning: a man would come by to pick up the guest list, and it would then be submitted for the approval of an agency responsible for security, the name of which she had not told.

This whole matter of security, Livia thought to herself, was becoming a genuine collective fixation. Now the secret police actually wanted to check over the guest list to a private party, a party that would be attended not by the Duce, but his daughter, probably not even accompanied by her husband.

A trolley went by beneath her window, honking its horn in counterpoint to the housemaid, who was singing a song called "*Presentimento*":

> *Dimme, e si 'e ffronne tornano*
> *Ca uttombre fa cade',*
> *Si tutto torna a nascere,*
> *Qua' primmavera ce pò sta' pe' mme?*
> *Cchiù 'o core è stracco 'e chiagnere*
> *Cchiù 'nnammurato 'o sento . . .*
> *Si mo' ce sparte 'stu presentimento,*
> *Pecché m'attacco a tte?*

Livia abandoned herself to the song, thinking how hard it was to concentrate on anything, in that city.

Even when the sun wasn't out.

XXII

Ricciardi followed Cristiano as the boy made his way up Via Nuova Capodimonte. It had started raining again. As they walked down the street he realized that in that part of town the boy was as much of a public figure as any member of parliament: the shopkeepers, the concierges busy mopping the front halls of the apartment buildings, the children leaning over the railings of the balconies all called to him loudly as he went past, greeting him fondly, though their expressions changed when they realized that the commissario was tagging along a short distance behind him. One thuggish young man even asked Cristiano in heavy Neapolitan dialect if he was having any problems, making it clear that if so, he'd be willing to help out.

When it was raining, the geography of urban business shifted. This was a city accustomed to working in the shadows, but always outdoors. The broad openings of the apartment building entrances leading out into the street, the stone arches through which passersby could glimpse courtyards full of plants, hosted the carts of strolling vendors with the tacit and well-remunerated tolerance of uniformed doormen.

Counterfeit monks, little match girls and women selling bouquets of flowers, men operating tiny floating casinos that consisted of nothing more than a wooden counter perched on a tripod—they all did their best to carry on their work even in the rain, competing for the best spots under the broad overhangs of stone cornices.

The uncovered street and the sidewalks, on the other hand, enjoyed the temporary expansion of available space; they were now open to speeding automobiles and gleaming wet horses pulling carts and carriages. As these conveyances went past, they sprayed jets of water into the air behind them, to the delight of swarms of *scugnizzi* who reveled in the unexpected cascades of water. The infrequent pedestrians stepped gingerly between the puddles and small ponds that were forming in the streets, doing their best to keep shoes and trouser legs dry and to cover themselves with cloth umbrellas that they'd lovingly waxed the night before with drippings from their candles at home.

Cristiano, like Ricciardi himself for that matter, seemed indifferent to the rain, clopping along in his wooden clogs through puddles of all sizes and depths, triggering the occasional imprecations of those he inundated as he passed. The commissario kept his eyes trained straight ahead, and he accepted the greetings of the dead in much the same way the boy took the greetings of the living: he saw the pair of adolescents and the despairing debtor, the familiar bridge-jumping suicides on the Ponte della Sanità, and he made a new acquaintance, a decorous, elderly woman dressed in black who had been crushed by the poorly secured load of a horse-drawn cart. The broad cavity in her crushed chest and her mangled left arm, still clutching her handbag, left no doubts as to how she had died and why. As Ricciardi walked past, she said: *my grandson hasn't come around for two months now.* I wonder if he came to your funeral, Ricciardi thought as Cristiano was benevolently and jocularly threatened by a strolling fruit and vegetable vendor. Everybody has the friends they deserve, the commissario mused bitterly.

They came even with a heavy wooden door, closed and locked. Cristiano stopped and waited for Ricciardi. They weren't far from the Tondo di Capodimonte, the piazza at the foot of the monumental staircase where Tettè had been found.

Without looking at the commissario, Cristiano said: "We come here to get a little something, now and then. It's a warehouse of good things to eat. We don't come all that often because the owner hides and stands guard; one time he caught one of the twins and pounded him within an inch of his life. He was in bed for the longest time, throwing up blood; we were pretty sure he was going to die."

Ricciardi observed the heavy bolt and padlock that secured the heavy door.

"But how do you get in here? It looks to me like it's pretty well locked up."

Cristiano smiled with a superior air and waved for Ricciardi to follow him. He turned the corner and slipped in through a doorway, vanishing from the commissario's view. Ricciardi stood motionless and disoriented in the dim dank half-light, until he heard a hiss and understood that the boy had slipped into a gap in the wall that had escaped his notice. He squeezed in after him and found himself standing in a narrow space between the two buildings, a sort of corridor where one person walking sideways could just barely get through. About ten feet farther in, the space widened into a large room stacked high with sacks and crates. They were inside the warehouse.

Ricciardi looked around in the grayish light that filtered down from the high windows: for the most part, the place was filled with grains and beans, as was clearly marked on the sacks; in one corner, though, he saw metal containers, slabs of dried fish and meat, wheels of cheese, and other foodstuffs. Cristiano seemed frightened: he stood there motionless, ears trained like an animal on the hunt, or a wary creature, potential prey to other larger beasts.

He silently pointed out to Ricciardi a series of small objects arranged in a semicircle on the floor near the goods; to the untrained eye, these were a number of tiny bread rolls. The boy picked one up and handed it to the commissario: a rolled-up ball of bread crumb and bits of cheese, odorless. Cristiano touched the commissario's arm and nodded his head in the direction of a large dead rat in the far corner of the storeroom. Ricciardi felt the weight of the edible ball in his hand: poison. This was what had killed Tettè.

He took a more careful look around, but saw no one: the boy hadn't died in the warehouse. Not that that added up to much, since he could easily have taken something and then run off to eat it elsewhere; but the boy's spectral shade wasn't there now.

Cristiano was increasingly anxious; he tugged at Ricciardi's sleeve, pulling him toward the narrow entryway they'd come in by. The commissario was turning to follow him when a muscular arm reached out of the shadows and grabbed the boy by the scruff of his neck.

Before Ricciardi could stop him, the man violently struck Cristiano twice in the face. The boy squawked in fright and tried to squirm free, while the man shouted:

"You damned thief, damn you, I finally caught you. You're done eating at my expense!"

Ricciardi finally recovered from the shock and shouted:

"Halt! Let him go! Police!"

This caused the man to yield momentarily, loosening his grip; Cristiano took advantage of the chance to sink his teeth into the hand that had held him in a vise grip just a second before. The man shouted out an oath and kicked his foot in the boy's direction, but Cristiano was by now well out of range.

Ricciardi stepped forward.

"Stop, I said! Who are you, sir?"

"Who am I? Who are you! If you're with the police, what are you doing in my warehouse? How did you get in, and why didn't you knock at the front door, like honest people do?"

By now, the commissario had regained control of the situation; Cristiano was standing safely behind him, massaging his neck and shooting the owner of the warehouse a defiant glare.

"I apologize for the way in which we entered, but it was necessary. This is a police investigation, and I'm Commissario Ricciardi of the royal police headquarters of Naples. Please be so good as to provide me with your name and surname."

The man continued to stare angrily at Cristiano and, holding his bleeding hand, he replied:

"Vincenzo Lotti's my name. And this is my warehouse you're in. I battle from morning to night with these shameless marauders: they're worse than rats and cockroaches. They slip in under the doors and steal everything in sight. I've already filed two criminal complaints, right where you work, at police headquarters, and no one even came out to see me, nothing happened, and they just keep on stealing with impunity. They're a scourge, I tell you: a scourge!"

Ricciardi did his best to be conciliatory:

"You're right: I'll show you where they get in, that way at least the boys won't be a problem for you anymore. You'll still have to deal with the rats, though. How do you handle them?"

He pointed to the carcass of the dead rat, midway between foodstuffs and front door. Lotti, a big strapping man in shirt-sleeves and wide suspenders, gradually changed his tone of voice as his anger steamed off:

"That would be great, Commissa'. To at least get rid of the problem with the boys, I mean. I understand that they're hungry, I ate constantly at their age, too, but I can't afford to satisfy their appetites. They aren't my children after all, are they? With the rats, now I'm putting down this poison I buy at the pharmacy and, as you can see, it seems like it's starting to work. But the poison's expensive, and the flour and cheese to make the poison bait aren't free, either. I've tried using traps, but you get a couple of them and then the others catch on quick as a blink. Rats, *scugnizzi*, they're the same thing. They learn right away how to steal."

Rats and *scugnizzi*, both just as bad; they aren't my children:

the man's words hit Ricciardi like a slap in the face. The back of Tettè's neck appeared before his eyes again, as thin as the neck of an Easter lamb, as the attendants were carrying him off like a piece of scrap wood to be discarded, and he felt a stab of pain in his stomach.

"I just hope for your sake that all your permits and papers are in order," he said in a harsh tone of voice. "Licenses, food rations, customs, everything. That the goods have all been purchased on the up and up and that you're issuing the proper receipts for your sales. Criminal complaints, you know, are a two-way street. Did you know that a few hundred feet from here, early Monday morning, at the foot of the Tondo staircase, a little boy was found dead? The investigation has shown that he was poisoned. Exactly what kind of rat poison do you use, in here?"

Lotti stood there openmouthed; his mind was trying to process the information he'd just received as quickly as it could.

"I . . . my permits? My permits are all in order, my brother-in-law, who's an accountant, takes care of them. I'm not so good at reading words, though I'm all right with numbers. And . . . a dead boy, yes, I heard about that, one of the kids from Santa Maria del Soccorso, I think. I was sorry to hear it, too. They may be thieves, but they're still God's creatures, and I have six children, so you can imagine my feelings about it, Commissa'. Poison? I buy it at the pharmacy, and it costs plenty. I don't know what kind of poison it is, but let me go get the receipt from the pharmacist. Just wait here for a moment."

He left through a door in the back. Ricciardi asked Cristiano how he felt, and the boy shrugged dismissively, as if to say: it takes a lot more than that to scare me.

Lotti came back with a paper envelope, the kind they sell stamps in, and a receipt. He handed it to Ricciardi.

"Take care, Commissa': if the pharmacist told me once, he

told me a hundred times to handle this stuff with gloves on. It's deadly poison, as you can see for yourself," he said, pointing at the dead rat.

The second the commissario laid eyes on the envelope he recognized the word he was looking for: strychnine.

"Where do you put them, the poisoned morsels? Think carefully, Lotti: it's very important for me to know."

The man shook his head decisively.

"Only in here, Commissa', I swear it. It wouldn't even make any sense to put them outside: they're expensive, and it would just be a waste of money. The only thing I care about is protecting my merchandise. If I keep losing product, I'll have to shut down my business; that's the only reason I would spend all this money on poison, you have to believe me."

Ricciardi looked him in the face and felt pity for him, too.

"Come on, I'll show you where the kids are getting in. If you hurry up and seal up that entrance, it will help everyone to sleep better: you'll stop losing merchandise, and they'll stop dying like rats."

XXIII

By a curious coincidence, less than a mile away from Livia, Enrica, too, was sitting at the desk in her bedroom, staring at the rain beating against her window; by an equally curious coincidence, she was thinking about the same person.

She had decided to take Rosa's advice and answer Ricciardi's letter. And that was an important step forward.

She smiled as she thought back on Ricciardi's *tata*: meeting her had been both an enjoyable and an encouraging experience. It showed her that there were moments in life when it was necessary to take the initiative, show some courage. She had been brave, in a way she would never have expected, and it had paid off.

She felt a shiver at the thought of herself running down the stairs of her building and out into the rain; arriving at Don Gerardo's shop, without needing to buy a thing (what would she have said, if they had asked her what she wanted? She would have had come up with something, she thought); waiting for Rosa to finish ordering; offering to help carry her groceries.

Above all, it struck her as incredible that she had been capable of talking about her feelings with that woman, who was, for all intents and purposes, a stranger.

And yet, thinking back on it now, as she looked through the rain at the window of what she now knew to be Rosa's bedroom, nothing could have seemed more natural than to find herself there, sitting on the sofa in his apartment, drinking a cup of coffee. And to smell his scent all around her, the aroma of his aftershave; to look at the marble tiles on which he walked, the big wooden radio he listened to. Even the door to his bedroom. She hadn't had the nerve to ask to see his window, *the* window; and to imagine herself embroidering, just fifteen feet away.

From now on, those fifteen feet would never be the same; now that she could picture it all in her head, now that she knew for certain what objects and what lines of sight her eyes were exploring. The barrier had been torn down, more by her visit to the apartment than by his letter.

The letter, she thought, dipping her pen for the umpteenth time in the light-blue inkwell. The letter that she now had to answer.

In her mind, she pictured him in the act of opening the envelope containing her reply. She imagined his remote gaze, his nervous hands, the lock of hair dangling over his forehead. What on earth could drive a man like him to live a life of such complete solitude? Why did he share nothing with anyone, ever?

She sensed, as she always had, that behind those silences and behind the wall he'd built around himself there was actually an infinite kindness and gentleness, an unexpected tenderness toward his fellow man. She had no real reason to think this, but she did think it: and her conversation with Rosa had confirmed it for her. If she won his heart, if she were able to get close to him and love him the way she could feel she wanted to, that tenderness would emerge, and he would become a different man.

She smiled at the rain. She'd never been with a man romantically, she'd always been reserved, disinclined to date or court: now she knew, for a certainty, that all her life she'd only really been waiting for a man like him. The time for hesitation and uncertainty was through; it had ended with his letter and with her visit to Rosa.

With a determination that she'd never expected from herself, she leaned over the blank sheet of stationery and wrote the salutation: *Gentile Signore*. Dear Sir.

As night began to fall, Livia heard someone knocking politely at her door. When she called out *come in!*, her maid, a lovely young girl in a black apron and a white ruffled lace headpiece, poked her head in:

"Signo', forgive me. There's a gentleman at the door, he wouldn't tell me his name. He says that you're expecting him, and that you already know who he is."

After a moment of puzzlement and annoyance, Livia remembered that she was expecting a visitor after all: the man from the security agency who was to review the list of guests for her reception.

She took a hasty look at herself in the mirror to make sure she was presentable, then she went into the living room where a distinguished but nondescript middle-aged gentleman with salt-and-pepper hair stood waiting for her, hat in hand and his overcoat wet with rain.

"*Buona sera*, I'm Livia Lucani Vezzi. And you would be . . . ?"

The man gave a slight nod of the head and smiled:

"Delighted to meet you, Signora. You are indeed enchanting, just as I was told. You'll have to forgive me but I can't tell you my name. You can call me whatever you like, just pick a surname at random."

Livia laughed nervously.

"Well, that's curious! I can't even know who's entering my home. It's a good thing that, as you must know, I have nothing to hide."

The man put on an aggrieved expression.

"I understand, Signora. This is standard procedure, you

know. But I don't want you to see this in any way as a lack of respect toward you. It's just that the agency . . . or, I should say, the organization to which I belong stipulates secrecy as a moral imperative. It's in your own best interests, Signora. Let's do this: why don't we say my name is Falco? It's a code name, and it's not really all that far from my real name. How are you? Well, I hope? Enjoying your time in our fair city?"

Though still uneasy, Livia's curiosity was piqued by this individual.

"I'm well, very well indeed, *grazie*. Even if the nasty weather we've been having recently does keep me from getting around. Signora Ciano's secretary had alerted me earlier that you'd be paying a call. Tell me, what can I do for you?"

The man looked around, admiringly.

"Nice place; the parlor is so large, perfect for a party with so many important people attending. Did you prepare the guest list as requested? If you're not ready yet, I can come back whenever you like."

"No, no, there's no need for that: I have it right here. Here you are."

The man opened the envelope and pulled out a sheet of paper.

"I took a look at the building. A magnificent choice: centrally located but not suffocated by the noise from the traffic or the open-air markets. And from our point of view, that is, in terms of security, it's just fine: a single entrance, which can be easily kept under surveillance from the street. And windows on the interior courtyard."

Livia was taken aback.

"Easy to keep under surveillance, my goodness! Do you really believe that there is any danger? And so much danger that you need to keep my home under surveillance! Should I be worried, then?"

"Signora, these are difficult times. The Duce and the Fascist

Party are carrying on a process of consolidation that is far from complete. There are numerous dissidents and they too are starting to organize, establishing alliances and making agreements. A picket line that takes the concrete form of demonstrations or even, still worse, violent attacks is not something we can afford to rule out. Naples has thinkers, intellectuals who have repeatedly expressed strong anti-Fascist views; there is no reason not to believe that they might have established alliances with anarchists and Communists, ready to do whatever it takes."

Livia laughed again, to undercut the drama.

"Now you're frightening me! I honestly haven't sensed this atmosphere, in the time I've spent in this city. If anything, everywhere I've gone, I've observed what seems to be a complete loyalty to the regime; for that matter, who would be so mad as to reject the future of prosperity and well-being that the Duce is building for the nation? Moreover, the Neapolitan police force strikes me as extraordinarily capable and vigilant, don't you agree?"

The self-described Signor Falco shrugged.

"The police do police work. They enforce ordinary laws, deal with evidence, and go after criminals: thieves, rapists, murderers. Things that are easy to track down and understand. We deal with a different set of problems, things that are underground, hidden. A professional of unquestioned rectitude, a man leading a normal, ordinary life, with a family and children; a factory worker, who rides his bicycle every morning to the Ilva steel plant in Bagnoli and comes straight home every night, and goes to bed early; a washerwoman, who sings at the top of her lungs as she slaps her sheets against a stone by a fountain in Vomero. People who walk down the same streets as you, brush past you on the sidewalk, tip their hats in greeting. These are our enemies, potential terrorists, dissidents. People ready to take up arms against the government, against the

Duce. Or against the Duce's daughter, for that matter. Our organization, Signora, tries to find these people, and to find ways to protect us all from them."

"I can't believe this, Signor Falco. It seems impossible that there could be situations like the ones you've just described."

The man smiled.

"And yet, Signora, all three of the examples I just gave you are true: three situations that actually took place, over the last year, and right here in this city. Three individuals now serving time in prison, far from here, all three of whom confessed their participation in seditious assemblies, where they plotted against the regime."

Livia sat openmouthed.

"Really? And how . . . by what means were you able to catch them? How did you do it?"

"Like I was saying, Signora: with extreme care and discretion. We have a network of informants that you couldn't imagine, not even in your wildest dreams. Dozens of people faithful to the regime who cover the entire city: strolling vendors, shopkeepers, teachers, professors, students. Normal people, just like those other people I described to you, who gather and report things they are told in confidence, personal impressions—sometimes something as simple as a criticism, blurted out in an unguarded moment. We sift through their reports and denunciations, and we do research of our own: we look for confirmation, we add up pieces of evidence. And then we proceed to questioning, and we conduct an interview or two. And we form an opinion, we come to a decision: it's in no one's interest to send an innocent person into domestic exile, or to prison, don't you agree? Surely you can see why we have to be careful."

Livia shuddered in spite of herself. A gust of rain shook the window.

"Yes, I do see. I imagine that your organization is necessary, too. In any case, my guest list is complete."

The man rapidly skimmed the list of names.

"Mm . . . yes, I'd say by and large that it corresponds to what we'd expected. There are a few small surprises . . . Garzo, the deputy chief of police, for example: small fry, among so many prominent figures. But if you like, feel free to invite him. All right, Signora. We'll examine it more carefully, and if no objections arise, you can send the invitations out as early as tomorrow afternoon. Among the guests there will be two of our own men. They'll introduce themselves to you with the utmost discretion, and I assure you that they will cause you no annoyance; but I'm sure you understand that it's necessary, to prevent any potential disagreeable developments. Even at the finest high society gathering, it happens that someone might get drunk, or take unacceptable liberties."

Livia didn't much like the idea of strangers in the apartment, carrying out surveillance on her friends' and her own behavior; but she concluded that there was nothing she could do about it. She hoped that the reason for all this vigilance was the presence of Edda, but regardless, from that moment on she'd always feel that she was being watched.

The man said farewell and turned to go. She stopped him, impulsively:

"Listen, Falco: there actually is someone . . . a man, who will probably be at the party, though I haven't included him on the list. I'm planning to ask him if he'll come, but I'll do it in person, not with a written invitation. This is a person that I'd be disposed to . . . whom I'd like to spend more time with, in the future. A man I'm interested in, in other words. Could you possibly provide me with a report on him? I understand that it's unusual, but I really would like to know something more about him."

Falco already had his hand on the door handle. He turned to look at Livia with a sardonic smile.

"Certainly, Signora. A prominent woman such as yourself,

and with friends in such high places, can make whatever use of us she sees fit. And if this man lives here in the city, it's quite likely that we already have something about him in our files. What's his name?"

Livia sighed, hesitantly. Then she said, all in one breath:

"Luigi Alfredo Ricciardi. He's a commissario at the police headquarters, in Via San Giacomo."

The man smiled.

"And in fact, we do know him. He's even had a couple of meetings with my boss recently. I doubt there will be any problems, Signora. I expect to have a response for you by tomorrow. Have a pleasant evening."

XXIV

On the short walk back to the parish church, Ricciardi and Cristiano had remained in silence. The boy had said only, after they had left the warehouse:

"Did you really have to tell him how we get in? If I'd known you were going to do that, I wouldn't have shown you."

Ricciardi had shaken his head.

"And do you all really have to steal? Haven't you seen what it can lead to? What happened to Matteo should have taught you a lesson, if you ask me. And that man was bound to kill another one of you kids sooner or later, the way he was standing guard over his merchandise."

Cristiano had shrugged in response: his favorite gesture, it would seem.

"The *cacaglio* was a fool, I already told you that. If he hadn't died from eating rat poison, he would have died from being run over by a car or a carriage. And that guy from the warehouse, even if he waited around all day with a gun in his hand, couldn't have killed us. We never go there at this time of day because we know he's there: we go late at night."

Late at night. Which corresponded to Tettè's presumed time of death. Cristiano concluded:

"In any case, we certainly don't eat his food. It's not worth it. Besides, what would we eat? Dried beans? We sell the food we steal."

Ricciardi spent the rest of the walk thinking to himself that it would be worth talking to the priest again, and this time the kid gloves would come off. It seemed to him that these kids were left to their own devices a little more than they should be. He'd have to do it without exposing Cristiano to the priest's reprisals, though. He'd need to move carefully.

Don Antonio had finished saying mass and was reading in the sacristy. Ricciardi walked in without knocking.

"Commissario, you're back, I see. Did you search the place thoroughly? Are you satisfied, now?"

Ricciardi stood with his hands in his pockets, looking at the priest. No emotion was apparent in his still eyes.

"Yes, I'm done for now, Padre. But no, I'm not satisfied, not even a little bit."

"Really? And why not?"

The commissario dropped the ironic tone.

"The conditions here—this is no way for children to live. And leaving them free to wander the streets, exposing them to all sorts of dangers, including life-threatening ones, hardly strikes me as a model of childcare."

Don Antonio leapt to his feet. Now he really was infuriated.

"Ah, so that's what you think? Then why don't you devote yourself to taking care of children? Why don't you spend your days with these poor little beasts, who've spent their lives fighting stray dogs and rats for scraps of food? Do you realize that if I were to shut down this house, most of these boys would probably die of typhus or some other disease before the year is out? Do you realize that if it weren't for parish priests like me, the ones who managed to survive would become criminals, and they'd wind up either with a knife in their gut or in one of your prisons?"

Ricciardi was unimpressed by the priest's outburst of anger.

"No, I don't know that. What I do know is that you keep them in a room that's filthy and cold. That two days after his disappearance, you had barely even noticed that Matteo was missing. And above all, I know that, from what I've heard around the neighborhood, your boys spend their days pilfering where they can and selling the things that they manage to steal. That's a fairly serious state of affairs, you know, Padre. A state of affairs that, I believe, would make quite a splash even in the curia."

The two men stood glaring at each other, eyes leveled, the priest's dark and flashing with rage, the commissario's green and unblinking. In the end, the priest was the one to yield.

"I see. Now, we have extortion, along with the rest. All right, Commissario. Go ahead: what do you want to know?"

"Tell me about the other boys, and relations among them. And if you please, the facts, Padre."

"They don't behave the same way when I'm not around. That seems natural enough, no? The bigger ones take advantage of the smaller ones, they command and the others obey. For instance, there are two cots, as you've seen: they were donated by the hospital. In theory, the two twins ought to sleep on them, because they both suffer from curvature of the spine, but Amedeo and Saverio, the two boys who've been here longest, have requisitioned them for themselves. Some things that happen I'm aware of, and I do my best to put a stop to them. Other times I'm not around to see, so I can't intervene. It isn't easy, you know, running this whole parish. And as for the sexton Nanni, he's incompetent; he can't be trusted to do anything."

Ricciardi considered what the priest had just told him.

"Where do you get the money to keep things going, Padre? I can't imagine that the offerings you get at Mass are sufficient, no?"

Don Antonio spread his arms wide in resignation.

"Don't be ridiculous, those aren't even enough to keep the church clean. We get some funds from the curia, though not much; and then there are the donations from the Ladies of Charity, who also come twice a week to tutor the boys. The gifts that come in, sweets or clothing, don't even pass through my hands. They just divvy them up directly among themselves."

Ricciardi wanted to get a clearer picture of things.

"And these Ladies of Charity, do they take turns, or are the teachers always the same? And just how many of them are there?"

"If only there were enough of them to be able to take turns. There are two of them, just two. If you'd like to meet them, you can come tomorrow morning: it's Thursday and they'll be teaching. They've been informed of Matteo's death; one in particular was especially close to the child. Let's hope she keeps coming: to lose her would be a tragedy."

What am I looking for? What the devil am I looking for?

Ricciardi kept asking himself this question on his way home. It was raining, surprise, surprise; and the temperature went on plunging from one hour to the next, as a persistent northern wind buffeted the city.

He didn't know what he was looking for; or rather, he knew but he couldn't accept it.

The Deed: the damned Deed, his curse, his cross to bear, for the first time was persecuting him even without showing itself. In fact, precisely because it had not shown itself. Poor Matteo—or perhaps he should say Tettè, the name they had given him to make fun of his stutter—was dead; that much was certain. And Modo had found traces of strychnine. And today he had even figured out where Tettè might have found it, just a few hundred feet from the step on the staircase where the milkmaid with the nanny goat had found him with his dog.

The dog. All he had to do was think of it and turn to look at the other side of the street and there it was, trotting along, indifferent to the rain. Ricciardi shivered as he realized that the animal materialized whenever he was alone. If only he could interview the dog, maybe that would give him all the information he needed.

His thoughts turned to the little boy. He could almost see him walking through the streets at night, in the rain, in the cold; he imagined the boy talking to the dog with his heart's voice, without stammering, easily and calmly. Tettè, you did have one friend. A friend who knew how to listen to you without needing to hear the actual words.

Cristiano, too, had melted Ricciardi's heart: the loneliness that he'd glimpsed behind the swaggering arrogance, the feigned confidence. The terror in the boy's eyes when the warehouse owner's grip had choked the air out of him. Children, refusing to grow up and face life.

He too had been a lonely little boy, he thought to himself, feeling the rivulets of rain streaking down his face. But he'd had someone to look after him, and he still did. He smiled in the dark, the sound of his own footsteps accompanying him down the empty street. Dear old Rosa, you've always been there, with your indigestible cooking, with your scent of lavender. Dear old Rosa, you're a warm room, you're fresh bread, you're woolen blankets. Dear old Rosa, I know you'll grumble for an hour when you see me drenched with rain, and you'll run to fetch towels of all sizes, and you'll complain about your aching bones, and predict the same aches and pains for me when I get old. Who knows if I ever will get old?

The Deed and its rules, he thought. And what if that rule simply didn't apply this time? What if Tettè died of fright, before the strychnine had a chance to kill him? Then I wouldn't see him, and I'd be looking for something that doesn't exist. The ghost of a ghost. Searching without finding.

Perhaps what I'm looking for is a reason. Something for myself, not for poor Tettè. He was thinking about this, when he finally glimpsed through the rain the corner of his apartment building, his home. Perhaps I'm looking for the reason that there are children who are dry and warm tonight, and then there are others with chattering teeth who don't even know if they'll find a dry place to spend the night.

Out of the corner of his eye he saw a white coat with brown spots moving in the rain. What do you have to say about it, dog? There are also children in caskets, waiting to be buried. But their memory will endure as long as you're around, dog, as long as you're following me and commanding me to find out why.

In a gesture that had become customary with him, before entering the front door of the building he turned his eyes up to the window of the kitchen of the Colombo apartment, and saw that it was lit up. Have you read my letter, *amore mio*? he thought. What future awaits you and what future awaits me, can you tell me that? Who were we as children, and what children will we become? And will there be children to whom we can promise love and safety? What would our children be like? What would their eyes see?

He brushed aside the wet hair that hung over his forehead, and he started climbing the stairs.

XXV

T he first morning of cold weather has a taste and a color unlike any other. Because the cold always comes in the night, when everyone's asleep, and it takes the city by surprise; and because it comes on the wings of the wind.

It comes, changing the taste of the rain, which used to smack of the sea and now tastes of ice, and turns into a shower of needles driving into one's flesh and eyes, replacing the light that was made up of yellow and black with a different light, a light that is gray and uniform.

Everyone gets dressed under the covers, on the first morning of cold weather: and that's the way it will be for the rest of the winter, as everyone twists and turns under the blankets to preserve the night's warmth down to the last gasp, fighting against the flannel nightshirt that gets caught in the sheets, keeping on the underclothes, the knee-length woolen underwear, slipping on the socks with garters, prudently left out the night before within reach of the bed.

Then a rush to the kitchen to wash up in the sink, down the icy hallway, while mothers and wives hurry over with clothing warmed on the stove, envying the lucky few with bathrooms in their apartments, as the line on the landing to use the shared latrine grows longer. Show up late and get ready to wait.

The mothers wake up the children, preparing the fingerless gloves that will leave their fingers freezing but able to write.

They'll wash the children, still dazed with sleep, uncovering only the surfaces to be washed, one after another, scrubbing with large chunks of Marseille soap, the same soap they use to do the laundry. The children will pee in the chamber pot, which will then be carefully emptied off the balcony later in the morning, when no one will be passing by below, to keep from obstructing the paths of those who have to go to work even today, on the first morning of cold weather.

The stoves are going full blast this morning. The firewood put aside over the last few days, in preparation for this first chill, is finally being burned. The people warm their hands on them, placing them on the stovepipe, insulated by a piece of wool cloth that fills the apartment with its scent. They rummage through cabinets and drawers in search of the heaviest uniforms to wear in the war against the first cold morning: no one worries about the color or the cut; those are concerns for warm weather, for the first days of spring, for summer swims. Now it's to war, because it's the first morning of cold weather. What's worse, it's raining; so the war starts with the shoes, a wooden sole and an old, orphaned leather upper, patiently nailed on, its original sole lost years ago; and those who have bought a new pair recently luxuriate in their wealth, carefully checking them over, sitting fully dressed on the edge of the bed and minutely observing the tiniest scratch, the slightest imperfection: and if a sign of wear is found, they curse the shoe seller or the incompetent cobbler, completely forgetting how long it's been since they made their purchase, that these have been their "new shoes" for several years now.

The first morning of cold weather, even though it's long been dreaded and awaited, will arrive unexpected; and it will catch the elderly off guard, with new aches and pains, and the certainty that this winter will be their last. The black shawl will be pinned at the neck, the beat-up hat will be worn even indoors, and there will be a new melancholy in their eyes. And it won't be just on account of the weather that a shiver will run up and down their spines.

The first morning of cold weather brings evil thoughts.

Garzo had a presentiment. He'd been feeling this sense of foreboding every morning for a while now, ever since he'd first learned of the Duce's visit.

His presentiment was the product of the nightmares that haunted the deputy police chief's agitated sleep. Each time his imagination gave birth to some new monstrosity, such as His Excellency's arriving ahead of schedule and tumbling down the steps of police headquarters, wet and soapy due to some last-minute mopping, or else the engine of the car conveying him breaking down, so that the Duce finds himself forced to help push the vehicle uphill all the way to City Hall, flanked on either side by hordes of mocking bystanders.

And invariably, when morning rolled around, his alarm clock caught him staring wide-eyed at the ceiling, his heart in his throat, with, in fact, a sinking feeling: something was bound to happen, and it was going to ruin everything.

On his way to the office in a trolley car crowded with wet and sniffling passengers, he decided that actually something good had happened: in one fell swoop, he'd not only gotten rid of the dangerous Ricciardi, who could have represented a problem with his unpredictable proclivity for making trouble, he'd also managed to wangle an invitation to a very exclusive reception at the new home of the widow Vezzi. A single fell swoop, in fact, the work of a master strategist. Still, he couldn't keep himself from feeling that creeping sense of uneasiness, as if something bad were about to happen.

When he got to the office, he'd just hung up his overcoat on a hanger to dry when he heard someone knocking on the door. Ponte stuck his head in with a face that was even more miserable than usual, an envelope in his hand. Garzo took it from him and saw his own name, written with a proliferation of swoops and flourishes. His first thought was of the invitation to the reception, which he'd been expecting any second; then he noticed the elaborate heraldic crest embossed on the stationery. He knew it well, he remembered the endless correspondence that had come and gone during the feverish days of the final negotiations on the Concordat, the Lateran Treaty. It was from the archiepiscopal curia of the city of Naples. The return address was on Largo Donnaregina, not far from the cathedral. He furrowed his brow.

The unpleasant sensation redoubled with every second it took him to get to his desk and take the silver letter opener in his trembling hand. He pulled out the letter and read it. Then he reread it. Then he reread it again. With each rereading, the famous violet patches spread further and further over his face and neck, of that distinctive hue that the staff at police headquarters liked to describe in a whisper as "Garzo-in-a-rage purple."

He finally staggered to his feet and made his way to the door, threw it open, and shouted into the deserted hallway:

"Maione!"

Climbing Via Santa Teresa, against the wind and the rain, Ricciardi arrived at the parish church. He ironically thought to himself that he'd been to church more often in the past few days than in the previous three years put together.

It was cold that morning, he thought. He didn't mind the cold: he'd grown up in the mountains, and cold weather reminded him a little of home. And experience had taught him that hot weather and sunshine encourage people to go out, to get together, and to feel an array of emotions: love, envy, jealousy. All emotions that served as accelerants for passions and, therefore, for murders.

Cold weather, on the other hand, slowed people's blood:

they tended to stay home, hunker down, let time pass. People clung to what they had, no matter how scanty; they became less interested in the possessions of others: money, jewels, clothing, women, husbands. There was less of an urge to go out on the hunt. When the weather was cold, murders tended to go into hibernation. Not all, but some of them.

He reached the sacristy where he found Don Antonio writing, next to a large stove, wearing a scarf around his neck and a woolen hat. He had fingerless gloves on, and he was blowing on the tips of his fingers.

When he saw Ricciardi, he gave him a look of surprise, which kindled the commissario's suspicions: hadn't they set this meeting just the night before?

"*Buon giorno*, Padre. I see you're suffering from the cold."

The priest surprised him a second time by smiling warmly at him.

"*Caro* Commissario. I hardly expected to see you here this morning, with this dreadful weather: rain and an icy wind—hardly the ideal conditions to come all this way from police headquarters."

"No, actually I came directly from home and, as you know, I live nearby. Plus I don't especially mind the cold. You'll recall that we agreed that I'd come by to meet the Ladies of Charity and the other boys of the house. It won't take more than a few minutes; I promise not to be a nuisance."

"Yes, that shouldn't be a problem, I imagine. They're in there having a lesson. Unfortunately, only one of the ladies came today; the younger one, the one I told you was fondest of Tettè, seems not to be feeling well. She's surely grieving over his loss."

Ricciardi held up his hand to stop the priest, who was just standing up from his chair.

"Just a moment, Padre. As long as we're here, there are some other things I'd like to ask you. You told me that the boys are apprenticed out to various artisans. Was this true of Tettè, also? And if so, could you tell me which artisan he was apprenticed to—perhaps you could give me his name?"

Don Antonio shook his head, regretfully.

"I'm sorry, Commissario, but that's something I don't know. As I told you, the boys are free to choose the trade they'd like to learn and, if necessary, I intervene to recommend them to someone. Tettè never asked me, so I'd have to guess he was working with some strolling vendor or artisan. He'd only been going out to work for a few months; his health wasn't terribly robust, poor child. Now, if you don't mind, I'll see you to the lecture hall. I need to get back to work on my sermon for Sunday."

What Don Antonio had pompously called the "lecture hall" was actually a room even smaller than the sacristy, with a few rattletrap desks and a table where the teacher sat, serving as the lectern. There was also a badly chipped blackboard with a crack running diagonally from one corner to the other. The place felt like an icebox. There were five children, the two biggest each with a desk of his own, the other three clustered at a single desk, huddling together for warmth. Ricciardi noticed that all their heads were shaved almost bald and they were wearing several layers of shirts, clearly every piece of clothing they possessed.

The woman who was teaching the lesson was a rosy-cheeked matron about fifty years of age, wearing a heavy overcoat with a fur collar and thick leather gloves. When the priest came in she smiled and invited the boys to stand, but her joyous expression vanished the instant she caught sight of Ricciardi; the commissario realized immediately that he'd been introduced in advance, in abundant detail, to the Lady of Charity.

Don Antonio said sweetly:

"*Buon giorno*, Signora De Nicola. At ease, at ease, children. This gentleman is Commissario Ricciardi, from police head-quarters. He's here to find out a few things about poor Matteo, and the misfortune that took him away from us. A tragic mishap, as we all know. Now, remember, Commissario: I want you to keep your promise not to take too much time away from their lesson."

With these words, he turned and left. Ricciardi noticed that as the priest left the room, several of the boys exchanged rapid glances, and then lowered their gazes again. No one had said a word, and they had remained on their feet. The commissario turned to address the lady.

"*Buon giorno*, Signora. I'm trying to shed some light on cer-tain aspects of Matteo's life, in the hopes of arriving at a better understanding of how he died."

"*Buon giorno* to you, Commissario. My name is Eleonora De Nicola Bassi, I'm a member of the Ladies of Charity of Capodimonte. We help these children, doing our best to lend support to poor Don Antonio, who's a saint in every sense of the word. Let me tell you first of all that I don't know much about Matteo's life, because our work largely consists of ensur-ing that donations come in and conducting these two weekly lessons, which unfortunately don't produce great results. The only reason the boys come at all is to get the sweets that we offer as a reward," and she pointed to two macaroons sitting on the table. "But, please, feel free to ask any questions you might have, and I'll do my best to answer them."

Ricciardi pointed to the door.

"I'd prefer to speak in private, if it's all the same to you."

The woman nodded and, after ordering the boys to main-tain absolute silence while she was gone, left the room.

"Now then, Signora: how long did you know Matteo?"

Although she answered politely, the woman could hardly conceal her hostility toward any man who dared to call into question the sainthood of Don Antonio; in fact, she probably wasn't even trying to conceal it.

"Not long. I've been working with the parish for two years, and my interactions have been primarily with Don Antonio, helping him with administrative work and with the many things he does for his community. We only started teaching the lessons a few months ago. The little boy, as no doubt they told you, had a very bad stutter. I don't have the patience for such things, and the more I lost my patience the worse his stutter would get. And so my friend, who's not here today, was the one who spent the most time working with him. Her name is Signora Carmen Fago di San Marcello. The news of Tettè's death devastated her: you see, she can't have children of her own, and she's a young woman. She had grown very close to the child, she cared for him and spoiled him, to an excessive degree, in our opinion. She was in no condition to come in today. She's at home, crying. It's heartbreaking."

Ricciardi did his best to return to the point.

"Yes, it is heartbreaking. Especially for the little boy. But did you notice any signs of bad blood among the younger boys, or perhaps with the older ones? Any episodes, fights, or . . . "

"Commissario, they're boys," the woman said curtly. "That's what males are like, they fight and they never get tired of mocking each other. Tettè is . . . was the runt of the litter, and what's more he stammered so much that he couldn't finish a sentence. It's only natural that the others would peck at him a little, don't you agree? But they meant no harm by it. Again, I just couldn't seem to be patient with him. I only saw him an hour at a time, once a week. The rest of the time, he was with my girlfriend."

"What about with adults? What were his relations with the sexton, for example, or even with Don Antonio himself?"

The woman visibly stiffened.

"Anyone who can't get along with Don Antonio just has

something filthy in their soul, take it from me. He's a saint, and he, too, is suffering a great deal over the child's death. I never saw any other adults with Tettè, except for the sexton, who never speaks to a soul. Never saw any adults with the other children, either. There aren't many of us, you know, who look after them."

Ricciardi nodded. On that point, unfortunately, he had to agree with the woman, however much he disliked her. Signora De Nicola concluded, brusquely:

"Are we done, Commissario? I'd like to get back to the boys. I'm all alone and I need to finish up; my chauffeur will be coming to pick me up in an hour."

Ricciardi shot a glance through the door of the schoolroom: the boys hadn't moved. But the two macaroons had vanished.

As he left the parish church, the commissario felt rather demoralized. True, he still had to talk with the other Lady of Charity, the one who was close to Tettè: but it was also true that he kept coming up empty-handed. As far as he could tell, a heavy curtain had been drawn around the boy's life, and it was impossible to see anything through it.

Unless, that is, he couldn't keep from thinking, there really was nothing to see: unless he was just losing his mind, driven mad by the Deed and its consequences.

The woman, this Carmen Fago di San Marcello, who had no children of her own and had therefore bonded with Tettè. Children with no mothers, children with mothers; real mothers and fake mothers; mothers who abandoned their children, mothers looking for a child. He thought of his own mother, for no reason in particular, as he walked home with the wind and gusting rain pushing him down the street.

He wondered if the madness that was taking possession of him was the same one that had killed his mother. He remembered her, white-haired even though she was still quite young, in the hospital bed where she was to die of what was hastily diagnosed as a nervous fever. In his memory he saw her eyes gazing blankly, with dark circles beneath them. She was barely conscious from the sedatives they gave her continuously. He remembered her light, delicate hand, holding his own: it seemed to be made of paper.

So what should we do now, Mamma? he found himself thinking. Should we just discard him entirely, poor Tettè, with his strange dog and his thin neck, along with the nothingness that seemed to surround him? No, he answered himself. I have to know. I have to understand. If it's the last thing I do, before they send me to the same hospital you died in. Because if there's one thing I know, Mamma, it's that I ought to have seen his image if he died where we found him. Just as you would have known it, if you'd been in my place.

Waiting outside the entrance to his building, awkwardly trying to shelter himself from the rain and wind, was a dimly lit silhouette familiar to Ricciardi: a very embarrassed, very wet Brigadier Maione.

XXVI

At the exact instant lunch was served, the doorman of Livia's apartment building blew loudly into the interphone. The maid went out on the balcony to see what he wanted and, irritated at the rainwater that had drenched her from head to foot in a matter of seconds, she walked into the dining room.

"Signo', that gentleman who was here yesterday is downstairs, the doorman says. He says that the man asked if he could come up, but if you're eating he can come back later. Should he send him away?"

Livia dabbed her mouth with her napkin and replied:

"No, Maria, have him tell the man to come right up. Put my lunch away and keep it warm, I'll finish it afterward."

When she walked into her living room, Falco was already there, as if he hadn't moved since the previous evening. He smiled and greeted her in the exact same way, with a slight nod of the head.

"*Buon giorno*, Signora. Forgive me for coming at this hour; I just thought I'd take advantage of a little free time at the office to bring you that report we talked about. I have to ask you to read it in my presence, though. I can't leave it with you, as I'm sure you can understand. But take your time. I'll wait."

Livia took the slim file that the man had pulled out of his leather briefcase. She noticed that her guest wasn't even wet, in spite of the fact that it was pouring rain outside. He must have come by car.

"Thank you very much. I hope I haven't caused you any inconvenience."

"None whatsoever, Signora. I merely made the request to Signor . . . to my superior officer, who was happy to oblige. Please, read away."

Livia sat down in the armchair, gesturing for the man to make himself comfortable; he declined the offer politely, standing and looking out the window at the rain so she could read in private. She was once again forced to appreciate the discretion that Falco wore like a second skin.

The report consisted of two typewritten pages, plus a hand-written note on a third sheet of paper.

In it she read that Luigi Alfredo Ricciardi, fourth baron of Malomonte, born in Fortino, province of Salerno, on June 1, 1900, resident of Naples, at Via Santa Teresa degli Scalzi, number 107, was unmarried. Livia learned that he lived with Rosa Vaglio, seventy-one years of age, who had been his wet nurse and now served as his housekeeper; that he was employed by the police with the rank of commissario, and had worked at the royal police headquarters since 1923, when he first joined the police immediately after graduating from university in Naples with a degree in law, summa cum laude, with a thesis in criminal law.

The person who drafted the report included a few bare bits of information about Ricciardi's childhood, at a boarding school run by Jesuits in Naples, then back in Fortino at the age of fifteen, when his mother died in her late thirties; his father had died when he was a child. Livia learned to her immense surprise that, along with the aristocratic title, which she had never heard him mention, Ricciardi also possessed a large fortune in real estate and farmland, but the report also clearly indicated that he was not at all involved in their upkeep or administration: his properties were looked after by Vaglio and several relatives back home, who reported directly to the woman.

His academic record, both at boarding school and at the university, had been impeccable. He'd always had top grades. The report explicitly expressed some bafflement about Ricciardi's virtually nonexistent social life: he did not seem to frequent women, not even casually, nor was there any reason to suspect homosexuality. He was friendly with one Raffaele Maione, a brigadier at police headquarters (married to Lucia Caputo, five living children, one deceased; see specific personal report), and with Bruno Modo (unmarried, medical officer during the Great War, on the Carso Front; see specific personal reports 127 and 15B), a physician at Pellegrini hospital: but these friendships were largely restricted to the professional sphere. Next to the note about his personal and social life there was a long red line, drawn in pencil.

Livia instinctively looked up at Falco, who hadn't moved a muscle and continued to look out the window. As if he'd been reading over her shoulder, he said:

"It means that it's strange. A man without women, men, or friends in his life. A man who lives only for his work. A man without vices. Strange, don't you agree? That's why there's that red mark in the margin."

The woman looked back down at the pages of the report. She found that man profoundly unsettling.

The report mentioned a number of cases brilliantly solved by Ricciardi, including the case of her husband's murder. It noted that he was viewed with dislike by his colleagues at police headquarters, probably due to professional envy; as a result it was a widely held belief that having any dealings with Ricciardi brought some kind of bad luck.

The report said that it was believed that he was slated for imminent promotions, but that there was no evidence that the man had made any applications for such promotions, as would be normal practice.

The last note in the report had to do with her. It appeared

that over the past few months Ricciardi had been occasionally seeing Livia Lucani, the widow Vezzi, who probably as a result of this acquaintanceship had decided to transfer her official residence to Naples, current address Via Sant'Anna dei Lombardi, number 112.

As she read these last lines, Livia felt a mixture of conflicting emotions. On the one hand, indignation at what she found to be an intolerable intrusion into her personal life. How dare those spies decide that it was "probably as a result of this acquaintanceship" that she had made the decision to change cities? What did they know about her loneliness, about the effects of the loss of her baby years ago, and later, of her husband, only the previous winter?

The other emotion was the excitement of learning that she was the only woman in Ricciardi's life. Of course, there was that other woman, the one "in his heart"; but she wasn't in his life, otherwise Falco's phantomlike organization would certainly have found out about her and meticulously revealed her existence in the report, perhaps erasing that red line.

She came to the last sheet of paper, which was handwritten. In the brief note she read: "Pay particular attention to the friendship with Bruno Modo, physician at the Pellegrini hospital, openly dissident, suspected of seditious activity against the Italian state."

She looked up and her eyes met Falco's; he was staring right at her. The customary cordial expression was gone from his face.

"Signora, my superior specifically asked me to bring you this last note, along with the report. I expressed my doubts about letting you read it, I have to be honest with you; but he insisted. He says that your commissario, whom he has personally met, strikes him as a good person and that he might well be harmed by this . . . acquaintance. Harmed seriously. And so he decided to take the risk and let you know, so that you might be able to do what you can to . . . extract him. Of course, it is your duty to say absolutely nothing to anyone about what you have read in this report, the very fact of its existence, as well as the existence of myself and the organization I work for. Are we agreed on that point?"

Livia was very upset. She nodded and handed back the file. Falco bade her farewell with his usual little nod and turned to go. When he had his hand on the doorknob, he stopped and said:

"Ah, I almost forgot. Your guest list is perfectly fine, Ricciardi included: you may certainly proceed with mailing out the invitations. Remember that there will be two additional attendees, one of them attending as a guest, the other as part of the household staff. They won't cause you any inconvenience. *Arrivederci*, Signora; and forgive me again for intruding on your lunch."

Once she was sure that Ricciardi had left the building, Enrica put on her overcoat and hurried downstairs, precariously balancing her umbrella in one hand and a baking pan wrapped in a cloth napkin in the other. She slipped through the street entrance of the building across the way and, her heart racing, she rushed up the stairs to the third floor landing and knocked on the same apartment door to which she'd accompanied Rosa the previous morning.

The elderly woman peered out through the narrow opening afforded by the door chain, and then opened up with a broad, welcoming smile, planting two loud kisses on the young woman's cheeks, which were now flaming red.

"Signorì, what a pleasure! How are you today? Come in, come in, don't stand out there in the cold. Can you believe the chill in the air this morning? Winter arrived overnight! It's like they say: 'Come All Saint's Day, put summer clothes away.' *Prego*, come right in."

Enrica was pleased with this warm welcome; the two women

had taken to each other right away, that much was clear to her, but she hadn't expected such expansiveness.

"Signora, I took the liberty . . . Since my father is very fond of this pastry I make for him, yesterday while I was preparing it I made some extra. That is to say, I didn't make more than I meant to, I made this special, but it was certainly no trouble. But please, I'd like you to sample it first, and then, only if you like it, you could give some to . . . you know, to him."

Rosa had pulled open the cloth and peeked in at the pastry with a smile.

"Don't be silly! That one eats like a wolf, he'll gobble down anything you set before him, I'm sure he'll like this. It's a *migliaccio*, isn't it? Ricotta and semolina . . . hold on, I'll cut us a slice and we can taste it. Make yourself comfortable, I'll be right in, you know the way, don't you?"

As she was waiting for Rosa to come back with the pastry, she noticed that the door to Ricciardi's bedroom had been left ajar. She glimpsed part of his bed, his writing desk, the window frame. She imagined him standing there, looking across the street at her; or bent over the desk, writing her a letter. The thought of the letter set her heart racing again.

Rosa brought in two generous portions of her pastry.

"I tasted it, Signori'. You're a good cook, truly: most of the time people use too much ricotta, to add to the flavor, but this is the real *migliaccio*. Very well done."

And they started chatting, like a couple of old friends. It didn't hurt that they happened to share the same favorite topic of conversation.

Without knowing it, Enrica learned from Rosa's lips the exact same things that Livia had read in the chilly bureaucratic language of the detailed secret police report; but the information she learned about Ricciardi's life, family, and past history was tinged with the immense tenderness and love that the *tata* felt for her *signorino*.

Enrica took a long and emotional journey through the childhood of the little boy with large green eyes, condemned to loneliness and solitude first by his noble birth and later by his personality. She was introduced to the two baronesses of Malomonte, the mother, who had taken Rosa from her peasant family, and the daughter-in-law, as slender as a little girl, her eyes filled with sadness. The boy went off to boarding school, years and years of studying without a friend, and then he was standing in the hospital room, holding the thin hand of that white-haired woman who left this life at such a young age. She saw Rosa herself, entrusted with the future of a man she couldn't understand but whom she loved wholeheartedly. She learned of a name as venerable as it was long, and of faraway wealth that would have allowed him to live his life comfortably, with a prominent place in society: all things he had contemptuously turned his back on.

From the folds of this long and heartfelt account emerged a man at once close to and yet so far from the one she had grown accustomed to dreaming of; and her heart swelled with tenderness and the desire to take him by the hand and lead him through life: she, of all people, who knew so little about life herself.

When she looked at the clock and saw that it was late enough that he might be home at any minute, she got up and kissed Rosa good-bye, realizing that she had tears in her own eyes and on her face, and finding several more among the *tata*'s wrinkles. She promised to come back, and before leaving, gave the old woman an envelope for him.

XXVII

Ricciardi came to a halt, face-to-face with Maione, who looked like a weeping willow, even though he was big as an oak. The brigadier looked away, scraped one foot on the ground as if he were trying to draw a picture, then heaved a sigh, raised his eyes to meet Ricciardi's, and said:

"*Buon giorno*, Commissa'. How is your vacation going?"

Ricciardi took the question under serious consideration.

"I'm sorry, Raffaele, but you come all the way up here from police headquarters, you're drenched and dripping with gallons of rainwater and you're probably catching pneumonia as we stand here, just so you can ask me how my vacation's going, in the middle of the street, not a full day after we said good-bye for the week? Why don't you come up to my apartment, first of all, and dry off a bit. Then you can tell me what's happened, because you have a look on your face like you were at your own funeral."

Maione started to object, saying that he didn't want to intrude, but then he sneezed and gave in. Once they got upstairs, he was immediately handed off to Rosa, who seemed to be in a particularly chatty mood. She made him take off his uniform jacket and shirt; since Maione's measurements were closer to the *tata*'s than to Ricciardi's, the brigadier, while he was waiting for his clothes to dry at least partially on the cast-iron stove, was forced to suffer the humiliation of wearing a dusty pink dressing gown.

To see him like that, gloomy and sopping wet, with his heavy boots poking out from underneath the hem of the lady's

166 · MAURIZIO DE GIOVANNI

dressing gown decorated with large tone-on-tone flowers, and with a steaming mug in his hands, worried Ricciardi.

"Now then, you want to tell me what happened?"

The brigadier's eyes flashed with anger.

"Commissa', I'm going to strangle him with my own two hands!"

"Who are you going to strangle?"

"Garzo, Commissa'. Him and that infamous lickspittle spy of his, that damned Ponte."

"Listen, Raffae': if you want me to understand what you're talking about, then you're going to have to start from the beginning. Otherwise I'm lost."

Maione heaved a long sigh.

"All right then, Commissa'. So this morning I came in to headquarters, so sleepy and dazed that I even forgot you wouldn't be there; I'm not used to you missing work. I even brought a cup of ersatz coffee to your office."

Ricciardi sighed.

"Well, that's the only piece of good news I've had today, that I was spared a cup of that slop. Go on."

Maione put on an offended look.

"What do you mean, a cup of that slop? I make the best coffee of anyone at headquarters! So anyway, at a certain point I hear him, Garzo, squawking my name like a brood hen: *Maione, Maione!* I pretend I don't hear him, I know the way things work in that building, and sure enough not two minutes go by before Ponte shows up at the door, out of breath. Didn't you hear Signor Garzo calling your name, Brigadie'? No, I said. I didn't hear him; why, do you have something to tell me?"

Ricciardi did his best to steer the conversation back to the main point:

"Raffaele, please: I don't care about Ponte when he's standing right in front of me, much less when he's a mile and a half away. Let's get to the point: What did Garzo want from you?"

"Commissa', you have to let me tell the story my way, otherwise I'm going to lose the thread and leave out something important. So anyhow, Ponte takes me to see Garzo. And let me tell you, I've never seen him in such a state: he was covered with so many red patches that it looked like he had scarlet fever, and the man couldn't speak. I thought to myself, let's leave this in the hands of God: now he'll die of a stroke and we'll all finally get him out from underfoot. Instead, he says: Maione, Maione. What am I going to do with the two of you?"

Ricciardi had lost the thread.

"Was he seeing double?"

Maione looked at him.

"Commissa', *you're* talking nonsense. But *he* wasn't. 'The two of you' meant you and me: the two of us, is what he meant. I said to him, I don't understand, Dotto'. And he starts waving an envelope under my nose. I thought to myself: if he gets any closer and slaps me in the face with that thing, I'll make him swallow it in a single gulp."

"And what was in the envelope?"

"He opens it up and reads it to me. To the attention of the esteemed Dottore Angelo Garzo, deputy chief of police et cetera. This letter is to respectfully request that you et cetera. We understand that on the date of et cetera . . . "

Ricciardi was starting to run out of patience.

"Raffaele, listen to me and listen closely: you're starting to make me anxious, and that's never a good thing. Could you possibly get to the point, please? I'm begging you."

Maione heaved a long, weary sigh.

"Oh, all right, Commissa'. If that's how you want it, that's how I'll tell it. To make a long story short, it was a letter from the archiepiscopal curia, signed by, if I'm getting this right, a monsignor, the personal secretary of Bishop Ascalesi. They were asking for information regarding an investigation that may or may not have been undertaken into the circumstances

168 · MAURIZIO DE GIOVANNI

of the death of a young guest, that's what they called him, a guest of the parish church of Santa Maria del Soccorso at Santa Teresa. They pointed out that, to the best of their knowledge, the pastor of the parish in question, Don Antonio Mansi, had been questioned repeatedly. And that, if this had actually taken place, it constituted a gross violation of articles thus and such of the Lateran Accords between the Italian state and the Holy See, on some date or other. In other words, an official complaint about our behavior."

Ricciardi scratched his chin.

"So that's why the priest was surprised to see me this morning: he'd calculated that the letter would already have reached police headquarters and that I'd have been immediately prohibited from going back to see him again. Go on."

"What am I supposed to go on with, Commissa'? He went nuts. He said that he told you loud and clear that the investigation shouldn't have been started in the first place. He said that he'd never authorized anything, and that this was a clear case of insubordination, and that he'd fix our wagons, the both of us."

"The both of us? What do you have to do with any of this?"

Maione put on a truculent expression.

"Why, wasn't I there, too, at the first examination of the crime scene? Didn't I go to see the doctor, at the hospital? And when we interviewed the priest, at headquarters? In fact I told him that we didn't do anything other than ask the standard administrative questions, the ones you'd have asked in any case of the kind."

Ricciardi was worried.

"You don't have anything to do with this matter, and you should have told him so then and there. This is something that doesn't concern you; you stopped when you were told to stop, period."

Maione regained some of his dignity, though it was partially undercut by the pink nightgown he was wearing.

"Commissa', I came here to tell you something else: I'm willing to call in sick, if you want me to help you in the investigation. The truth is, I've been thinking, and I think that the reason that poor child died is because he was wandering the streets by himself, left to his own devices to find something to eat, and what he found, he ate; but at the same time I've worked with you for too many years now not to know that when something doesn't sound right to you, then you're probably onto something. So even if that idiot Garzo sent me to tell you that if you dare to do anything that results in another word of complaint from the curia, he'll toss you out on your ear, I'm here to give you a hand."

Rosa, standing in the kitchen doorway, said, "Bravo!"

Ricciardi looked at her.

"Excuse me, aren't you supposed to be going deaf? Into the kitchen with you, go on, and mind your own business. No, Raffaele, I already told you: you're more useful to me if you're at headquarters, ready to allay suspicions."

"Commissa', then let me do something! Just sitting around unable to help you—all it does is make me worry. And besides, lately everyone is busy polishing brass doorknobs for the Duce's visit, and I don't have anything to do. And when I have nothing to do, I put on weight, and that's no good."

Ricciardi pretended to be overwrought.

"No, that's no good. All right then, maybe you could try to gather a couple of pieces of information that the priest didn't want to give me. First: they say that Tettè worked as an apprentice to someone, an artisan or a strolling vendor. I need to find out who that was, and what he does. Then I'd like to learn a little more about this parish priest of ours; he strikes me as just a little too uncooperative, and I'd like to know if there's something behind it. But be careful: use outside channels, nothing that could get you in hot water back at headquarters."

Maione smiled broadly.

"That's it, Commissa', now you're talking. I'll take care of it, don't you worry: you'll have all the information by nightfall. We can meet at Gambrinus in Piazza San Ferdinando, at the end of my shift, let's say 8:30, is that all right? Be careful, though: if that Garzo sees us talking, he'll put two and two together. I mean, he's a cretin, but not that much of a cretin. Now, if you don't mind, I'm intruding, and I should be on my way. My clothes must be dry by now; it's got to be a hundred degrees in here with that enormous stove."

Ricciardi nodded.

"In the meantime, I'm going to take a walk and pay a call on an old friend of ours. Let's see if I can wheedle a little interesting information out of him."

Maione slapped his forehead.

"That reminds me, Commissa'; I almost forgot. This morning Signora Vezzi—you know, the widow—came by looking for you. She wanted you to go with her to pick out a dress for that soiree. She'd forgotten that you weren't at headquarters. I didn't say a thing, naturally."

Ricciardi shot a worried glance toward the kitchen.

"And what did she say?"

"Nothing, nothing. She said that she'd take care of it on her own, that it might actually work out better that way, so that she could surprise you. To be sure, if you don't mind my saying so, Commissa', that's one beautiful woman. Whenever she comes around everyone from the sentry at the door to the last custodian and janitor seems to find some excuse or other to come by and take a look at her. Some of them more than once. And then she's the only one who seems to be able to get Garzo out of our hair. If you ask me, you ought to give her some thought; she seems to have a real crush on you."

Ricciardi cut in brusquely:

"All right, all right, you stop worrying about it. The important thing is that you didn't give her my address."

"No, I wouldn't have dreamed of it!"

"Good work. Now get dressed and go do what I told you to do. Tell Garzo that I wasn't home, that I've gone back south to Fortino to take care of some family matters. Ah, and Raffae': *grazie*. Thanks for everything."

Maione took a bow, which, along with the dressing gown, made him look remarkably like a sumo wrestler.

"Don't give it another thought, Commissa'. Always at your service! But you should tread lightly, especially with that priest."

Just ten feet away the *tata*, who on some occasions proved to be anything but hard of hearing, was processing the information she'd just learned with a very worried expression.

XXVIII

He ran through the streets and *vicoli*. He ran barefoot, dodging cars and carriages, trolleys and handcarts. He ran through the market, leaping over obstacles and bumping up against fat women selecting apples. He ran on the sidewalks, splashing puddle water onto office workers trying to keep their pants dry on their walk to work, thus setting off curses and angry cries in his direction.

Cristiano ran, not caring who or what he slammed into along the way, indifferent to the icy drizzle he was dashing through; running warmed him up, and he liked to breathe in the rain.

He ran because he was looking for someone, and he went from one place to another where he thought he might find that person. And then he found him.

Cosimo Capone was a *saponaro*, a soap seller. It was a trade that encompassed many others, as he always liked to say. In theory it consisted primarily of barter, swapping junk for junk, with the difference in value paid in irregularly shaped chunks of brown soap, as difficult to handle as they were slow to dissolve. In theory. But in practice, Cosimo did more chatting than anything else.

He chatted with everyone, but especially women. He knew that he was charming, with his handsome smile and his gift of gab, and that a couple of nicely phrased compliments did wonders to soften the hearts of housewives and washerwomen; and with the softening of their hearts invariably came the opening

of their coin purses. If you added a pretty song to the reassuring handcart piled high with raggedy old clothes and copper
pots, the items practically sold themselves.

According to Cosimo, going around with a little kid in tattered clothing was a great idea for someone in his line of work;
and the skinnier and hungrier he looked, the better. Women
are mothers, or else they'd like to become mothers: an ill-fed,
ill-clothed child is an irresistible appeal to their pity, and therefore to their generosity. And then if the child looks much
younger than he really is, has such a bad stammer that he can't
even speak, and is accompanied by a stray mutt in worse shape
than he is, then you've hit the jackpot.

For Cosimo, Tettè constituted a genuine gold mine; depend-
ing on the situation, he'd either tell people that Tettè was his
son and that the boy's mother had died in childbirth, or else
that he'd found the boy on the street, or that he was the son of
a comrade-in-arms who'd died in combat. He was quite astute
at guessing the nuances of grief and pain in the life of any
woman who approached his handcart, and he knew how to
play the innermost chords of her soul; the haggling eased up
and the earnings were always much greater than he had any
right to expect.

But this wasn't the only thing that made Tettè the ideal
assistant. The other thing, the most important one, had taken
months of training: an investment of time and effort that had
only recently begun to pay off, and which Cosimo, conscien-
tious businessman that he was, wasn't willing to lose without a
fight.

When Cristiano, dripping with rain and out of breath,
caught up with him, Cosimo was using his running patter on a
mistrustful middle-aged woman leaning halfway out the
ground-floor window of a *basso*.

"Signo', this morning you're a sight for sore eyes: you're
such a vision that if I look at you I'll be blinded, I'll have to

stumble my way through the *vicoli*, I'll run my handcart straight into a brick wall. But tell me, how do you do it—how do you keep yourself looking so pretty?"

The woman, who had a beard and whiskers a cadet might envy and looked to weigh as much as a cartload of bricks, narrowed her eyes.

"Your magic isn't going to work on me this morning, Cosimo. I've got this handful of rags, and what I need is a large bar of soap. If you want to give it to me, fine; otherwise clear out, because your handcart in front of my window is blocking my air."

"Donna Carme'," he sniveled, "you're trying to ruin me! A large bar of soap is worth at least a shirt, and a shirt in good condition, or at least a frying pan without any holes in it. What am I supposed to do with a couple of tattered footcloths? Put at least a five-cent piece next to them, and that way you'll send me away a happy man! Don't take advantage of me, now that I've fallen head over heels for you!"

The woman showed that she was a tough nut to crack; it had been thirty years since she'd last received a sincere compliment, and she wasn't about to be made a fool of.

"Nothing doing. So go on, make up your mind and make it quick. I have things to do."

It was then that Cosimo noticed Cristiano's presence. After catching his breath, the boy said:

"Don Co', I can work with you, I'll go into the apartments, that *cacaglio* won't be coming anymore!"

Donna Carmela narrowed her eyes to slits and asked, in an even warier voice:

"What did the child say? What apartments is he going into?"

With the speed of a rattlesnake, the junk seller's hand shot out and grabbed Cristiano's shoulder, crushing it in a violent, viselike grip. The boy immediately fell silent.

"No, this child must have me confused with someone else, Donna Carme'. I've never even met this *scugnizzo*. You know that the only one I keep with me is my stepson, Tettè. You remember Tettè, don't you?"

The woman's scowling face suddenly brightened into a smile.

"Of course, how could I not? The lovely quiet little boy with the brown and white dog. Always so polite, the way he bows to me if I give him a cookie. Why isn't he with you today?"

Cosimo put on a worried expression, without letting go of Cristiano's shoulder.

"He's sick, a few lines of fever. If he doesn't feel well, I don't take him out with me, especially in this weather, no? You have children yourself, don't you, Donna Carme'? In other words, you can understand me."

The woman grew cautious again, but her voice had softened at the thought of little Tettè.

"No, I don't have children, I never got married, because there was never anyone who was right for me. But I have nephews and nieces, and your little boy reminds me of a little nephew of mine who died, years and years ago. All right, let's not waste any more time: here are the rags and a five-cent coin, give me the soap and get out of here, I've got work to do."

Once the transaction had been completed, the woman slammed the window shut with a bang. Cosimo spat angrily on the ground and, once they'd turned the corner, began shaking Cristiano.

"Who asked you to open your big mouth? What on earth made you think you could speak to me without permission? I ought to kill you with my own two hands!"

The boy stood there, wide-eyed and speechless. He was terrified. Cosimo went on, in a hiss:

"You know that I'd do it, too, eh? You know that all too well. Where's your little friend? Why hasn't he been around for the past three days, him and that disgusting dog of his? If he turns up and he's been out scavenging food, I'll break every bone in his skinny body, I swear it as God is my witness!"

Cristiano caught his breath and said, the words tumbling out:

"Don Co', that little *cacaglio* won't be coming anymore: he's dead. He ate rat poison and died, and they found him at the Tondo di Capodimonte. So I wanted to take his place, and come around with you. I don't want to go work with the cobbler anymore. I'm fast, I can run. And that thing in the apartments, I can do it better than he ever did!"

Cosimo turned deathly pale; he looked around in terror and, after making sure that there was no one around to see or hear, he grabbed Cristiano by the throat.

"What are you saying? What do you mean, he's dead? Who knows about this? And what do you mean by 'that thing in the apartments'? What do you know about it, who did you talk to?"

Now Cristiano really was afraid: he hadn't expected that reaction from the junk seller, and in the dark stretch of alley where the man had taken him there was no one to call to for help. Animal of the street that he was, he recognized the cold determination in the man's eyes, and he understood that his life was in danger.

"No, no, let me go, I won't breathe a word to anyone. And no one else knows. The *cacaglio* himself told me, he told me that sometimes when you were out on your rounds together, he'd sneak into the apartments and grab something while the women were talking to you. But he only told me, and I'm not going to tell anyone else. Now let me go. I told the priest that I was coming to talk to you for a minute and then I'd be right back."

Cosimo thought fast, and he loosened his grip. The red imprints of his fingers were clearly visible on Cristiano's throat. The man ran his hand over his face to wipe away the rain: he'd come within an inch of killing the boy.

"Go on then, get back to the priest. And don't let me ever lay eyes on you again. But remember this: if anyone finds out anything, I'll come track you down wherever you're hiding, and I'll finish what I started this morning. You understand? Now, get out of here!"

Cristiano didn't have to be told twice, and he took off running, slipping on the wet cobblestones.

Cosimo flopped down onto his cart, with a faint clanging of copper pots. He's dead, then, he thought. He's dead.

And now what am I going to do?

XXIX

Ricciardi entered the church of San Ferdinando in an entirely different spirit from the one he'd been in as he entered the church of Santa Maria del Soccorso. He almost found it funny, all this going around to churches, so far removed from his personality; but this time he was happy to be calling on an old friend.

Actually, not that old a friend; he'd first met Don Pierino, the assistant parish priest of the beautiful church in the city center, when he was investigating the murder of Livia's husband, the tenor Arnaldo Vezzi. The murder had caused an uproar in the city, especially among the many impassioned opera lovers. Don Pierino was an opera lover himself, and he had been at the Teatro San Carlo the night that the murder had taken place.

The two men couldn't have been any more different; perhaps that was exactly why they had hit it off so well. Don Pierino countered Ricciardi's grim materialism with a simple and absolute faith, which in his interactions with society at large took the form of a constant effort to help the weak and the vulnerable. Thus the two men arrived, by very different paths, at the same heartfelt involvement in the things they saw in the grim underbelly of the city.

Ricciardi didn't like opera, and in general tended to shun the portrayal of false emotions. He was far too well aware of how devastating and lethal real passions could be. Don Pierino loved opera and music, in part because their beauty struck him as a testimonial to God's love toward all mankind. The commissario had found an important guide in the little priest, and Don Pierino had been invaluable in the course of his investigation. He'd never have been able to solve the mystery without him.

In the dim light of the central aisle, Ricciardi saw the figure of the assistant parish priest emerge from the confessional. Don Pierino was a short man, with a belly that was becoming more and more prominent, but which did nothing to keep him from being constantly on the move, as energetic and vigorous as a restless child. There was a look of weariness about him now, until he noticed Ricciardi and his face lit up with joy.

"Commissario, how happy I am to see you! It's been a long time since you thought of your friend here, eh? You're soaked through, is it still raining out? I've been hearing confession for three hours now, and it looks like I'm finally done."

Ricciardi shook the priest's hand.

"How are you, Padre? You look tired? Can it be? Do men of the cloth like you get to the point of exhaustion, too?"

Don Pierino joined his hands on his belly, in a gesture that was common with him.

"Any priest can tell you, Commissario, that nothing wears you out like hearing confession. You have to look straight into the hell that every person carries within, you have to delve into it, you have to understand it, and you have to forgive them in the name of God: a forgiveness that many don't even want, because they'd rather be forgiven by their fellow human beings. It's draining work, and sometimes it's atrocious, believe me. But how about you: how are you doing? When I think of you, and I think of you often in my prayers, I always remember that you promised that you'd let me take you to the opera sometime."

Ricciardi made his customary grimace of exasperated annoyance.

"Padre, I know, I said I would: but believe me, the opera that this city manages to stage on a daily basis keeps me from making good on my promise. And that, along with the pleasure of seeing you again, of course, is what brings me here this evening."

Don Pierino turned serious.

"I know very well how much pity and compassion you have for the poor; that is why I'm always glad to help you with your cases. If it were strictly a matter of sending someone to jail, I don't think I'd be so happy to talk with you. These are strange and difficult times, Commissario, and no one knows that better than you: certain so-called criminals are far more innocent than the men who prosecute them."

Ricciardi nodded.

"I know that, Padre. I know it all too well. But some victims are certainly innocent, too. I'm not sure if you heard, but Monday morning a little boy was found . . . "

"Yes, at the Tondo di Capodimonte, I heard about it. One of those poor children from Santa Maria del Soccorso. I was told by a parishioner of mine, a woman who works in a shop over in that part of town. How pitiful."

"Yes, Padre. Truly a pity. In any case, I'd like to get a clearer picture of what happened. Not that there's any doubt about how the boy died, to be clear: he ingested rat poison."

Don Pierino sighed.

"Hunger. Damned hunger. Things like this shouldn't happen; much less to children."

Ricciardi agreed:

"That's exactly right. In short, I asked around to get a better idea of just how this child was living, mainly to keep such a thing from happening again. But to my surprise, I encountered a great deal of resistance from the parish priest of Santa Maria del Soccorso."

Don Pierino was astonished.

THE DAY OF THE DEAD · 181

"But why all these questions, Commissario? Do you think that . . . that someone could have . . . Forgive me, but I just can't believe it. A little helpless child, a poor orphan . . . "

Ricciardi waved his hand to dismiss the idea.

"No, no, Padre. No doubts there. It was an accident, unquestionably. But what I wish I understood better is how and why a child like this one could be allowed to sneak into a warehouse, by night, evidently with the intention of stealing something to eat, and instead wind up dead after eating a poisoned piece of bait, like a sewer rat. And so my questions dealt with this aspect."

The priest shook his head.

"I understand that. The parish priest of Santa Maria, Don Antonio Mansi—I know him. We even studied together and were classmates for a while. He was a good student. A good student and . . . quite the diplomat, too. One of those with a gift for getting the professors to like him, if you know what I mean. Then we fell out of touch, but every so often I run into him on the street and we have a chat."

Ricciardi was afraid he'd been indiscreet.

"Padre, the last thing I'd want is to create difficulties for you. Nor is it my intention to speak badly of Don Antonio, whom I met just briefly a couple of times. It's just that his reticence on the subject struck me as odd. He went so far as to ask the curia to intervene to put a halt to my investigation. Doesn't that strike you as absurd?"

Don Pierino made a strange grimace.

"No, it doesn't strike me as absurd. You see, someone looking at us from outside might think that priests are all alike. But that's not the way it is. We're human beings, every one of us with his own shortcomings, a few small vices, some obsession or other. I, for example, am a music lover, as you know: and there are times when this passion of mine leads me to do things I shouldn't, like the time we first met, when I was hiding on the steps of the back utility staircase behind the main stage at the Teatro San Carlo. Do you remember?"

The commissario waited, patiently, for Don Pierino to wrestle with the obligations of his conscience before setting forth his doubts about Don Antonio.

"In some cases, the vices can be quite serious, and our superiors intervene to set things right. There are priests who fall in love with women, others who have crises of faith; those are things that keep you from being a good priest, and it is right that they should be sent away for a while, don't you agree? Then there are priests who have a certain . . . propensity, some talent that might strike some as a defect, but which proves useful to others. That's all."

Ricciardi said: "And in Don Antonio's case, what is the talent, Padre?"

Don Pierino looked pensively at the church's frescoed vault.

"Don Antonio is a first-rate administrator. Very good at accounting, let's just say that. His parish seems to produce very generous donations, and so he's made himself practically financially independent, and the curia is very grateful to him for that, from what I've heard. He's on excellent terms with everyone, wealthy families in his parish and his superiors at the archiepiscopal see. He's universally respected and esteemed. He has lots of friends, in other words."

"Well? Why would you consider this to be a defect? And I'm pretty sure you do consider it a defect, if I know you at all."

Don Pierino laughed.

"Yes, you do know me. I think that, these days, if you're working in this city, especially if you're working with children, then the money that comes in ought to go straight back out. That's all."

"And instead, he rakes off a profit."

THE DAY OF THE DEAD · 183

The priest protested forcefully:

"No, no, Commissario, that's not what I said. Don Antonio is an excellent priest, he takes children in off the streets and, in many cases, as you and I both know, that means saving their lives. It's just that, when a family adopts one of these children, or makes a large donation to the church to cleanse their conscience, he donates that money to the Curia instead of improving the lives of the older children, who aren't likely ever to be adopted. That's something that I just personally dislike. Just that, nothing more. But, let me repeat, what he does for the children is important; that's what counts."

Ricciardi nodded.

"Sure. That's what counts. Thank you, Padre. It's always a pleasure to talk with you."

Don Pierino studied Ricciardi's face.

"Same for me, Commissario. Let me ask you one question, though: why all this interest? If this is an accident, plain and simple, why would someone as important as a commissario from police headquarters take the trouble to ask all these questions? I see something in your face: like a sadness, some kind of pain. What's going on?"

Ricciardi fell silent for a moment, then he replied:

"Padre, you know it yourself: going around this city and witnessing the things that happen here, you can't help but be sad. The day it no longer saddens me to see such a small child dead and discarded like an old rag; the day it no longer grieves me to think that seven- and eight-year-old children are starving to death or, as was the case with this child, being reduced to eating poisoned rat bait out of hunger; the day I stop asking why a little boy was wandering the city alone in the rain late at night, barefoot; the day I find it normal to find a corpse sitting on a staircase at dawn, with only a dog to watch over it: that day, I swear to you, Padre, I'll give up this profession and go home to the village where I was born."

Ricciardi had spoken under his breath, whispering in the cold, dank silence of the church of San Ferdinando; but to Don Pierino it had seemed as if he were shouting at the top of his lungs. He couldn't help laying a hand on the arms that Ricciardi had crossed over his chest, as if he were suffering from some stabbing abdominal pain.

"You know, Commissario, you may be the only person I learn something from every time I see you. And even though you say that you're an unbeliever, you're more of a Christian than the many people who fill these pews every Sunday just to show off their new clothing. You're right; and forgive me for not having understood. Just one thing: be careful, very careful; Don Antonio has powerful friends in the Curia, precisely because of the stream of money he brings in. He can make a great deal of trouble for you."

XXX

G ambrinus was crowded that evening. The rain and the cold made it impossible to sit at one of the outdoor tables and people were in the mood for something warm.

Ricciardi, who had arrived ahead of the time agreed upon with Maione, had to wait to be seated at his usual table, which was located off to the side, near the plate glass window overlooking Via Chiaia. He watched a steady stream of people go by, doing their best to stay dry under the rain as they headed home from the shops and offices in the city center.

He saw a woman begging, almost out of his field of view: she was sitting on the pavement, drenched and ill-clad, her open hand extended. Behind her was a little boy, in the shelter of the overhanging cornice, wrapped in a blanket. The mother, if indeed that's what she was, mumbled an appeal to every person who passed by, though Ricciardi couldn't hear what she said; just a couple of people tossed her a coin or two, and they did so without even slowing down.

Some ten feet away, a well-dressed young man in a white suit stood noisily mocking someone as a gash in his elegant waistcoat pumped out a gushing stream of dark blood. He kept saying: *Come on, I'd like to see you. I'd like to see if you have the nerve.* Ricciardi remembered the street fight, two months earlier: the young man in white had been stabbed to death by a friend, his best friend, in fact, who was sick of being derided for his nonconformist style of dress and his alleged cowardice. Just another way of expressing a difference of opinion among *guappos*, foppish young toughs, on the subject of men's fashion.

If there was one thing that tormented Ricciardi when it came to the Deed, it was being forced to recognize the complete pointlessness of certain deaths. Not that there was any such a thing as a useful death, of course; he was perfectly in agreement with Modo on that point. But the sheer futility of certain motivations for a stabbing or a suicide offended him deeply.

As he sat waiting for Maione to arrive so he could order, he mused on the contrast staged before his eyes: the little boy's desperate attachment to life, as he shivered under his blanket at his mother's side while she took advantage of the spectacle of her son's misery to stir pity in the hearts of the passersby, and that raucous laughter that served as the final exclamation mark in the life of the stabbed *guappo*. One life struggled for; another life casually discarded. But a life was a life, one the same as the next. Or was it?

His thoughts were interrupted by the arrival of a wet and circumspect Maione, who warily scanned the room like an adulterer operating in flagrante.

"Commissa', *buona sera*. We're going to have to be really careful here, the atmosphere at police headquarters is becoming more suffocating by the minute. All we needed was that letter from the archbishop's secretary. Garzo and Ponte look exactly like a couple of ballerinas from the Teatro San Carlo: they're constantly leaping around en pointe, the doors of offices fly open and one of them goes in and the other goes out."

Ricciardi shrugged his shoulders.

"I'm glad I'm not there, then. Sit down, I was waiting for you to get here before ordering. What'll you have?"

"Nothing, Commissa', I have to get home for dinner; Lucia and the children are waiting for me. Maybe just three little zeppole, a *sfogliatella* with a cream filling, and a glass of rosé, *grazie*."

"Good, that way you'll have plenty of room for your wife's ragù, eh? I'll just have the usual *sfogliatella* and an espresso, *grazie*."

After placing his order and dismissing the waiter, Ricciardi asked:

"All right then, were you able to find out any of the things I asked you?"

Maione flashed a fleeting smile.

"Are you really asking me that, Commissa'? What, can you think of a single time that I set out to learn something and came back empty-handed? All right: it occurred to me that Patrolman Antonelli has a son, a young man, and I know that the kid spends time in Capodimonte; there's a girl, a *guagliona* that he's sweet on, who lives around there. So I sent for the kid and his *guagliona*, and I asked them a few questions about the parish church and Tettè. Everyone knew the boy, he tugged on people's heartstrings, he always had his dog with him, and they'd see him go up and down the street. At first they thought he was mute because they never heard him say a word, but then they realized that he had such a bad stutter that he could only converse with the dog. And precisely because of his stutter, the *guagliona* told me—she works in a shop right by the church—all the other boys in that house pushed him around and made fun of him and beat him up. That poor child's existence really must have been a living hell."

Ricciardi nodded.

"I suspected that from the moment that the priest told me, before saying anything else, that everyone loved the boy. An unsolicited bit of information. Go on."

"In any case, the boy never fought back. He was starved for affection; the girl remembers how he'd stand there, trying to catch people's eye in hopes of a smile, any gesture of friendship. And when the boys saw that, they just treated him worse. Boys can be cruel, sometimes, as we well know. I even found out who Tettè worked with; and it was a pleasant surprise. He was going around with Cosimo Capone, an old acquaintance of ours. He sells soap in the streets, a wandering junk seller in other words, he makes the rounds with one of those handcarts piled high with all sorts of merchandise, you know what I mean, they call out 'get your rags here, get your soap here,' but he's visited our offices more than once, and I remember him clearly. Silver-tongued devil, smooth as the soap he sells, with a bright smile: a pure unadulterated stinker, a *fetente*. Word on the street is that when he was a youngster he killed a man, he never faced formal charges, but he likes to boast about that piece of lore to throw a scare into people who are dumber than he is. Ah, *grazie*, just put that here."

Once the waiter had left, Maione went on with his story:

"So in other words, Tettè wasn't exactly a full-fledged apprentice. He was just a kid Capone took along with him to soften up the housewives, and to chip higher prices out of them. But when we got to this point in the conversation, young Antonelli's *guagliona* started getting a little evasive, so I took a little walk around to talk to our colleagues who take in criminal complaints in that part of town, between Capodimonte and the Sanità, if you follow me. And I found out that three or four reports of minor thefts committed during the day had come in, and they involved our friend Capone. There's something to it, in other words; it could even be that the kid found that poison when he was 'on the job' with this gentleman, and he accidentally swallowed it."

Ricciardi was listening with intense focus.

"Do you think that he was using the boy to burgle apartments?"

Maione answered with his mouth full, spraying sugar in all directions:

"You know how it is, Commissa', in the *bassi*, our ground-floor apartments in the alleys and *vicoli*: if I've got a talent for making chit chat, then I keep the housewives' attention focused on me, and a small boy capable of moving fast can easily get in and out again without anyone noticing. Quick and painless, as our Dr. Modo likes to say, no? Maybe, and I'm just saying maybe, that's what that bastard Capone was doing. Otherwise, I can't imagine what trade Tettè could have been learning, much less what good he could have been to that man; he couldn't talk because he stuttered, and he couldn't carry anything heavy because he was small and weak. The only thing he was good for was inspiring pity."

The commissario nodded as he looked out the plate glass window at the child wrapped in the tattered, rain-drenched blanket.

"Yes, you're right. Inspiring pity was all he was good for. The next thing is to talk with this Capone; maybe we should throw a scare into him, to see if he had anything to do with the boy's accidental death."

Maione shook his head, swallowed a *zeppola* in a single gulp, and said:

"I don't really think Capone had anything to do with this though, Commissa', to tell you the truth. For two reasons: First off, he's one of those guys who's all talk but would never hurt a fly, because he's too much of a coward. Second, he lives in the Vomero, a long way from where we found Tettè; he comes down into town in the morning to work, if you can call what he does work, and then at night he climbs back up the hill to go home. It's a two-hour walk, and on Sundays he doesn't come down at all. The boy's death, and the doctor was very clear about this, took place late Sunday night. If Capone had been out and about at that time of night and on a day that would be so unusual for him, someone in the quarter would have noticed it, but no one saw him. I checked."

Ricciardi took a sip from his demitasse, thinking. Then he said:

"This Cosimo Capone strikes me as a character we need to keep an eye on. We can't be sure that he had nothing to do with it. What about life at the parish church, anything else about that?"

Maione carefully scooped up the mortal remains of his *sfogliatella* with his fingers, cream filling included.

"Yes, Commissa'. The *guagliona*, Antonelli's son's girl-friend, like I told you, works in a shop whose customers include the parish church. She had quite a lot to say about this priest, Don Antonio, and about what life is like in there generally."

Ricciardi said:

"It's so nice the way nobody minds their own business in this city. One can always rest assured that if there's something to know, in the end, it'll be found out."

Maione agreed, philosophically:

"True enough. In any case, it seems that the priest likes to go over all the accounts personally, checking the weights of the merchandise and so on. He's someone who cares a lot about money, according to what the girl told me. And she also said that he's terribly harsh when it comes to punishments. The boys are terrified of him. It seems that when someone does something they weren't supposed to, he locks them up in a broom closet outside in the courtyard, where it gets suffocatingly hot in the summer, and freezing in the winter, and it's full of rats and bugs. The minute he mentions the broom closet, even just as a threat, everyone falls right into line. I could use a broom closet like that at my house, because when I talk and I talk to my kids, it just goes in one ear and out the other. In other words, that priest is a Fascist, only he uses the broom closet instead of pouring a gallon of cod liver oil down the people's throats."

Ricciardi decided that all these lovely details were really starting to enrich Don Antonio's character for him. He looked out the window and noticed that Tettè's dog was sitting outside, between the beggar woman and the murdered *guappo*, looking at him. He shivered.

"You caught a chill, eh, Commissa'? Of course you did, with all the rain that's falling these days, and you without a hat or an umbrella. The girl told me one important thing right at the end, just as she was leaving: apparently the main reason that the other boys were so hard on Tettè is that he was the favorite of one of the Ladies of Charity, and she used to pick him up and drive him around in her car. She said that this lady—the *guagliona* didn't know her name—gives so much money to the parish that the priest lets her do whatever she wants. And she didn't have children of her own, so Tettè was a sort of son to her."

Ricciardi nodded.

"I know, they more or less told me so, both the priest and the other Lady of Charity, a woman with a winning personality that's just not to be believed. Money to the parish aside, if you want to know the truth."

"Obviously, the other boys were very jealous of him; but more than making fun of him and knocking him around a little every once in a while they didn't do, because the kid shared everything the woman gave him and the priest was determined to keep this idyllic arrangement going, because of the money it brought him. Who knows how he'll manage now to keep his claws in that hen that lays the golden eggs: it seems to me he'll have to get her a new little kid."

"In effect, our tunic-wearing friend struck me as a little worried about that. That lady's another one I wouldn't mind talking to."

"I think you'll have a chance to talk to her pretty soon, Commissa'. Dr. Modo phoned in earlier this evening: he sends his best wishes and says he hopes you enjoy your vacation; he even wanted to recommend a place for you to spend some of your time off, but I think I'd better not tell you where. He says that the boy's funeral is scheduled for tomorrow morning, and it should be quite a deluxe affair, all paid for by a certain rich lady, I think the very same lady we've been talking about. In case you wanted to attend."

Ricciardi sat looking out the window, thinking. The stream of people heading home had started to ebb. The beggar woman grabbed the blanket and the little boy as if they were a bundle of rags and walked off toward the *vicoli*. Left behind to watch over the street were the mocking dead *guappo* and the dog.

"Very well. I'll go attend the last earthly carriage ride of Matteo Diotallevi, known to his friends as Tettè. Except that he didn't have any friends."

Sitting with his back to the window, Maione added, with a sigh:

"Except for the dog."

As if on cue, the dog that had been Tettè's only friend on earth got up and trotted off through the fine cold drizzle.

XXXI

Seven days earlier, Thursday, October 22

T ettè is running.

He's running at breakneck speed, running barefoot and holding his wooden clogs to keep from falling.

He's running and he's risking his life, though he'll lose that anyway, barely dodging car tires and carriage wheels. Horns honk in annoyance.

He's running, dodging the walking sticks of gentlemen who swing their canes to punish him for forcing them to step aside.

He's running, unintentionally splashing water on the nannies pushing tall perambulators, and they curse at him with incomprehensible words, uttered in the accents of unfamiliar dialects.

He's running, and other scugnizzi try to trip him so that they can laugh at his calamitous fall, but he knows what they're thinking and leaps over their outstretched feet, and stays upright.

He's running, and the plate glass windows seem to be running along beside him, with shopgirls dressing mannequins who smile at him.

He's running, and two little boys in smocks carrying bookbags and holding their mother by the hand watch him, envying him his freedom.

He's running through the alley, and the dog is running after him, light, effortlessly, its ears fluttering like handkerchiefs waved from a departing train. It zigs and zags exactly like the boy, *choosing the same trajectories as if it had some kind of advance notice of the route, as if they'd mapped it together.*

They're running, the dog and the boy: the same jutting ribs, the same eyes squinting in concentration, the same mouths half-open from the effort.

They're running, and they hope they'll get there in time.

Cosimo is standing next to his handcart in a little piazzetta where four vicoli run together, in the Spanish Quarter. He always follows the exact same route, so Tettè knows where to meet him at this time of day. One time, when he was being nice to the boy, Cosimo told him that by following the same route, passing through the same places at the same times, the women get to know him and they wait for him, and they set aside the best items for him, and it's good for business.

In fact, there are times when Cosimo is nice to Tettè. At times like that, perhaps when it's getting dark and business has been good that day, he starts telling stories. Tettè listens happily, and thinks to himself that Cosimo could be his papà, and he could be Cosimo's child. One time Cosimo even gave him a coin, all shiny, and Tettè never spent it; he just kept it in the pocket of his britches and, every once in a while, would pull it out and look at it. Then one day Amedeo saw it and took it for himself, but Tettè could still summon it in his memory.

Tettè thinks; he can't really talk, but he thinks. And he remembers, he remembers everything. He remembers good things and bad things, but he doesn't go into the bad things in his head. He holds on to them, because they might turn out to be useful someday, but he doesn't go there. He goes into the good things, and in the good things there's Cosimo telling him a story as night falls.

But this time Cosimo isn't going to be nice to him. He knows it from the look he gives him when he sees Tettè arrive, even though he doesn't look at him again right away, otherwise the women standing around will notice something is wrong.

He knows one of the women and in fact, when she sees him coming, she celebrates his arrival. Here comes Tettè, she says: hello, handsome, why weren't you here this morning? And here's the dog, too, but aren't you ever going to give your little dog a name, Tettè? Don't you know that animals get names, too?

Tettè says nothing, but he smiles. He says nothing because he's worried about the way Cosimo looked at him. And besides, he doesn't want to give the dog a name. He talks to the dog, they spend time together. They're equals. And if they're equals, how can he give the dog a name, Tettè thinks to himself. It has a name, in its dog-language. When the dog is ready, it'll tell him its name.

But the dog can't talk; so what? thinks Tettè. I don't talk, either: just with him. And I told him that my name is Tettè. He already knows.

The fat woman who greeted him when he arrived caresses his head. Cosimo notices, and he starts saying how he loves the boy like a son, and starts telling the story of his friend who died in the war, next to him in the trenches: how with his last dying breath, he had told him to take care of his son.

One time, Tettè got up the nerve to ask him, ask Cosimo, if the story was true: if his father had really died in the war. Cosimo slapped him hard in the back of the head and called him a stupid, ugly fool of a cacaglio, and added, You're an idiot. I never went to war, I have a heart that skips a beat. I just say it so the women will take pity on me and give me more money for the soap. Who knows what kind of good-for-nothing your father must be; your mother is probably a worthless wench. And the slap in the back of the head is for making me waste all this time, standing here waiting for you to squeeze out two words.

Now, to show the women how the boy is like a son to him, Cosimo has put his hand behind Tettè's neck. He pinches him, good and hard. Tettè doesn't cry, because he knows if he cries it'll be worse for him, but his eyes fill with tears. Oh, how sweet he *is, look, says another one of the women, when he hears someone talk about his father, he still feels like crying. He wipes his eyes with his shirtsleeve and pretends not to feel the terrible pain.*

The dog lets out a low snarl and bares its teeth. Only Cosimo notices, and he loosens his grip. After bartering copper saucepans for soap, the women walk away, and Cosimo says lots of bad words to Tettè, because he got there late and Cosimo had to tell the woman, the one they talked about yesterday, that he'd come back later. It's Tettè's fault that he'll have to run another risk. And, he adds, if that bastard dog of yours snarls at me again I'll kill it; I'm capable of snapping a neck with my bare hands, why don't you ask around, Tettè, everyone knows that I killed a man when I was just a boy.

They come to a wooden door with a decorative inlay. They walk through it and into the courtyard, Cosimo calls his wares, a number of women lean out their windows, the concierge comes out of her apartment on the ground floor. They start chatting, Cosimo catches and holds her attention, he starts to show her the goods he has in his handcart, the women laugh, he tells his jokes. He's good at what he does, Cosimo is: he knows what women want to hear. One of them caresses Tettè hastily, another one plays with the dog.

At a certain point Cosimo starts to tell a story he's heard, about a certain lady in Santa Lucia who has a lover, and her husband caught her with him, and so on and so forth. This is the agreed-upon signal: Cosimo always says that women can't resist, when you start to tell them stories about husbands and lovers. Sure enough, the women form a circle around Cosimo, and stand there listening, openmouthed.

Tettè slips carefully into the concierge's apartment. He doesn't have much time and he knows it. The dog sits just outside the door: if anyone came near he'd start barking and Tettè would know. They've done this plenty of times.

It's dark inside, but warm. There's a pot boiling on the fire, and a wonderful scent wafts across the room. Tettè can feel his stomach rumbling. As soon as his eyes get used to the dark, he takes a look around: he sees a drawer and pulls it open. Inside are forks, knives, and spoons that look like they're made of real silver. Tettè grabs three and slips them under his shirt. There are some linens, freshly pressed with a coal-fired iron. He grabs an embroidered handkerchief and puts it in his pocket. The secret, Cosimo tells him, is to take just a few things: the women won't notice right away, it might take them a few days, and by then it won't occur to them that we were here.

Before leaving, on tiptoe in his bare feet so that he makes no sound at all, he sees a piece of pastry that someone dropped on the floor near the table. He takes it and puts it in his pocket, too.

Now Tettè is outside, and the second Cosimo sees him, he concludes his story to the laughter and astonished "ooohs" and "aaahs" of the assembled women. He sells a few items at a good price and sends his customers away happy. They turn and wave as they walk off.

They walk until they're a good long way away, to be safe. Cosimo says nothing, he smiles at the people they encounter, and every once in a while he shouts out his wares. Tettè gives the pastry to the dog, a crumb at a time, and saves the last little bit for himself. It tastes good, even if there are a few ants in it. All you have to do is take them out first. Tettè does this carefully.

They come to a corner by a field, where the streets end and the countryside begins. Here there are no prying eyes. Tettè pulls out the three pieces of silverware and the embroidered handkerchief. Cosimo grunts with satisfaction: the utensils are solid silver. Look at that, he comments: who knows where the concierge stole them from.

Tettè talks to him. The serpent slithers up from his stomach and knots itself around his neck, as always; but this time Tettè has something important to say. He tells Cosimo that the reason he was late was that he had to serve Mass that morning. Cosimo is in a good mood, he says that it worked out fine all the same, everything is all right. But Tettè has something else that he needs to tell him. He does his best to breathe; when he breathes properly, the serpent hangs back and lets him speak. Sometimes.

He tells him that the priest, Don Antonio, has been talking about people who steal. He said that people who steal go to hell, and they burn for all eternity. One time he burned himself, Tettè says, when he was trying to get warm near a fire in the entrance to an apartment building, and it hurts, it hurts so bad. He shows him the mark on his arm, where the skin was scorched away and never really grew back. Tettè says that he's afraid of burning in the flames of hell, and that he doesn't want Cosimo to burn in them either. And so he begs him, he begs him not to make him steal anymore.

Cosimo seems to be listening with interest. But then he suddenly reaches out and wraps the fingers of one hand around his throat, and then he squeezes and lifts the boy off his feet. Tettè hangs there, his feet dangling in midair, grabbing at Cosimo's hand to keep from choking to death. The dog jumps to its feet and starts snarling and barking. Cosimo glares at the dog and sets the child's feet back on the ground, but he keeps his hand on his throat.

Listen to me carefully, you fool of a cacaglio, he says. Listen good, because I'm only going to tell you once. If you try to tell anyone about what we do, I'll kill you. I'll kill you, capisci? And I'll kill you in a way that no one will ever be able to tell that it was me. I've done it before, I told you, and I never went to jail for it. Do you understand?

First I'll kill your dog, and I'll make you watch it die. In fact, you know what I'll do? I'll light a big fire, since you say you're afraid of fire. And then I'll throw your dog in the fire. That way, you'll get a good idea of what it means to burn in hell. You'll get it into your head once and for all. And then I'll kill you.

He lets go of him, with a hard shove. Tettè falls and vomits water and the little bit of pastry. The dog comes over and licks his face.

XXXII

Anyone who walked into the third-floor office at police headquarters, at the end of the corridor, would have been greeted by the sight of a diligent deputy chief of police at work poring over reports in surroundings gleaming with order and cleanliness. A stirring tribute to the efficiency and dedication to hard work that defined the New Fascist State.

But the reality was somewhat different. His eyes scanned the typewritten lines, but his mind was flying elsewhere, lost in his own grim thoughts.

Garzo shot a fleeting glance at the telephone that enjoyed pride of place on his desk. In his mind he heard the odious nasal voice of the chief of police, alerting him to the impending arrival of an official from an organization not otherwise identified; the man needed certain information from him in view of the Duce's upcoming visit to the city, information having to do with security and, more generally, any investigations currently under way at police headquarters. The matters in question belonged to the domain of common criminality, since that was the field in which Garzo worked.

He didn't like it, not even a little. And for a variety of reasons. First: What was this organization? Did it not have a name? Was it an agency under the Ministry of the Interior? Was it some kind of branch of the army? Second: What was the phrase, "the domain of common criminality," supposed to mean? What other domain and what other kinds of uncommon crimes were being kept under observation that didn't fall under the jurisdiction of police headquarters? Third: Was the security to be discussed in this interview that of the Duce and of his entourage? And who was this official? How would he know him, if he hadn't even been told his name?

The deputy chief of police was one of those people who can't stand unexpected developments: they gave him a sense of chaos, and they got in the way of his planning. He liked to move along the rutted path of procedure, where everything that happened had a precedent one could go back to and an outline that could be followed, right down to the last detail. And this visit, announced and yet unannounced, was completely unprecedented, as far as he could remember.

As he was skimming the report without reading it, he heard a discreet cough to his right. He jerked in his chair in a spectacular fashion: his pen flew out of his hand, leaving a trail of ink in midair, and then a light drizzle of black drops on the desktop; his eyeglasses fell off, luckily without breaking; and he emitted a—quite mortifying—falsetto shriek.

Right in front of him, standing with a coat draped over his arm and a closed umbrella in his hand, was a middle-aged man with thinning salt-and-pepper hair, dressed in a rather nondescript dark suit.

"Who . . . who the devil are you? And what are you doing in my office? How did you get in here? Ponte! Ponte!"

The stranger gave him a half smile.

"Be calm, Dottore. There's no problem. Ponte's not here: he was sent on a break prior to my arrival. An order from you, which you'll be so good as to confirm later. I'm the person you've been expecting. You may call me Falco. I belong to the organization that's making all of the necessary arrangements for the Duce's visit."

Garzo hadn't yet resumed breathing normally, and he sat there staring at the so-called Signor Falco, his eyes bulging.

"But . . . but . . . this is hardly the way! Haven't you ever heard of knocking on the door? I could have had a stroke!"

Falco showed no sign of contrition.

"We can't afford to linger in hallways for extended periods of time, Dottore. This means, in some cases, an act of apparent rudeness. Shall we discuss the matter at hand, now? I imagine that you've been briefed about what we need to know."

After recovering a minimum of self-control, Garzo did his best to think as quickly as he could. This specter who had suddenly appeared before him was certainly with the secret police, the subject of much fevered speculation in every police station in Italy, as well as in those seditious publications printed in secret and tossed into crowds anonymously. This meant that he had to be careful, very careful; he'd heard of people and even entire families vanishing into thin air, leaving not a trace from one day to the next. There was no choice but to comply with their wishes.

He put on an off-kilter smile, placed his glasses back on the bridge of his nose, and said:

"*Prego*, have a seat and tell me what you need to know."

More than three hours later, they'd minutely planned every single second of the Duce's visit, evaluating alternative routes to the ones that would be announced, people to be invited to the meetings, official and private moments. More than once, when Garzo expressed his concerns about the number of men available for a given function, Falco was dismissive, saying:

"That's not going to be a problem. Don't worry about it."

The deputy chief of police realized that there would be a very sizable contingent of armed men serving as a protective cordon, in plain clothes and incognito. This made him uneasy rather than reassuring him; but he realized that it was better to be safe than sorry.

In the end Falco, who hadn't even unbuttoned his waistcoat, asked:

"Now tell me something, Dottore: how many investigations into serious crimes are currently ongoing? Please tell me about each. We like to have the situation entirely under control, as you must surely have gathered by now, and we certainly don't want to have some problem rising to the surface just when the highest-ranking government official after the king as well as all the top officials in the ministry are present, do we?"

Garzo fiercely returned the man's gaze.

"No, certainly not. There haven't been any events recently, heavens be praised, and the investigations now under way have to do with petty crimes, property crimes. This city, my dear man, is running efficiently and in perfect order."

Falco stared him in the face for a long, uncomfortable moment, after which the notorious red patch appeared on Garzo's neck and began spreading in a northerly direction. Finally, Falco nodded and said:

"Very good. In fact, that's what we hear. Your staff is all present, I trust?"

Garzo pulled out the personnel registries and leafed through them in front of his guest.

"We have suspended all regularly scheduled vacation time. The only person absent is Commissario Luigi Alfredo Ricciardi, who requested a few days off but will return to duty the day prior to the Duce's visit. We decided to authorize that vacation because he is seeing . . . that is, he is friends with a person who is close to His Excellency's family, a girlfriend of his daughter, who will be hosting a party which Donna Edda is expected to attend."

Falco assumed a thoughtful expression.

"Ah, Signora Ciano. That's another problem, though it doesn't concern you directly. The daughter is far less easily controlled than His Excellency, unfortunately. She resists all attempts to rein her in, and she's very dynamic and strong-willed. She needs to be protected without being made aware of it."

Garzo immediately decided that anything he said was likely to be used against him and kept his mouth shut. Falco went on.

"Of course, we know about this reception. And we also know about this Ricciardi, and his friendship with Signora . . . Vezzi, no? The widow of Arnaldo Vezzi, just recently arrived in the city. A beautiful woman, held in very high regard in Rome. Your Ricciardi is a lucky man."

Garzo thought he'd sensed which way the wind was blowing, and jumped in enthusiastically.

"One of our finest men, no doubt about it. Capable and trusted, and an indispensable support to me. I don't know how many times he's successfully concluded exceedingly complex investigations, with my guidance, of course."

Falco nodded.

"Certainly, certainly. I've heard this as well. But not all his acquaintances are so eminently praiseworthy; certain individuals he is close with are causing us some concern, to be perfectly frank. For one, the medical examiner, Modo. A man who never misses an opportunity to shout to the four winds bitter criticism of the regime. Which, as you can imagine, we are none too happy about."

Garzo gasped like a dying trout and performed an impressive 180-degree turn.

"Ah, but of course I have no relationship of any kind with Ricciardi outside of work! Indeed, let me tell you, Your Excellency, there is a dark side to that man's personality that I don't like one bit. I intend to keep him on a tighter leash in the future, you can rest assured."

Falco stood up with a faint smile.

"Let's not go overboard, Garzo. And don't call me Excellency. In fact, you will be so good as to forget that this conversation ever took place, and pretend you don't know if we were ever to cross paths in the street, though that's highly unlikely to happen. *Buona sera*, and enjoy yourself with your wife at the widow Vezzi's reception. Don't worry: it will be a delightful and carefree evening, without unexpected developments of any kind."

With that he left, as silently as he had come.

When he was alone, Garzo started trembling; he couldn't even manage to light a cigarette. He felt like a man who'd just narrowly escaped death and was only realizing it now, after an improper delay. He pulled open the drawer and looked at the envelope from the Curia, with its request for clarification regarding the alleged investigation into the boy's death. He ran his hand through his hair and unbuttoned his shirt collar, letting out a long sigh. It was necessary, absolutely indispensable, to make sure no one even thought of bothering the parish priest of Santa Maria del Soccorso again. He'd see to it personally, if necessary.

He thanked the Lord above that Falco's organization knew nothing about that letter.

XXXIII

Friday, October 30

Ricciardi arrived at the hospital quite early. He wanted a chance to talk to the doctor alone, to have a calm, leisurely conversation before Tettè's funeral began.

It was raining, for a change; but that morning the rain was mostly atmospheric, a light, constant drizzle that colored the air gray, as it did people's souls. The perfect color, thought the commissario. He hadn't seen the dog along the road, and he wasn't surprised; he found it exactly where he'd expected to find it, in the courtyard outside the hospital morgue, off to one side, sitting in a nook in the outside wall. Smoking a cigarette under the overhang stood Modo, looking at the dog.

"I find that dog unsettling. I see it all the time now, ever since the kid was brought here. Every once in a while it leaves, as if it had been summoned; but then it comes back. The other night I was working the night shift and it never moved the whole time I was here. I offered it something to eat, but it wouldn't come near me. It waited for me to walk away, and then it gobbled down every last speck in a minute."

Ricciardi nodded.

"Yes, I've noticed. I've come across that dog several times in the past few days. It goes the same places it went with Tettè."

Modo gave him an ironic look.

"Tettè, eh? So you've become fond of the boy, now that he's

dead, with all the digging you've been doing. Come to think of it, it suits you: the macabre Ricciardi who gets along with the dead better than with the living. You know, you may have picked the wrong profession; you should be in my line of work. Or maybe you should do what those gentlemen do."

He nodded toward the white hearse drawn by a pair of horses, next to which a couple of men were smoking and stamping their feet to keep warm.

"It seems money was no object. Would you look at that? Whoever paid for the funeral wanted only the very best. Nothing overstated, nothing pompous, but high quality all the way. The last trip he takes will be in a horse-drawn carriage, your—what did you call him? Tettè. Just a kid, but truly a noteworthy exit from the stage."

"By the way, Bruno, do you happen to know who's paying for the funeral? The priest didn't strike me as one inclined to make much of an outlay for pomp and circumstance."

Modo snickered.

"And right you are. These priests even take money for proffering the illusion of Paradise; the last thing they'd do is pay a red penny to bury a little orphan boy. No, certainly not the priest. I asked the undertakers: the funeral arrangements were made and paid for by a certain Signora Fago di San Marcello, who it seems is also a Lady of Charity at the parish church of Santa Maria del Soccorso. Evidently she has money to burn. She could have spent that money better by feeding the child when he was alive; then he wouldn't have been driven to swallow morsels of poisoned bait, and he'd still be alive now, playing with his dog."

Ricciardi shook his head.

"Always a cynic and a materialist. I find it comforting that, at least now that he's dead, there's someone who weeps for him. You know, asking around a bit, all I could find out was that no one gave a damn about the poor child."

"A phantom, in other words. Just one of the thousands, perhaps hundreds of thousands of phantoms in this city. The ones no one sees."

That's what you think, thought Ricciardi. There *is* someone who can see them, the phantoms. Unfortunately.

"That's right, Bruno. But they have a right to a few answers, at least once they're dead."

Modo took a drag on his cigarette.

"And so Commissario Ricciardi, knight errant and defender of lost souls, begins to dig. Be careful, though: don't forget that your commander in chief, jackboots, Fascist regalia, and all, will be here soon, and he'll want to find everything in tip-top order. He'll end up grabbing you by the ear and explaining, with a round of sharp kicks and a few bottles of cod liver oil, that actually everything is just fine, that the city is marvelous and neat as a pin, and that the steaming mess being served is first-rate and plentiful."

Ricciardi shook his head.

"You're getting old, Bruno. And in your old age, you've become fixated on some unpleasant things. These days, whatever I talk about with you, you turn the conversation to politics. You realize that this makes you not so different from those you hate? They also talk always and exclusively about politics. I'm not interested in politics in the slightest. I'm interested in doing what I can. If everyone did that, perhaps all this talk of the chief world systems would become obsolete. At last."

Modo laughed.

"Luigi Alfredo Ricciardi, alias Saint Francis of Assisi. *Bravo!* You, too, can shrug in indifference; we can just leave it to them to take care of everything. Not that that's not what they're already doing."

Ricciardi shrugged:

"Enough, enough, please. I've learned my lesson: always

agree with you right away; that way I can change the subject. Speaking of changing the subject: beyond the manner of death, the other day you mentioned that the child was in very poor shape. Would you mind telling me a little more about that?"

Modo crushed his cigarette butt underfoot, exhaling a last puff of smoke.

"All right, let me remember: he was skinny, terribly skinny, but you could see that for yourself. The subcutaneous adipose layer was just the thinnest possible film, like cellophane. Abrasions on the knees, bruises on the legs, but all things from days or weeks before, nothing that could be dated to the time of death. A burn on one arm, fairly serious but old, dating back one or two years. Deep, though. A nasty mark. One strange thing: a few bruises on the neck, from three or four days prior to death, because the marks were bluish, not red: someone had grabbed him by the throat. These boys engage in terrible fights to survive, often among themselves. But he wasn't returning the favor: his hands were in good shape, his nails weren't broken, no bruises on his knuckles. He was taking it, and that was it. The skin on the soles of his feet, on the other hand, was thick as the sole of a shoe from habitually walking around barefoot."

Ricciardi listened with his usual attention.

"So nothing very recent. Nothing that would suggest a struggle prior to death."

"No, I told you. The ingestion of the bait was voluntary, not forced. The oral cavity, the esophagus, the interior of the cheeks: all intact. The injuries I listed for you were war injuries: the war that a child like that one fights every day to survive, in this lovely Fascist city of yours."

"It's your city, too, though. At least until the day a couple of men dressed in black show up to take you away, after which no one will ever hear of you again."

Modo rubbed his hands together to warm them up.

"I'm told that internal exile is usually to hot, seaside places as often as not. But the best thing of all would be never having to look at your ugly face ever again."

They stopped talking as the small cortege from the parish of Santa Maria del Soccorso arrived. Leading the procession was a somber Don Antonio, complete with vestments and round ecclesiastical hat; following him were the five boys, wearing their Sunday best but still quite down-at-the-heels, their shaven heads glistening with rain; and bringing up the rear was the sexton, with a flat cap tugged down over his ears and his hands in his pockets. The parish priest locked eyes with Ricciardi and Modo and coldly nodded in their direction before entering the hospital chapel.

A few moments later a cream-colored torpedo-body limousine pulled into the courtyard, driven by a uniformed chauffeur. The man got out and, doing his best not to get mud on his uniform or shoes, he opened the rear door. Out stepped Signora De Nicola Bassi, as majestic as the conveyance in which she'd arrived, but dressed in a dark-brown overcoat; behind her was another woman, younger, dressed entirely in black. Ricciardi looked at this second woman curiously. She was slender, very elegant, and he could tell that she was fair-skinned behind the black veil draped over her hat. Her shoulders were bowed and she held a handkerchief clutched to her mouth: she was the very picture of grief and suffering.

The two women entered the church. Modo and Ricciardi followed them in, but remained standing at the far end of the little nave. In the center, on a raised bier at the end of the aisle, stood a tiny white casket. Dead and in his coffin, Tettè seemed smaller still.

The boys were all crowded into the same pew; they did their best to stay as far from the casket as possible, as if death were contagious. Passing by it on her way to the front pew,

210 · MAURIZIO DE GIOVANNI

supported by Signora De Nicola, the other woman burst into heartfelt, choking sobs. Don Antonio approached her, supporting her by the arm and helping her to her seat.

The funeral service was short and solemn. It didn't seem to Ricciardi that Don Antonio showed any real feeling, even though he spoke beautifully; but he attributed the impression to his prejudice against him. Throughout the service Carmen Fago di San Marcello—that was the full name of the other Lady of Charity—never stopped sobbing and coughing. That kind of grief couldn't be feigned; the commissario immediately felt deep empathy for such profound suffering.

When it was over, the undertakers came in, carried the coffin out, and placed it in the hearse. In the meantime, several floral wreaths arrived, with ribbons identifying them as having been sent by Signora De Nicola and the Ladies of Charity. On one wreath, the finest one, only these words appeared: *to Tettè, with all my love*. Signora Fago came over, pulled out a white rose and kissed it, then laid it gently on the small casket, shining wet with rain. Ricciardi approached her, bowing his head slightly in her direction.

"Signora, my name is Ricciardi. Believe me, you have my sincerest condolences for your loss. I never knew the boy, but you have my sympathies nonetheless."

The woman lifted her veil, uncovering a pair of swollen eyes, red with crying, and a pretty face that was, however, creased and worn with grief.

"The commissario; yes, of course, they told me about you. I'm Carmen Fago. Thank you. It's everyone's loss really. There's no one who didn't love Tettè. It would have been impossible."

"I'm certain of that. I apologize for having to ask you this now, but it would be very useful to me if I could speak with you, after . . . when the ceremony is over."

Signora De Nicola, who had come over to tell Carmen that

the funeral procession was about to depart, shot Ricciardi a scorching glare.

"Does this strike you as an appropriate time for this? You certainly are insensitive—heartless, I'd say. Can't you see that my friend is distraught?"

Carmen Fago laid a gloved hand on her friend's arm.

"No, Eleonora: please, I *do* want to talk to the commissario. He wants to understand, and so do I."

The older woman did her best to object.

"Carmen, I've already told you, there's nothing to understand. It was an accident, a terrible accident. Why do you insist on tormenting yourself?"

The younger woman shook her head, with determination.

"I saw him, just two days before it happened. I saw him and he was fine, you understand? He was fine. He was my little boy, the one who gave me a feeling of tenderness that nature has denied me. I can't and I won't just put him in the ground without knowing."

She turned once again to Ricciardi.

"Commissario, I'll be with you right afterward, once Tettè . . . once we've said good-bye to him. Please, wait for me."

XXXIV

The hearse rumbled off, emerging from the hospital courtyard into the crowded quarter of Pignasecca, with its mix of working-class and poor inhabitants.

Despite the fine drizzle, the market was teeming with people, accompanied by a relentless wave of noise: vendors' cries, quarrels, loud haggling; but when the white hearse emerged a spectral silence fell and the crowd opened, forming two walls of humanity. The horses knew their job, and even though their cargo was light, they proceeded at a proud and cadenced pace.

Don Antonio led the cortege, aspergillum in hand. After him came the twins, in their altar boy vestments. Their bearing and appearance—identical to the last detail as long as the one missing his front teeth kept his mouth closed—was quite choreographic.

Next in the procession was Carmen, who couldn't stop weeping, held up by a serious, stately Eleonora.

The three other boys walked with their heads bowed. Cristiano shot a furtive glance at Ricciardi, then fixed his eyes on the pavement and kept them there. A step behind them was the sexton, following their every move like a prison turnkey.

Ricciardi and Modo, one bareheaded, the other with his hat tugged firmly down around his ears, brought up the rear. Behind them, roaring like a panther about to lunge, was the torpedo-body limousine in which the two women had arrived at the church.

The men lining the procession's path either doffed their

hats or saluted smartly, fingers to the hat brim; the women made the sign of the cross, and a few even pulled out their rosary beads and began to pray in silence. Many people curiously inquired of their neighbors whose funeral this might be; the poor exited this world with much less grandeur, certainly without carriages and flowers, and when the child of a wealthy family died word spread quickly, as a rule.

When they reached the corner of Spirito Santo, where the street ran into the larger Via Toledo, Carmen opened her black purse and pulled out a handful of white Jordan almonds, flinging them to either side as if she were sowing wheat. Instantly, a horde of ragged, barefoot children silently lunged to collect the sweets, with little squabbles breaking out among them.

Ricciardi was familiar with the custom, and exchanged a glance of understanding with Modo: the Jordan almonds represented the happy occasions that the dead child would never celebrate: first communion, confirmation, and wedding. The two men observed those children, hungry and festive, following the funeral procession. Death and life, intertwined for all eternity.

Saverio, one of the boys from Santa Maria del Soccorso, followed his instincts and pounced on a handful of almonds, which immediately put him into a noisy clash with a pair of *scugnizzi*, but the sexton quickly grabbed him by the scruff of the neck and shoved him back into line.

The cortege stayed in formation until it reached Piazza Dante, and there it halted and dissolved. One of the undertakers approached Carmen, who pulled an envelope from her purse; the man touched his hat and climbed back into the hearse, which then departed in the direction of Poggioreale cemetery. Ricciardi waited with Modo off to one side, while Don Antonio lingered in ceremonious conversation with the two ladies. The elegance and speed with which the priest concealed in the folds of his tunic a second envelope, which

Carmen had extracted from her purse, did not escape the commissario's eye.

After a few minutes spent exchanging condolences, the priest headed off toward Capodimonte, followed by the boys and the sexton. Before leaving, he turned to look at Ricciardi, briefly looking him in the eye. The commissario returned the stare, until the priest dropped his gaze.

Modo squeezed Ricciardi's arm.

"This is where I bid you farewell, my friend: after having accompanied a dead boy, I'm off to see if I can be of any assistance to a few of the living, who may not stay that way for long. Take my advice: be careful. I worry about you, even though I have to say that this new Ricciardi who does his own investigating is a refreshing development."

Ricciardi shot him the grimace that he often wore in place of a smile.

"We always end up urging each other to be careful when we say good-bye. We both must be doing something wrong."

He approached the two women. Eleonora glanced briefly at him with a look of hostility and spoke to Carmen.

"If you like, I'll wait for you in my car. When you're done, I can take you back home."

The younger woman shook her head.

"No, don't worry about it: you go ahead. I'll ask the commissario to see me home. I live nearby; it can't be more than a ten-minute walk, and it's hardly raining at all. Besides, I'd like to get a little fresh air. *Grazie*, Eleonora. Perhaps I'll give you a call on the phone later."

Continuing to glare severely at the impassive Ricciardi, Eleonora nodded.

"All right, if that's what you prefer. Give my best to your husband. I'll talk to you later."

She turned and left, without a word of farewell. Ricciardi said:

"I'm afraid your friend doesn't really like me. She interprets my questions about Matteo's life as casting a shadow on the way Don Antonio looks after his boys, and he seems to share her feelings."

Carmen replied in a voice still hoarse from weeping:

"Well, isn't that the case, Commissario? Just what is the motive behind your questions, if not that?"

The two of them headed off, walking up Via Toledo, retracing the route of the funeral procession in reverse. Carmen had opened a charming little umbrella to ward off the fine drizzle. Ricciardi realized that she was young, probably no older than thirty, but there was a look of unbearable grief in her eyes.

"No, Signora," he replied, "I have no suspicions about Don Antonio. I think that he could do better, that's true; still, he does a great deal. Nor do I doubt that Tettè's death was the result of a tragic accident, as far as that question is concerned. What I want to understand is if and how I can prevent such an accident from happening to another one of the boys. And in order to find that out, I have to know more about the child's life, that's all."

Carmen blew her nose into the handkerchief she kept tucked into her glove.

"I see. You should know, Commissario, that I'm infertile. Ever since I was a little girl, I've only had one dream: to have a child of my own. I come from a humble family. My father was a schoolteacher, my mother kept house. I watched her and dreamed of being the way she was with my little brother: a mother, nothing but a mother. Then I met my husband; I would have liked to have ten, twelve children with him. One of those big, happy, healthy families. But that's not what happened. No children came."

Ricciardi could hear the incessant surge of sadness in the woman's voice: a flow that reminded him of the sea's undertow, calm yet somehow terrible.

"I couldn't tell you how many physicians we went to see, how many sanctuaries we visited. My husband is rich, you know: very rich. He could have afforded to adopt hundreds of children, but I never wanted to. I wanted flesh of my flesh to hold in my arms, the fruit of *my* love, not other people's. After ten years, I finally resigned myself; we both did. We'd grow old together, and we'd be the last ones to bear my husband's family name. I turned to charity. This city needs it, and desperately, as I'm sure you know, Commissario."

Ricciardi nodded. He was perfectly aware.

"Then, after about a year, I met Tettè. He was the smallest one there, and with his stutter he couldn't even speak. But he had a smile, Commissario, a smile that loosened a knot in my chest that I didn't even know was there. I remember it . . . forgive me . . . "

Carmen stopped talking and burst into tears. Ricciardi waited for her sobbing to subside.

"We understood each other instantly, all it took was a glance. He never spoke to anyone; his difficulty with speech made most adults lose their patience, even Eleonora, and the other boys just made fun of him. I'm not a particularly patient person, and I never have been; but I was patient with him. We'd sit together for hours, he'd draw and I'd speak sweetly to him, and toward the end he almost never stuttered with me anymore. He was able to talk to me about his world, his life. We'd tell each other stories. It was as if our two lonelinesses had finally met, after waiting for each other for all those years."

Ricciardi listened in silence. Then he said:

"Did you see him often, Signora? I mean to say, aside from the lessons you gave him twice a week."

Carmen sighed. She smiled through hers tears as she spoke.

"I used to go pick him up at least once a week; he loved my car, he was so excited whenever he got a chance to ride in it. I'd bought him a suit of clothes that they kept for him at the parish, and they'd have him wear them whenever he came out alone with me. I'd take him out to eat, but he'd get full right away, because his stomach was so small. I'd drive him around, without my chauffeur. He loved the way the wind would come in through the window and toss his hair, and in the summer we'd put the roof down and laugh, oh how we laughed. Those were the happiest moments, for him and me. He was the son I'd never had, Commissario. God had given him to me, after all."

XXXV

Seven days earlier, Friday, October 23

I t's cold in the big room, freezing cold. It's still early, but Tettè has been awake for a while now, curled up under the burlap sacks that he has for covers.

The rain patters against the shutters, still closed, and the dampness in the air ought to depress him; instead Tettè smiles happily. It's the most wonderful day of the week. The day his angel comes.

Tettè daydreams and waits. When Nanni opens the door and yells out the morning wake-up call, he leaps out of bed and starts folding his makeshift covers, pulling his shirt and britches from under the pallet. He shivers as he puts them on. They're icy cold against his bare skin.

After the sexton has made sure that even the most stubborn ones are out from under the covers, he approaches Tettè and gestures for him to come with him into the other room. Tettè follows him, joyfully. The other boys watch them go, and the twins exchange a knowing glance.

In the other room, it's even colder, because no one sleeps in here; it's a little room that the sexton always keeps locked. There's a table with two chairs and a small, rusty metal cabinet, also locked. The sexton pulls the key out of his pocket and opens it. Tettè can't wipe the smile off his face, and Nanni shoots him an ugly look.

The man pulls a pair of short pants and a little sailor's blouse *out of the wardrobe, a cap and a pair of black leather shoes. The clothes are spotless and neatly ironed. Nanni sets them down on a table like a series of relics and then sits down to watch Tettè change.*

Tettè doesn't like the way the sexton looks at him; he has one of those gazes in which you can't read a thing. His eyes are always red; Tettè knows, as do all the other boys, that the man gets drunk every night in a tavern down by the harbor. They've seen him snoring openmouthed in the gutter on summer nights many times.

You're getting to be a big boy, says Nanni as he watches him. Such a big boy. Tettè gets dressed as quick as he can, putting the clean clothing on hastily, and in his haste he loses his balance and almost rips the short pants. The man lunges forward and slaps him hard.

Stupid cacaglio, *he says to him: those pants are worth a lot more than you are. You have no idea what Don Antonio would do to you if you tore them. Tettè's ear is ringing from the slap the man gave him, but he chokes back his tears. All he wants to do is get dressed and leave the room.*

Nanni goes on talking: remember that I know your secret, cacaglio. *The secret that only you and I know. Just remember that I can always tell that secret, and if I do you'll lose everything, you fool of a* cacaglio. *Which means you also won't get to wear your new clothes and drive in the car with the signora anymore.*

Tettè wants to answer him: he longs to say, no, I don't want the secret, you can have it! All I want is to be with my angel, nothing more. Why can't you leave me alone?

That's what he wants to say; but the serpent immediately comes up from his belly and coils around his throat, choking off his breath. And, as always, it keeps him from speaking.

The man laughs, and he opens his mouth wide, showing his rotten teeth. A foul stench of wine wafts over Tettè. Tettè shuts his eyes and thinks: it doesn't matter. In a couple of minutes, I'll be out of this room. In a couple of minutes, I'll be out on the street, holding Don Antonio's hand, in my new clothes, waiting for the car to come and pick me up.

I'll be with my angel.

XXXVI

C armen had stopped near a doorway, the entrance to one of the most opulent apartment buildings on Via Toledo, just before the Largo della Carità.

"The son I never had. I don't know why I formed such a strong bond with the boy. I could have picked a younger child, a . . . healthier child, a child without defects. I could have picked a little girl, one I could teach good manners to and dress up like a doll. Lots of women do it, you know, Commissario. I have plenty of girlfriends who have a favorite, a child on whom they lavish their maternal instincts, as a kind of release. But I wasn't looking for a toy, and in fact, Tettè wasn't one."

Ricciardi remembered the exchange of white envelopes and asked:

"I noticed that Don Antonio approached you, at the hospital and also at the end of the funeral service. He told me that he was worried you might stop coming to see the other boys, now that Tettè is dead. Is that true?"

Carmen smiled bitterly. Her blind grief was slowly giving way to dull melancholy, a process with which Ricciardi was all too familiar. The melancholy would take a long, long time to ebb away; and it might never go away entirely.

"Money. All Don Antonio cares about is money, do you think I don't know that? I know it very well; but I don't care. I have much more money than I need. And as you said yourself, at least he's doing something for these children. I don't know if I'll ever be able to go back to the parish. I'm not sure I could stand to see that place at the desk without . . . "

She burst into tears again. A few passersby turned to stare: her black dress was indicative of a recent loss, and so people exchanged looks of commiseration. Carmen recovered and went on.

"I'll never love a child again, Commissario. I know it. I would caress his head, and he'd press it against my hand, so that he wouldn't miss a second of it. I'll never be able to caress another child as long as I live."

Ricciardi felt a great surge of pity for the woman, deprived first by nature and later by cruel fate of the one feeling she dreamed of experiencing.

"Signora, you shouldn't talk about it now, with this loss so fresh in your mind. You should wait; on this point I have to agree with Don Antonio. There are so few people who do anything for these lost children. You can't give it up."

Carmen wasn't listening. She was reliving her memories.

"I had bought him a sailor's suit. When I went to get him for our outings I asked Don Antonio to dress him in it. He was a sight to behold, and so happy. I understood from the fact that the clothes never showed any signs of wear that they only let him wear them to go out with me. How can it have happened, Commissario? Could he really have been so hungry that he ate rat bait? Wouldn't he have said something to me? I'd have given him anything he wanted."

Ricciardi shook his head.

"I don't know, Signora. I'm trying to figure it out myself. Earlier, I was talking with Dr. Modo who performed the . . . the necessary examinations of the child's corpse. He found many marks, bruises, and contusions. Nothing dating to the time of death, though, or immediately before it."

Carmen opened her eyes wide.

"I didn't have the courage to see him dead, Commissario.

Eleonora told me . . . she was scandalized. She said that it was horrible, to torment the poor body of a dead child like that. I . . . I don't know what to say about it, to tell the truth. I can't even believe that I'll never see him again. But tell me, what kind of marks? What were they, these injuries that he had?"

"No, Signora, not full-fledged injuries. Let's just say, marks of abuse. For instance, someone had taken him by the throat and choked him, a couple of days before his death."

The woman raised her gloved hand to her mouth, as if to stifle a scream.

"Really? By the neck . . . then someone wanted to kill him? That means his death could have been . . . oh my God!"

Ricciardi held up a hand, as if to put a halt to that chain of thought.

"No, no, Signora. That's not how it is. I repeat, his death was absolutely accidental. There are no signs of involuntary ingestion. Tettè meant to eat them; he just didn't know they were poisoned rat bait. But what I'd like to know from you is whether he told you about any kind of mistreatment recently. Any fights, or violent quarrels. In other words, if there could have been someone who had it in for him."

Carmen tried to remember.

"I know that life at the parish wasn't easy, certainly. He didn't like to talk about it; perhaps he was afraid that I'd lodge some complaint with Don Antonio and that there would be retaliations against him. The other boys made fun of his stammer, they took it out on him because he was the smallest, the most defenseless. One time there was a bruise on his face, but he refused to tell me what had happened; he said he tripped and fell but I didn't believe him. So I told the parish priest and he promised to look into it, but I never heard back from him."

Ricciardi took advantage of the opportunity:

"Did he ever tell you about the other people in his life and the things he did? For example, about his apprenticeship;

about the sexton, about Don Antonio himself; whether he ever went anywhere in particular, or frequented some establishment or other, I don't know, with that junk seller, Cosimo Capone, or anyone else?"

Carmen ran a trembling hand over her eyes and tried to remember.

"I don't know, really. Right now, I'd say no . . . It hurt me to think of him left to his own devices, and he knew that, so after a while he stopped telling me things. That man, the junk seller to whom he was apprenticed, for example: one day I happened to see them out together. I saw Tettè first; I felt so sorry for him, he was so tattered, with that little dog of his. But he was smiling; he didn't strike me as unhappy. The man was odd, dressed in a ragged old tailcoat and a dented hat. I think he was reciting a poem, and the people around him were laughing. Well, I left to keep Tettè from seeing me. I knew how much he cared about being clean and nicely dressed when we saw each other. Still, he didn't strike me as a bad man, and again, Tettè was smiling."

Ricciardi insisted on the point:

"And aside from his rounds with the junk seller, did he go anywhere else? For instance, do you know if he went anywhere at night?"

Carmen furrowed her brow and tried to remember.

"No, Commissario. That's the oddest thing of all: the thought of Tettè going out at night strikes me as absurd. He didn't like the dark; he was afraid of it. I can't imagine him out on the streets on one of these rainy nights, with thunder and lightning. And in any case, not anywhere strange, places he didn't usually go. My God, Commissario, I can't stand to think about it: that he's dead, and that perhaps his death could have been prevented."

Ricciardi decided that it was time to put an end to that conversation. The woman seemed to be on the brink of a nervous breakdown.

"Signora, let's stop talking about it, for now. You're exhausted, you need to get some rest. If anything should occur to you, you'll find Brigadier Maione at police headquarters. I'm going to be out for a few days, but he'll know how to get hold of me."

Carmen nodded, still pensive, and walked toward the entrance of the building. Then she turned around and came back.

"There is one thing I want to tell you, Commissario. Perhaps you're thinking that if I loved him as much as I say I did, I should have adopted Tettè and brought him to live with me."

"Signora, I . . . "

The woman interrupted him, raising her gloved hand.

"I know that you have to be thinking it. I think it myself. And I meant to do it, as God is my witness. But you should know that my husband is ill, very ill. His sickness has rendered him a complete invalid, and to bring a child home, in these conditions, would have meant doing him harm."

Ricciardi became uncomfortable as she confided these details.

"Signora, I beg of you: I have no right to have an opinion, or to judge. I only want to understand whether there is anything, in the deplorable death of this child, that can possibly explain it. And that's all."

Carmen nodded.

"But I'll be damned for all time, Commissario. I'll be damned by the thought that if he'd been with me, that night, and not abandoned to his fate, right now Tettè would probably be alive. And I'd still have had a chance at happiness."

She turned and walked away, carrying with her an immense burden of grief. Ricciardi felt pity for her, because he knew that what she'd said was true.

XXXVII

Seven days earlier, Friday, October 23

Tettè lets go of Don Antonio's hand and climbs into the car. He closes his eyes halfway: the smell of the leather upholstery, the hot motor oil, the gasoline. The roar of the speeding car, the light breeze from the window.

Ciao, amore mio, *says his angel. He smiles at her, head over heels in love. He adores every instant that he spends with her, wherever they are, wherever they go. He feels a pang of regret for having left the dog behind, but he knows he understands because he explained it to him: it's just a matter of minutes, he whispered into the dog's ear as he petted him, an hour or two at most.*

She strokes his hair, he holds the cap in his hand. Where do you want to go? she asks him. Would you like a yummy pastry? Yes, he replies. Yes, of course.

He thinks to himself that the other boys never have moments like this one. They dream of moments like this one. One of the first times he went out, they asked him to tell them about it: come on, you fool of a cacaglio, *tell us where you went with Signora Carmen. And he wished he could have told them, but the serpent rose up out of his stomach and he just couldn't do it; so they beat him up, the twins holding him down and Saverio kicking him in the belly, Amedeo laughing. But Cristiano left the room, so he didn't have to watch.*

Tettè likes Cristiano. He thinks that they could even be

friends, if only Tettè were able to talk. Cristiano's the only one who protects Tettè sometimes, the only one who intervenes.

Ever since that time, whenever they go out together, he asks the angel to let him take something back with him, a pastry, some cookies, a piece of candy. That way he can give it to them, they'll eat it, and no one will hit him.

All of them seem to hate him, because his angel loves him. But since each of them gets something in return, they seem to leave him be, let him have this thing, and they don't beat him to a pulp or say something false, something bad to her.

As the car pulls up in front of the pastry shop and comes to a stop, Tettè thinks back to what Nanni, the sexton, said to him. He thinks about this bad thing that's happening, this secret that he never wanted, and the fact that if his angel ever found out, according to what Nanni told him, she'd never want to see him again.

Tettè could lose everything. He'd even lose the dog, and he's crazy about that dog, the dog is the only friend he has. But he'd never give up the time he spends with his angel. Never.

Now they're in the pastry shop, the proprietor bows to them, he entrusts them to the care of a waiter who leads them to a nice little table. The angel asks hims what he wants, and he points to a cream-filled pastry.

He eats, but he doesn't finish because he can't eat it all. His angel laughs, she says but how can it be that you're so hungry, you're so skinny, and yet you eat like a baby bird. He laughs: like a baby bird! He begs his angel to have them wrap up the half pastry that's left over so he can take it back to the other boys. She is moved, and full of tenderness she says you're so good to think of other children less fortunate than you. Tettè thinks: that's right, and plus that way no one will beat me like a drum at the Festival of Piedigrotta.

He thinks that maybe he can even save a little piece for the dog, but he'll have to find a new place to hide it, now that they know about the loose brick in the wall.

228 · MAURIZIO DE GIOVANNI

His angel asks him all the usual questions. How are you? How are they treating you at the parish? Is anyone hurting you? What about the junk seller?

What can Tettè say? Should he risk ruining these moments, so longed for, so dreamt of? Should he speak of the hatred, the mockery, the pranks? Isn't it better, Tettè thinks, to keep the two lives separate, to enjoy these moments of pure heaven?

No. He shakes his head and smiles. Everything's all right, my angel.

Everything's all right, as long as you're with me.

XXXVIII

Livia decided to make a visit to police headquarters to find out where Ricciardi was and what he was doing. She had played a crucial role in helping him to get that time off, but in the days that followed he hadn't even bothered to give her any sign that he was still alive.

The information she'd learned through Falco's organization, from the report that she'd read, had given her plenty of food for thought, and the allure that the commissario exerted over her had only increased as a result.

So, the man was a wealthy aristocrat; with a standing that would easily have allowed him to play a prominent role in high society. He wasn't a homosexual, which confirmed what her instincts had told her. There was no woman in his life. He'd chosen to live modestly, with his old *tata*, and in a part of town that was hardly chic, far from the center. Even his friendship with Modo, dangerous though it might be, showed that Ricciardi had values above and beyond those of self-interest.

That man was a living mystery. Fascinating, thought Livia as she stepped out of the car door held open by her chauffeur. Absolutely fascinating.

Ponte, Garzo's oily assistant, materialized in the lobby, evidently standing watch for any new developments.

"Signora, welcome. Dottore Garzo will be delighted to see you. *Prego, prego*, come right this way and I'll show you to his office."

Livia certainly hadn't come to see Garzo.

230 · MAURIZIO DE GIOVANNI

"No, *grazie*. I'm actually here to see Commissario Ricciardi."

But Ponte had seized her by the elbow and wasn't about to let go.

"But the Commissario isn't here, Signo'. He's on vacation, don't you remember? If anything, I would think you've seen more of him in the past few days than we have, no? Come along, come along. Just for a moment, the dottore will say a quick hello and then you can be on your way. If he finds out that you were here and I let you get away without stopping by his office, you can imagine the temper he'll be in!"

He continued to chatter away as he led her up the stairs and then down the hall to Garzo's office. The deputy chief of police saw her coming through the half-open door.

"*Mia cara signora*! At last, a ray of sunshine, on this dark, damp day! Come in, come in, *prego*, please have a seat!"

Now Livia was bitterly sorry she'd had the idea to visit police headquarters.

"No, Dottore, I really don't want to take up your valuable time, with all the things that you must have to get done. I just dropped by to . . . I just had something I wanted to tell Ricciardi, but your assistant tells me that he's not here, so . . . "

Garzo had practically forced her down into the chair, and then he'd closed the door behind her.

"But, just five minutes, it's never a waste of my time to speak with you, and especially not to see you in person. How are you? How is everything going?"

"Fine, just fine, *grazie*. I've almost finished furnishing my new home."

Garzo was doing his best to seem charming and sophisticated, which made him appear to Livia's eyes even more insipid than usual.

"Ah, speaking of your new home, how are the preparations going for your party? No one in Naples is talking about anything else. I personally refrain from mentioning the fact that you and I have discussed it, and that you were so kind as to express your intention to invite me and my wife, but I listen to everything I hear with great interest."

"Yes, I know that people can even be far too interested in these unimportant little social gatherings. For me, it's nothing more than an opportunity to see an old girlfriend and to introduce her to my new acquaintances, that's all."

The deputy chief of police put on a conspiratorial air.

"Let's put our cards on the table, Signora: your position and your presence in this city are the subject of considerable observation. Very, very attentive observation."

A moment of silence followed this statement, which seemed to cast the functionary in a new light: could it be that this insignificant man, this conceited bureaucrat, possessed information about the activities of the mysterious organization Falco worked for? After all, it was a kind of police force, and police headquarters might well be keeping tabs on its work. In that case, perhaps Garzo, in his eagerness to curry favor with her, might be able to provide her with a little more information about the degree to which Ricciardi was in their crosshairs. In a strange way, Livia felt that she might be able to protect the commissario.

She decided to let on that she was aware of the secret police's surveillance, hoping that this would prompt Garzo to confide new details.

"Certainly, Dottore; I'm well aware that the Duce's daughter—and by extension this insignificant friend of hers—must be protected and therefore kept under watch. These are difficult times, and who would know that better than you? But since we have nothing to hide, it is reassuring to feel that we're being protected. Especially when those who are watching over us are so thoughtful as to inform us of the fact. As far as the reception is concerned, it will be kept extremely secure, and therefore, as guests, you should certainly feel safe."

Garzo's face lit up; hearing explicitly that he would be among the invited guests, and finding out at the same time that not only did Livia know about the secret police's surveillance, she was happy about it, was more than he could have hoped for.

"Signora, I know it, too, and I'm very pleased. You put it perfectly: when a person has nothing to hide, being under surveillance is actually quite reassuring."

It wasn't true, and they both knew it. Too many rumors had been circulating about innocent people who, without the slightest idea why, had been hauled off to secret locations and subjected to trials that inevitably resulted in guilty verdicts; but neither one trusted the other enough to express their fears.

"Dottore, I came by in search of news about Ricciardi, whom I haven't seen since the last time I was here. Have you heard from him? He's a latter-day scarlet pimpernel, that man!"

She followed her words with a cheerful laugh, to keep from betraying a hint of concern. Garzo shook his head.

"No, Signora. In fact, I don't mind telling you that I'd like to know a little more about what he's up to. As long as we're talking confidentially, I should say that sometimes the man takes personal initiatives that put him at serious risk of trouble. Certain behaviors of his, certain people he spends time with— they might give the wrong impression. You and I, who are his friends, ought to urge him to be more careful."

Livia immediately understood that Garzo possessed the same information that had been given to her. What else did he know?

"So true. That's exactly what I intend to do, when he finally decides to show his face. But let me ask you, Dottore, do you have any idea as to what commitments might have induced him to ask for this time off? How could I get in touch with him, if I wished to speak with him?"

The deputy chief of police seemed uninterested in going any further. You could never know for sure: what if Livia herself was an informant for Falco and his associates? After all, she came from Rome, and he couldn't be sure she hadn't been sent by someone to investigate him and police headquarters.

"Well, I really couldn't tell you. You were here the last time I saw him. And as you know, it's hard to say with Ricciardi. I just hope he doesn't get himself into some mess that I can't help him out of, because—and this is something you should know about me, Signora—no matter how I like and respect him, I'd never do anything that might conflict to the slightest degree with the wishes of the regime."

Livia refrained from expressing her disgust. The man was a coward, and he clearly thought that even she might be an informant.

"I'm more than sure of it, Dottore. *Grazie*. But now I really have to go, there's still so much left to do."

Garzo stood up to see her to the door.

"Certainly, certainly, I completely understand. Well, then, *arrivederci*, my dear Signora. I'll look forward to receiving . . . mail from you."

Livia flashed him her most dazzling smile.

"And you most certainly will. Have a pleasant day."

Just as her car was leaving the building, Livia glimpsed the massive silhouette of Brigadier Maione. She told the driver to stop. She got out and approached him.

"Brigadier, good afternoon. How are you doing? I was just held captive for a short while by your Dottor Garzo, who doesn't know a thing about Ricciardi. Would you happen to know what's become of him?"

Maione looked around. He seemed conflicted.

"No, no, Signora. How would I know where to find the commissario? He's on vacation, as you know, the lucky dog. And not here slaving away like the rest of us."

234 · MAURIZIO DE GIOVANNI

Livia dismissed the brigadier's reticence with a wave of her hand.

"Let's skip the playacting, Brigadier. Ricciardi's welfare and health are as important to you as they are to me. What kind of mess has he gotten himself into, if I may ask? A man doesn't just disappear from one day to the next, and I know that you wouldn't just stand idly by without knowing anything about it, nor would he fail to keep you informed. So tell me: what's going on?"

Maione was a married man; he was all too familiar with womanly determination, and he knew that his personal strength was inadequate up against that kind of resolve. Better tell her something, he thought to himself; I'll toss her a bone and see if that satisfies her.

"Signo', perhaps you'll remember that the commissario made some reference when you met—after all, I was there, too—to the death of this little boy at Capodimonte. He was an orphan, poor thing. The last time I spoke with the commissario he was looking into this death, but informally, just trying to get a clearer picture. He'd asked Dr. Modo to do an autopsy; he wanted to know how the child had died, that sort of thing. That's all I know. Forgive me, Signo', but I have to leave you now. My shift is over, and before going home I need to make a stop somewhere. It's been a pleasure to see you. Have a good evening."

And, touching the tips of his fingers to the visor of his cap, he walked off into the rain under an enormous umbrella.

When she heard the doctor's name, Livia grew more worried still. With all her strength, she hoped that Ricciardi wasn't getting himself into serious trouble.

For the hundredth time, Enrica walked past the window and shot a look across the street. Dark. There was no glow of light from Ricciardi's window. It was torturing her, because she had no way of knowing whether her letter of reply had been read or not.

She'd chosen a courteous tone, cordial but not overly warm, and in the letter she'd informed Ricciardi that she didn't mind in the slightest if he chose to greet her, and that it was just as much a pleasure for her to see him and say hello in turn. She cited good neighborly relations, as well as her own upbringing. With apparent nonchalance, toward the end of the one-page letter, written in the clear, precise script of a left-handed girl who had resisted even the nuns' efforts to make her change hands, she had made it known that there was no one else he could offend by saying hello to her, and she hoped the same was true for him.

Now she was very worried. She was afraid that with that allusion to the lack of a fiancé on her part and the lack of a fiancée on his, she might have seemed a little too aggressive, leading him to think that she was angling for a more serious and definitive commitment. What if he were to think that the fact that she was unmarried at her age had turned her into a manhunter, on a desperate campaign to land herself a husband? What if he took fright and withdrew? If he never wrote her again, what would she do?

She sighed. For a person as patient as she was, this anxious waiting was a new experience, and she found it difficult to bear. She decided that, unless she heard from him directly by the next day, she'd go back to Rosa for advice.

XXXIX

Panting his way up the hill and cursing the rain dripping down the back of his collar in spite of his umbrella, Maione reflected on the current situation and worried. Livia's questions, the growing tension that he sensed at police headquarters, Ricciardi's terrible propensity to plunge head-first into trouble: all made him fear for the commissario.

What bothered him most of all was that he couldn't seem to understand the reason that the commissario continued to delve into the life of that poor child. He'd become accustomed over the years to accepting Ricciardi's intuitions without discussion; he couldn't always follow his boss's reasoning, but it often corresponded to exactly what had actually happened. The analytical approaches, the mental processes that seemed to inspire such mistrust among his fellow policemen—who superstitiously avoided all interactions with his superior officer, whom they never missed an opportunity to bitterly describe as a Jonah with an evil eye—were, as far as Maione was concerned, just so many truths handed down from on high, and far be it from him to question them.

And yet, this time, he thought to himself as he struggled up the last part of the climb, the risk was enormous: a semiofficial note of protest from the Archiepiscopal See, delivered, moreover, during the very sensitive time immediately preceding the arrival of Mussolini himself, put a very dangerous weapon in the hands of that idiot Garzo. What had Ricciardi glimpsed in the tragic death of that young orphan? What subtle clue, what feeling that there must be something else concealed beneath the surface?

He didn't understand; but precisely because he was unaccustomed to questioning Ricciardi's orders, he intended to accompany him on this dangerous path. Everything else could go to hell, as far as he was concerned.

He looked up disconsolately at the steep flight of stairs that still loomed before him; the commissario had asked him to go out and gather information, and he'd turned to the finest informant at his disposal. And if that informant had the somewhat eccentric habit of agreeing to meet with Maione only and always at her own apartment, which in fact stood at the top of the stairs in question, which in turn could be reached only by climbing the steepest hill in Naples, he was determined to go there all the same.

It was therefore a tired, rain-drenched, sweaty, starving Brigadier Maione who finally knocked at Bambinella's door.

The true name of this particular individual was known only to a very select few; the nickname, by which she was universally known and renowned in all the city's most sordid *vicoli*, derived from a song by Raffaele Viviani that had been in vogue over the last few years. The protagonist and namesake of the song was a beautiful prostitute who was in love. The figure that answered the door, wrapped in a garish floral silk kimono, her face heavily made up, did possess lovely features and might very well be in love; nonetheless, under the thick layer of rouge, one could clearly see a veil of dark stubble, which only contributed to the cognitive dissonance induced by the individual's sheer height and strapping broad shoulders.

"Why, Brigadie': what a lovely surprise to see you here, and in weather I wouldn't send a dog out in! I was resigned to not seeing you at all, at this hour. Please come in, *prego*: make yourself right at home."

The low, throaty voice was unmistakably masculine; but the

modulation, fluting and affected, left no doubt about the speaker's absolute femininity. Bambinella walked, breathed, and lived perfectly at her ease along a fine boundary line: something that was only possible here, in the world's most tolerant city. And she was so much a part of that city that she managed, given her natural propensity for gossip, to learn everything about everyone in record time, information that she shared only and exclusively with Brigadier Raffaele Maione, in the name of an exceedingly odd and particular friendship between two people who couldn't have been more different from each other.

"Bambine', I have to tell you: of all your twisted ways, this insistence on only talking to me at your apartment, which happens to be on top of a mountain, is the one I can tolerate the least. One of these days, you're going to give me a heart attack, and then you'll have me on your conscience, you will."

Maione flopped down into a small wicker chair that groaned under his weight, loosening his shirt collar and fanning himself with his handkerchief. Bambinella sat down across from him, coquettishly angling her sheer-stocking-clad calves to one side.

"Sure, that's all we need, to have our little conversations together in a café, in plain view. Then someone will slice my gut open with a knife, and at the very least they'll go tell your signora that they saw you with the loveliest *chanteuse* in Naples, and she'll slice you open, too."

Maione's panting was starting to subside.

"You have a point, and that's why I'm willing to come all the way up here. But there is one other possibility: I could always arrest you, that way we could chat comfortably any time I like, without climbing a single step. What do you say to that?"

Bambinella clapped her hands.

"*Bravo,* Brigadier, now you're talking sense. That way I'd have free room and board, and you'd get what little information I could scrape together in jail. What do you say, is that what you're looking for?"

Maione snorted.

"All right, all right, I'll let you go free for now. Let's see if what you have for me today is sufficient, otherwise I might have to rethink my decision. Well?"

Bambinella looked up at the ceiling, as if to summon the information to her memory.

"Now then, what was it you wanted to know? Ah, yes, Cosimo the *saponaro*. Now, why are you interested in him? He's just a poor wretch, without skills or money. What could he have done wrong?"

"I told you already, Bambine', you need to remember to mind your own business when you're dealing with me. But only with me; as far as the rest of Naples is concerned it's your job to stick your nose in, and if you fail to do that, I'll have to throw you in jail."

"*Mamma mia*, what an oaf you are! But all right; I have a soft spot for a man in uniform, and I just can't say no to you. Now then, about Cosimo: You were right about him, I got confirmation from a dear little girlfriend of mine who works in the building at the corner of the Largo San Giovanni Maggiore and Via Sedile di Porto. She saw him do it; he does pilfer from apartments. The method is a simple one: he starts chatting with these women, because he does have a nice running patter, he tells them stories he's just made up then and there, he pays them compliments, and the women get distracted. That's what fools we are, the weaker sex: we fall hard for the first man to come along and pay us a compliment."

Maione considered the sheen of stubble on Bambinella's face, and the coarse hairs poking out from under the silk kimono that her powerful hand held tight to her chest, and said:

"You're exactly right. That's just the way you women are. Go on."

"Well, while he was talking, the little kid that he brought with him on his rounds, who was the same poor child you found dead at Capodimonte, would slip stealthily into their apartments and steal a little something. Nothing spectacular: a fork, a knickknack, a pillowcase. All things that would then show up on the *saponaro*'s handcart, but in some other part of town, or else someone might catch on to what he was doing. Little things, eh: but they help make ends meet. The question is what he's going to do now without the little boy."

Maione scratched his head.

"So there was crime, if little more than a minor felony, in the life of this child. Though experience tells me that two-bit thieves are rarely capable of murder."

Bambinella sat up straight in her chair, her eyes flashing.

"Murder? Why, what are you saying, that the child was murdered? Oooh, *madonna mia*, and you think that Cosimo did it?"

"No, Bambine', calm down, for Pete's sake! That's not what I said at all, and besides, I already told you, the child died after eating rat poison, accidentally. I'm just trying to figure out why the commissario wanted to know these things, that's all."

Bambinella sighed.

"That commissario of yours. Every time he has a doubt about something, it turns out in the end that he was right. *Mamma mia*, what a handsome man he is! Too bad he's such a grouch and he brings bad luck, heaven protect us, or I'd be willing to take him out for a spin around the block, since you continue to spurn my advances."

Maione groaned.

"No, in fact, I don't want you, Bambine'! I'm only here so that I don't have to arrest you, and you know it. Your profession, out on the street the way you practice it, is illegal. And don't you dare go around saying that my commissario brings bad luck or I'll lock you up, information or no information."

Bambinella picked up a fan and started fanning herself coquettishly.

"Ooh, what a fiery temper you have! All right, I'll stop saying that he brings bad luck, even if everyone at police headquarters says so. And as for my profession, Brigadie', it's not my fault if the legal bordellos only take girls whose identification papers have the letter *F* in the box marked "sex." How is a girl supposed to make a living? She has to do what she can, don't you agree?"

Maione waved his hands in a gesture of surrender.

"Fine, fine, I give up, you're right; as long as you go on with what you found out. What else?"

Bambinella listed the items:

"Now then: Cosimo I told you about, he's a miserable wretch; at the very worst, he might lose his temper, get drunk, and pester some poor woman he meets on the street. But if you ask me, he wouldn't hurt a fly. Word is that he killed a man when he was young, but I also know that it wasn't him, it was another man who later fled to America. I asked around about what life is like for the boys in the parish church, and I got confirmation on what you've already heard. I also learned that the priest, Don Antonio, lends out money at interest. Nothing big, a little here and a little there, and he threatens those who are late in paying that he'll spread the word about them. You have no idea what people will put up with just to keep word from getting out that they're dying of hunger. And I've also heard that he buys and sells houses, apartments, and shops, and that he puts them in the names of stand-ins, fronts who collect the rent and then hand it over to him. In other words, he's a profiteer who does a little work as a priest on the side."

Maione shook his head in disgust.

"How lovely. Doesn't practice what he preaches: the expression is certainly apt in this case. What else?"

Bambinella smiled unctuously.

242 · MAURIZIO DE GIOVANNI

"I got another nice tidbit from a girlfriend of mine who does old women's hair, right in the Santa Teresa quarter. She says that the sexton, a filthy drunk named Nanni, not only drinks but also has a bad habit of putting his hands where they don't belong . . . where they *really* don't belong, if you follow me . . . on women and, get this, on little boys. In other words, he's obsessed with that stuff. My girlfriend heard about it from an old bag of bones, a woman who told him where to get off— but my girlfriend says that it would have been smarter for her to accept, because that old woman is so old and ugly, when is she going to get another chance like that? Anyway, he was seen trying to wrap his arms around one of the bigger boys while he was drunk, and the boy kicked him and ran off. Now I don't know if this last bit of information is of any use to you, but I wanted to let you know."

Maione put on a thoughtful expression.

"Well then, nice place, this parish church of the Soccorso. What a foul mess; in this city it seems like any manhole cover you lift, you find something filthy underneath it. All right, then, I think that's everything. *Grazie*, Bambine'. If I need anything else I'll let you know. And in the meantime, take my advice: behave yourself and don't let anyone stab you."

Bambinella had gotten to her feet to walk Maione to the door.

"Brigadie', you know that you're always welcome here. I've told you before, there's no danger of being seen, and if you were, I'd just say that you were a loyal customer."

Maione shot her an angry glare.

"You just dare to say such a thing, and if I don't kill you, I'll throw you in jail for the next thirty years, *capito*?"

"I get it, I get it. All right then, I'll just say that you come to see me incognito and you don't want word getting around, is that better?"

Maione's shoulders sagged in defeat.

"Say whatever you like! If you hear anything else, send me word."

Just as the brigadier was walking out onto the landing, Bambinella called him back:

"By the way, I almost forgot. I should tell you that a client of mine, who sells fruit and nuts from a handcart—a fine strapping young *guaglione* who never has any money because he has six children, so I charge him half price because he breaks my heart, poor thing—he says that the boy who died used to go around with a little dog, is that right?"

Maione nodded, turning around and standing on the threshold.

"Yes. So?"

"He saw him not far from the parish church last Saturday. My client remembers because he'd only ever seen the boy on his own, just him and his dog. Sometimes he'd give the boy a walnut, or a cherry in May; he felt sorry for the kid because, as I told you, he has little ones of his own. But this time, the boy wasn't alone."

"So who was he with? With the other boys, with the sexton?"

Bambinella shook her head.

"No, no. He was with a tall man, elegantly dressed: a gentleman, in other words. And one thing that made an impression on my client was the fact that he didn't walk right, in other words, he walked with a bit of a limp. And my client thought: well, look at that, a *cacaglio* and a *zoppo*, a boy who stutters and a man who limps. What a lovely pair."

XL

Nothing like one of Rosa's dinners when you have a headache, thought Ricciardi; her cooking is so devastating that your stomach, in its grueling efforts to digest it, demands so much of your attention that any other minor discomfort fades into the background. And there's no choice about whether or not to eat every last bit: she'll start sulking and the atmosphere at home will become intolerable.

That night she'd inflicted upon him, in an alleged attempt to raise his body temperature to what it ought to be, a *zuppa maritata*: in a bowl roughly the size of a small city piazza, there sailed sausages, lard, beans, celery, and a number of other objects that could not be readily identified. There was a perfect storm of garlic and onion, as he had been able to tell the minute he walked into the lobby downstairs. Ricciardi estimated that digestion wouldn't be complete until forty-eight hours out, unless he died before then.

The thoughts had never stopped running through his mind, even as he battled the unholy stew under the cook's vigilant gaze, standing as she always did in the kitchen doorway and watching him eat. The faces of Don Antonio, Carmen, and Eleonora, the downcast gazes of the boys, and the ambiguous figure of the sexton followed one another through his thoughts, alternating with the mysterious junk seller, the owner of the food warehouse, the thousand suspicious and malevolent eyes that looked out at him from the shadows of the *vicoli* as he went by, like the eyes of the young tough who'd asked

Cristiano if he needed any help. He couldn't seem to put together a complete picture of the dead boy's life: there was something that continued to elude him.

He was starting to understand the dull, powerful yearning for affection that drove Tettè to comply with those who surrounded him, and which pushed those same people to take advantage of him, to persecute him; everyone except for Carmen and the dog. The thought of the dog sent a shiver down Ricciardi's spine, as he listened to the arabesques of a jazz orchestra on the radio. He couldn't get used to seeing that dog appear just ten feet away, sitting silently, barely visible through the rain. In some strange way, it seemed to him that this little spotted mutt, with one ear cocked, was commissioning him to pursue this investigation.

He coughed, and his throat clutched painfully. Too much rain and too much cold wind: it seemed to be the onset of a head cold. He could feel the weariness in his limbs that always precedes a fever.

It was painfully ironic to think how reassuring it would have been to glimpse the little boy's ghost, possibly in a *vicolo* not far from where he'd died.

Perhaps a man on his way home from work late at night had found the corpse outside his own apartment building, in the rain, and in order to avoid getting involved in a police investigation and having to give answers about something he knew nothing about, he'd picked the little body up, carried it to the monumental staircase, and left it there, after positioning it respectfully and tenderly.

Perhaps a woman had found him dead in the atrium of an apartment building and had lacked the courage to raise the alarm so she chose to put the dead child where the first passerby would be sure to see him.

Perhaps the boys from the parish, his companions in his nightly raids, had brought him there from some distant corner of the city where they'd stolen something. After all, Cristiano had taken Ricciardi straight to the warehouse, without any hesitation.

But the image of the Deed had refused to appear. And it hadn't been in the large room at the parish, nor along the street that ran into the Tondo di Capodimonte, nor anywhere else he'd been in the past few days, as he retraced the steps of Tettè's life.

The thought took him back to that lolling neck and the pain of mingling lonelinesses. Pardoxically, he thought, it would have been comforting to experience once again the extreme anguish of death, to feel the Deed taking hold of him, and to hear the last sorrowful words of the child's departure from this earthly life. Perhaps to see the boy in the throes of the immense burning pain of the poison, the convulsions, the yellowish foam on his lips, his limbs seized in one last terrible spasm. He would watch him, his own eyes locked with the boy's dull, dead ones. He would listen to his last words, as always in keeping with the last moment of a life, once again revealing how, when a person dies, he goes into nothingness looking back at life.

Then at least he'd know; then he'd be able to make peace with it. He'd approach the dog, give it something to eat, and then each would go his own way. Each with his own intolerable memories.

The radio presenter announced that a certain brand of rhubarb liqueur was bringing their listeners the next song, *Polvere di stelle (Stardust)*: and the orchestra struck up a melancholy tune.

He got up from the armchair, his head on fire, his throat on fire, his stomach on fire. Unaware that he was being watched by a pair of curious eyes from the kitchen, he spotted a sealed envelope on the table by the door that he somehow hadn't noticed before. He picked it up hesitantly; he immediately guessed what it was, and was instantly overcome by a fierce wave of fear.

Enrica's answer. She'd written back.

His head spun, and he felt a surge of nausea, but he concealed his queasiness lest Rosa inflict upon him some terrible herbal tea from Cilento that would deal the coup de grâce to his precarious condition. There was still a flimsy chance he could avoid vomiting, and he wasn't taking any risks.

He asked Rosa:

"Who brought this letter? It didn't come by ordinary mail: it isn't postmarked."

The *tata*, who hadn't missed a single move Ricciardi had made, pretended to be startled.

"*Mamma mia*, you scared the life out of me! I thought you were asleep in the armchair. That letter? How would I know who brought it? I just found it in the mailbox, downstairs in the front hall of the building."

"Ah, you did, did you? And since when have you been collecting mail from the mailbox?"

Rosa put on the same truculent expression she wore every time she found herself with her back to the wall.

"What, I can't look in the mailbox? What about the bills that come from the village, the invoices and all the other documents that need to be dealt with in order to manage the farmland, who do you think looks at them, the *signorino*, by chance? Don't I take care of those things, even though I'm old and my eyes are shot, and every bone in my body aches?"

Once he realized his misstep, Ricciardi abruptly changed gears:

"For heaven's sake, forget I ever said it. Of course you can look in the mailbox: why shouldn't you? I was just wondering who might have put it here, that's all."

He entertained the notion of some complicity between Rosa and Enrica, but dismissed the idea immediately. It was incon-

248 · MAURIZIO DE GIOVANNI

ceivable that his *tata* knew that he watched her from his window, much less that he had written her that letter. He'd been very careful; she couldn't possibly have noticed. He excluded it categorically.

Feigning indifference, he sat back down in the armchair. His hands were trembling, but he didn't want to run the risk of tearing the letter along with the envelope. He waited until he'd calmed down a little to open it. The handwriting immediately stirred a feeling of tenderness in him: it slanted to the wrong side; she wrote with her left hand. Absurdly, he thought about how she'd managed to resist any efforts to correct this aspect of her personality—and, needless to say, he liked it.

He couldn't bring himself to read it. He'd glimpsed the signature at the bottom, which meant she'd only used one side of the paper, and it read: "*Cordially yours, Enrica Colombo.*" Not very long; but for that matter, his hadn't been either. He was afraid: there's nothing quite as concise as a flat refusal.

He'd been turning the sheet of paper over in his hands for more than a minute when Rosa spoke up.

"Well? If I want to know what a letter says, I read it."

His *tata*'s voice was like a rifle shot, and Ricciardi started.

"I'll read it, I'll read it. It's for me, it's something . . . something having to do with work, that's all. Office business, nothing to worry about. Go on, go to sleep, it's late. *Buona notte.*"

His *tata* replied with a gruff "*Buona notte.*"

But she smiled as she headed for her bedroom.

Finally, Ricciardi read the letter, all at once; then he reread it, and when he finished he reread it again, savoring each word, pronouncing them in his own mouth as he read, going over them in silence, like a poem he was trying to learn by heart. In them he found the exact image he'd formed of her: tranquil, sweet, serious, but quick to smile.

Now he knew the most important thing of all: she wasn't engaged; she hadn't promised her heart to anyone else. He knew that she wanted a family one day, and a home of her own, where she could move around, at her ease, calmly, quietly.

That she found him neither annoying nor disgusting, that she was not bothered by his crudeness or the ineptness he knew he suffered from in his personal relations. That she liked his eyes, even though they were accustomed to observing pain and grief and to recognizing their sounds.

Just like every time he thought about it, the rational part of him ordered him to keep his distance, to tear up that leter, close the shutters, and never see her again; to stop dreaming of a future in which the Deed would perhaps be passed on to innocent children, in which he'd have to share his curse with those he loved most.

The other part of him, the one that with each passing day yearned more and more for a normal life, the everyday existence that only he had been denied, pushed him instead to run to the window, throw it open, and call Enrica at the top of his lungs.

Of course, he chose the middle path. He stood up from the armchair, turned off the radio and the overhead light, went into his bedroom, and stepped over to the window; he looked across the street to a window with a light on, as he did every night; he waved slightly with one hand, and in return he received a lovely tilt of the head from the girl with glasses, who was doing needlepoint with her left hand.

He smiled, hesitantly, and held up the sheet of paper with his trembling hand. She blushed and dropped her embroidery to her lap for a moment. Then she picked it up again, with a smile on her face, too.

Ricciardi decided that he definitely had a fever.

XLI

Saturday, October 31

For the past few days, Maione had liked going to work less and less. He thought about it as he walked, doing his best not to slip on the slippery black cobblestones, glistening with rain, along the steep hill down from his home to police headquarters.

First of all, he wasn't used to working without Ricciardi. Not that the commissario was much company, to be clear: not even Maione, the only one there who was fond of him, would have claimed that. But he was still a constant point of reference, a landmark, a center of gravity around which the brigadier's workday revolved.

Then, there was another thing: he didn't like atmosphere that he'd been sensing at police headquarters and throughout the city for the past few days. It was a sort of menacing euphoria, an unrelenting state of feverish excitement over the impending visit of the Duce. With each passing hour, as painted slogans and portraits appeared on the walls of buildings all over the city, as posters were put up singing the praises of Mussolini, and as groups of idlers strolled arm-in-arm through the streets singing anthems and fight songs, Garzo became increasingly hysterical, testing the nerves of the entire headquarters staff. It was not merely annoying, it was also dangerous: in those combustible conditions, all it took was a spark, and in fact in the past few hours there had been brawls at several points around town, with emergency calls and squads of patrolmen summoned to the scene, usually too late to do anything more than tot up the damages and injuries.

Last of all, and no less disagreeable than the other factors, was the weather. It had been raining and raining for almost two weeks, with only rare, brief breaks in the downpour. Hard rain, drizzle, and wind. Water got in everywhere and caused flooding, collapses, bad falls, and car crashes. For a policeman, there was nothing worse than rain.

Caught up in these grim thoughts, and taking care not to slip himself, Maione almost failed to notice the figure waiting for him, standing beneath the overhang of a cornice at the corner of Via della Tofa, some fifteen feet from police headquarters.

"Hey there, Commissa', what are you doing here so early? I was just thinking about you, and here you are before my eyes! How are you? Everything all right?"

In effect, Ricciardi wasn't much to look at: he was pale and his eyes were red. He looked feverish.

"I'm fine, *grazie*. A little bit of a headache, but it'll pass. I wanted to talk to you before you went in to work; could I buy you an espresso?"

Maione shot a quick look around. He wanted to make sure that they were safe from prying eyes, that no one could report their meeting to Garzo. He lacked the patience to let himself be interrogated by the deputy chief of police about just how Ricciardi was spending his time off.

He followed the commissario into a small café already open and serving at that hour of the morning. They sat down and ordered, Maione, as usual, something to eat, and Ricciardi a glass of red wine. The brigadier looked at him in surprise.

"Commissa', I don't think you ought to be out on the street in the rain, if you don't feel well. If you ask me, you have a fever, too, and a glass of wine first thing in the morning isn't enough to set you right."

"It helps take the chill off. I've got the shivers; this damn water never seems to stop. But why don't *you* tell *me*: Did you find anything out?"

Maione relayed in detail the information he'd received from Bambinella about the junk seller, the priest, and the sexton. Everything fit in with what they'd come to believe about the actual life that the child led, in spite of the rosy pictures painted by those they'd interviewed.

Ricciardi said, thoughtfully:

"All these people are violent individuals. People who might have an outburst of rage, or hurt someone, no doubt about it: but crudely. They may well have been responsible for the marks and bruises on poor Tettè's body—bruises, cuts, even a burn mark on one arm. And no doubt they were. But I can't imagine them committing a premeditated murder. After all, what reason could they have?"

Maione broke in forcefully:

"And in fact, they didn't do it, Commissa'. No one murdered that poor child. You yourself admitted it, no? And the doctor said the same thing, I believe. I still don't quite understand what it is we're looking for."

Ricciardi decided he needed to tell Maione something; if for no other reason than to motivate him in the investigation he was carrying out on his behalf.

"I have reason to believe, Raffae', that Tettè's corpse was moved. I'm not trying to say that anyone killed him, let that be clear; but I don't think that he died there, where we found him."

Maione opened his eyes wide. He was truly surprised.

"Really? But what makes you think that? What marks did you see?"

Ricciardi had an answer ready:

"No actual physical marks, which is to say, no evidence; otherwise you'd have seen them yourself or I would have told you about them immediately. But, first and foremost, death from strychnine poisoning causes convulsions—Modo said so—and I don't think that dying of convulsions would leave a person sitting, still and serene, with their legs stretched out straight and their hands in their lap the way we found Tettè, looking sad-eyed into the middle distance. He would have fallen over, wouldn't he? We would have found him sprawled out on the pavement, in the rain. Then there's the problem of the dog."

Maione was increasingly baffled.

"The dog? What does the dog have to do with it, Commissa'? Come to think of it, which dog?"

Ricciardi tapped his forefinger on the empty wineglass

"Do you remember the dog that we found near the boy? Everyone we talked to told us that Tettè and that dog were inseparable; which means the boy must have fed the dog, no? In that case, why would the dog still be alive? The dog should have been poisoned, too, don't you think? But it wasn't, it was sitting there calmly, watching over that poor dead child."

Maione nodded, pensively. He wasn't entirely convinced.

"Sure, that's odd, I admit. But still, don't you think it's possible, Commissa', that the child snuck into the warehouse by himself, grabbed several different things to eat, and only by chance, or misfortune, in the dark, he also grabbed one of those poisoned morsels, just one. The doctor said that just a few grains of poison would be enough to kill such a small child. Now, as for the convulsions . . . the child was already so weak, maybe he died right away of a heart attack and didn't have time to suffer. Which would be nice to think, no?"

Ricciardi nodded.

"Sure, it would be nice to think that. But until I'm certain I want to try to figure it out. I told you, there's no evidence; it's more of a feeling that I have. But you know what I'm like: if something doesn't look right to me, I want to figure it out. That's all."

Maione smiled.

"Yes, I'm all too familiar with your hardheaded ways, how could I not be? All right, Commissa', let's proceed; also because, according to the information I got from Bambinella, and as you know she's always reliable, there's a disgusting world behind all this, and those kids are right in the middle of it. The most important piece of intelligence that she gave me, though, is something I haven't told you yet: and it has to do with what a *verdummaio* saw, a strolling fruit and vegetable vendor who's a client of hers: he told Bambinella that he saw the boy, exactly a week ago, with a strange individual."

And he told Ricciardi about the tall, well-dressed man with a limp, and his meeting and discussion with Tettè. The commissario immediately became more attentive.

"What do you mean, discussion? Were they arguing, or talking calmly? And what did this person look like? How old, more or less? And how tall?"

Maione threw his arms open wide.

"How would I know, Commissa'? We're talking about something glimpsed in passing by a strolling vendor, a week ago, in the middle of the street. It's already a miracle we even know about it, and it's thanks to Bambinella, who seems to me to be the central clearinghouse for information in this city. If you ask me, the newspapers ought to hire her. She could write the whole paper, from the front page to the back."

Ricciardi ran his hand over his forehead. It was burning hot.

"We have to find out who this gentleman was. Something strange, and unusual for him, the very day before he died: that's extremely important. And it strikes me that at this point it's necessary to speak directly to two people I haven't interviewed yet: the *saponaro* and the sexton. And we should also talk to Cristiano, the boy, who I know will be a tough nut to crack."

Maione spoke decisively:

"Then we'll have to split up and work in parallel, Commissa'. Maybe you can talk to the sexton and I'll go see the junk seller and the kid, because when they see the uniform, it puts the fear of God in them; and as you know, fear loosens the tongue better than a glass of wine."

Ricciardi objected:

"That's out of the question. You know what the atmosphere's like at headquarters. That's all we need now: for you to get charged with insubordination and thrown in jail. Let me take care of it, *grazie*."

But when Maione made up his mind about something, there was no changing it.

"No, Commissa'. This is how we're going to do it this time. First of all, because you don't look strong enough to me to be running all around town in this weather; second, because in any case I don't trust myself to hang around at police headquarters, with that maniac Garzo on the warpath; and last of all because we'll almost certainly have to talk to Bambinella again, and as you know, she refuses to talk to anyone but me. So face the inevitable and do what I tell you for once, instead of the exact opposite."

Ricciardi raised his hands.

"All right, I surrender. You go ahead, and I'll talk to the sexton, Nanni. Let's not waste any time: I have a feeling that the more time goes by, the less evidence we're going to come up with."

XLII

Seven days earlier, Saturday, October 24

Tettè is happy because he managed to successfully smuggle in the piece of pastry that he didn't finish at the pastry shop the day before; now he's outside and he's with the dog, seeking shelter from the rain in the entrance hall of an apartment building.

With his fingers he breaks the stale pastry into three small pieces. He eats one himself, and he gives two to the dog, which wolfs them down.

Suddenly something blocks the faint light, looming up between them and the front door. Tettè looks up in surprise and sees the man with the limp. He holds his breath in terror. He's very afraid of that man.

Ciao, bambino, he says. He always speaks in a low voice, he looks around, he seems to be on the verge of taking to his heels. He's never done him any harm, and yet Tettè is still afraid of him. The man rears up in front of him like a ghost when he least expects it, and never when he's at home, at the parish.

Ciao, bambino, he says. What are you doing, are you and the dog having something to eat? Who gave you something to eat?

The serpent quickly slithers up and coils around his throat. Tettè doesn't even try to answer him. He shakes his head no, he doesn't even know why.

Then the man looks around, tells Tettè to get up, says let's get out of here. Tettè doesn't want to leave, because he doesn't know *where the man wants to take him; so the man grabs him by the arm and yanks him to his feet.*

The minute the dog sees that the man has laid his hand on Tettè, he leaps to his feet and snarls loudly. The man has a walking stick in one hand, and he uses it on the dog: one sharp rap, on the dog's back. Both Tettè and the dog whine together, almost the same sound. The animal backs away, but stands there snarling and watching the man with the limp, even as he continues to yelp in pain.

If you're good I won't hurt you, says the man with the limp. I won't hurt you, or your dog. You know that. But you have to do what I say. For example, you have to answer my questions. If you don't, you know what will happen.

Tettè knows, and how: Nanni has said it a hundred times over if he's said it once, in the week that's passed since he came to fetch him and take him outside, around the street corner, to where the man with the limp was waiting for him. If you tell someone, anyone, about this meeting, about the fact that the man with the limp comes to talk to you, I'll talk to the blonde woman. And then you'll never see her again, never ever again. I'll tell her certain things and she'll take to her heels in horror, she won't even come back to teach school. But if you go with the man with the limp and talk to him, I won't say anything to anybody. It's a secret, you fool of a cacaglio: *just a little secret. You'll know it and I'll know it, and if no one else ever knows then everything will be fine. But if someone finds out, you're the one who'll be worse off. Just you.*

The man with the limp drags him by the arm, and with his other hand braces himself against his cane. Every so often the end of the cane slips on the wet street, but the man with the limp never falls. Tettè walks fast, otherwise the man will lift him off the ground and that hurts his arm.

The dog follows at a distance, still snarling; he's walking normally. Thank goodness, the man with the limp didn't hurt him too badly, Tettè thinks.

They stop by a vicolo. The man with the limp gets all nice again, he smiles, he pats Tettè's head. Bravo, he says, you really are a good boy. Would you like a piece of candy? Look, I brought you a piece of honey candy. Tettè takes it and puts it in his pocket. He thanks him, seriously, the way his angel taught him to do. Aren't you going to eat it? asks the man with the limp. Later, he replies: I'll eat it later.

The man with the limp starts asking questions, in a relaxed tone of voice: that's how he always begins. What do you do? What do you eat? How old are you? How long have you been at the parish? And then, the way he does every time, he starts to delve into the memories that Tettè doesn't have: Don't you know who brought you here? Didn't the priest ever tell you anything? Don't you have anything, a piece of clothing, a sheet? What do you remember from when you were a tiny little boy? But how can it be that you don't remember a thing?

Even with the serpent coiled around his throat, Tettè answers. The man with the limp isn't patient, but he waits. His face is polite, but he squeezes Tettè's arm.

He starts with the questions that scare Tettè most: Who comes to see you? Is there anyone at church who looks at you with greater interest than the others? And when you go out with her, with the blonde woman, where is it you go? Where does she take you? What does she say to you? What do you talk about? And what do you answer her?

Tettè doesn't want to tell the man with the limp about the time he spends with his angel. He's afraid that the man will somehow take it away from him, that precious time. Plus, he's jealous; that's his business and he doesn't want to say anything about his angel.

And so the man with the limp realizes that Tettè doesn't want to answer, and he starts to get mad. His hand clutches the end of the cane very tight; Tettè can see creases appear in the man's white gloves. The man's lips grow thin and bloodless, and his eyes narrow to a pair of slits.

The other hand squeezes his arm hard, harder, and harder still: Tettè can't feel his hand anymore, and he whines in pain.

The dog takes a step forward, snarling again, and the man with the limp raises his cane in his direction. The dog stops where he is, but he goes on snarling, the fur on his back bristling, the tail still, the ears flat against his head. He looks as if he's about to lunge, cane or no cane.

Talk, says the man with the limp. Talk, you stuttering idiot, you ugly retard.

He squeezes too hard: Tettè cries out long and loud, just as a fruit vendor passes by with his handcart out on the street near the vicolo. *The vendor hears the boy cry out and turns, squinting to see into the shadows.*

Who's there? he shouts. What's going on?

The man with the limp turns around and immediately changes his expression. He lets go of the boy's arm and tousles his hair. Poor little children, he says to the vendor. The things they'll make up, just to get a few pennies. The vendor glares at him from under the visor of his flat cap, standing with a hand on each handle of the cart. He says nothing. He has children at home, and he doesn't like it when gentlemen come down into the vicoli *to do strange things.*

The man with the limp realizes that the vendor isn't going to go away unless he goes first. He stares hard into Tettè's eyes, gives him a grimacing smile, and then lifts his gloved forefinger to his lips, opening both eyes wide. Be careful, he whispers. Be careful.

And he limps off, with his cane slipping on the wet cobblestones.

XLIII

At the end of Mass Maione hid around the corner from the parish church of Santa Maria del Soccorso. He'd reckoned the time that it would take Cristiano, after serving Mass in church, to come out and head for the streets.

Right on time, almost down to the second, the boy sauntered past, his hands in his pockets, his eyes on the pavement, whistling a popular tune. The brigadier took a step and emerged from the shadows, coming to a stop right in front of him, in all his considerable size. Cristiano almost slammed into him.

The boy's first instinct was to run. Maione had expected that, and his hand shot out and grabbed the boy by the arm. Cristiano tried to twist out of his grasp, but Maione held him firm.

"If you hold still, we can be done with this in a minute and then I'll let you go. Otherwise, I'll take you down to police headquarters and we can do our talking there. Which will it be?"

This proposition, hissed into the boy's face like a slap, had the desired effect. Cristiano stopped and stared insolently into the brigadier's eyes.

"I didn't do anything wrong. What do you want with me?"

Maione glared back at him.

"Since when do you have to have done something to be brought in to police headquarters? You know how it works: I can always find an reason. I'll just ask around a little bit. But all I want now is to have a little chat, nice and easy."

Cristiano look around circumspectly; being seen talking to a policeman wasn't an especially healthy thing in his world.

Maione sensed the boy's unease and nodded his head toward the dark alley where, a week earlier, the man with a limp had dragged the terrified Tettè.

As soon as they were safe from prying eyes, Cristiano regained the arrogant confidence that he liked to put on.

"I've done nothing and I know nothing, I already told your colleague. I've got nothing to say."

Maione grabbed the skin under the boy's chin between his fingers and squeezed hard, but Cristiano didn't blink.

"Listen, handsome: my colleague, who's not my colleague at all, but a police detective, a commissario, has been a little too gentle with you, because you're alley fodder, *carne da strada*. I know your type well, and I know when you're telling the truth and when you're talking nonsense. Most importantly, I know how to make your life a living hell. Now then, I'm going to ask you once, and once only: What can you tell me about what might have happened to your friend who died of poisoning? And don't tell me that you don't know anything, because that would make this the day that you disappear from the street for a good long time."

Cristiano evaluated Maione with a critical eye. He was barely older than a child, but he'd been out on the street for so long that he had become very good at appraising whoever he was dealing with, and the advantages and risks that a situation could entail for him. This time, his appraisal led to nothing good. He darted to one side, confident that Maione's attention had dropped off, but the brigadier's leg shot out fast and tripped him. Before Cristiano hit the ground, Maione had grabbed him by his shirt collar and set him back on his feet.

"Careful: you'll fall and hurt yourself. Don't you look where you put your feet? Try that one more time, and I'll make sure you can't walk home on your own two legs. You got that?"

Cristiano looked at him again, rubbing his neck. He'd known what would happen, but he still had to try it.

"What do you want from me, can I ask? What am I supposed to tell you?"

"I told you. What happened to your friend?"

The boy smiled mockingly.

"My friend? That fool of a *cacaglio* was no friend of mine. He was just another kid in the house, the runt of the litter. That's it."

Maione went on staring at him.

"Really? And yet someone told us that you were the only one he talked to, now and then. The only one who didn't torture him."

"Talked? The *cacaglio* never talked. When he tried to, he'd get stuck and say the same thing over and over: *ma-tte-tte-tte* . . . which is why they called him Tettè. But we called him the stupid *cacaglio*."

"And why did you call him that?"

"Because he was a *cacaglio*, and because he was stupid. He believed everything, if you told him, go over there, someone's calling you, he'd go. He never learned, he always fell for it. And the others got the better of him, and had fun playing pranks on him."

Maione listened attentively.

"What would they do to him?"

Cristiano shrugged.

"Just pranks. They'd put dead animals in his bed, steal food from his plate. Put dogshit in his shoes. Things like that."

"What about you? What did you do to him?"

Once again, that contemptuous gaze.

"I didn't waste my time playing pranks on the *cacaglio*. One prank's enough to show everyone what a fool he is: once everyone knows, what's the point? And then I felt a little sorry for the *cacaglio*."

Maione asked:

"Why did you feel sorry for him?"

"I told you, he fell for everything. He was looking for someone—how can I put this so you'll understand?—looking for someone who wouldn't hurt him. Always searching, looking you in the face with those eyes, never saying a word. It seemed pointless for me to pile on."

A simple explanation, but clear. Maione nodded.

"All right. Then let's talk about the night before, about the last time you saw Tettè. What do you have to say about that?"

"What should I say about it? It's not like we all look after each other. The *cacaglio* was minding his own business, and I was minding mine. At a certain point he went out and I didn't see him again. That's all there is to say."

Maione thought he'd noticed a slight hesitation.

"Think harder, try to remember; it's in your own interest. Did anything strange, out of the ordinary, happen? That day, or the day before?"

Cristiano shrugged.

"I don't remember. I don't think so."

"You don't think so, eh? Well, I've been doing some thinking of my own, and I think you know something that you don't want to tell me. It seems to me that the air down at police headquarters does a world of good for kids like you. Come on, let's go there and do some more talking. Maybe the air'll be good for your memory."

Cristiano twisted free from Maione's grasp.

"What do you want from me, anyway? The *cacaglio* was a fool, period. He died because he was a fool. It was all his fault, his fault, I tell you!"

Maione went on trying to get him on the ropes.

"I on the other hand think you know something. Tell me about the rat poison, then: How is it possible that one of you kids, who know the streets cobblestone by cobblestone, would make a mistake like that and eat a poisoned piece of food, like some stupid stray dog?"

The boy was starting to get exasperated.

264 · MAURIZIO DE GIOVANNI

"How am I supposed to know? We all knew about them, the poisoned morsels of food at the warehouse. Everyone. In fact, some of the boys even used to bring them back and feed them to cats, just for the fun of watching them die, with all the twisting and jumping they would do. We knew what they were, and the last thing we'd do was eat them ourselves. I don't know if the *cacaglio* knew about them, because he never came with us; he was a *signorino*, the teacher's pet, and she'd take him to the pastry shop on the Via Toledo to eat sweets. But if he didn't know what they were, if he didn't know that eating one would kill you, then he was even more of a fool than he seemed."

Maione insisted:

"And you didn't notice anything unusual at all? Am I really supposed to believe that you just can't remember when he went out and why?"

Cristiano gave him a defiant look.

"Brigadie', you can go ahead and take me to prison if you like; I have no idea where the *cacaglio* went that night. And I don't know why he went to eat rat poison; maybe he ate it because he wanted to die, or else just because he was a fool. I didn't hate him, the *cacaglio*. He wasn't a bad kid, plus he was little, and people who pick on little kids are cowards, and they turn my stomach. So I never did him any harm. What do you think, officer, aren't people who pick on little kids cowards?"

Maione stared at him for a long time. Then he released his arm, a disgusted grimace on his face.

"Get out of here, beat it. But remember: I'm still looking. And if I find out that you lied to me, I'll come get you in church if I have to."

Cristiano ran all the way to the end of the *vicolo*; then he turned around, looked back at Maione, and emitted a loud raspberry. Then he turned and vanished.

The brigadier couldn't help but burst out laughing.

XLIV

Seven days earlier, Saturday October 24

The rain has decided to take a little break.

The boys are standing in a knot near the food and grain warehouse, which is closed.

By now, night is falling. It's the time of the evening when the colors disappear before the light itself: you can still see, but everything's gray. From the woods of the royal estate around the palace comes a wind carrying the scents of trees and damp and winter.

A little off to one side is Tettè, with his dog. He's petting him, whispering into him ear. Amedeo nods his head sharply and Saverio sets off for the street entrance, behind which is the passageway to the interior. The others wait. One of the twins hops from one leg to the other, partly in excitement, partly to keep warm. The other one has a bag in his hands.

After a moment, Saverio emerges from the entrance. He's holding something.

A loud thunderclap bursts overhead; it's about to start raining again. A horse-drawn cart goes by, its load covered by a wet canvas tarp. The drayman wrapped in a tattered old overcoat is nodding off, his hat tipped forward to cover his face. The smell of the wood burning in the potbellied stoves hangs in the air. Darkness is falling, minute by minute.

Amedeo takes a couple of pellets from Saverio's hands. These are the poisoned morsels that Lotti, the owner of the warehouse, has laid out to kill the rats that have been eating his merchandise. When he gives a signal, the twin opens the bag and pulls out a bony, mangy cat with a length of twine tied around its neck. The cat tries desperately to break loose, but unsuccessfully, because the boy is holding the piece of twine tight. Tettè is standing up now, one hand resting on the dog's head.

Amedeo offers the cat one of the poisoned morsels. The cat sniffs at it and then turns away. The boy snickers, then gestures to Saverio to help him. Cristiano is standing with his arms crossed, glowering, away from the rest of the group but on the opposite side of the boys from Tettè and the dog. In the distance they hear the sound of an automobile coming closer, then whizzing past without slowing down.

Saverio holds the cat's head and pries open the mouth; Amedeo force-feeds the animal the poisoned morsel. Then they put it down on the ground and take a few steps back, still holding the cat by the twine leash tied around its neck.

The cat takes two steps and then stiffens; it goes on walking, legs extended, comically, like a windup toy. Amedeo starts laughing, and all the others laugh with him, except for Tettè, who clutches the head of his immobile dog, and Cristiano, who looks away.

The cat slams to the ground and its whole body starts contorting, leaping belly-up. Amedeo, Saverio, and the twins are all laughing uncontrollably by now, slapping each other loudly on the back. A yellowish foam issues from the cat's mouth.

The convulsions go on for a minute, then cease. The cat gets up, dazed, takes a couple of steps toward the street, as if to make its escape, then its legs stiffen one last time and it slams into the pavement again. The boys start laughing again, until the animal, with one last horrible contraction, dies, its paws straight up in the air.

They all go on laughing for another couple of minutes, then they fall silent. In the distance, a woman is singing. There's another rumble of thunder, closer this time.

Amedeo tells Saverio to give him the other poisoned morsels, and then he turns to face Tettè. Filthy cacaglio, he says: bring that bag of fleas that follows you everywhere over here, right now.

Tettè looks at him and tries pleading with him with his eyes; no, he wants to say, please, he's not like the cat, he's my friend. He's the only friend I have. Tettè wants to say to him: I talk to him, you know, and he listens to me. He talks to me, too, and I understand what he tells me. The dog knows the way I pet him, he licks my hand, we share everything we find that's good to eat, when the rest of you force me to give you my meals.

That's what he'd say, if he could speak; if the serpent hadn't slithered up from his belly, and weren't trying to suffocate him from within.

Tettè would try to say something, but all that would come out would be a single guttural consonant, and everyone would laugh at him and do just as they pleased, like always. But not this time. This time Tettè has to stop them.

He looks around in desperation; there's no one going by. Saverio starts walking over to him, but Amedeo stops him: no, he says. He has to bring the dog here to me, with his own two hands; and he has to give it the poison pellets, he has to feed them to that bag of fleas, otherwise it'll bite us. Get moving, you fool of a cacaglio, hurry up; we need to get this out of the way before it starts raining.

Tettè looks at Cristiano, begging him with his eyes. But Cristiano turns his gaze away, and starts studying the night sky over the forest.

But then he intervenes, saying: come on, cut it out. The dog might bite your hand in its death throes, or piss on you. Amedeo turns to look at him, and asks if he'd like a good hard kick in the ass. No, wait, let's do this instead, he says: cacaglio, if you don't bring us the dog and feed it the poison, then you have to eat it. That's what I've decided: either the dog dies, or you die.

That way we'll see what kind of sound a cacaglio *makes when he eats poison. If you ask me, he says, he'd be harder to understand than the cat.*

They all start laughing again, except for Tettè and Cristiano.

Cristiano turns and speaks to Tettè: come on, cacaglio, *don't be more of a fool than you already are. Give the poison to that damned useless dog, and let's go home before it starts raining.*

Once it becomes clear to Tettè that no one is going to defend him, he drives the dog away with a kick. The dog, surprised and hurt, yelps and runs off, just ten feet or so. Then Tettè picks up a rock and throws it at the dog, and it turns and trots away along the wall, heading in the direction of Santa Maria del Soccorso.

Tettè turns to face Amedeo, and he glares at him with a light of defiance in his eyes. He can't speak, because the serpent is suffocating him, but he looks him in the eye all the same.

Amedeo looks around and says: then you'll have to eat them, you filthy cacaglio. *You'll have to eat the poisoned morsels.*

You, or your damned dog.

XLV

Dragging his feet loudly on the floor, Nanni entered the church through the sacristy door, a scrub brush in one hand and a metal bucket full of water in the other. As he walked along he looked at the floor and muttered to himself, his forehead creased, his shoulders bowed.

When he reached the corner at the far end of the nave, near the main entrance that let out onto the street, he noticed a man standing in the shadows, his hands in his pockets, his hair dangling over his forehead. He noticed him because he saw his eyes shining in the dark, like the eyes of a cat. Green eyes.

"You're the sexton, aren't you? Nanni, that's what they call you. I need to talk to you; come outside with me."

Nanni recognized him: it was that police commissario who kept asking about the *cacaglio* child. The sexton took fright: the policeman's face was pale, with purplish circles under his eyes. It looked like *he* was dead.

"Who do you want, Don Antonio? Is that who you want to talk to? I'll go and get him for you, he's resting just now, he has Mass in two hours."

The dead man shook his head.

"No, I don't want to talk to Don Antonio. You're the one I want to talk to. Come outside with me, I said."

His tone was cold, emotionless. Nanni felt uncomfortable. That man was scaring him more and more.

Outside there was a damp chill in the air. The temperature had dropped even lower, and heavy clouds were gathering, portending another night of rain. It seemed like the rain would never end. They stopped just outside the church, on the steps, under the overhanging wooden shed roof that kept the entrance dry.

Ricciardi got straight to the point:

"Listen closely, because I have no time to waste. I need information about Tettè's life, what he did here and who he saw."

Nanni laughed nervously, a high-pitched titter.

"Those aren't things you should be asking *me* about. I'm just the sexton, I see no one and nobody talks to me. You ought to ask Don Antonio; he's the one who spends the most time with the boys. I don't know anything."

Ricciardi's face was a mask.

"I told you I don't have any time to waste. I've already talked to the priest: now I'm talking to you. In fact, the priest doesn't need to know anything about what we're discussing right now. Nothing at all."

Nanni dragged his feet back and forth on the ground, more anxious than ever.

"Commissa', forgive me, try to understand: I can't . . . Don Antonio gives me work, surely you understand that . . . "

Ricciardi spoke in the same tone of voice, whispering as if they were still inside the church, so that Nanni had to strain to hear what he was saying:

"I must not have made myself clear. Don Antonio may give you work, but I'm keeping you out of jail. You just try keeping the things I want to know to yourself, and tonight you'll be sleeping next to twenty people, all of them worse than you, and eager to get to know you. Take your pick."

Nanni tittered again, as if he'd just been told a funny joke.

"Me, in jail? Why on earth would I go to jail, if I haven't done anything wrong?"

"Nothing wrong, eh? I can file three criminal complaints

immediately, from women you've molested when you were drunk. Or men, if it comes to that. These days, we don't need a guilty verdict: it's enough to spread a rumor. Even if you got out of jail the next day, you'd never work again, and certainly not in a place like this. And you'd find yourself face-to-face with a nice squad of jackbooted enforcers, who'd beat you to death to help keep the streets safe. So what'll it be?"

The sexton ran his tongue over his chapped lips, looking around as if in search of help. He was in a transitory state of sobriety and knew that the commissario was right: if he felt like it, he could toss Nanni into a world of trouble.

"What do you want to know, Commissa'?"

"You just need to tell me what you know. I want to know anything and everything that Tettè did that was different from the other boys, no matter what it was, even things that seem unimportant. And fast."

Nanni ran his tongue over his lips again: evidently a habit with him, and an especially disgusting one.

"The *cacaglio* . . . the child was good, he never did anything wrong. But the others picked on him, they made fun of him because he was a *cacaglio*. They played pranks on him."

"I know all about that. Go on."

"He was the favorite of one of the two ladies, the younger one. She'd given him a new suit of clothes. Don Antonio put the clothes away in a little cabinet. He kept it locked, and we only got them out when the child was going on an outing with her. The signora was fixated on him. She petted him, she kissed him. I don't understand: why didn't she just have a child of her own?"

Ricciardi let the comment go unacknowledged.

"That's not what interests me, and it's none of your business, either. Go on."

"The priest, Don Antonio, he exploited this thing, this fixation of the signora's. Because she's rich, very rich, and when

Don Antonio smells money, he grabs on to it and never lets go. Every time she'd talk to us, she'd say, the child needs this, the child needs that, and she'd give us money. One time, she even gave me a gift, when the boy had a fever, to make sure I'd keep an eye on him and give him his medicine."

Ricciardi was so keenly focused on every word that he didn't even blink.

"How did Don Antonio act with him? How did he treat the boy?"

Nanni waved his hand.

"That Don Antonio only cares about money. He doesn't care about the children at all. To him the *cacaglio* was just another kid; if you ask me, he barely knows one from the other. But the child was his way of getting money, so he punished him a little less. Only when it was necessary; otherwise the others would have killed the *cacaglio* out of envy."

"Why, if he punished Tettè the others wouldn't envy him? They wouldn't envy what the signora did for him, the gifts and the outings: didn't they envy him for that?"

"Of course they did; but it worked out well enough for them, because he'd always bring back something for them, too. Now that the *cacaglio*'s dead, they don't get any more treats."

That must have struck the sexton as funny, because he started tittering again. Ricciardi's icy glare shut him up immediately.

"Now I want you to tell me something else. I need you to talk to me about the man with the limp, the man who came to see Tettè."

A silence fell between them, as cold as the air that surrounded them. Nanni looked at Ricciardi, afraid to breathe, his eyes open wide. How could that damned policeman know about the man with the limp? Who could he have talked to, if the *cacaglio* was dead and he himself hadn't told a soul? He tried to stall for time.

"What are you talking about, Commissa'? I don't understand."

Ricciardi said nothing. Then he said, all in one breath:

"Very well then. Then let's go get your things. You're coming with me."

The sexton turned pale and staggered, as if he'd been slapped.

"Commissa', I beg you, don't ruin me. I wouldn't know where to go, if they kicked me out of here."

"Then don't make them kick you out. All you have to do is tell me everything you know about the man with the limp. This second."

The man looked down at the ground. His tongue darted first in one direction, then in the other over his lips.

"Ten days or so before the . . . death of the *cacaglio*, this man stopped me, just outside the church. A gentleman, well dressed, with a walking stick with a handle made of bone. He gave me money to bring the child to him."

"Which child? Tettè in particular, or just any child?"

"No, that one, the *cacaglio*. I thought that . . . sometimes it happens that a gentleman, or even a lady, sees a boy and wants him. They say it's just to do a little work around the house; I don't believe them, but what does it matter to me? If they give the boys gifts, money, and there's a little something in it for me, then everyone wins, right? I just thought that it was the same thing with the *cacaglio*. I brought the *cacaglio* to meet the man with the walking stick. But I never heard anything more about it."

Ricciardi realized that rarely in his life had he been in the presence of anyone slimier and more repugnant than the sexton.

"How many times did you arrange for them to meet? How many times did Tettè see the man with the walking stick?"

Nanni concentrated, trying to remember.

"Three, four times, as far as I know. No more. Then he died."

Then he died. Ricciardi shivered. He was increasingly finding the dead less frightening than the living. The man was disgusting, but he didn't seem to have the courage to actually hurt anyone.

It was becoming more and more important to find out who the man with the limp was, and what he wanted from Tettè.

He turned on his heel and walked off, leaving the sexton standing on the church steps, filled with new fears. As for him, he was even more baffled than before.

XLVI

Maione tracked down Cosimo the *saponaro* late that afternoon, after asking around a little in order to reconstruct his route. It wasn't very hard; he was a fairly well-known local character.

He caught up with him outside an upper-class apartment building, over Montecalvario, addressing a little crowd of half a dozen women. He watched Cosimo from a distance for a while, without making his presence known. The junk seller's whole manner was contrived and affected: he gesticulated wildly to emphasize the nonsense he was spouting; he was wearing an ancient, tattered frock coat, with a crooked, slightly dented top hat; he displayed his wares as if they were fine jewelry; and somehow he managed to come across as attractive rather than ridiculous. Maione thought once again that he lived in a city of actors.

He waited until nearly all the women had left, many of them carrying something, a saucepan or a rag. One woman stayed behind, and Cosimo grew confidential; he took a quick look around, then furtively pulled open a secret compartment in his handcart and extracted a bundle, which he unwrapped. A metal object of some kind emerged, perhaps a piece of silverware. It gleamed in the grayish light. Maione chose that moment to step forward.

"Good evening. What are we talking about, over here?"

At the sight of the brigadier, the good-looking young woman's eyes opened wide.

"Oh, *buona sera*, Brigadie'. You'll forgive me, I was just about to leave; my signora wants dinner served early tonight. *Arrivederci*, Cosimo. I'll see you the next time you come through."

The junk seller was conflicted between his desire to complete the transaction, which he felt sure he was about to close, and his fear of the cop. After a second's hesitation, his fear won out decisively.

"My good Brigadier, what an honor! I was just passing the time of day with this lovely young *signorina* at the end of my rounds, to finish the day with a face that's so easy on the eyes. But now, as you yourself just pointed out, it's evening, time for weary workers to rest their bones, and so I think I too had better be going; it's been a long, hard day. If you'll excuse me, then . . . "

Maione stared at him, his hands in his pockets.

"Not so fast, Cosimo Capone. I have a feeling your weary bones aren't going to get to rest just yet. First we need to have a little conversation."

The junk seller's mind registered the fact that the oversized brigadier, whom he had never met, seemed to know him very well, first name and last. A long shiver ran down his back, and the dampness in the air had nothing to do with it.

"Have we met, Brigadie'? I don't remember being introduced, but such a notable and important personage as yourself would certainly have stuck in my memory. I guess I'm just getting old, is all."

Maione smiled satanically.

"I know you, and that's all that matters, Capone. I know you and I know your sort. That's my line of work, people like you: the same way you work with copper pots and washerwomen."

Capone put on a baffled expression.

"Brigadier, I don't know what you mean. I'm a hardworking man who spends all day on the job, pushing this handcart all over Naples, just to get a crust of bread to eat. I have a family to feed, up on the Vomero. What are you talking about?"

"I also have a family to feed. Everyone has one. And they feed theirs without slipping their sticky fingers into other people's possessions."

A scandalized expression appeared on the junk seller's face.

"I don't know what infamous wretch told you that, but it's a lie! I swear on my honor, Brigadie', that I've never dreamed of stealing a thing! I've been accused in the past, but all due to the malevolent envy of some son of a good woman bent on destroying my reputation. I'll let you speak to my customers, all good women who love me dearly and have been buying from me for years, and they'll tell you . . . "

Maione broke in with a curt wave of the hand.

"Capone, you can't charm your way out of this one: you're a burglar and a thief. And the worst kind, too, because you don't look like a thief. I have a certain respect for thieves who creep out at night, with their jimmies, dressed in black. We catch them and we throw them in a cell; it's our job to be policemen, and it's their job to be thieves. They don't deny what they've done, and once we've cornered them, they resign themselves and come along quietly. They're proper thieves. It's their profession. Thieves like you, on the other hand, will be the ruin of this city. You pretend to be honest but you're rotten to the core."

Capone was starting to get genuinely scared.

"Brigadie', I don't understand. Why are you saying these things to me? What are you accusing me of?"

Maione shrugged.

"I could easily find a reason to lock you up. And I wouldn't rule out the possibility that, once I'm done with the case I'm on now, I might come pay a little call on you and search this handcart thoroughly."

278 · MAURIZIO DE GIOVANNI

He landed a kick at the approximate location of the compartment from which the junk seller had pulled out the bundle
to show the young woman. A rattling of metal came from
inside. Capone's face turned white, and he tried his luck, playing the wrong card entirely:

"Brigadie', don't ruin me. I'm a father, with a family to provide for. I have some valuable merchandise in there; let's just
do this, I'll give you half and you . . . you can return it to the
rightful owners on my behalf. And we'll each go our own way."

At first Maione couldn't believe his own ears. That half-man
was trying to bribe him! He shut his eyes tight and counted to
ten. Then he reached out his hand and grabbed Capone's arm
in a vise grip. The man emitted a cry of surprise and pain.

"Listen up and listen good, you useless bag of bones: I'll
break every bone in your body and then I'll throw you in jail,
and I'll just say you resisted arrest. A lie for a lie, that seems
like a fair trade. You aren't even worthy of looking me in the
face, you know that? Much less doing business with me."

The junk seller started stammering:

"But . . . but . . . B-Brigadie', what on earth did you think I
meant? I would never dare . . . Let me go, you're breaking my
arm!"

Maione loosened his grip and heaved a deep sigh. Then he
resumed his relaxed tone of voice.

"All right, let's get this over with, since it disgusts me to
have to talk to you. I'm not interested in you; you're practically
worthless. What I want is information about the boy, and it'll
go better with you if you tell me what I want to know, and right
away."

Capone looked thunderstruck.

"The boy? What boy?"

"Tettè, the boy from Santa Maria del Soccorso. The little
boy you used to take on your rounds, the one who died."

The junk seller was now completely confused; it was getting

dark and that enormous brigadier seemed to be out of his mind, and he was really scaring him.

"Certainly! That boy was like a son to me. He used to help me out, I was teaching him the business, and . . . "

Again, the vise grip.

"Capo', do you still think you can go on pulling my leg? I told you I want the truth! I know what you were doing, I know what you were using that poor child to do, that you sent him into people's apartments to steal while you distracted your little audience of idiot housewives with your gift of gab. I know everything."

Cosimo felt like he'd fallen into a nightmare.

"But if you already know everything, what do you want from me? I'll say I'm sorry, I'll promise I'll never do it again! If you'll let me go . . . "

"First, you have to tell me about the little boy. Everything you know about him, everything you did to him."

The junk seller stiffened in terror.

"What is it you think I've done, Brigadie'? I absolutely refuse to stand by while you think this horrible thing! Besides, I heard that the boy ate poison—I had nothing to do with it!"

Maione looked at him gravely.

"Go on. I want to know what this child was like. And don't try telling me that he was like a son to you, because fathers don't send their sons out to steal."

By now Capone had finally gotten it through his head that he needed to tell it straight, and do his best to shorten this nightmare:

"He was just a boy, Brigadie'. A boy, like thousands of other little boys, living on the streets. He never talked, and when he tried, he stuttered; but he was small, and he melted women's hearts, so he came in handy to me. I . . . I told him that if he told anyone anything about what we did, I'd hurt him, but I never would have, never. After all, it was hardly in my interest, was it? After I'd taught him how to do what . . . how to do what he did, why should I get rid of him?"

Maione was disgusted, but inclined to believe him.

"Tell me about the last few days. When did you last see him? Did you notice anything strange or unusual? Did you see anyone with him? Talk!"

"No, Brigadie', I haven't seen the boy since Thursday. I just assumed he'd gotten sick, he was so skinny, so weak, it always looked as if he was about to fall to the ground, or blow away with the breeze. I didn't know what had become of him, and I didn't go looking for him because I didn't have time. Then, the day before yesterday, his friend, Cristiano, the other boy from the parish, comes around, and he tells me that Tettè is dead and asks if I can take him to work in his place. That's how I found out he was dead. And there was never anyone with him, just that bastard dog that used to follow him everywhere. That's all I know, I swear it!"

The brigadier looked at him long and hard. He wanted to make sure that his contempt seeped into the man's soul and stayed with him, like a threat: if he found out that the man had lied to him, if he and the man crossed paths again, if he ever heard that the man had stolen or burgled or mistreated another living soul, that would be the end of him. Capone understood, and looked down.

"I can track you down, Capone. The same way I found you just now, I can track you down whenever I want. Remember that. And you'd better just pray to God that you haven't lied to me."

The junk seller looked up again.

"I didn't lie to you, Brigadie'. It's one thing to steal, it's another thing to murder, or to let someone be murdered. I don't know anything about what happened to the child; and I wouldn't even know who to ask. I told you, he was just a child like so many other children, living on the street."

On his way back to police headquarters, Maione couldn't seem to get the *saponaro*'s last words out of his head: a child like so many other children, living on the street. With a shiver, he realized that he'd thought the same thing, when he couldn't seem to figure out the reason for Ricciardi's fixation on this death.

The thought terrified him: a child like so many other children. What if he, Maione, had died the same way his son Luca died, his son the policeman, stabbed to death by a criminal? Then would his children, his sons and daughters, have wound up like that, "like so many other children, living on the street"?

Once again, he thought, the commissario had been right. Children living on the street were somebody's children; in fact, they were everybody's children. And he, Maione, was ashamed not to have seen that right from the start. You can't write off a child's life with a couple of words in a police report. You have to understand it. And as their investigations had shown, some strange, dark things had happened in Tettè's short life.

As Maione went by the corner of Via della Tofa, where he'd found Ricciardi waiting for him that morning, he heard a faint whistle and instinctively turned around. Bambinella was waiting for him in the shadows, with a handkerchief on her head and wrapped in an overcoat that had been patched and repatched, mended and remended.

"Bambine', is that you? What are you doing here? Is something the matter?"

Bambinella the *femminiello* had a serious expression on her face that Maione had never seen before, with deep creases at the corners of her mouth.

"Good evening, Brigadie'. I need to talk to you."

XLVII

S ignora? Signo', well, which one will it be?"

Livia shook herself out of her thoughts and for what seemed like the hundredth time tried to focus on the two dresses that the seamstress was showing her. This seamstress had been recommended to her by a new Neapolitan friend, the Marchesa De Luca di Roccatagliata. She was happy with the two samples, but she couldn't quite make up her mind as to which one she liked best.

But her mind was wandering chaotically, returning repeatedly to the rain-streaked window. The few words she'd managed to pry out of Maione had put her in a state of anxiety and alarm for Ricciardi, especially concerning his relationship with Dr. Modo, a subject of special interest to the secret police.

She'd gone to police headquarters specifically to let Ricciardi know, without saying it in so many words, that seeing the doctor socially could expose him to a very serious risk: it took next to nothing, these days, to find yourself shipped off to internal exile.

But then Maione had spoken to her of the dead boy, and this, too, had gone straight to her heart. She'd been a mother herself, if only for a short time, because her baby boy had sickened and died. The fact that a man could become so passionately involved in finding out the reasons for the death of a little orphan boy only increased her interest in Ricciardi, if such a thing was possible.

From the street below, along with the sounds of the pouring rain and passing cars, came the cheerful yells of the *scugnizzi* splashing in puddles. Anyone who feels love for children
has a great deal of love to offer, she decided. She smiled at the
seamstress.

"They're lovely, just beautiful; I'll take them both."

In the same little café where he had met with Ricciardi earlier, Maione was sitting with Bambinella, who was warming her
hands around a cup of tea. The expression on his informant's
face worried him: Bambinella was usually all smiles, playful
and affectionate in a vulgar fashion, given to rough humor and
teasing; now she was serious, grim, pensive.

"Well, then, Bambine': What's going on, will you tell me?
You're always telling me how dangerous it is for us to meet out
in the open, and now I actually find you standing on the street
corner by police headquarters saying you want to talk to me?"

Bambinella set down her teacup and picked up a napkin
with her long fingers, her polished nails.

"Brigadie', it's about the death of the child, the little boy
from Santa Maria del Soccorso. I heard something and, since
it struck me as an interesting piece of information, I came to
tell you about it. Did I do wrong?"

"No, no, you did right. It's just that you have a face . . . well,
not the usual ugly face I'm used to seeing on you."

Bambinella grimaced.

"I know, I just left the house the way I was, without even
touching up my makeup. But if a girl is pretty, she's pretty no
matter what, Brigadie'."

Maione smiled.

"Exactly—if a girl is pretty. So tell me all about it: What did
you find out?"

"All right, Brigadie', listen carefully: This morning that
client of mine came by, the *verdummaio*, the strolling vendor

who told me that he'd seen the boy with that well-dressed man, the man with the limp, you remember?"

Maione nodded.

"Go on."

"Well, he'd already told me that he'd had the impression that the man and the little boy were having an argument, and that the man with the limp was holding him by the arm and rousting him, shaking him a little, in other words. He'd even thought about stepping in, because it seemed to him that the little boy needed help."

"Yes, you already told me about that. So?"

Bambinella went on patiently:

"Well, today he told me that he'd seen him again, the man with the limp. He'd seen him come out of an apartment building, in Via Santa Lucia, number twelve; and he asked just who that gentleman was. The doorman, who was a friend of his, told him that the man lived there, and that his name is Sersale, Edoardo Sersale. He's a nobleman, and he comes from some venerable family or other, my client didn't really understand that part. The name rang a bell for me, and after the *verdummaio* left, I went down and talked to a girlfriend of mine who works in a bordello in Via Torretta."

Maione spread his arms wide.

"I don't know what to say, you have a girlfriend working in every single corner of this city, as long as the place is sufficiently filthy and disgusting. Whorehouses, taverns, gambling dens, you name it."

Bambinella nodded.

"It's true, Brigadie'. And it's a good thing, too, because as always I'd remembered correctly: my girlfriend had told me about one of their customers who was really hooked on one of the girls. I know her by sight, too; she's pretty enough, but if you ask me she's just a bit vulgar, with a pair of tits like this, and a mouth . . ."

Maione interrupted her vehemently:

"Listen, do you really think that I should be sitting here with you, at the risk of having someone see me and making me look like a fool, and being mocked until the day I die, just so I can find out what kind of tits a whore who works at the bordello in Via Torretta has? Will you get to the point, yes or no?"

"You're right, you're right, Brigadie', forgive me; that's just the way I am, I get distracted. In short, this client of the friend of my girlfriend answers the description perfectly, the limp, well-dressed, and so on. So I asked this girlfriend of mine if she could arrange for me to talk to the girl, whose name I'm not going to tell you—sorry, but I swore on Our Lady the Madonna of Pompeii, and as you know I'm a very religious girl. Well, to make a long story short, the name matches. And this guy Sersale is in trouble, too. Big trouble."

Maione perked up his ears.

"What do you mean, in big trouble?"

"Well, he may be an aristocrat, but he's up to his ears in debt. He likes women, bordellos, and cards. He's gone through a fortune, and now he's in the hands of the loan sharks, and they've told him that if he doesn't pay up, every last cent, they're going to fix him good."

"What does that have to do with the little boy?"

"Ah, that I couldn't say, you'll have to find out for yourself. But the fact remains that the girl said her friend had changed completely in the past few days. He was laughing and giddy like he used to be; he seemed to be happy again. He told her that it wouldn't be long now until he expected to have all the money he needed to pay off his debts and straighten out his situation. And when the girl asked him how he expected to do that, he said: I've found the boy. That's all."

Maione was baffled.

"What's that supposed to mean: 'I've found the boy'? What

286 · MAURIZIO DE GIOVANNI

did he mean by that? Tettè was an orphan boy, he didn't even have food to eat, and in fact he was so hungry that he even gobbled down rat poison. What could he have given to a man like that?"

Bambinella shrugged her shoulders.

"That's something I couldn't say, Brigadie'. But my heart tells me that this bastard with a limp fits in with the death of that poor little child somehow, and that he's in it up to his neck."

Maione agreed.

"Whether or not he was involved, we'll certainly have to investigate him. *Grazie*, Bambine': you were right, this is very valuable information, and it needed to reach me right away. But can I ask you something? Why did you do it? Why did you go out hunting, all the way to Torretta in the rain and then here, to wait for me on the corner, knowing I might not come by here at all?"

Bambinella drank her last sip of tea and smiled sadly.

"Because I was a little orphan boy myself, Commissa'. No father, no mother, abandoned in the middle of this city's streets. I know it what it's like, when you're nothing; when it doesn't matter whether you live or die, and nobody gives a damn. I had to earn my living in scraps and mouthfuls of food, just like that poor creature you found dead at Capodimonte. Let's just say it was a flower I placed on that child's casket. A flower from Bambinella."

Enrica's hands flew over the bowls, plates, and utensils as she set the table for dinner. And the same way her hands were flying, her heart was soaring, high above the rain-dense clouds that were louring over the city.

She'd received another letter. Her father had handed it to her with a conspiratorial smile, having pulled it out of the mailbox with a rapid sleight of hand that his wife failed to see: a knowing smile that had made her turn red as a ripe tomato, until she managed to escape to her bedroom.

This time the tone was gentler, although it remained well within the bounds of discretion that she'd established with her own letter. Ricciardi apologized awkwardly for his shyness, which perhaps had been excessive, and had prevented him from stepping forward and speaking to her directly, as many other men surely would have done in his place.

She shouldn't doubt, however, that all his thoughts were focused on her: what he felt, and what he hoped one day to be able to tell her, was something very important (and here Enrica had been forced to stop reading, because her heart felt suddenly as if it were trying to leap out of her ears). It's just that he wasn't comfortable in this kind of situation, as he'd never experienced anything of the sort before.

He concluded the letter by saying that he sincerely hoped that she, too, thought about him from time to time, and that her thoughts resembled his own. He truly hoped so. And he closed by wishing her every good thing in the world, with all his heart.

Enrica couldn't remember ever being so happy in her life. Ever. Not even close.

She just hoped that she'd be able to put all her feelings into the letter she was about to write in response: she, too, would be more affectionate this time.

She wondered when he'd ask for a meeting.

XLVIII

The population of Gambrinus changed at the dinner hour.

The clients who came in for an aperitif, those who lingered over their afternoon chats, and others who met there for encounters more or less clandestine had all returned home by now, to punch the domestic time clock, and now sat around groaning dinner tables, carrying on uninteresting conversations with a bunch of strangers who bore their same surnames.

The evening clientele, which consisted of those who wanted to hear music played by live musicians rather than the tinny sounds emitted by the wooden box known as the radio, others who wished to exchange glances with those of the opposite sex and lay the foundations for future liaisons, and those who hoped to take advantage of the giddy atmosphere to establish profitable business relationships—this clientele had yet to arrive.

Dinnertime at Gambrinus was a no-man's-land. The same waiters and barmen were sharpening their tools of the trade for the evening, while calculating the day's profits and losses. They were starting to tot up the day's tips, repairing rips in their tailcoats, reknotting bowties that were sagging from the feverish pace of the afternoon rush. At the monumental cash register, the bell of the cash drawer was dinging a little less frantically, and there were fewer caps and top hats doffed at the entrance, as customers entering met others on their way out.

Even the smells changed at Gambrinus when the dinner hour arrived. As His Majesty King Coffee had reigned triumphant all morning and the scents of cooked tomatoes, mozzarella, and eggplants had wafted through the air at lunchtime, followed by those of pastries and savory treats in the long afternoon's rounds of vermouths and rosolios, now the aromas all blended together, with no one smell clearly victorious, none entirely vanquished, since they'd thoroughly seeped into the silk upholsteries and woven wall hangings that day, ready to take up the battle again the next.

At Gambrinus, sounds played their part, come the dinner hour. The cheerful piping melody of morning and the dreamy strains of afternoon had evolved, on the keyboard of the handsome concert grand piano, into quizzical arpeggios, a harmonic training session without any clear meaning. A babbling brook of musical notes, a drifting dust of falling stars surrounding the crystal fixtures, too delicate to make them vibrate, a music of expectation and faint regret.

The air was oddly clear, under the lights at Gambrinus, when the dinner hour came. Cigars and cigarettes were a lingering memory of the afternoon, when they had blended with the scent of the rain and the silvery sound of women laughing and little spoons stirring tea in teacups; they would come back over the course of the long night that lay ahead, serving as a misty backdrop to the whispered words and the sensual despairing tangos danced in the center of the room, surrounded by tables piled high with hungry eyes and sugary *sfogliatelle*. But at that hour, at the dinner hour, the light of the immense crystal chandeliers played over the gold and the silver of the walls and the counters, arriving intact, just as it was when it set out from the thousand tiny lightbulbs.

Dinnertime doesn't last long at Gambrinus: from the last glass of vermouth tossed off and left empty on the table to the first nighthawk who walks in and looks around in disap-

pointment, less than an hour will go by. But it will be a very
long hour.

Because it's the dinner hour.

Maione entered Gambrinus circumspectly, but there were
very few people: no inconvenient encounters to be feared.

A few tables were taken, of course; but then, it was a big
place. A woman sitting alone, her makeup slightly smeared, an
angry glare. An elderly man, the watery eyes of a drunk, every
once in a while an incongruous giggle. Two men with stiff
starched collars, intently eating dishes of something, never
once looking each other in the face. A couple, the man reading
a newspaper and the woman staring into the middle distance,
saying nothing. How dreary, thought the brigadier.

He saw Ricciardi sitting at his usual table, a steaming cup
on the table in front of him, his hands in his pockets and his
eyes gazing raptly out at the rain-slick street, striped with
bands of light from the streetlamps. He was frighteningly pale,
and now and then his lower lip quivered with a tremor.

"Commissa', you're not at all well; and these aren't nights
to spend out in the streets, if you're not well. You've got a raging fever, you can tell right away. Let me walk you home. Trust
me on this: if you're unwell, you're no good to anyone."

"Don't worry about me, I'm fine. I'm the kind of person
who just gets sicker if he tries to take care of himself. I ordered
you a *sfogliatella* and an espresso. But why don't you tell me
what you got up to today, and then I'll tell you about my day."

For more than half an hour, they exchanged information
about their reciprocal investigations. Ricciardi talked about
the sexton, without being able to conceal his revulsion at what
a disgusting individual he had proven to be; Maione talked
about Cristiano and his hard outer shell, so sad to see in a boy
so young, and about Cosimo and his grimy self-interest. Each
of the three prompted a potential theory of murder, in each of

the three a potential for violence lurked; but in none of the three did they see a likely poisoner.

Then the brigadier told the story of Bambinella lurking in wait for him, and the news that the *femminiello* had brought him about the man with the limp, a man who could now perhaps be pinned down to a Christian name and a surname and an address.

Maione shook his head in dismay.

"Commissa', none of this is leading anywhere, we're just spinning our wheels. Even as for the man with the limp, what solid evidence do we have? A confidential tip from one whore to another. And maybe the man's nothing but a pervert, in which case we can certainly go pick him up and throw him into jail, after pounding him black-and-blue, obviously."

Ricciardi still seemed dubious.

"But you tell me: Would someone who's in that much trouble—piled high with debts and loan sharks on his tail, desperately looking for money—really waste his time venting his passions on a little boy? And even if so, what would it have to do with his remark about having found the money he needed because he'd found the little boy? No, this theory about him being a pervert doesn't add up as far as I'm concerned."

"All right, then, let's go back to square one, Commissa': the theory of accidental death. The deeper we dig, the more disgusting the things we find, I agree with you. Horrible things, things that make you want to puke. Let me say it again: let's do a little cleaning. Let's throw the *saponaro*, the sexton, and the man with the limp in jail. We'll take a fine-toothed comb to the priest and see what we find, once Thunder Jaw leaves town, because till then they won't let us move an inch; in other words, let's really clean house. But the boy's death was an accident, God rest his soul in peace, and now he's an angel up in heaven. Let's leave him there."

Ricciardi fell silent. He looked out at the street; it was cold and rainy, but the dead *guappo* was still standing sentry, his heart pumping out blood as he repeated the same words: *Come on, I'd like to see you. I'd like to see if you have the nerve.* He thought to himself that that's the way things are: there they stand, firm and immutable; but there are some who see them, and others who don't.

He turned to look at Maione.

"Tomorrow's the Feast of All Saints, Raffaele. And the day after that is the Day of the Dead. You have two days off, why don't you stay home with your family. I thank you from the bottom of my heart for having kept me company in this crazy investigation that's probably—no, certainly—just another one of my misguided obsessions."

Maione studied the commissario's face.

"You're not well. First of all you've got a fever that could knock out a horse, and the weather's rotten, so if you insist on going out on the streets you're going to catch pneumonia. In the second place, I know you pretty well—no, I know you very well, and you're not capable of letting go of a case like this, not at this point. But do me a favor, Commissa': give yourself a rest. We don't have any hot leads; for now, unfortunately, this case is dead in the water. We've seen what we can see, and there's nothing more that we can do. Let's wait until Tuesday, and then we'll get back on the trail."

Ricciardi half smiled.

"Yes, I doubt there's anything else we can do. Don't worry."

That wasn't enough to placate Maione.

"No, you have to promise me, Commissa'. Otherwise, I'm not letting you leave Gambrinus. No initiatives, no contacts until you and I see each other again. You know that if I go with you, it's better for everyone involved. Please, do me this favor and put my mind at ease. You know that at my age worrying can be bad for the health."

Ricciardi shook his head.

"I never make promises; you know that. But I will tell you, one last time, don't worry, because there's really nothing left to do for the time being. I'll wait for you. Now, you go home, and I'll take an aspirin and get to bed."

The whole way home, shaking with fever and a headache that was rapidly becoming intolerable, Ricciardi thought of Enrica. He thought about her as a refuge from the torment of seeing the image of the dead boy in his mind, and the sexton running his tongue over his lips, and Bambinella talking to Maione about the man with the limp, and the junk seller with the silver hidden in his handcart.

A thousand tiny details, some connected, others isolated, and an overall picture that refused to coalesce.

When he walked through the main entrance of his building, he turned to look behind him, and there was the dog, patiently watching him through the rain, which had once again started to fall.

XLIX

A rainy Sunday is a whole other thing.

It puts you in touch with things you'd forgotten, things you'd rather not think about. It keeps you from diving out into the streets, into the crowds, prevents you from intoxicating yourself with color and light, from being pushed aside by fat nannies in the public gardens or young couples in the cafés in the Galleria. A rainy Sunday will keep you from going to fill your lungs with salt air, listening to the cries of the fishermen as they call their wares, inviting you to buy the fish they caught last night.

A rainy Sunday shuts all the doors. It filters light through the slats in the shutters, it dampens the walls and floors, it makes its way into your soul, rising through your feet and clutching your heart in its fist. A rainy Sunday knows how to toy with hope and loneliness.

A rainy Sunday will make you want something different, whatever is it you don't have. It'll make you look out the rain-streaked windows and everything you see will become distorted, altered. A rainy Sunday even denies you a view of the outside world, with which you could fill your long hours deprived of strolls and encounters with other people.

If you're an old physician with war wounds carved into your soul, a rainy Sunday will find you already awake when day dawns. You'll get out of bed and shuffle around in your slippers, wandering through the rooms of an apartment that's too large for you, chilly drafts making you shiver in your nightshirt, heavy socks on your feet. You'll sit and smoke, looking your age-old loneliness in the face, without shame but with plenty of fear; contemplating the dark future you may never even have. You'll think of the long-ago fogs and rains of your childhood and youth, filled with games, devoid of frustrations; and perhaps you'll decide to go ahead and get dressed and go to the hospital, even though it's not your shift. Because the sick and their suffering are all you have left.

A rainy Sunday has its weapons.

If you're a young woman in love, you can't wait for something to happen, but a rainy Sunday makes time stand still, in a void that seems to stretch out into infinity. You'll read and reread a letter, comparing it with the hopes you secretly harbor, and the cold gray light filtering in through the windows will make you fear the worst. You'll make lunch with remote, distant gestures, and your family will sense your inexplicable agitation and they'll look at you with worry or annoyance. You won't even notice them, as you return over and over to the window like a fish staring through the plate glass of an aquarium, fearing and dreaming of a world in which you might no longer be able to breathe.

A rainy Sunday is ridden with fears.

If you're a woman in a man's body, perhaps you'll spend the day lacquering your nails, removing every single hair from your body. You'll feel a burst of rage over the fact that you can't go out in a summery flower-print dress, to shout to the world that you're strong and beautiful, in defiance of nature, which refused to listen to you. Perhaps you'll think back to how you were as a child, on the streets, rejected and mocked, humiliated by the very same men who now come to you begging and panting like hungry dogs. Some will come furtively to call on you, drenched with rain, eager and out of breath, and they'll

look around when they come in and again when they leave, in
fear of being seen; but you don't care, because that, too, is love,
and if it pilfers a few moments now, eventually it will return
them to you.

A rainy Sunday gives strange gifts.

If you're a beautiful woman from another town, you'll look
out on your unfamiliar new city in the pouring rain. You'll
think to yourself that for the land of sunshine, it certainly rains
a lot here. But even the rain is different, gusts of rain alternating with shafts of light filled with music. You'll decide to go
out anyway, and you'll drive around in your car through the
empty streets, enjoying the silent *palazzi* overlooking the sea,
the froth of the waves washing up onto the streets, the air
charged with electricity. You'll think to yourself that you want
a man, when at the café a dozen eager hands reach out to light
your cigarette and a dozen doting smiles leave the other ladies
glowering with envy; but the man you want isn't here, and your
mind can only cultivate one hope at a time.

A rainy Sunday narrows your field of vision.

If you're a brigadier on your day off, you'll laze in bed for a
change, while the rain hammers at the shutters. You'll make
love to your wife in the morning, without haste, losing yourself
in the blonde hair and light blue eyes and soft skin of the
woman you've loved, you love now, and you'll always love,
unflaggingly, until the light leaves your eyes. And later you'll
welcome five little pixies into your bed, while she prepares
breakfast, and you'll tell all those wide-eyed little ones about
the dazzling adventures of the heroic policeman who arrests
bad guys. And maybe you'll have a thought for someone who's
gone away, and you'll send him a tear and a smile, reminding
him that in your heart, the heart of a father, there's a big, beautiful, light-filled room just for him, and there always will be.

A rainy Sunday has plenty of guests.

If you're an aging *tata* filled with aches and pains, you'll watch your *signorino* getting dressed to go out, even if today is Sunday, even if today is the Feast of All Saints, even if today it's raining cats and dogs. And you'll protest, you'll complain, but you'll be ignored. He never listens to you. You'll look into his eyes glistening with fever, you'll listen to his dry cough. You'll feel the anguish of no longer being up to the task, your fear of his pain. You'll pin your hopes on the fact that you've seen him write when he thinks you're not looking, the fact that he keeps a folded, rumpled scrap of paper in his inside jacket pocket. Close to his heart.

A rainy Sunday has a few shreds of hope, amidst the loneliness.

Ricciardi was walking, and his footsteps echoed as if it were late at night, even though it was early morning. The rain was keeping people indoors that autumn Sunday.

He would gladly have stayed home himself that day, within the comfort of four thick walls. He was a wreck, his throat was on fire, his head felt like it was wrapped in cotton balls; but he knew that he couldn't rest until he had figured out who the man with the limp was, and what part he had played in the last days of Tettè's life.

The sexton had been nothing but a middleman. The other boys couldn't possibly know anything about the man with the limp, and in any case it would be difficult if not impossible to pry any information out of them. Don Antonio certainly knew nothing about him, besides which Ricciardi could no longer talk to him after that letter from the Curia. There was only one person left in whom the child might have confided.

The doorman of the building on Via Toledo was quite mistrustful: that bizarre individual who had come in from the rain, without a hat, his green eyes shining with fever, struck him as far too odd to be given easy access to his masters, on a Sunday morning, no less. He was just telling the man to come some other day because the signora wasn't in when none other than the signora called him on the interphone, ordering him to send up that strange visitor.

Ricciardi walked up a flight of stairs and found Carmen waiting for him at the door to her apartment, with a maid ready to relieve him of his overcoat.

"Commissario, *prego*, come right in. Luckily I saw you from the window, otherwise that hellhound of a doorman, Alberto, would have turned you away, without even asking me. I'll have to have a talk with him, one of these days."

Ricciardi followed her through a succession of rooms until they reached a parlor lit by a large crystal chandelier. The apartment was large and opulent, full of carpets, tapestries, and old paintings. It emanated a solid prosperity, the feel of a fortune dating back generations and rendered stable by its successive heirs. The decorations, statues, and even the furniture spoke of travel to exotic lands and exquisite tastes.

Carmen followed Ricciardi's gaze.

"The money isn't mine, Commissario. It comes from my husband's side of the family, as I told you the last time we spoke. And this place, all the other houses, all this wealth ends here, with us. Because of my infertility."

The commissario looked at her. Her grief didn't seem to have left her, though it might have passed from the phase in which it rages like a stormy sea shrieking in the soul to a dull background noise. Her delicate face was reddened and worn, crisscrossed with lines from crying; there were dark circles under her eyes, and her slender fingers never seemed to stop picking at her handkerchief. She was wearing a black dress, identical in every way to the dress she wore to the child's funeral, or perhaps it was one and the same.

"I can't stop thinking about it, Commissario. It's like a knot, right here in my chest, and it hurts every time I breathe. I hadn't realized myself just what that child meant to me. Even though I saw him only two or three times a week, the thought of being with him gave me a strength I'll never have again. What will I do now?"

She sighed and stared into empty space. Ricciardi again felt an acute sense of sympathy for that immense loneliness. The woman was all alone, surrounded by her wealth, far more so than poor Tettè had been in his life of poverty and despair, a life that lasted little more than the space of one breath.

"Signora, I didn't mean to intrude. I realize how hard all this is for you."

Carmen looked up.

"I've thought a great deal about what you told me, Commissario. You're right: I should have brought Tettè to live with me. I should have overcome my fears, my pettiness. I should have given him the life and the well-being that you're supposed to provide for your children, because that's what he had become for me: the son that God wouldn't let me create. I was afraid, and now I've been punished. But the punishment was too harsh."

Ricciardi tried to comfort her:

"No, you mustn't think that. You should blame the streets for Tettè's death, the general neglect of these unfortunate creatures. We should blame our general indifference for Tettè's death, not yours; after all, you were the only one who even felt the urge to go to his aid."

The woman shook her head.

"No, Commissario. Unfortunately, it's not that simple. I might have started out with that intention, but in time Tettè became something else for me, something different, something deeper. I was interested in him, not the other boys, not all the poor children who live on the street. And I'll never be able to forgive myself for leaving him alone, to die."

"Why are you tormenting yourself, Signora? Why are you accusing yourself of cowardice?"

Carmen stood up.

"Come with me, Commissario. I want to show you something."

Ricciardi followed the woman down a long hallway and then up a flight of stairs. At the top of the stairway was a door. A male nurse in a white lab coat sat reading a newspaper; the second he saw the signora he got to his feet.

"No, no, stay seated. I just wanted to show the commissario something. Open the peephole."

In the center of the door there was a small, hinged panel, with a knob so it could be pulled open. The man took a quick look, then stepped aside. Carmen stood looking for a long moment, then made way for Ricciardi, with a sorrowful look on her face. And he looked in.

The room was shrouded in dim light; windowless, it was illuminated only by a weak electric light set into the wall and protected by a metal grate. The only piece of furniture was a bed, in the middle of the room. A man was sitting on the mattress, dressed in a nightshirt.

His age was impossible to say, he could have been thirty or he could have been seventy. Sparse clumps of fading black hair covered his head. His eyes darted continuously over the walls, as if following the movements of nocturnal animals. From his constantly moving mouth dangled a streamer of drool, dripping onto his neck and his nightshirt. Through the peephole, which was covered with a pane of glass, he could hear a murmur, a stream of meaningless words. Carmen shut the little door.

The nurse said:

"He's already had breakfast and taken his medicine, Signora."

"How was his night?"

"Peaceful, for the most part. The day nurse, Stefano, will be here soon to take over. Do you need anything else, Signora?"

Carmen sadly shook her head, and gestured for Ricciardi to

follow her. When they were seated once again in the living room, the woman smiled bitterly and showed the commissario a photo in a silver frame.

"I should have said: I'd like to introduce you to my husband. This is what he looked like when we were married, and you've just seen what he looks like now. It's a disease of the nerves, and the doctors tell me that it might even be hereditary. Perhaps it's just as well that I'm infertile."

The photograph showed a smiling man, tall and handsome: nothing in common with the human vegetable in the room at the top of the stairs. He stood arm in arm with a younger, much happier Carmen, dressed in white.

"It wasn't that long ago, Commissario. But to me it seems like a century. I wanted to show him to you so that you could understand, at least to some extent, why I didn't bring Tettè home with me immediately, to live here. Nurses, medicines, locked doors. I thought, what kind of place is that for a small child? And yet if I hadn't raised these objections, he'd be alive today. But that's not the only thing that condemns me to this living hell. In truth, I was selfish, deeply selfish."

"Why, Signora?"

"My husband has relatives. Greedy souls, interested in him only for his wealth. If we were to adopt, that would have foiled their hopes of one day laying their hands on all that we now possess. They'd have done anything to prevent that from happening; and the last thing I wanted to do was to inflict upon my husband, in his present state, the pain of seeing his entire family turn against him. I preferred to give donations to Don Antonio, to provide Tettè with a little bit of welfare in this indirect manner. In other words, I was a coward. And now I'll never be able to forgive myself."

Ricciardi pitied the woman; but he couldn't comfort her. She was right: if he were in her position he'd have carried the burden of his own well-being on his conscience.

"Signora, forgive me: I came here to ask you something. From the information we've been able to gather in the past few days, we think that Tettè met with a man. Do you know anything about that?"

Carmen blinked in bafflement.

"A man? Tettè? No, I don't know anything about that. What man?"

Ricciardi did his best to be precise:

"Apparently he was a tall, well-dressed man, and he came into contact with the child through the sexton. This man is said to have seen Tettè at least two or three times in the week leading up to the child's death. He would visit with him outside the parish church, and I'm pretty sure that neither Don Antonio nor the other boys knew anything about it. I thought that perhaps Tettè might have mentioned it to you."

"No, absolutely not. I'm surprised; he told me everything. What was he like, this man?"

"I told you: tall, well-dressed; apparently, he walked with a limp, and he carried a walking stick."

Ricciardi observed the immediate change in Carmen's expression: she'd opened her eyes wide, and she'd raised her handkerchief to her mouth. Her other hand had suddenly clutched the arm of her chair, so hard that her knuckles were white.

"What are you saying, Commissario? Are you sure of this?"

"Yes, Signora. Other information, which we have yet to verify, suggests that the man lives on Via Santa Lucia. I intend to go there later today."

Carmen stood up. Her voice was quavering with agitation and grief.

"I know him, Commissario. I know who that man is!"

Ricciardi stood up in his turn, staring into the woman's face with an inquiring expression. She went on:

"He's my husband's half brother, Edoardo. His name is

Edoardo Sersale. And he hates me, he hates me with every bone in his body."

Carmen fell back into her chair, and burst into desperate sobs. Ricciardi waited for her crying to subside, then asked:

"Why would you think that it might be him, Signora? I have to tell you that the name also matches the information in our possession. I didn't want to tell you until I'd checked it out personally."

Carmen seemed to be crushed by her own thoughts.

"It's him: my poor mother-in-law's son by her second marriage. She died of a broken heart because of him. He swore to me that he would have his revenge. He'd asked me for money, since I administer my husband's fortune—after all, you've seen what condition the man is in. Edoardo is a dissolute wretch, wallowing in vices: easy women, gambling, horse races; all the sins a man can commit he has committed, and then some. I told him he'd had enough, giving him money was like throwing it down a well, there just was no end to it. And that's what he said to me: I'll take my revenge."

Ricciardi stared at the woman, baffled.

"What do you think he could have done? What did Tettè have to do with it?"

"Don't you see, Commissario? He hurt me by taking away the one thing I loved: my little boy. In a single fell swoop he eliminated the danger of adoption and took Tettè away from me. My God, Commissario . . . if it was him, then that means that the reason the child died . . . it was my fault! It was all my fault!"

Ricciardi stood staring at the sobbing woman as her shoulders shook, with no idea of what to say to console her.

Outside, the rain was covering everything: people and objects.

L

A s the churchgoers exit after Mass, Tettè looks up and scru-
tinizes the sky. It's not raining right now, but the ground
is wet and there are dark clouds in the sky overhead.

*What kind of day will this be? he wondered. Will I see my
angel? Perhaps she'll come and get me, even if she hasn't sent word
to Don Antonio; perhaps she'll just feel like seeing me, she'll come
and I'll be with her for an hour. We'll go for a ride in the car, and
I'll sit in the back as if she were my chauffeur. And she'll take me
to get something yummy, and I'll laugh, and she'll hug me tight.*

Like a mamma *with her child.*

*As he thinks these thoughts, he notices the dog, curled up at
the foot of the church steps. The moment the dog sees him it
leaps to its feet and wags its tail. Tettè throws his arms around
the dog, hastily, then heads for the corner to get out of sight. He
pulls a ball of bread out of his britches pocket, and he gives it to
the dog. The dog chews and swallows it almost instantly.*

*Suddenly the dog starts to snarl, looking up past Tettè's shoul-
ders. The boy spins around and finds himself looking into
Amedeo's eyes. They're dead eyes, expressionless. Tettè is terrified of those eyes.*

*Amedeo gestures with his head, and Tettè sees that behind
him are all the others, the twins, Saverio, and Cristiano. The
twins step forward and grab him, one by each arm. Saverio slips
a rope noose around the dog's face and head; it has a slipknot,*

and Saverio tightens it with a yank. The dog snarls louder and bites Saverio's hand, lightning quick: the hand starts bleeding. Saverio curses and hauls savagely on the rope. The dog's eyes bug out, and it starts to cough.

Amedeo shakes his head no, and lands a slap to Saverio's face. Saverio loosens the noose.

Amedeo turns and starts walking; behind him the twins drag Tettè along. The dog hesitates, then follows the little group obediently. The rope is loose, there's no need to pull him.

Cristiano turns to look at Tettè only once. There's fear in his eyes, too. Tettè wishes he could scream, but he can't: the serpent squeezes, and he can barely breathe.

The little procession continues along until the road opens out into a tiny piazza at the foot of a double staircase, not far from the food warehouse. No one's around. Angel, my angel, where are you?

Saverio brings the dog around in front of Tettè. The dog whines, just once, then settles back on its haunches. It waits. The twins loosen their grasp on Tettè's arms, without letting him go.

Amedeo says: it's time for breakfast, you filthy cacaglio. *Don't you remember that I promised you a nice breakfast? What did you think, that we'd make you something good to eat? Save', out with the breakfast.*

From the pocket of his old overcoat, a coat that falls almost to his feet, Saverio pulls out the poisoned morsels. Here you go, he says. Breakfast is served. They all start snickering, except for Cristiano. Amedeo dries his tears and, laughing again, says: well, you filthy cacaglio, *have you made up your mind? Who's going to eat this breakfast, you or that bastard bag of fleas? Come on, talk. Or can't you speak?*

Cristiano says: come on, Amede', why don't you drop it. This is something that's going to cost us, every one of us. Nothing good's going to come of it. We'll even lose what the cacaglio *brings us when the signora comes and takes him out.*

Amedeo replies: Cristia', shut up. I'm sick of you, too, you're afraid of your own shadow. Or do you like the cacaglio, *too? Have you turned into a faggot like the sexton? If you want, I've got a little morsel for you too. That way it'll look like there were two fools who didn't know these things were full of poison, instead of just one.*

Cristiano *falls silent and takes a step back. He looks down.* Tettè *on the other hand looks up at the sky and thinks, angel, angel of mine, forgive me, but I won't let them poison the dog. The dog's my friend, and I won't let them poison my friend.*

Just as he's about to say: me, I'll eat the breakfast, he hears a brusque cry: hey, guagliu', *what are you doing here? Why are you holding that little boy?*

They all turn toward the sound of the voice, and they see that a tall man is standing at the entrance to the piazza, wearing a stern expression. The man walks toward them, limping. He points his cane at Saverio *and says: untie that dog. Untie that dog immediately, and let it go.*

The boys exchange glances, uncertain what to do now. There are lots of them and only one of him, and there's no one else in the piazzetta *to see what's happening. They could even make him eat the poisoned bait.*

But he has his cane, and a grim expression on his face. They realize they'd probably better do what he says. Amedeo *makes a sign to* Saverio, *and he removes the noose from around the dog's neck. The animal snarls, takes a few steps back, but doesn't run away. The twins let go of* Tettè's *arms and wait for instructions from* Amedeo. *At a certain point, one of the twins turns and runs away. The other one watches him go, looks at* Amedeo, *and moves off, backing away.*

Amedeo *says to* Tettè: cacaglio, *we're not done with you. We'll see you later. And he walks off angrily, followed by* Cristiano *and* Saverio, *who spits on the ground.*

The man with the limp walks over to Tettè. *The boys stop just beyond the* piazzetta *and stand there watching.*

LI

Sheltered from the rain in a building entrance, Ricciardi waited. It might take hours, or it might take just a few minutes. His job demanded patience and a willingness to wait.

He felt like laughing every time he was at the movie theater and he chanced to see his imaginary American counterparts leap through windows, pistols drawn, to the frantic accompaniment of an out-of-tune piano; or whenever he read cheap pulps with stories of terrible shoot-outs, or policemen laying out armies of thugs with their fists. Most of the work he did consisted of just this, waiting in the rain, often waiting for nothing, while most of the rest of it involved filling out reports that no one would ever read.

He sneezed and then felt a stabbing pain in his temples from the sudden jerk of his head. Perhaps he should have kept the promise he'd refused to make to Maione and spent his Sunday in bed, sipping one of Rosa's horrible steaming brews. He could have gone over to the window every now and then and looked out, and he might even have caught a fleeting glimpse of Enrica. Perhaps she would have smiled at him, and he would have known that she'd liked his most recent letter.

Instead, his policeman's feet had dragged him out into the rain, to Santa Lucia, to wait for a man he'd never seen and who might not even have anything to do with what he was looking for.

Right: what *was* he looking for? The phantom image of a dead boy, which might not even exist. In fact, it almost certainly didn't exist, outside of his own diseased mind.

My diseased mind, he thought; and the sad spectacle that he had witnessed through the peephole at poor Carmen's apartment flashed before him: a man who'd lost his mind, a human vegetable constantly conversing with a world of ghosts that only he could see. Deep down, how was Carmen Fago di San Marcello's husband any different from him? He wasn't. Perhaps only to the extent that while that poor man now saw nothing but specters, Ricciardi still possessed some feeble connection to the real world.

What would you tell me, ghost of Tettè? Would you tell me to pet your dog, so it might stop persecuting me? Would you say that you're finally getting enough to eat? I wonder what Signor Fago's phantoms say to him. We really ought to exchange our impressions.

The street door that he'd been watching suddenly opened. A tall man emerged, more or less the same age as Ricciardi, perhaps a few years older. He wore a hat and an expensive overcoat, and he carried a cane. He walked with a limp.

He looked around, cautiously. When he saw that the street was empty, he seemed to be reassured and closed the heavy door behind him.

Before Ricciardi had a chance to move, three figures emerged from the shadows of the *vicolo* that ran alongside the building the man had just exited. They rapidly surrounded him. Two kept a lookout while the third pulled something out of his pocket, something that gleamed dully in the light of the rainy day. The man with the limp turned pale with terror, and lifted his arm to protect his face.

Ricciardi snapped to and acted as fast as he could. He stepped out of the doorway and walked toward the little knot of men, shouting:

"Halt, police! Drop your weapons!"

The man who was standing lookout in his direction gave a cry of warning and took off running, followed by the other two. The one with the knife waved the sharp tip threateningly toward the man with the limp, as if in warning, before turning to run.

Ricciardi approached the man, who was leaning, white as a sheet, against the jamb of the closed door.

"You saved me. *Grazie.* Did you see? A knife, they had a knife."

"I'm Commissario Ricciardi, from police headquarters. You need a good strong drink. There's a tavern at the corner, come along."

Keeping an eye on the man's expression, Ricciardi registered only relief when he identified himself. Clearly the man had more to fear from other quarters than from the police.

They reached the tavern; the man with the limp walked fast, even over the slippery cobblestones, leaning on his cane and shooting worried glances in the direction of the *vicolo* down which his three attackers had vanished. He kept muttering to himself, under his breath, "This is how far it's come, this is how far they're willing to take it . . . "

They sat down at a table. The man knew the proprietor, who greeted him affably and looked suspiciously at Ricciardi; the man must be used to Sersale's bad company.

"Commissario, you arrived just in the nick of time. They would have wounded me, perhaps slashed my face. *Grazie* again."

Ricciardi waved his hand dismissively.

"This neighborhood is a mecca for armed thieves. These are hard times."

The man laughed bitterly.

"Those weren't thieves. I know who sent them. Forgive me, I haven't introduced myself: my name is Edoardo Sersale. And I thank heaven above that you happened to walk past my building just then, otherwise I would certainly have wound up in the hospital."

"I didn't just happen to walk by. I was waiting for you, Signore. Just like the three of them, though obviously with different intentions."

Sersale looked at him curiously. He was surprised but not frightened.

"Really? And why would that be? The police are the only people in town I don't owe money. And I've never defrauded anyone."

Ricciardi carefully studied the way the man reacted.

"You said that you knew who sent those men after you. Who was it, and why do you think you know?"

Edoardo had ordered a carafe of wine. He poured himself a glassful and downed it in a couple of gulps.

"Well, Commissario, I'm not going to tell you that, of course. If I were interested in filing a complaint, I would have come down to police headquarters months ago; and I'd almost certainly be dead now as a result. These are nasty people, that's all you need to know. People who want the money I owe them, and want it now. Money I don't have."

"But not long ago you confided in a girl, somewhere, that you expected to come into the money soon. How do you expect to get it?"

Sersale was increasingly curious.

"Incredible! How do you know that? Have you been following me? How long have I been under surveillance?"

Ricciardi decided to come clean.

"No, you haven't been under surveillance. I'm on a case . . . that is, I'm interested in a situation that may involve you: the death of Matteo Diotallevi, a young boy, an orphan at the parish church of Santa Maria del Soccorso in Santa Teresa. Does that sound familiar?"

The man jumped back and recoiled as if he'd suddenly been slapped hard in the face.

"He's dead? Tettè is dead? But how on earth . . . That can't be, I saw him just last week! And he was fine! It's impossible, Commissario; if this is a joke, it's in very poor taste."

"I wish it was a joke. The boy was found dead Monday morning at dawn, at the base of the monumental staircase leading up from the Tondo di Capodimonte."

Sersale ran a hand over his face.

"Poor child . . . but how . . . how did he die?"

"He seems to have accidentally ingested rat poison. But there are a few dark spots, and that's what I'm looking into."

Looking him straight in the eye, Ricciardi realized that Sersale was genuinely upset.

"At this point, I need to tell you the way things stand, Commissario. I've told you about my debts. I should also tell you that my family . . . "

Ricciardi broke in:

"I already know about your family. I've seen . . . your half brother. His wife was very fond of the little boy, and I've talked to her a number of times. She's the one who confirmed your identity."

Sersale's face hardened in anger.

"That harpy. She wouldn't dream of missing the opportunity. But please bear with me, Commissario: Why don't you listen to my version of events?"

Ricciardi nodded his head and gestured for the man to go on.

"I was injured in combat in the Great War, and I was left . . . like this, the way you see me now. I have to walk with a cane, and when the weather is as damp as it's been, my wound hurts so bad it practically drives me crazy. I haven't been able to work, or be as productive as I used to be; or maybe I've just taken advantage of my condition to do nothing, like my poor mother used to say. I'll admit I like living the good life; and I like beautiful women. But that doesn't mean I'm a gangster, and your family is supposed to help you when you fall on hard times. That woman . . . For as long as my brother's been in this condition—and I wouldn't rule out the possibility that she did this to him, with some spell she's cast, witch that she is—all communications between us have ceased, because of her. All the family's wealth, and therefore my own, remains in her hands."

Ricciardi listened attentively. The man continued.

"I'd lost all my ambitions, and I went through a long and difficult time. But I've recently been in touch with one of my old enlisted men, who's started a business with northern Italy that . . . in other words, I can think about my future again, if only I could wipe out the debts I've run up. You saw them, those three . . . they wouldn't kill me, because if they did they'd never get their money. But hurt me, cut my face, yes, they'd do that: that's the way they make their point."

"So you asked your sister-in-law for the money."

"Who else could I go to? She's in charge of it all, the witch. And she turned me down, said that enough was enough, that it was time for me to face up to my responsibilities, and so on and so forth. I was beside myself."

Ricciardi tried to bring the conversation back to what happened to the boy.

"And how does Tettè fit into all this?"

Sersale smiled wearily.

"He fits in, Commissario. She told you that she's infertile, didn't she? That she can't have children. That her life has been a living hell. A few months ago, by chance, while rummaging through a steamer trunk in search of a book, I stumbled upon a pack of old letters tied with a ribbon. The trunk was from my brother's home, and it contained my mother's clothing. That witch couldn't wait to get rid of it, and she shipped it off before my mother's corpse was cold. Somehow these letters, which had evidently been hidden all too well, wound up in the trunk. They were from the doctor who was in charge of my brother's care, and they date back ten years or so, to immediately after the war. In short, he and my sister-in-law had been having an affair. It went on for years, at the same time that my poor brother was losing his mind. You see, Commissario? You see how shameful?"

Ricciardi shrugged.

"These things happen. It doesn't strike me, in any case, that you're in the best position to preach morality to others, no?"

Sersale blanched, but recovered.

"It's not a matter of morals: Did she have an affair, yes or no? Was she unfaithful, yes or no? Then perhaps she has no right to grab my family's wealth for herself. Those letters were the proof. So I started to follow her, determined to find out whether she was still having that affair with the doctor, or if she'd found herself another lover to take his place."

Ricciardi nodded.

"And you found out about the child."

"Yes, I did. And it just seemed odd to me, how attached she was to him. This bottomless love she had for a little bastard boy . . . forgive me, Commissario. Poor little thing, after all. But I came to the conclusion that this child might be something else to her, something different, something more. Perhaps this was her son, the child born of that affair. Even if he wasn't, I still could blackmail her with those letters. You know it yourself, Commissario, in this city, defamation moves mountains. I could insinuate the suspicion, based on the fact that she'd had the affair."

Ricciardi was putting together the pieces of the puzzle.

"So you started to dig."

Sersale nodded.

"Precisely. I gave a little money to that disgusting pig of a sexton, a truly filthy creature, just so that I could get a chance to talk to the boy alone. I met with the boy several times; the sexton simply assumed I was a pervert, and let me tell you, I came very close more than once to beating his repulsive face in with with my cane. I have to admit that the little boy was pitiable: he was a little runt, skinny as hunger itself, and with a stutter that would break your heart. It took him half an hour just to get out a couple of words."

Ricciardi was starting to see where Sersale was heading with this.

"You were trying to find out whether the woman had a special attitude toward the boy, weren't you? Signs of motherly love, in other words."

"Yes, that's right. I tried everything on him, blandishments and threats, though I never hurt him, so I could find out what I could about how she behaved; but there was never anything solid, Commissario. Clearly, she loved the boy, but she never said anything special to him, never gave him anything unusual. The boy called her Signora, he adored her, and he was enormously devoted to her. But he would have bonded with anyone, like he did with the stray dog that used to follow him everywhere, and I was even sorrier for the dog than the boy. But it was just because she was the only one who treated him decently."

"So you gave up."

"That's right. I was hoping to use the letters and the boy, but I finally realized that I wouldn't achieve anything more than dragging my brother's name through the mud, with nothing in return. But no, I haven't given up. I'll talk to her again, the witch, and I'll threaten to make the letters public. Without the boy, it'll be harder, I know: especially because she'd never made a move to adopt him, or at least take him home to live with her."

Ricciardi thought to himself that it was for exactly that reason that Carmen had condemned herself to eternal regret.

"One more thing, Sersale: Who, as far as you know, would have had any ill will toward Tettè? Was there anyone, for instance, who could have faced suspicion if the corpse had been found near a private home or a shop?"

Sersale thought it over, then shrugged.

"The other boys didn't much care for him, that much is certain. They had it in for him and for his dog. In fact, the last time I saw him, I had the distinct sensation that they were about to do him or the dog some harm. The sexton, too, let me say it again, struck me as the kind of guy who would sell you his sister for a couple of lire. But who could have any reason to care about a little kid like him?"

Ricciardi nodded, sadly. Who could have any reason to care about a little kid like him?

"Watch out for yourself, Sersale. Folks in the *vicoli* don't kid around. They might leave you with more than a warning, next time they catch up with you. If you change your mind and decide to tell us the names of the loan sharks, you know where to find me. In the meanwhile, until we settle all our questions about Tettè's death, I'd recommend you not leave town."

LII

Seven days earlier, Sunday, October 25

The man with the limp drags Tettè toward a parked car, at the corner of the street. The knot of boys has moved off and is now watching from a distance, eager to find out what's about to happen.

The dog, however, takes up a position on the sidewalk on the other side of the street, sitting on his haunches. Tettè thinks: run, dog. Run away. If those boys catch you they'll poison you, like that poor cat that hadn't done anything wrong. But the dog doesn't run away. He sits and waits.

The man with the limp puts him in the car, in the front seat, and then goes around and gets in on the other side. It doesn't feel to Tettè the way it does when he goes for a drive with his angel; she puts him in the backseat, like a wealthy young master being driven by his chauffeur. Plus, he doesn't like this car. It stinks of smoke, and it's dirty.

The man with the limp grabs him by the arm and twists it, hurting him. Listen, you retard, did you think about what I asked you? What does Carmen say to you, when she takes you out? What do you talk about? What did she tell you?

Tettè speaks, in spite of the serpent. He understands that if he doesn't say anything, it'll just be worse. We talk about me, about my life, about school, he manages to say, with great effort. It takes him a long time to say it. And now it's started raining, fat drops landing on the car windows and windshield.

What do you call her? What does she tell you to call her? I call her Signora, says Tettè. I call her Signora, what else should I call her? He thinks to himself that he also calls her my angel, but he keeps that to himself.

The man with the limp looks him hard in the eye, and nods his head. He understands.

What does she give you? What gifts does she bring you?

Tettè's eyes fill with tears. Where are you, my angel? he wonders. The group of boys hasn't moved, in spite of the steady rain. His arm hurts, in the man's grip.

She doesn't give me anything, he says softly, as the serpent coils around his throat, choking him. Nothing. She just buys me food. One time, he wants to say but can't, she gave me a wooden toy car, tiny but just like hers, only Amedeo saw it and he stepped on it and crushed it; then I gathered up all the little pieces of wood and tried to put it back together, but it fell apart.

So then, Tettè would like to say but can't, one time when I was stealing in an apartment for Cosimo, I saw a toy car on the floor, maybe it belonged to the child of the signora who was laughing with Cosimo. And I took it, but that was the only time I stole anything for myself.

And I keep it in the cabinet, I colored it with my school pencils. It's not as nice as the one my angel gave me that Amedeo stepped on, but it makes me think of my angel's car. And the happy hours we spend together.

That's what Tettè would have said, if the serpent hadn't been coiled around his throat; and if his thoughts formed into words, instead of confused images that got mixed up and overlapped in his mind.

The man with the limp gives him a disgusted look and says: you're useless. You're a useless thing. And you're getting my car filthy, too, with all the mud and slime you have on you.

Get out, he says. You're useless, and you disgust me.

He opens the car door, pushes the boy out onto the pavement, and drives off.

Tettè looks up and sees the gang of boys, Amedeo leading them, heading straight for him.

Behind him, the dog starts to snarl.

LIII

A lone again, and back out in the pouring rain, Ricciardi thought back over the conversation he'd just had with Sersale, the man with the limp.

His problems, the life he led, and the company he kept aside, the man struck him as sincere; but experience had taught him what extraordinary passions need can stir in the darkness of the human soul. He'd seen terror painted on the man's face, in his eyes, when he was being attacked, and Sersale himself had told him that the only source of funds available to him was his brother's estate, kept securely under lock and key by Carmen.

It might be, and Ricciardi certainly wasn't willing to rule it out, that Sersale had approached the woman and threatened to harm the child and, when his threats were ignored, he'd gone ahead and carried them out; even Tettè's death might have been a skillfully arranged setup, to keep anyone else from figuring out what the child meant to his benefactress and the man who hated her.

He felt a stab of sorrow pierce his heart. Perhaps the little orphan had just been a pawn on a chessboard, where the stakes were tawdry and all too material.

He ran a hand over his forehead, which was hot with fever. Perhaps that's not how it went at all, and all the internal struggles of the Fago family aside, the boy had just died accidentally, the way everyone had said from the outset; and then a merciful hand had gathered the poor corpse from the gutter where it was lying and placed it in a more dignified position where it could be easily found. That, too, was a possibility: he couldn't blame anyone who was afraid to say that they'd found a dead child on their front doorstep.

The streets were deserted, under the once-again heavy rain. Everyone was enjoying their Sunday inside the four warm and cozy walls of their own homes. From the venerable old apartment buildings and from the *bassi* came the smells of burning firewood and the holiday banquets that were being devoured, garlic and onions, sauces that had burbled away for an entire day in heavy pots to delight the palates of those who now rested, comfortably listening to the radio and sipping ersatz coffee.

He walked past a *vicolo* where a tragedy had taken place the week before: a room below street level, where a very poor family was sleeping, had been flooded by a surge of sewer water; the heavy rain had swept down from the hillside a large branch wrapped in dead leaves and garbage. This plug had effectively stopped up the sewer, causing the water to back up. For the parents and the two children, caught unawares in their sleep, there'd been no escape. Their bodies had only finally been found two days later, due to the difficulty of draining the liquid waste from their home.

Ricciardi saw them now, standing translucent in the pelting rain, at the door of the place that had been their home. They were murmuring indistinctly the words of their dreams, through lips gaping open to reveal blackened tongues, mouths gasping in the attempt to get a final mouthful of air. The little girl was the only one who had woken up, Ricciardi saw, but no one had listened to her. She was shouting: *water, Mammà, wake up, the water's coming in*. They were all drenched with filthy water.

The street is populated with the dead more than with the living, Ricciardi mused as he strolled along with his hands deep in his trench coat pockets, as icy rivulets ran down his back, penetrating through his clothing.

Loneliness, he mused, is an infectious disease. I'm infected, and I carry it within me. Or perhaps it is loneliness that carries me within it.

He sensed movement behind him; he half turned and out of the corner of his eye he saw Tettè's dog, following him some twenty feet back. How can I rest, he wondered, and enjoy my Sunday off, if my client is so eager to see how much progress I'm making? It's just that I'm not really making much progress at all, dog, as you can see for yourself. I'm right back where I started.

Carmen, he thought: I have to ask her. She alone, since she knows him, can tell me whether Sersale threatened to harm the child; whether she thinks her brother-in-law would be capable of doing such a thing.

A powerful wave of dizziness swept over him, and he staggered. His fever was climbing and he felt as if he were walking in a dream state. He could feel his strength ebbing away. He looked around, spotted a bench, and fell down onto it. The neighborhood looked vaguely familiar, though he couldn't have said why. There was no one in sight. Even the dog seemed to have vanished: that is, unless I dreamed it up in the first place, he thought to himself.

As he sank into a stupor, he saw around him first his mother, then Rosa, Enrica, and Livia, their loneliness, and he decided that he must have infected them with his disease. He thought he saw himself playing alone, imagining the playmates and friends he'd never had. Only when he turned to look more carefully did the child have Tettè's hollow, absentminded face.

Then came darkness.

Wrapped in her warm housecoat, Livia was smoking a cigarette and allowing her thoughts to roam freely. She'd always been afraid of Sunday afternoons, just before nightfall; it was the time when loneliness reached out its fingers, just like the darkness, expanding into people's lives, placing people face-to-face with their souls, stripping away any last possibility of continuing to lie to oneself.

During the years of her marriage, she'd been so terribly alone; her husband was always traveling, gone on endless concert tours, with the clear understanding that the last thing he wanted was for her to accompany him; he liked the freedom to be with his countless lovers. Not that she was any less lonely when he was home, she thought with an ironic smile.

Even now, I'm alone, she realized; but the color of my loneliness has somehow changed. Then I was in despair, and now I'm full of hope.

She walked over to the window, which rattled from the rain, and thought back to the winter night when she had looked out from her waterfront hotel room and seen Ricciardi, on the street, in the swaying light of the streetlamps, in the foam from the storm-tossed sea. What that man did to her soul was pretty close to what the wind had been doing to the sea that night. She smiled at herself, because she'd just imagined she'd glimpsed him, sitting on a bench in the pouring rain, right outside her front door.

And then she realized she wasn't imagining a thing. It was really him.

Enrica was uneasy. She couldn't have said why; Sunday had gone its wet, gray way, a wet Sunday Mass in the pouring rain, no stroll in the Villa Nazionale, just lunch and the radio, followed by a light dinner. Nothing out of the ordinary.

But she felt wrong, somehow: a vague tightness in her chest, a fear of some kind, an anxiety. Really, she should say, a sense of anguish.

She'd finished her reply to Ricciardi's letter. To tell the

truth, she'd finished it at least five different times, having rewritten it whenever she thought of another thing to say, another thing to explain, another thing to leave unstated. She sensed that this would be the last push, converting the glances out the window, the tentative waves, and the smiles from a distance into a full and actual acquaintance: a transformation into her dream of strolls hand-in-hand, movie theaters, and downtown cafés.

Then why this sense of anguish?

She put the idea of a presentiment out of her mind. She didn't believe in those things, and she didn't like to think about them. She went to the window to look out at the rain; through the wet glass, she saw the building across the way, the windows of Ricciardi's apartment.

In one of them, the one in the living room that she now knew so well, she saw Rosa, looking out.

Livia was drying Ricciardi off, using a large cotton towel.

The maid stood watching from the door of the bedroom, concerned and uncomfortable: she had seen her own mistress run out of her bedroom, grab an overcoat from its peg, and shoot out of the apartment, leaving the front door wide open behind her; from the window she'd seen her rush out onto the street, in the pouring rain, in her slippers and wearing her housecoat beneath the overcoat, bareheaded; then she had seen her signora approach a man sleeping on a bench, quite possibly a hobo or a panhandler; she'd seen her throw her arms around the man and help him to his feet; then she'd seen her help the man along as he stumbled woozily. And bring him into the building, and then into the apartment.

Now her mistress had removed his trench coat, his jacket, his tie, his shirt, and even his undershirt. The articles of clothing were strewn across the floor, in puddles of water; and she was drying him, rubbing his head and his hair with a dry towel.

He was staring blankly, his eyes red, with dark circles underneath them. A skinny man, pale, and possibly quite sick.

Livia turned and spoke to her maid, in a state of extreme agitation.

"Adelina, hurry: go summon Arturo, the chauffeur. Tell him that I need him. And bring me another dry towel . . . no, first heat it up on the stove. And hang up these clothes to dry, right away. And make a cup of herbal tea."

She turned her focus on him now, as Adelina left the room:

"Ricciardi, answer me . . . what's wrong, why were you out in the rain? What happened to you, tell me!"

He looked at her as if he had no idea who she was.

"The child, the child . . . that's me, don't you understand? He's dead, but I can't see him, I just can't see him. And I don't know what he'd say to me, and the dog, what does the dog want from me?"

Livia looked at him and didn't even try to understand. He was feverish and delirious. He was trembling and muttering.

"No, don't try to get up. Calm down, you have a fever, a very high fever. Here, lie down, don't worry about a thing. I'm here, I'll take care of you."

Adelina returned with the herbal tea, accompanied by the chauffeur who was hastily buttoning his uniform.

"Arturo, go and summon the doctor . . . what's his name, the physician who lives downstairs? Mirante, that's it. I know that it's Sunday, but that doesn't matter! Tell him that I need him here immediately. Make sure he comes directly. And you, Adelina, help me, let's get him into a bed, in the guest room."

In her terrible concern for the fever that she could feel in every part of Ricciardi's body, even though she couldn't understand a word he said in his delirium, Livia couldn't help but think that now she was no longer alone. Not anymore.

Now she had someone to look after.

LIV

D r. Mirante came in a hurry; he was a short, middle-aged man, with a large mustache, a careful comb-over on top of his cranium, and a prominent belly. Being invited into the home of the beautiful and mysterious neighbor whom everyone was talking about, so late at night, had flattered him, making him hope that the reason might be quite another. And so, when he found himself in the presence of a feverish Ricciardi, he made no attempt to conceal his disappointment.

After examining the patient and administering a generous dose of quinine, he pulled the belt of his damask dressing gown tight and said:

"It's nothing but a powerful cold. His larynx is badly inflamed. But now the fever ought to fall, and then he'll need a few days of undisturbed bed rest."

Livia was wringing her hands with worry.

"But quinine . . . are you afraid he's contracted malaria?"

The doctor dismissed that possibility in no uncertain terms:

"No, absolutely not. I just gave it to him for its antipyretic properties. Don't worry, Signora: your . . . friend will certainly recover, if he's given adequate care. Were you planning to look after him yourself? Were you going to keep him here?"

The chance to supply that harridan of a wife of his with succulent new gossip was too tempting an opportunity to pass up by just saying goodnight and leaving. Livia realized exactly what he was up to and she didn't like it one bit. As usual, she reacted with a counterattack:

"I certainly hope to, doctor. If he'll let me, then I really hope to. But Commissario Ricciardi from the police headquarters of Naples, that's his name and rank, does as he chooses. We'll see how it goes. In any case, I thank you for your courtesy, and once again I apologize for having asked you to come up on a Sunday night. I hope you'll give my warm regards to your delightful wife."

Mirante read between the lines and gave in.

"Why, it's no trouble at all, Signora. As you know, the doctor's life is a mission that has no holidays or time off. If you like, I'll be glad to drop by tomorrow morning and take another look at that larynx. I'll certainly convey your regards. Good evening."

Ricciardi collapsed into a deep sleep, populated by disconnected specters and images. His fever came and went, leaving behind it scattered thoughts that blossomed into nightmares.

The dog was always there in his dreams, looking at him from a distance and every once in a while emitting a single mournful howl, just as it had when the morgue attendants first took the dead Tettè away. The little boy never appeared—at least his face didn't—but Ricciardi met with the image of his dangling neck, and the rivulets of water dripping off it onto the pavement, an image that was always accompanied by the sadness it had instilled in him from the outset.

In his dream, he looked out the window and saw Enrica doing her needlepoint. He called to her but she couldn't hear him; so he went to Rosa, but she couldn't see him either. It was as if he himself had become a ghost. Rosa would glance at the pendulum clock on the wall, sigh, and brush away a tear. Ricciardi could tell that his *tata* was worried about him, but he had no way of reassuring her.

Then he found himself back out in the rain on Via Toledo. He saw Maione go by; he called to him but he couldn't seem to make himself heard, so he chased after him, trying to catch his attention, unsuccessfully. The brigadier walked past Sersale but didn't recognize him, because he'd never seen him before. Ricciardi tried to warn him, but no voice issued from his lips. I'm a ghost, he thought. A ghost, and no one can see me.

Livia went to check his temperature every half hour; around one o'clock it seemed to her that his temperature was rising, and she decided not to leave the guest bedroom again. She took off her housecoat and stretched out next to him.

The light from the streetlamps filtered in through the open shutters, allowing her to glimpse Ricciardi's profile. His clenched expression told her of the nightmares he was still living through. She wished she could enter into his dreams and somehow heal them, give him peace: the peace that he refused himself when awake, at least to quieten his nights.

In the partial darkness Ricciardi's features struck her as even more handsome: he looked like a very young man, lost in thoughts of something much bigger than him. "The boy," he seemed to be murmuring; "tell the dog that I can't see him." Still in the throes of delirium.

She dampened his brow with a wet cloth, and he fell silent, perhaps comforted. Then she ran her fingers over his lips, his throat. She caressed his chest, and he seemed to breathe more easily. She felt a certain languor, a tightness in the pit of her stomach. She found herself wondering when she had last made love, and not being able to remember.

She pulled the sheets aside and let her fingertips slide down his belly.

The clock in the hall chimed. Outside, the rain lashed against the window.

Ricciardi dreamt that he was back in his own office, with

Livia. He could smell the scent of her cinnamon perfume, he saw her face, her full lips, her fascinating, mysterious smile, even in the dark. She was beautiful, and he felt his usual blend of attraction and fear.

She got up from her chair, took off her hat, and walked toward him, circling around his desk. Her feline gait, her heels echoing on the floor, her dark, liquid eyes, staring into his. Ricciardi wanted to stand up and move away, but in his dream he was incapacitated: he sat there, motionless, his fingers digging into the armrests of his chair, his heart racing furiously in his throat.

When she was finally right in front of him, she caressed him, long and slow, with a smile. She was as desirable as she'd ever been, but he was also terrified of her. He couldn't move, as if hypnotized by her gaze.

His thoughts tried to turn to Enrica, but without success.

Livia placed her lips on Ricciardi's mouth. She was lying down next to him, her hand on his belly. She could feel the warmth of his body, his racing, feverish heartbeat.

She realized that what she was doing wasn't right, that she should have respected his wishes, that he was sick and might be dreaming of another woman, the other woman he claimed to have in his heart. But still, she was a woman, and she'd been alone for far, far too long. She, too, had her dreams, and that man was at the center of them.

She kissed him, long and slow, tenderly and with growing passion. She sought him in the depths of the shadows, she took him by the hand, and she led him out of the storm, into still waters. She felt him react to her with a long shiver. And in the end, he uttered her name.

In the mists of fever and dreams, Ricciardi saw Livia sitting upon him, her magnificent long legs sheathed in sheer stockings. He felt himself immersed in her scent and her stunning, breathtaking eyes.

He called out to her, telling her to stop—telling her not to stop. He wanted to be strong and he wanted to tell himself to be weak.

Then it was silk and warm velvet, under the trembling flesh of his hand; it was snow crystals and wind, and a slow climb up to a highland, and looking down into the bottomless precipice in the absurd realization that he could fly.

All around him, all the sorrows of the countless deaths that plagued his existence took a step back, in silence, to keep from intruding; and for once life, with all its deafening noises, fell silent.

Between dreaming and full waking, with the scent of spices and her sighs penetrating his soul, he sampled all her flavors, both sour and sweet, and found them at once alien and familiar.

He surrendered to her flesh, hoping in some hidden part of him, the part that insisted on keeping watch, that this was nothing but another dream, less painful than the others; but the whole time knowing that it wasn't.

To hear her name on his lips as she kissed him reassured her and made her happy. He was thinking of her, perhaps in a fever dream, perhaps in the depths of a soul finally stripped bare; he was thinking of her.

And then she remembered everything about being a woman. She lingered in full awareness that she was teasing out a very fine gossamer thread, tugging it ever so carefully, because it might snap at any moment. She took pains not to frighten him; the last thing she wanted was for him to regain consciousness and retreat from her once again, rediscover the principles and thoughts that always kept him so remote. She took her time. With every fiber of her being, she hoped that

Ricciardi might not simply be dreaming, but that he was too lost in sleep to withdraw into his distant world—no, not that, not now that she could feel him as a man and herself as a woman, in a way that she'd missed for far too long now.

She forgot that she'd ever been selfish and shallow, and discovered that she could be generous and nurturing. She guided his hands, his mouth, his body: calmly, gently. This was even newer for her, who had had lovers in the past, than it was for him, who had always denied himself everything.

She took the pleasure she'd been dreaming of, the pleasure that she'd missed for so long, the pleasure that she considered to be her birthright. She took for herself the moment of heaven that she'd been yearning for, and when she was done, she plunged her mouth into her pillow and let out a long, muffled sigh.

At last, she smiled in the darkness, gentled now like a sated tiger.

LV

At dawn, the rain took a break, transforming itself into a myriad of drops suspended in the cold air. As if it were aware of the sadness of this day, it colored everything a melancholy gray.

Ricciardi walked out the entrance to Livia's building and into the empty street. He felt exceedingly weak but decided he no longer had a fever.

He'd found his clothing neatly folded on the armchair by the bed, a bed he couldn't remember getting into the night before; they were still slightly damp but warm, because there was a hot stove nearby. The hollow he'd found in the mattress, a body-sized dip beside him, and a black hair on the pillow had immediately revealed to his analytical mind, now finally lucid, that what he remembered all too clearly had not been a mere dream, fueled by his raging fever.

He'd dressed and left the apartment without making a sound. As he walked past Livia's bedroom he'd seen her silhouette, stretched out on the bed in the half-light, and his head had started spinning.

He was confused; he felt a deep sense of guilt toward Enrica, feeling deep down that he'd betrayed her, but also toward Livia, for having taken her without feeling true love for her.

But what do you know about true love? he thought. Have

you ever experienced it? Have you ever shared all your thoughts, desires, and hopes with another person? That sentiment that moves the dead lips of those who killed themselves or were murdered for love, that emotion you've dismissed as absurd so many times; have you ever really felt it?

Inconsistent. As he walked in that strange watery suspension, as if swimming beneath the surface of an airy sea, he felt inconsistent. He hadn't had the strength to push Livia away when he realized that her hands upon him were no dream, that his lips upon hers were all too real.

If possible, Livia was even more beautiful than she'd seemed when she walked into a room and attracted the gaze of every man present, like a powerful magnet.

Even now as he was doing his best to push her memory away, he understood the sensations she could impart, he was more aware than ever before that she embodied everything a man could possibly desire in a woman: she was educated, captivating, wealthy, and passionate.

Then why did he feel that he'd been nothing but a weakling and that, out of weakness, he'd allowed something to happen that was profoundly wrong?

With a shiver, he thought of Enrica, the letters they'd exchanged, the relationship that, amidst endless second-guessing and fears, especially on his part, was so laboriously germinating between them. He thought of how this fragile, new love was growing in spite of everything that he'd always believed, in spite of his certainty that there was no woman upon whom he could inflict his curse.

Now what would he do? How could he talk to her about this, if they'd only exchanged the occasional stilted greeting until now? And how should he act with Livia, for that matter? How could he pretend he didn't remember what had happened?

At the corner of Via Toledo, in the empty dawn street, he

saw Tettè's dog. It was sitting on its haunches, alert, one ear cocked as if to catch his footstep. It had been waiting for him.

Ricciardi's heart lurched as his mind went back to the little boy, his death, and the fact that just the night before he'd spoken with Sersale, the man with the limp; it was the last thing he could remember, before Livia. His ears echoed with the man's hatred for his sister-in-law, who stood between him and his half brother's fortune.

He'd finally become convinced that the boy's death had been the result of neglect and hunger, those stubborn, age-old enemies; but it was possible that Carmen herself might be in danger, and he wanted to warn her as quickly as he could. He remembered that he'd been heading for her house, to tell her about Sersale and his ham-handed attempts at extortion, and to find out whether she thought that her brother-in-law could be capable of such extreme acts of vendetta. He had seemed to Ricciardi to be well aware of the woman's love for Tettè, a love similar to what a mother might feel for her son.

Like a mother. His thoughts turned to Rosa; he never failed to let her know if he would be out late, and this time he'd neglected to do it. He hoped she'd gone to sleep and was sleeping still, so that he could just tell her he'd come home late and gone out very early in the morning: a little white lie, to keep her from feeling she was no longer up to the job of looking after him. He decided that that's exactly what he'd say to her, when he got home.

But first he wanted to see Carmen. He thought he knew where he could find her, since today was the holiday of the commemoration of the dead. He'd wait for her there, by Tettè's grave. He headed off toward Poggioreale cemetery, his heart heavy with new worries, a new sense of disquiet.

Rosa woke with a start to the mournful sound of the first bell from the nearby church. She looked around, baffled. Then she

334 · MAURIZIO DE GIOVANNI

remembered: she'd fallen asleep in the armchair in the living
room, facing the front door, waiting for Ricciardi, who hadn't
come home the night before.

She understood that he was a grown man now, with a right
to take the time he needed for men's pursuits, and that, of
course, the work he did sometimes entailed staying out all
night, and indeed that had happened a few times before. But
this was the first time that he'd failed to let her know before he
left, or send a man to inform her.

The behavior she'd noticed over the past few days had been
worrisome; and Maione's visit and the snippets of conversation
she'd overhead had done nothing to reassure her. And there
was a woman mixed up in this, a woman who brazenly went to
call on him at police headquarters. A signora, what's more: not
even a respectable signorina.

She laboriously raised herself up from the armchair, doing
her best to ignore the excruciating complaints of her creaky
old bones. There was nothing she could do except wait to hear
something. She forced herself to rein in her worries. The *signorino* was a respected and responsible person, a commissario
in the mobile squad. He certainly wouldn't run unnecessary
risks.

She went into her bedroom, planning to lie down for a few
minutes. She glanced out the window and saw, wrapped in a
blanket, another person looking out of her bedroom, across
the street in the Colombo apartment, in the uncertain, misty
half-light of dawn, on the Day of the Dead.

Enrica hadn't been able to rid herself of the oppressive
sense of anxiety that had accompanied her the whole night
through. She had slept badly, with long stretches of wakefulness, lying there listening to the rain rattling against the shutters.

She was a rational, no-nonsense young woman, and feeling

worried for no good reason was something that she found hard
to take, something she found disorderly and objectionable. But
then, when the light in Ricciardi's window had failed to come
on for their little evening appointment, it had become clear to
her that her anxiety was perhaps an inexplicable form of pre-
monition.

At dawn, she'd gone into the kitchen to get a glass of water,
because her throat was parched. She'd looked at the building
across the street through the half-opened shutters and she'd
realized that the curtains in Ricciardi's bedroom hadn't moved
since the night before. That never happened; he always pulled
them closed before going to sleep. And the faint light in Rosa's
bedroom, which normally stayed on all night long, was also off.
What was going on?

Her growing worries would certainly keep her from falling
back asleep; and so, wrapped in a blanket, she sat down by her
bedroom window to wait for any sign of life from the apartment across the way.

Outside, the rain had been transformed into a strange gray
light.

Livia had never found a daybreak to be quite as magnificent
as the gray morning of the Day of the Dead.

At first, of course, she'd been disappointed: she hadn't
found him in the bed, where she'd left him sleeping easily, just
before dawn. She'd gone to her own bedroom to lie down for
just a few minutes, but instead she'd dropped into a deep,
serene sleep, filled with that gentle weariness that she thought
she'd forgotten. When she woke up, she found that he'd left,
and knowing him as she did, it hardly came as a surprise; he
surely needed to do some thinking, to delve deep down inside
himself to discover the true significance of what had happened
the night before.

Stretching like a cat, she smiled happily. If he had asked her, she would have been capable of telling him exactly what had happened.

Love, she would have told him, is a strange, dark thing: you think of a hundred or a thousand possibilities and you imagine so many situations, only to discover that there's just one element that needs to be understood, to be taken into consideration: being together. Faced with the naturalness of touching each other and kissing and being one inside the other, all the structures that the mind and society spend so much time and energy building simply collapse, like a castle made of playing cards.

What was supposed to happen between the two of them had finally happened. She knew it, she'd always known it, and in fact, that's how it had been. And it had been wonderful, like a dream; if it had been that way for her, it must necessarily have been the same for him.

He'd gone away, but he'd come back to her. This would no longer be a time of loneliness.

Her thoughts turned to the reception that she'd be holding in just two days, and the people who would be attending. That would be a magnificent opportunity because, beyond all the pointless formalities and empty words, everyone would be able to see how radiantly happy she was. She'd want him by her side, so that there could be no doubts about the reasons for her contentment.

She shook her head at the thought of his shyness and intractability, both qualities she had come to know well. He would probably be unwilling to advertise their relationship until it was on a sounder footing. She'd try to talk him into it. But if she couldn't, she didn't care. She'd do without it; the only thing that mattered to her was to see him again, as soon as possible.

Smiling, she decided that it was time to really get to work planning her party. She summoned the maid.

LVI

The trolley that went to the cemetery was the number 31, and it left from Porta Capuana.

Ricciardi had to walk for half an hour to reach the end of the line, but he didn't mind; it helped to clear his head of the contradictions and inconsistencies of the past few days. He still didn't feel well; his sore throat was very painful and every so often a dizzy spell would make him feel queasy. Then he'd have to stop and rest, but his mind remained clear.

Not that that was necessarily a good thing, he thought with a hint of irony. A clear mind is no help in understanding certain events. Livia, for example: the conclusions she'd leap to, after what had happened. Enrica, with whom he was still not on sufficiently intimate terms to discuss certain topics; in point of fact, they'd never even spoken, but she was so important to him that he wanted to be sincere with her from the very beginning. So how could he tell her that he'd betrayed her, before he'd even declared his feelings for her?

With an effort, he tried to turn his thoughts to the story of Tettè, Carmen, and the man with the limp. It was a grim distraction, but a distraction nonetheless, he told himself.

Desperation, he knew well, could lead to acts that were entirely out of keeping with a person's nature. Sersale hadn't seemed to him to have a violent character, and the fear he'd read in his face during the attack was umistakable. But fear itself could trigger a sudden, out-of-control act, a brutal reaction to, say, being cut off from the family fortune; which meant Carmen might be in real danger.

And as for Carmen, Ricciardi felt genuine compassion for her. She'd been unfortunate, in spite of her great wealth: no children, a deranged husband, and a family of in-laws with whom she had nothing in common but the wealth over which they squabbled. A malignant, toxic loneliness, an ironic fate that had taken from her the only true love she'd managed to find in life.

Then his thoughts went to Tettè: an even deeper loneliness, a small, brief life that had ended who knows where—and so tragically. And then there was the body, moved roughly, the same way he'd seen the morgue attendants carrying him on the stairs of the Tondo di Capodimonte, and placed where someone would be sure to find it.

The trolley was full of people, even though it was still early. Many carried bouquets of flowers; the women were dressed in black, their hair gathered beneath knotted handkerchiefs, while the men wore black armbands and black neckties, a black button on their lapels: all signs of mourning. Many had dark circles under their eyes from weeping.

The trolley car made its way along the tracks, screeching as it passed over switches, in the damp morning air that promised rain, just like every morning before it. Inside the car there was a silence unusual for such a crowd, at least in that city. Death was a passenger on that trolley: today was His day. Ricciardi looked out the windows and watched the quarters of the city stream past, the streets filled with knots of silent people, all walking toward the same destination as him: the Vasto district, Via Foria, Piazza Carlo III. A populace united for once by an absence, the wish to remember.

At the cemetery entrance, Ricciardi inquired where a certain Matteo Diotallevi might have been interred: a recent arrival, only here since last Friday. A bored attendant checked a ledger book and told the commissario that the child was a guest of the Fago di San Marcello family chapel, and pointed him in that direction. He was touched by Carmen's gesture: she hadn't had the chance to welcome Tettè into her home while he was alive, but she'd chosen to do so at least after his death.

He walked up the tree-lined lane that would take him to his destination, shooting fleeting glances at chapels and tombs that were gradually being populated with visitors. Every so often he had to look away, because among the living and the statues he occasionally glimpsed the dead.

This was why he always avoided trips to the cemetery, if he could. There were many who found life no longer worth living after the death of a loved one, often choosing to put an end to their own lives on the very spot where the last remains of the one they had loved now reposed. And autumn, the saddest time of the year, was their season.

Ricciardi saw an elderly woman kneeling in prayer on her son's grave, a stream of blood flowing slowly from her wrists. She kept saying *just a little longer, my son, just a little longer and I'll kiss your face again.* Not far away, almost invisible because of the time that had passed since his demise, a man stood with a pistol in his right hand, the right side of his head almost obliterated, as he thought of the woman he had loved and lost to death: *I'll always love you, I've always loved you, and I love you still.* To Ricciardi's eyes, the man oozed despair and gloom.

This was also a gift that the Deed had given him: the exact feeling that certain people had of how impossible it was to survive certain events. The opposite of the instinct that led to most crimes, the survival instinct. Both impulses, in most cases, seemed to him pointless causes of death.

He recognized the chapel by the many fresh flowers arranged outside. The door was open and he glimpsed Carmen sitting inside. Already here, at this early hour.

The woman recognized him and smiled, hastily drying the tears that were running down her cheeks.

"Commissario, thank you so much for coming. *Prego*, come inside. You see, Tettè is here, and when I die I'll be here with him. I couldn't stand the thought of him lying next to just anybody, in some potter's field. And I didn't ask anyone's permission: I just brought him here, that's all."

"*Buon giorno*, Signora. I didn't expect to find you here so early. But I wanted to talk to you, and I knew that you'd come sooner or later, today."

Carmen smiled sadly.

"Where else could I have been, on a day like today? You see, Commissario, I'm not an old woman, I'm just a little over thirty. But my loved ones—aside from my husband, and you've seen the state that he's in—are all here. I went by my parents' grave, because, God rest their souls, they passed away many years ago, and now I've come to see Tettè. I brought flowers, as I do every week, to my in-laws; not that they cared much for me, truth be told, but I'm happy to do it on my husband's behalf. Did you want to talk with me? Are there any new developments?"

Ricciardi was still standing, his hands stuck in his pockets.

"Yesterday I met your brother-in-law, Signor Sersale. I wanted to understand what kind of man he was, what walk of life he occupied. I was just approaching him when . . . well, when he was attacked by three individuals, tough characters, who took to their heels when I showed up. But then I had a chance to talk to him. He really is in dire straits, as you no doubt already know."

Carmen stared back at Ricciardi, scowling.

"I told you, Commissario. Gambling, prostitutes, shady dealings. Think of something illegal or immoral, and he's done it."

Ricciardi nodded.

"Yes, Signora, I realize that; and to tell the truth, he doesn't deny it. If anything, he seemed fully aware of the situation he's gotten himself into, as well as the fact that the only funds that could help him get out of debt are in your hands. He told me that he discussed this with you, unsuccessfully, and that he therefore tried to find a way . . . in short, tried to find evidence that he could use to blackmail you. And he found certain letters."

Carmen continued to stare at him.

"Letters? What letters?"

"These matters are none of my business, let me make that clear, Signora: but I believe that it might be useful for you to know just what your brother-in-law has in his possession, what weapons he intends to use against you."

Carmen seemed to have been turned to stone.

"But why, Commissario? Why would you want to help me?"

Ricciardi sighed.

"You were kind to the boy, Signora. The only good thing in his life. It seems to me that I owe it to you, on his behalf. This investigation of mine is not a proper police investigation, as you know. In fact, I'm working on it in my own free time; I'm not on duty now. But the work I did to understand the days of Tettè's life helped me to get to know him, you see: and his life wasn't an easy one. So take it as a gift from him, if you like."

The woman nodded, pensively.

"The letters. That's why I couldn't find them. So he has them. So what? What does he want to do with my letters?"

Ricciardi shrugged.

"He followed you. That's how he managed to find out about Tettè. He hoped to obtain some evidence that your . . . friendship with the man who wrote those letters might still be going on. He wanted to find out from Tettè whether you'd said anything to him, if you'd mentioned this man, anything he could turn to his own advantage. For purposes of extortion."

The woman could barely contain her rage. The knuckles of the hand clutching the handkerchief were white with strain.

"Damn him. Damn him. Just because he has a black heart, he assumes the same about everyone else. He wanted to use the boy to hurt me. What could that blessed soul have ever told him? What could he have known about it?"

Ricciardi waited, in silence. She went on:

"I had a love affair, it's true. I had an affair, and I don't regret it a bit. My husband . . . you've seen him. He's been like that for many years, too many years. And I'm infertile, so I couldn't have had a child to devote myself to. There was this man, a physician . . . for a long time we'd hoped he could cure my husband, find the cause and keep him from vanishing into that world of his, that world of monsters, slowly, inexorably. We grew closer, without realizing it. We fell in love. I was married, he was married; I was unhappy, he was unhappy. Sure, I had an affair. A wonderful love affair. And I'd have been willing to give up everything, my money, my comfort, for him. But he wasn't willing. He couldn't bring himself to abandon his wife, his children, and his work. That's the whole story."

Ricciardi was increasingly uncomfortable.

"Signora, I have no right to know these things. They're none of my business. I only wanted you to know, so you could defend yourself. That's all."

Carmen ran a hand over her eyes.

"I don't need to defend myself, Commissario: not anymore. This is something from long ago; it's over, dead and buried, just like my poor, sweet Tettè. And like Tettè—whom I was too afraid to adopt and bring into my home when I still could have, and ought to have—it's something that will weigh only on my conscience, and for the rest of my life. These are all things that Edoardo, wallowing in his poverty and misery, couldn't understand. But, Commissario, are you all right? You're absolutely ashen."

Ricciardi waved a hand dismissively.

"Just a touch of fever, Signora. Nothing serious. These have been trying days, and with this nasty weather I just caught a bad cold, that's all."

The woman looked at him with a note of concern in her eyes.

"If I were in your shoes, I wouldn't be so dismissive. You don't look a bit well. Let me drive you home; my car is parked just outside the cemetery entrance. I was just going home now. Unfortunately, nothing's going to change here."

Ricciardi tried to refuse her offer, but the signora wouldn't hear of it. Truth be told, he didn't mind sparing himself the trolley ride back. The car was sure to be full of people returning home from a visit filled with grief and regret. Once Carmen had locked the chapel gate, the two of them headed toward the entrance.

LVII

As they walked up the tree-lined lane, Ricciardi wondered what difference there was between the woman walking beside him and the one with slit wrists he saw dying over her son's tomb, just some fifteen feet away.

They were both alone, both in the depths of despair. Both tied to life only by bonds of obligation that over the course of time had come to seem increasingly meaningless. Love, Ricciardi mused, can tie you to life or evict you from it entirely. Without love, there's not much difference between living and dying. Carmen had struck him as an empty shell, devoid of any strength. Tettè's death, the memory of her lost love, the steadily declining condition of her mad husband. No worldly fortune, no amount of money could make up for those losses.

They came to the car, in the cemetery parking area. The woman walked around to the driver's side.

"I prefer not to have my chauffeur drive me, Commissario. I like not having to depend on anyone else. Tettè liked it too, you know? It was a game we played, to go for a drive, as if I were his own personal driver."

As they did every time she spoke about the boy, her eyes filled with tears. Ricciardi realized that her lost child could easily become a burden too heavy for her to bear, and that poor Carmen might well have more to fear from herself than from any blackmail her brother-in-law could even dream of. He got into the car and sat beside her.

As the woman shifted the car into gear and pulled away, and

as the roar of the engine filled their ears, Ricciardi detected a slight movement directly behind him, in the backseat. He turned around and stopped, openmouthed, horrified by the sight that met his eyes.

Maione stepped out of the trolley, holding Lucia's arm and followed by their five children. The second of November was a painful recurrence: the only day of the year in which the entire family came together, both the living and the dead.

They'd dressed in silence that morning. No one felt like talking; everyone was busy remembering.

Luca, who'd been Lucia and Raffaele's firstborn son, was one of those boys who fills the lives of those around them. He was blond and had his mother's blue eyes, with his father's sunny, extroverted disposition. He never tired of playing pranks and cheerfully teasing the rest of the family, including his siblings, who worshiped him. He was loved by one and all in their quarter; his funeral was memorable for the sheer number of people who attended. So many of them with tears in their eyes.

Maione let a smile escape him as he approached the cemetery entrance: the *brigadiere panzone*, the big-bellied brigadier, that's what Luca used to call him. And Maione would chase the boy through the apartment with a wooden clog in one hand, calling: If I catch you I'll break your head open and put some good manners in there; and Luca would scream with laughter, and then turn to him with a serious face and say: I'll grow to be big, you know, Papà. I'll be bigger and taller than you, and I'll be a policeman, too.

The brigadier remembered how proud he'd been every time his son said those words; and how many times he'd cursed himself for setting him that example.

It was that example that had resulted in Luca's death, from a cowardly stab wound in the back, in a cellar where a wanted thief had been hiding out. The grief that he felt today, the third year running that he'd gone to visit his son at the cemetery on the Day of the Dead, was still as shiny and new as a piece of polished silver.

He looked over at his wife and, as always, she sensed his eyes upon her and smiled back at him. How beautiful you are, Luci', he thought. And how close I came to losing you, too. In the long months of silence, grief and sorrow had taken over their lives, creating an archipelago of islands separated by waves of salt tears. He'd been so close to leaving home, a place where it had almost become impossible to breathe.

But because love exists, and in the long run it can win the age-old struggle against grief, they'd found each other again that spring; and now they were closer than ever, bound together in part by the memory of Luca, and by the constant, aching loss that they both felt.

As always, the thought of Luca took Maione's mind back to Ricciardi, the only one who had understood that the best and only way to help the brigadier was to catch his son's murderer. He thought back to how close the two men had been on that occasion, and how close they had remained ever since.

He wondered how his commissario was doing, whether he'd kept his promise to abandon his strange investigation until the two of them could work together again. A search for something that was nonexistent, in the life of a poor orphan boy, in his world of desperation. Maione hadn't understood and still didn't understand what Ricciardi was looking for, but what he feared above all else was that he might run unnecessary risks, the kind of risks that it was Maione's job to protect him from.

Just as these thoughts were going through his mind, he saw a powerful automobile race down the curving road that led away from the cemetery, going just a little too fast. There was a woman driving, and he had the odd sensation that he'd seen her before somewhere, but he couldn't remember where. Seated beside her, incredibly, he saw none other than Ricciardi. He raised his hand to wave, but he realized that the commissario was looking behind him, toward the backseat, which was, however, empty.

He raised his hand to wave, but stopped mid-gesture when he saw the look of absolute horror on Ricciardi's face. It was over in an instant: the car shot off, leaving a trail of mud and exhaust. Maione felt his heart race furiously in his chest, and he responded to the impulse of the moment. He squeezed Lucia's arm, murmured that he'd join her afterward at Luca's grave, and set off at a dead run toward the taxi stand.

There you are, thought Ricciardi. At last, there you are.

For the first time since he'd become aware of the Deed, the name he gave his peculiar ability to perceive the grief of the dead who were killed, he had sought it out instead of fleeing from it.

He'd tried to explain the absence of Tettè from all the places he might reasonably have expected or hoped to find him; he'd walked the same streets the boy frequented, the same dark *vicoli* and alleys. And now, just when he'd given up the hunt, just when he'd decided to set his soul at rest and stop worrying, here he was, in all the atrocity of a slow, painful death.

The boy was contorted in excruciating convulsions, which forced him to straighten and then fold over at the waist continuously; his eyelids were pulled back and his eyes were showing the white of the corneas; he was grinding his teeth from the tremendous suffering caused by the poison. Yet at the same time, a sweet, loving phrase kept issuing from his lips: *thank you for the cookies. I love you, Mamma, you know that: you're my angel.*

As was often the case, the greatest horror of all lay in the contrast between the contortions of the body at its moment of extreme suffering and the dead boy's last delicate, loving thought. Ricciardi couldn't seem to tear his eyes away from Tettè's ghost, and from the terrible implications of seeing him there of all places, and of the phrase that he continued to repeat.

He turned to look at the woman.

He turned to look at the killer.

LVIII

It had once again started to rain. A peal of thunder had shaken the air and a violent gust of rain slammed down onto the pavement.

Carmen was a nervous, jerky driver, and she paid no attention to the slippery surface of the road. She seemed lost in other thoughts, which drew her far away.

Ricciardi wondered what could possibly have driven her to such an act. Why had she done it? Suddenly he felt a terrible weariness come over him, and after the brief cease-fire that the fever had accorded him, it was back, and worse than ever. The commissario's soul was filled with the dead boy's suffering and sorrow, his last dying hope, all the love he'd felt for the woman who'd killed him.

Without thinking about the words he was saying, he murmured softly:

"Thank you for the cookies. I love you, Mamma, you know that: you're my angel."

He couldn't even be sure if he'd really said it, or if he'd just imagined he had. But Carmen jerked in her seat as if she'd been bitten by a snake. She turned to look in terror into the back seat, and then gazed, aghast, at the commissario. The car swerved dangerously, knocking a handcart standing by the side of the road into a ditch, but then miraculously returned to the road. The woman didn't even think of slowing down. In fact, she jammed her foot down hard on the accelerator.

350 · MAURIZIO DE GIOVANNI

And, through tears and shrieks of sorrow, she began to tell her story.

So you knew all along, then. You knew. I realized it immediately, when I first saw you at the funeral: somehow you'd figured it out, that he hadn't just died by accident. And now you're here with me, to hear me confess it, and to take me down to hell.

Because I know, I know who you are: you're the devil. With those unblinking eyes of yours, that pale face, with death all around you. I know, I know who you are.

But I'm not going with you to hell, and you know why? Because I'm already familiar with hell. I've lived there and I live there still, in hell. Do you know, devil, what it's like to live with a lunatic? Do you know that, before locking him up, ashamed that word might get out, we used to pretend that he was normal? He'd stub out cigarettes on my arms; he'd wake me up at night and beat me bloody; he waited for me around every corner, in the dark, and lunged at me, fists clenched. He used to say that I was his enemy, a monster. But the real monster was him.

I lived like that for five years. How bad can you make hell for me, devil, how much worse than what I'd already lived through? But I put up with it. I put up with it all.

Because, you see, devil, I was born poor. I put up with privations because my father gambled away every penny we had, because my mother didn't know how to do anything but cry. And now that I finally had everything I'd ever dreamed of—wealth, comfort, status—I wasn't going to let anyone take that away from me.

That's right. The little boy was my son.

Born of an illicit affair, the child of a love without a future, two people writhing together in the dark. We made love while the lunatic was screaming and pounding at the door of his cell. We made love while everyone else thought we were hunting for the cure, as if there could be a cure for that monster's madness.

I really did think I was infertile. I'd tried, with all the treatments available, back when the monster still seemed to be a normal man. Nothing. But with him, with the doctor, I got pregnant right away. He took fright, he was as penniless as I was, all his money was in his wife's name. A lovely pair of paupers we were, rich only with other people's money.

We came up with a spa cure for the lunatic, far away, in Tuscany; Matteo prescribed it for him. Did you know that, devil, that his name was Matteo? So now, do you understand why my child bore that name?

I gave birth all alone, assisted by the chambermaid in a hotel. Like an animal. Like a stray bitch.

After that, what else could I do? I went back to my life, to my gilded cage. I placed the child with a family in the country, people I secretly sent money, but who didn't even know my name. Then the woman died of typhus, and the man began to drink. I couldn't leave him there anymore.

I searched for and found Don Antonio, that slimy, money-hungry priest. I paid the child, every month, plenty of money; but at least I could see him, I could practically raise him myself. I made the best of it, teaching school to those other bastard children, as long as I could be near him: near my son.

I couldn't keep him with me, you understand that, devil? It would have been easy for the monster's family to put two and two together: that wastrel of a brother, that coward who wants to get his hands on my money, now that the monster is finally dying, now that I finally have a chance to live my own life, a decent life.

And now he's found the letters.

I thought I'd destroyed them; I didn't remember that I still had them somewhere. He came to see me, he threatened me. I gave him a little something, but that was as much as I was willing to give him. So he followed me, and he found Tettè.

I knew everything, you understand, devil? He never stuttered with me. It was only with me, with his *mamma*, that he could talk. And the things he didn't tell me, I understood on my own. I knew all about those little bastards, the way they tormented him, what they put him through. I knew about the priest, the sexton, and the dark broom closet they used for punishments. I knew about the dog.

He'd told me about the poisoned tidbits in the food warehouse, how afraid he was that his dog might eat them. And toward the end he'd told me about the visits from my debauched brother-in-law, Edoardo.

The fear of losing everything obsessed me. If anyone found out that he was my son, a little orphan left to rot in a parish church, wallowing in filth and hunger, I'd have lost everything. They'd have tossed me out on the streets—perhaps they'd have thrown me in jail. What could I do? The child told me about the relentless demands, the questions that the damned man with the limp kept asking. It was only a matter of time; everything was coming to an end.

I had waited. I had been waiting for the lunatic to die and finally make me the mistress of all my wealth. Then I'd take the boy home to live with me, I'd give him everything I'd never had as a child; but now I'd been found out, and now I could no longer afford to wait.

For days and days, I was in a state of utter despair. I couldn't make up my mind. I had to choose between remaining rich and lonely or becoming poor and desperate, with a mentally deficient child to raise, and no skills, no way to make it on my own.

I just couldn't make up my mind. So I decided to leave it to fate. I baked him four cookies, two of them poisoned, and two safe. I made up a wrapper of cookies and took them to him. He loved it when I made him things with my own hands. I thought to myself: if he doesn't pick the poisoned cookies, that'll mean we're destined to go forward together, to fight side by side, even if we're left with nothing but each other.

We'll fight the man with the limp, we'll fight the lunatic, we'll take on the whole world.

But he grabbed the poisoned cookies without hesitation. I watched him eat them eagerly, smiling at me, right here, in the backseat of this car. And he said those words. The words that no one knows but you—because you're the devil—and me. And I'm his mother.

That's all he said.

Then he died.

LIX

Ricciardi listened to Carmen's story as if in a nightmare. His head was pounding painfully; the fever was devouring him.

And as if that weren't enough, the incessant hammering sound of Tettè's voice rang in his mind, piercing his soul, without passing through his ears. *Thank you for the cookies. I love you, Mamma, you know that: you're my angel.*

He'd seen so many things in his time: sons murdering mothers, brothers slaughtering each other, wives killing their husbands as they slept. But a mother who'd abandoned her own child to his fate and then poisoned him, letting him die an atrocious death, writhing in nightmarish pain—that was beyond his wildest imaginings.

Even without looking back, as the car hurtled at reckless speed up a steep dirt road leading to Posillipo, the wheels sliding in the mud, he still could sense the contractions of Tettè's body, the convulsions induced by the strychnine. And at the same time, he could sense his words of love. *I love you, Mamma, you know that: you're my angel.*

It dawned on him that the woman was referring to him as the devil. He almost laughed at the irony of the thing, until he realized that she might well be right. His otherworldly perceptions, the Deed: it was possible they came directly from the chief demon, might be a sign of his own damnation. Absurdly, he thought of Don Pierino, and his simple faith made up of a blend of truth and lies. Here you are, then, Padre: one angel and one devil, sitting side by side in the same car hurtling through the rain at breakneck speed. But you tell me which is which.

As the woman wept and muttered her delirious rantings, Ricciardi understood that their fate was sealed: Carmen was no longer looking at the road ahead of them, and she seemed to be jerking the steering wheel at random as she pressed the accelerator to the floorboards. Sluggishly, as if through a headful of drifting vapors, the commissario found himself thinking that at least they were now out of the populated districts. There was no one in sight, the road running straight uphill high above the coast was deserted; if nothing else, at least there were no other innocent lives involved.

Behind him, his voice gentle and unhampered, Tettè was once again thanking his angel.

The last thought, Ricciardi reflected. My last thought, so that if someone like me were to happen past, he'd hear it. My last thought, a legacy, a memory. A dead man's last thought, his farewell to a life he never really lived. That's my sin.

The car hurtled into a tight curve. The rain poured down furiously; visibility would have been limited even if Carmen's eyes hadn't been blurred with tears, her eyelids half shut. She said: child, my sweet child; forgive me, forgive your mother.

Around the curve, in the middle of the road, motionless, sat a dog on its haunches, still as a statue. Its eyes were leveled straight at the car that came swerving, tires spinning uselessly in the rain-slick mud, around the curve like a snarling beast. The dog didn't move. Carmen shouted Tettè's name and yanked the wheel hard in the direction of the railing, toward the sea far below, toward the sheer cliff.

As the car was hurtling toward the void, next to the woman who was sobbing out the name of the son she'd murdered, with the ghost of the little boy calling his mother his angel from behind him, Ricciardi squeezed his eyes tight shut and thought of Enrica, with every fiber of his being, trying to ensure that his thoughts would be there if someone could hear them, so someone could convey them to her: *love, oh my love; what a pity, what a shame.*

LX

Rain accompanied the silence of the evening of the Day of the Dead, falling heavy in the courtyard of the Pellegrini hospital.

The air, which was normally full of the cries of the vendors at the neighboring market, was now still, as if expectant. Maione shivered under the entrance awning. He wanted to know, but he was afraid.

For the hundredth time, he pulled out his pocket watch, looked at it, and put it away: it had been almost six hours. Commissario Ricciardi had been fighting for his life for six hours now, in Dr. Modo's operating room.

It's all my fault, he thought. I knew that he'd go on investigating, that he wouldn't stop; that he'd already made up his mind not to stop. I knew it, but I left him alone. If I'd been there with him, none of this would have happened: he wouldn't have gotten into that woman's car; he wouldn't have been with her on that absurd, desperate chase to Posillipo; he wouldn't have been in the car when it flew into the empty air.

For what seemed like the hundredth time, he saw himself in the taxi, pulling up too late; he saw the car wheels still spinning in the furious downpour, the overturned vehicle teetering on the brink, held back from that nightmarish final plunge only by a few stubborn shrubs; he saw himself extracting Ricciardi's body from the wreckage with the help of the taxi driver and a passing coachman; he saw the dead woman, her body half ejected through the shattered windshield of her automobile,

358 · MAURIZIO DE GIOVANNI

blood and brains oozing out of her broken skull under the driving rain. He ran a hand over his face. The rush to the hospital, the doctor's surprised and grief-stricken expression. And that had just been the beginning of this nightmare, this endless wait.

He'd sent a local boy to summon his eldest boy, who'd already returned home from the cemetery without news of his father, and through him he'd gotten word to Lucia and police headquarters. Then he'd ordered a patrolman to go get Rosa and bring her to the hospital.

He went back into the waiting room where the woman sat. She'd been accompanied to the hospital by a young woman whom Maione remembered as a neighbor of the commissario's, someone they'd questioned once in another case. Colombo, Enrica Colombo. That's how she'd introduced herself.

She was waxen, overwrought; she was supporting Rosa, who looked as if she'd been carved in marble. Sitting still, glassy-eyed, her lips whispering a prayer, her rosary in her hands.

Baroness, I know that you can hear me. You remember, you always heard me, even when I was sure you were sleeping; even with your eyes closed, you smiled and you'd tell me things in response to the things I was thinking. I never knew how you did it.

If you can hear me, Baroness, then you know where I am and what I'm doing here. We're in the hospital, because they say that your son, the *signorino*, is dying. I don't know if he's really dying. Those aren't things I'd know how to judge for myself. I'm ignorant and I don't even know how to read, I only know my numbers. And I don't know if you're mad at me, Baroness, because you entrusted your son to me, and I haven't been able to keep him safe. But I will tell you that he's my life, and that if he dies, I'll surely die too.

At the start, you gave me this responsibility, and I gladly took it. He wasn't an easy child, and he isn't easy now. He's hardheaded, stubborn, and you've always got to do things the way he says; he's thirty-one years old and he's all alone, leaving aside the fact that I'm an old woman and I'm going to die one day soon and he'll be left all alone like he is now. Even now that he's come to know this poor girl who's sitting here beside me, and who's insisted on coming with me through all that rain to the hospital, who rushed out into the street when she saw the patrolmen who came to get me, and even now he won't make his mind up to come out and tell us that he's fine and that he'll live to be a hundred.

Baroness, you're in the other world, the world of truth, and you can speak with the living and the dead, so try to find him wherever he is and tell him to come back to us, that he can't die now, that it's not true that he's alone; there are people who love him, and they couldn't go on living without him.

Tell him, Baroness. Tell him that he doesn't dare play this miserable trick on me, a poor old woman. That in all the years of making me lose my temper, I've never once raised my hand to him. Tell him for me that if he dares to do this to me, I'll fix him so he'll remember it for all eternity, whether it's in this world or the next.

Tell him, Baroness; tell him to come back to me.

Enrica was sitting by herself, in the shadows. The hospital waiting room was cold and the rain was hammering against the plate glass of the front entrance, determined to come in and cover with a film of water all the emotions and all the suffering that sat waiting there.

When she saw the two patrolmen approaching Ricciardi's apartment building, she'd given a name and a color to the anguish that had been persecuting her since the night before. Something had happened. She knew it. She saw Rosa leave, bundled into an overcoat, with a scarf on her head; even from a distance and through the rain, she could tell from her pallor that she was distraught and terrified.

Enrica didn't think twice: this was no time to stand on ceremony and formalities. She pushed her mother aside, as she stood there asking where Enrica thought she was going, and in this foul weather, and she hurried recklessly down the stairs, putting on her overcoat as she went. Rosa welcomed her with unruffled simplicity, linking arms with her. He's in the hospital, she told her.

Enrica prayed, listening to the rain hammer at the glass and waiting to learn whether she'd have to give up her dream forever.

She wondered if she was praying for Ricciardi's life or for herself, for her own life. Then she realized that it amounted to the same thing.

The silence was broken by the roar of a car engine pulling into the courtyard, with a sharp screech of brakes. After a few seconds the front door flew open and Livia rushed in, followed by a wet and unusually disheveled Garzo.

"Maione, you're here; I came the minute I heard, though first I swung past and picked up Signora Vezzi. Can you tell me what the devil happened? What was Ricciardi doing in a car with Signora Fago di San Marcello, a Lady of Charity at Santa Maria del Soccorso? Didn't I say it was time to close that damned investigation? In fact, didn't I say never to start it in the first place?"

Maione had gotten to his feet, and now he was staring at Garzo with an expression that couldn't promise anything good.

"Dotto', I don't know what the commissario was doing in that car; but I can assure you that if he was with that woman he had his own excellent reasons for it, as is proven by the way in which the accident took place."

"Exactly what do you know about the mechanics of the accident?"

Maione was clenching and unclenching his fists.

"What I know I know because I saw them go by and then I caught a taxi and followed them. The woman was driving, and she seemed very upset. Why, I couldn't say."

Garzo waved one hand, having finally understood that it was not a good idea to push the brigadier any further on this topic.

"Very well, we'll ask Ricciardi himself. Can we speak to him?"

Maione took a step toward Garzo; he seemed to have made up his mind to pick up the man by the scruff of his neck.

"Ah, Dotto', in that case you don't understand what's happening here: the commissario, as we speak, is in the operating room. Dr. Modo is performing surgery on his head. He's in critical condition. The last thing that he cares about, the last thing that any of us here who love him care about, is determining exactly what he was doing in the car driven by Signora What's-Her-Name. Have I made myself clear? Now, if you want to say here and wait, do me a favor: take a chair and keep your mouth closed. For once, take my advice: sit down and shut up."

He'd spoken softly, practically in a whisper, but his voice had carried throughout the waiting room like a clap of thunder. Garzo seemed to deflate, then he staggered backward and flopped down in a chair, without another word.

Livia stepped forward, her eyes filled with tears.

"Brigadier, what did the doctor say? Do you know anything, what damage . . . how is he, in other words, how is Ricciardi?"

Maione spread his arms wide in a gesture of helplessness.

"We don't know anything, Signo'. I brought him here by taxi, his eyes were closed, he seemed like he was dead, and blood was pouring out of his head. He wasn't talking. His pulse was faint, you could barely feel it. Luckily, it was the doctor's shift; the minute he saw him he put him on a gurney, had him wheeled into the operating room, and ran right after him. We're in the hands of God, and of that doctor."

Livia wrung her hands; she seemed to be on the brink of despair. Tears began to roll down her cheeks.

"But the doctor . . . are we sure we shouldn't take him somewhere else? I can arrange for immediate transportation to Rome, perhaps by plane. I can call someone, I have highly placed friends . . . They'd all be glad to make themselves available immediately, in other words. The best doctors in the country, the Duce's personal physicians. Wouldn't that be better, Brigadier?"

Maione smiled and shook his head.

"No, Signo', trust me: you're not going to find a better doctor anywhere than our Dr. Modo. The commissario wouldn't have chosen anyone else, if it had been up to him. And now it's too late, don't you think? He's operating on him now. We just have to wait, and pray, for those who are believers."

Livia bowed her head and put her face in her hands. Rosa and Enrica stared into the distance, expressionless.

Maione started pacing back and forth, like a caged lion. An hour went by. Then another. Garzo stood up, went over to Livia and, after saying a few words, mere formalities, which she barely heard, turned and left.

Enrica watched the panes of glass shiver with the gusts of rain. Let him live, she thought; that's all I ask. Let him live, let him breathe and walk and laugh and cry. If You do that, if You let him live, I'll give You my dream of happiness.

And now I'll never see him again.

A distant roar of thunder warned that the storm was drawing to an end. Night was falling, and the cold hospital lighting was coming on. In the courtyard, far from the eyes of one and all, a dog with a spotted coat sat on its haunches.

Suddenly, without warning, the door swung open and the weary figure of Dr. Modo appeared on the threshold. Everyone leapt to their feet, scrutinizing his exhausted expression. He smiled, looked at Maione, and said:

"Go ahead. He's asleep, but you can see him."

Livia was the first to run in, as light as the breeze, followed by Maione, who was holding up a weeping Rosa by the arm. Enrica murmured her thanks and left, in happiness and despair.

On the pane of glass, she glimpsed the last rain of autumn. Like a tear. Like a drop of blood.

And the winter started again.

ACKNOWLEDGMENTS

At the end of this fourth season of his, Ricciardi has many people to thank.

First and foremost, Fandango Books: in order, Domenico, Tiziana, Manuela, Francesca, Manuela, for the road we've traveled together. Mario Desiati, in the fullness of his world, with all the sensibility of the remarkable writer that he is, and the smile of the friend who's like a brother to me. And Gianluigi Toccafondo, a magical, marvelous artist.

Francesco Pinto, for having conceived of the whole distance when no one else had even thought of setting out.

Antonio and Michele, who think up his stories and the air that he breathes.

Professor Giulio Di Mizio, through whose eyes he sees the dead and hears them speak.

Rosaria De Cicco and Peppe Miale, who possess his voices.

Francesca Filardo, who imagines his clothing and fabrics.

Monica Biglietto, who looked for the poison and found it.

The fantastic team of the Corpi Freddi: Serena Venditto, Aldo Putignano, and Stefano Incerti, who are the first to hear his heartbeat, and smile when they recognize it.

Thanks to you all, from Ricciardi.

I have just one thank you of my own to say, but it's immense.

To the author of my enchantment, to the bearer of my song: to Paola.